GALLEON

"Your Excellency," Ned said crisply, having decided that it was time to put his cards face-up on the table, "Europe is one world and the Caribbee another. Treaties signed in London, Madrid, Paris, Lisbon or wherever you care to name, do not have the slightest effect on us out here . . .

"Originally we were Royalists escaping from Cromwell's regime, or men and women he had transported, prisoners of war or those sick of Puritanism. Now we have settled down here, trying to remake our lives again."

"A pretty speech," Luce said sarcastically, "but how does it concern me?"

"Because," Ned said slowly, now enunciating each word very clearly and carefully, "whatever the Spanish say in London and Madrid, whatever treaties they might sign, whatever agreements they might make with England, out here in the Caribbee *there is No Peace Beyond the Line*."

Also in Arrow in the Yorke series

BUCCANEER

ADMIRAL

Galleon

Dudley Pope

ARROW BOOKS

Arrow Books Limited
62–65 Chandos Place, London WC2N 4NW

An imprint of Century Hutchinson Limited

London Melbourne Sydney Auckland
Johannesburg and agencies throughout
the world

First published in Great Britain by
The Alison Press/Martin Secker & Warburg Limited 1986
Arrow edition 1987

Printed and bound in Great Britain by
Anchor Brendon Limited, Tiptree, Essex

ISBN 0 09 949320 9

For Alex and Harry Jonas
who were in Marigot
when it happened

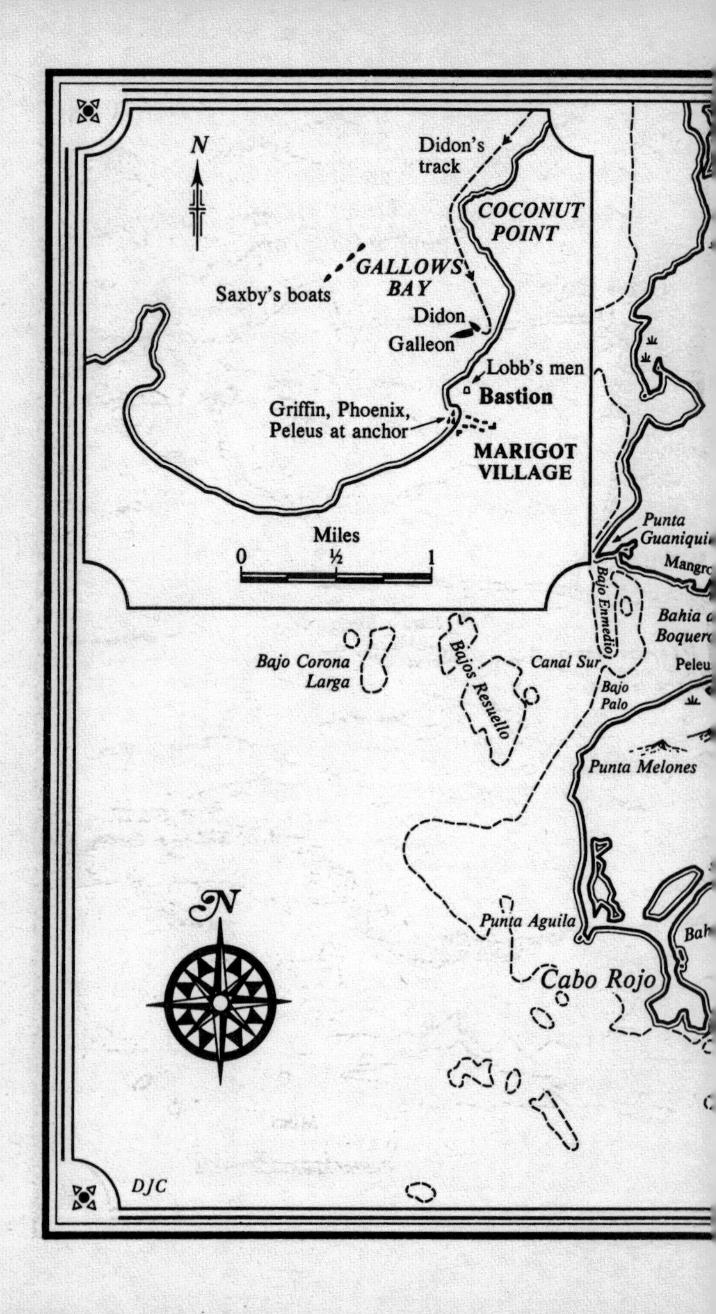
N
Didon's track
COCONUT POINT
GALLOWS BAY
Saxby's boats
Didon
Galleon
Lobb's men
Bastion
Griffin, Phoenix, Peleus at anchor
MARIGOT VILLAGE
Miles
0
½
1
Punta Guaniqui
Bajo Enmedio
Bahia
Boquer
Bajo Corona Larga
Bajos Resuello
Canal Sur
Bajo Palo
Punta Melones
N
Punta Aguila
Cabo Rojo
DJC

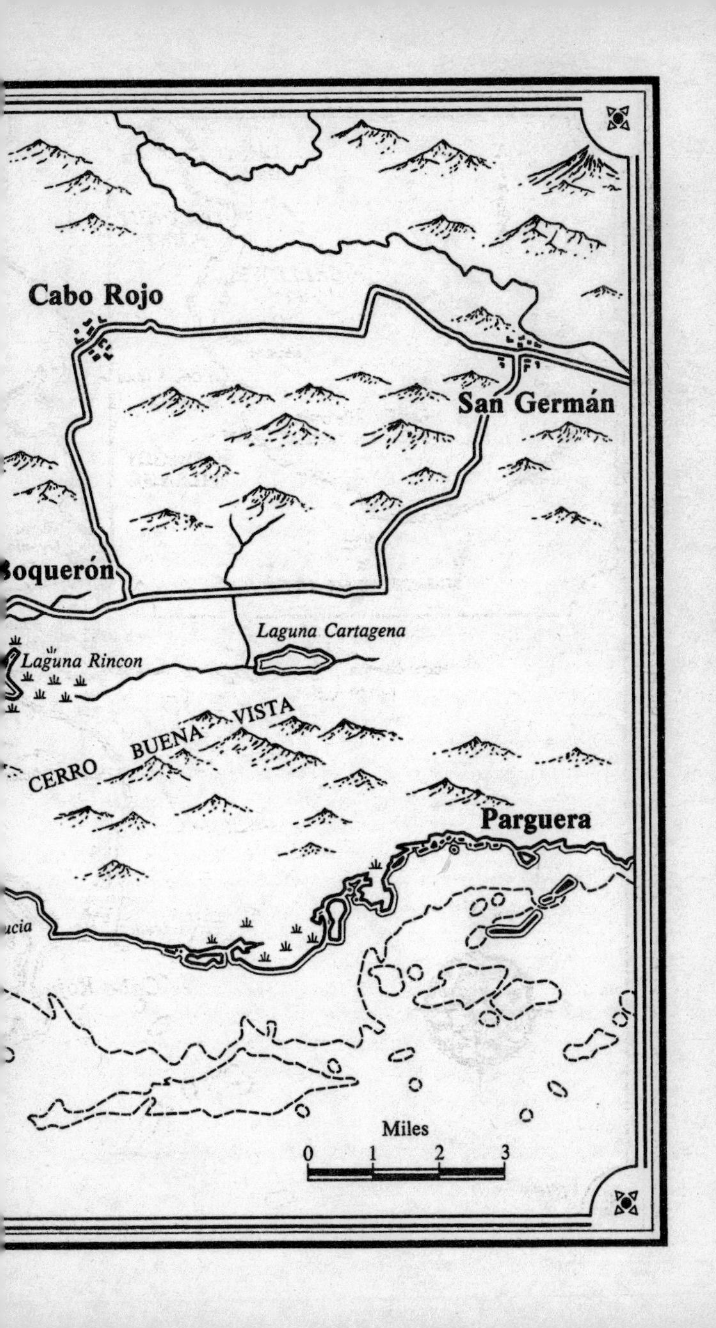
Cabo Rojo
San Germán
Laguna Cartagena
Laguna Rincon
CERRO BUENA VISTA
Parguera
Miles
0 1 2 3

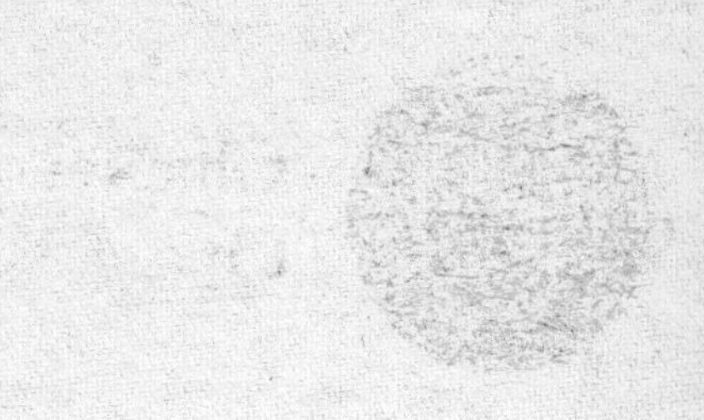

Chapter One

Aurelia examined the inked lines portraying the new house, drawn with geometric precision on the parchment scroll, and then looked round once again at the rough field on the top of the cliff where it was to be built. No matter how hard she tried, she found it impossible to picture the thin, insubstantial lines as a stone house standing four-square, proof against hurricanes, marauding pirates and tropical downpours.

However, Ned had chosen the perfect position. From seaward a lazy swell rolling in from the north thundered to its death against the cliffs below, the breaking water slipping white lace collars round each rock.

Inland the mountains stretched like folded pastry, alternate crests and valleys rising and falling and eventually disappearing in a distant blue haze. From the northern sea horizon to the farthest mountains in the south she could see three distinct broad ribbons of colour: the almost unbelievably vivid purplish-blue of the sea, the green merging into parched brown of the grass and bushes where they were standing, and the blue-grey of the mountains, a colour which she wished could be produced on cloth.

She waved the parchment. "I can't believe we'll ever see this house built and actually live here, Ned. Just imagine, those rollers lulling us to sleep, and then we wake up in the morning and look out to sea ... Something dreadful will happen to spoil it all."

Ned shrugged his shoulders. Aurelia seemed able to look into the misty future at will, yet sometimes the view alarmed her. As a rule, he reflected, she accepted life as they all accepted the Trade wind clouds parading past in neat lines of white cotton balls – they were there on most days of the year, and if they vanished it heralded a change in the weather.

He gestured at the deep rectangular pit across which was placed the thick trunk of a mahogany tree. One perspiring sawyer stood astride on top with his mate in the pit below as they pulled and pushed the great two-handed saw, slowly slicing off yet another plank, and sneezing from time to time with the sawdust.

"Just listen," Ned said, pointing towards a small, circular pit, like a pond except that it glowed red with charcoal, the Trade wind making bellows unnecessary. A couple of men fished out a strip of red-hot iron with long tongs and took it to a small anvil. They hammered it into shape with strokes which sounded curiously flat out in the open, Ned noted; presumably because his ear was expecting to hear the echo inside a blacksmith's forge.

Several long strips of blackened, forged metal were already scattered in an untidy pile near the charcoal pit. Each had a scroll-like twist at one end and they were window, shutter and door hinges beaten into shape during the last few days. Nearby and covered with palm fronds to keep off the sun – the heat would otherwise split the unseasoned planks – were piles of sawn wood: mahogany for the most part, but there were shorter planks and beams of bullet wood, light red now it was freshly cut, but it would turn dark brown as it seasoned. It was enormously hard (and hated by the sawyers, who had to sharpen the teeth of their saw after only a few strokes across the fine, straight grain). Yet its very name showed why it was used for shutters over the windows: gun loops would be cut out later, like giant keyholes, once the shutters were hung and the carpenters could be sure of the size and positions, because the sole purpose of the gun loops was to allow defenders inside the house to aim their muskets at attackers.

Further inland, muffled by a clump of trees, there was a regular clinking from a newly opened quarry as a dozen men with picks, crowbars and hammers cut and levered stone for others to shape into blocks.

Already a flat space of land just beyond Aurelia was marked

out with wooden pegs and pieces of marline linking them, to reveal a shape similar to the drawing on the parchment, the foundations of a large house.

"You know, Ned," she said, pressing a finger on the parchment as she tried to hold it flat against the tug of the wind, "I think I'd sooner have the kitchen at the other end. It'll be easy enough to change, won't it? Saxby and Simpson can move the pegs and restring the marline."

Ned took the plan from her and rolled it up. "Darling, it took us a week to agree on *this* plan, so let's leave it as it is."

"But the kitchen: surely we can –"

"The kitchen is fine where we've put it!"

"Yes, but I want to have a room on the west side, just there, where we can sit in the evening and watch the sun setting . . ."

"*Chérie*," Ned said drily, "do you want to sit and watch the sun set with the stink of boiling vegetables and cooking meat and smouldering charcoal in your nostrils?"

"Of course not!"

"Well, that's what you're proposing. Remember, the wind usually blows from east to west –" he gestured up at the clouds and down at the gently swaying bushes, "– so we decided to put the kitchen on the west side of the house, then all the cooking smells blow clear, and we have the sitting and drawing rooms on the south side, which begins to cool as the sun goes round . . ."

She bit her lip, angry with herself for not thinking before turning a sudden whim into words: she had lived in the Tropics long enough to know elementary things like that. She realized that standing up here on the cliff had suddenly given her the idea of watching glorious sunsets from the drawing room of her own house . . .

As though reading her thoughts, Ned said: "Darling, it's going to be your house – your first real home – so you can have exactly what you want. But remember, we have balconies on three sides, and you can always lie in a hamaca . . ."

"And get eaten alive by mosquitoes and sandflies!"

"Yes," he protested, "but they come into the rooms to bite you just as much. We beat them simply by having tobacco leaf smouldering outside. The smoke will keep them away just the same as it does inside."

Aurelia laughed and took his arm. "Yes, you're right as usual: I've been living in a ship so long that I've forgotten about itching insects. When will the house be finished? I want to start planning the beds and chairs and tables, and mosquito nets, and the cooking pots for the kitchen, and the china and cutlery, and –"

"Concentrate on the bed," he said, and as she blushed he added: "Large, and with a mosquito net as big as a tent hanging over it. A *square* bed," he added as an afterthought. "I want some compensation for all the time we've been squeezed up in a bunk."

"You can explain that to Saxby," she said. "I shall be too embarrassed." A *square* bed. The more she thought about it though, the more attractive the idea became: she admitted that and was startled when Ned muttered: "I wish we had one now, this minute!"

"*Chéri*, we have a long ride back to the ship, so concentrate on that."

"That dam' bunk is so narrow."

"This is the first time you've complained about it," she reminded him. "You always say how snug it is."

He grinned at her. "Yes, but that was when we couldn't even consider a real bed – a big *square* bed."

She sighed and she seemed content, and yet he thought he detected a certain nostalgia too, and perhaps uncertainty.

"You are sure that you really want to come on shore and live in a house?"

"Oh, Ned, I don't know what I do want. Well, yes, I know I want to be with you, but do I want to sail off somewhere in the *Griffin* or be the mistress of this house? Arranging beds of flowers, arranging a *square* bed for us," she said with an impish smile. "Do I want to look down at the sea from our own house, or cross the sea in our own ship? I don't know.

"Ask me now, and I say the ship. In a few hours' time, when we are on board again, I shall crave for the house and the smell of the herbs and the flowers, and the booming of the rollers down there. In fact," she admitted, "sit me down in Port Royal and I'll change my mind every ten minutes." She shook her head and the blonde hair, seeming almost white in the bright sun, the colour of an ash twig just stripped of its bark, streamed out in the wind gusting over the edge of the cliff. "Oh, Ned! I'm spoiling it for you just as your dreams are coming true."

He shook his head and took her hand. "I feel the same," he admitted. "Ever since Cromwell and his Roundheads drove us out of Barbados and we had to leave the Kingsnorth plantation, I've dreamed of saving enough money to start a new plantation. Well," he said ruefully, "thanks to the Brethren of the Coast we have plenty of money, and now we have two thousand acres here in Jamaica."

"And we've started building a house with a kitchen at the western end," she added. "Cromwell is dead, the King is back on the throne, and the new Governor has just arrived. We should be content!"

"Yes," Ned said gloomily, "but instead we may find that our troubles are just beginning." He caught sight of two riders approaching in the distance. "Ah, here come Diana and Thomas: they've been looking over their acres, too."

"Diana feels the same as me," Aurelia said. "Changing with the wind. Women are weathercocks."

The woman slid off her horse into Ned's arms. She was the only woman he had ever seen ride astride – she wore men's breeches and riding boots that were very new. Port Royal now had a good bootmaker who, Ned realized, must have the finest selection of leather at his disposal. Certainly Diana's boots were made of leather as soft as cloth and at this very moment the cobbler should be busy at his last, making a similar pair for Aurelia.

If Nature had wanted to find an opposite to Aurelia, the search would end with Diana. Lady Diana Gilbert-Manners had black hair and deep brown eyes, a wide, sensuous mouth and a body where everything – breasts, thighs, slim legs – seemed emphasized without her appearing to notice it. She was, Aurelia had once commented (sympathetically, not maliciously), someone who would, like a succulent rose just before it bloomed fully, have to watch her weight in a few years' time.

Now, tanned, flashing-eyed, high-spirited, it was obvious she was deeply in love with Thomas and again Aurelia had summed it up: they loved each other in bed and out.

The contrast with Aurelia, Ned saw, was only a physical

one: Aurelia was as lively (but quicker-witted?) and as loving and loved, but in contrast to Diana's her hair was so blonde that from a distance in bright sun it seemed white. She was slim; her bosoms were firm and high, the nipples small and pink, compared with the big-bosomed Diana, who had large, dark nipples, Ned's knowledge of them being gained because the four of them, refusing to accept the usual warning about the sun, had screened areas on board their ships where they could lie in the sun and become tanned all over, and then never had to worry about being sunburned.

Aurelia's deep tan emphasized her blonde hair and blue eyes, but the same tan on Diana emphasized her body. Why? Was it more intriguing speculating about Diana's tanned breasts? Ned neither knew nor cared; he loved Aurelia and Diana was attractive, and he knew the reverse was true for Thomas, and that was how it should be.

"Darling Ned, being in your arms – even for a few moments – is ecstasy!" Diana looked across at Aurelia and winked. "I won't tell him that being in anyone's arms is ecstasy after sitting on that damned horse for hours. It's like being astride the barrel of a cannon."

By now she was kissing Aurelia in an affectionate greeting and Sir Thomas Whetstone, a burly man with a thick square beard, flowing moustaches and long black curly hair, had dismounted, kissed Aurelia's hand with a flourish and slapped Ned on the back.

"Diana's taken against horses," he explained. "She prefers to sit in a boat and be rowed everywhere. Give her a barge and she'll be the Cleopatra of the Caribbee."

"I *haven't* taken against horses," Diana protested, "it's just this Spanish saddle. No wonder portraits always make *hidalgos* on horseback look so haughty; the poor fellows have been battered into capons . . ."

Whetstone was looking across at the wooden pegs driven into the ground with the lines indicating where the foundations of the new house would be. "Yours looks bigger than the drawing, Ned – and that's a relief, because ours seems enormous. I was beginning to think we'd made a mistake in the scale on the plan."

"Aurelia, do tell him (because he won't listen to me) that a house can't be too big," Diana said. She had a surprisingly deep and rich voice, a complete contrast to Aurelia's lighter tones and slight French accent.

"The Devil take the house, what about the bed?" Thomas boomed. "I've had enough of ships' narrow bunks."

"I think Ned feels the same way," Aurelia said. "In fact he is designing a special one for us."

"A *square* bed," Ned said.

"I should think so," Whetstone said in a tone which took it for granted that anything else was unthinkable. "By the way, Ned, this isn't a social visit. The new Governor has finally decided to introduce himself to the peasants tomorrow. We're bidden to the presence of m'lud Luce, along with Heffer and probably half a dozen others, mostly tradesmen no doubt. Is your land grant confirmed?"

The question sounded casual, but Ned understood Thomas well enough to know that he was avoiding alarming the women.

"Yes. Heffer signed and sealed the papers last week. Yours?"

"Same, thank goodness."

However, the casual tone had not fooled Aurelia. "Why do you ask, Thomas?"

"I gather the new Governor has either some fancy ideas or special orders from the Privy Council. Either way, from what I hear, he thinks he's going to announce the beginning of Jamaica's 'Golden Age'. Still, gold or dross, I think we'd better start back to Port Royal . . ."

Sir Harold Neil Luce, for the past few months a knight, was an ageing survivor; one of a small group of crafty politicians who had managed to back the political horse both ways by dividing their stake. They had lost half with the collapse of the Protectorate in the first race; but they had won handsomely on the second with the Restoration, switching allegiances with that facility limited to politicians and whores.

Small and sandy-haired, narrow-faced and thin, he looked like a ferret; he had a high-pitched voice that became shrill, particularly when challenged about something of which he was uncertain. Luce had been appointed Jamaica's first Governor because the King, the Duke of Albemarle, the Secretary of State and members of the Privy Council's Committee for Trade and Foreign Plantations could no longer stand the sight of his face nor the whine of his northern accent. Like a tout for a brothel, he had seemed to be everywhere, accosting, begging for preferment, pleading, making new offers.

There was now a powerful group of men at Court, those who had always been Royalist and who had followed the King into exile, who resented the way that Luce (and others like him) fawned, bribed and lied into being tolerated, if not accepted, at Court once the King had been restored.

As soon as the Civil War had started, Luce had vanished from his estates, hiding his silver and sacking his servants. In fact he had gone into hiding – not because he thought the Roundheads would fail to win a complete victory and make the country a Puritan republic (which meant an ascetic, bloodless, laughterless one) but because he was waiting to see who in the new republic emerged with the power.

Once he had identified the man beyond all doubt as Oliver Cromwell, he swiftly decided to pay the price for his tardy allegiance and he compounded, the euphemism for paying the Roundheads a large sum of money for forgetting that during the actual fighting he had sat not on, but behind the fence (Royalists paid much more), and was allowed part of his estate back. For the next ten years "Mr Luce" had lived as close to Cromwell as he could, currying favour and sniffing out Royalists with revolutionary zeal.

When the Protector died he tried to transfer his allegiance to the son Richard, who was not interested in the succession. Then suddenly (or so it seemed to Luce, who was trying to see where and how much he could benefit from the Army's discontent with Richard, although it was nearer two years) General Monck, one of the late Oliver Cromwell's great generals, had gone across the Channel, brought back the King and put him on the throne. While almost everyone was hailing the Restoration, devout Roundheads hid under their beds and prayed even more fervently than they had under the rule of the Lord Protector.

Luce gave a silent cheer while former Roundhead friends disappeared into the countryside, as discreetly as he had himself a dozen years earlier. But as he watched the activities of his fellow turncoats who had compounded with the Roundheads, he saw how General Monck (now created Duke of

Albemarle) was quietly squeezing them out, while advising the King against revenge. Yet Luce was quick to understand that, whether the country was a republic or a monarchy, it took the same number of men to administer it. He saw that the task was impossible without using men who had the administrative skills, even though as former Republicans they were tainted, and anyway the King had declared a general amnesty.

Luce came back into public life stealthily. His compounding was explained away to anyone who remarked on it as a method of *survival* (as it had been in the case of many genuine Royalists); close friendship with Cromwell and his Puritan cronies was excused as the only way of existing. In fact it had been part of the glory-and-riches-for-Luce policy which he pursued all his adult life with the tenacity of a hungry debt collector. Before the Restoration he had been angry because during Cromwell's dozen years in power he had never been able to get his hands on even one of the Royalist estates confiscated by the Lord Protector and given to his favourites. Two estates in particular (one of them bordering his own) had taken Luce's fancy, and he was furious when the neighbouring land went to a wild-eyed parson famous in the county not for the quality of his sermons or the attention he gave his flock, but for the zeal with which he smashed, in all the churches within a day's ride, everything he regarded as "idolatrous". The sound of his mason's hammer chipping fine altarpieces, the shrill orders which started off the pecking of chisels and the thud of mauls to deface wooden carvings, and the shattering of stained-glass windows wrought to the glory of God two centuries earlier by artists and artisans produced in him a secret fervour usually reserved for old men in bordellos and won him a public reputation as a sound Puritan – and Luce's envy.

At the Restoration, when the priest vanished, Luce's hopes of ownership once again ran high – but the original Royalist owner of the estate (who Luce had been sure was killed at Marston Moor) had been with the King during the whole of his exile and returned home to miss the decamping priest by less than a week. Luce later heard that the priest had discovered from a servant (whom he had installed as one of his mistresses, assuring the bewildered girl that although she might fear pregnancy – she carried three children – she was obeying God's will and thus there could be no sin) where the silver had been hidden when the Royalist had fled. The priest had apparently regarded it as part of his secular duty to take the silver with him, packed in panniers on two mules, deciding he preferred the certainty of receiving his reward on earth.

One way and another, Luce decided, the Restoration had so far added nothing to his fortune, but he was cunning enough to admit that General Monck's virtual amnesty (the King's rather) meant that Luce's head stayed on his shoulders. He knew, during the darkest hours of the night, that he had been guilty of treason, but in the bright sunshine of the Restoration it was being overlooked, as though the Roundheads had not been regicides.

Then with all the zeal found in devious converts, Luce assured himself that the country wanted a monarchy and set about being an ardent Royalist; so ardent that Monck, now the Duke of Albemarle, when considering the future of Jamaica (about which few people knew anything), saw it as just the exile he needed for Luce, thus beginning the long tradition of using Caribbee governorships as the dumping ground for men who were incompetent or otherwise an embarrassment to decent society or the government in London.

So Commodore Mings had just returned to Port Royal with a frigate, delivering the new Governor. Luce's first call once the anchors had splashed down had been for Major-General Heffer, a survivor of the Roundhead force which had originally captured the island and who (to his own surprise) had eventually found himself in command of the island as acting Governor. Since those heady days following the island's capture, Heffer had died a hundred times in his own imagination, prey to every rumour about Cromwell's health, Richard's intentions, impending Spanish attacks, the starvation of his garrison – and mutiny.

Originally the garrison had been (in Cromwell's mind) the powerful force which would carry out his Western Design, starting with the capture of Hispaniola. That attack, Heffer readily admitted, had been a débâcle won by the Spanish and vile diseases like cholera and dysentery.

The Roundhead survivors had reeled away to leeward, and captured Jamaica as a sop to the Lord Protector, driving out the small and startled Spanish garrison and accidentally acquiring, without realizing it, one of the most strategically important islands in the West Indies, one that was as effective a threat to the galleons carrying the treasures of the Main to Spain as a knife at Philip IV's throat.

However, this was not how Heffer saw it. When General Venables and Admiral Penn, the leaders of the original expedition, hastily departed for England to make their excuses and claims over Hispaniola to an unsympathetic Lord Protector, Heffer had found himself left commanding an island garrisoned by disaffected and sickly troops and facing a threat from Spain that could only be driven off by the very ships of war that Venables and Penn had taken home. Not only that, he told Luce almost tearfully, his officers turned against him. By an oversight all the cattle and hogs on the island had been let loose and driven up into the mountains and the *Cimarróns*, the Indians made slaves by the Spaniards and who were expert in hunting them, had also been driven off, and his officers would do nothing to encourage their troops to till the land and plant the crops that would provide food – and make it easier for them to stay.

When Luce had asked how his soldiers had survived so far, General Heffer admitted that he had managed to buy several hundred tons of maize from some pirates who had bought it from the Spaniards and smuggled it over from the Main. When asked whence came the cannon which Luce saw in some forts and batteries protecting the port, Heffer once again had to admit that the guns, powder and shot came from Santiago, in Cuba, and had been captured specially for the purpose by the same pirates.

"Pirates?" Luce had exclaimed. "Seems obvious to me that these 'pirates' saved the island while you and your wretched army squabbled. You admit your officers won't do anything that could result in them being left here. No sense of duty or honour, that's obvious! You leave the defence of Jamaica to the pirates, while your officers want to abandon it altogether, eh?"

Luce's anger frightened Heffer, who had long ago lost his always flimsy confidence. First, there had been the rumours of the death of the Lord Protector, whom Heffer had come to regard as a talisman. Then after his death there had been a brief reprieve, when Richard Cromwell succeeded, but the rumours telling of that also told him that Richard had no liking for the job. Then had come the news that even now Heffer found it hard to credit – General Monck had crossed the Channel and brought back the King: Cromwell's most successful general had restored the monarchy. And for Heffer there had been the weeks and months of waiting in Jamaica, never knowing when a frigate would appear over the horizon, never sure whether the orders it brought would set in motion Heffer's hanging, reprieve, promotion, recall or what . . . Now the frigate had finally arrived, bringing Sir Harold Neil Luce, Kt.

Chapter Two

After taking a cold and dispassionate look across the table at Heffer, Luce finally decided that he had made a dreadful mistake in accepting the governorship of Jamaica. In London at the time it had seemed exciting (romantic almost), and when whirling from drawing room to drawing room taking his farewell, he was the centre of congratulations (but far too naïve and self-centred to realize why so many influential people were glad to see him go). Then sailing in a special frigate which was waiting for him at Portsmouth . . . ah, governors were men of considerable importance!

On the long voyage to the Tropics he had pictured the Governor's residence in Jamaica as large and airy, high-ceilinged, the walls covered with rich hangings (he understood they liked them in the Tropics), plenty of servants, and all the tradesmen living there only too glad to welcome him and give him credit as they fawned their way to favouritism – yes, he was looking forward to that, and speculated what it would mean in terms of "presents".

Heffer with his long sheeplike face symbolized all of Sir Harold Luce's disappointments: there was no Government House, no one apparently gave a damn that the new Governor had arrived and certainly no one was in a hurry to beg favours.

This damned man Heffer, who had occupied the only house of consequence near the harbour (Luce had yet to explore the capital, which was inland) and had immediately been made to surrender it to the new Governor, was a typical

Puritan: the whole damned house was whitewashed like a monk's cell or a Roundhead privy. In fact, Luce was both intimidated and intrigued because Heffer's austerity and cold disapproval of just about everything seeped through the house like the reek of sewage, even creeping invisibly into rooms he had obviously never used.

On the voyage out here, Luce had imagined a large and well furnished room, probably panelled and with a long and polished table, at the head of which he would sit, with his newly chosen island executive council seated left and right in order of seniority. Servants would bring in refreshing drinks as diligent clerks wrote minutes or prepared letters and copied them into the letter book. Life would be conducted (leisurely) by a snap of finger against thumb.

So much for imagination; Luce had now to admit that the reality was quite different. The new council chamber would have to be this wretched little room that Heffer used as an office, little more than a rabbit hutch with one tiny window, a desk and chair, and a small table at which five could be seated. Six, if Heffer could find another chair.

Work with Heffer . . . well, that's what his orders said, but they might as well have told him to bring out a shepherd's crook: Heffer was a man who always lost; that much was clear to Luce who, by playing a waiting game, had so far always won.

Luce looked down at the list of items he had written down in preparation for this first meeting with the acting Governor (from whom he was taking over and who was to become his deputy) and a few leading citizens chosen by Heffer. Ah, how he had thought about it all during the long and very tedious voyage from England: he had made list upon list, tearing up one after the other as new ideas came to him and new problems emerged.

He need not have bothered. Instead of Sir Harold Luce, Kt, Governor of Jamaica, etc., etc., consulting with his deputy Governor (granting him an occasional audience, Luce had supposed) the whole thing was taking on the tone of a local parson questioning the grocer about overcharging – and doing it in the potting shed.

And the heat. And the damnable insects – the mosquitoes he could see and hear and they were biting, but the sharpest stings, like stabs with red-hot needles, came from wretched little things he could not even see, and which Heffer casually dismissed as "only" sandflies, explaining that the soldiers called them "no-see 'ems", and the worst itching soon wore off. And the humidity. And the hurricane season. And no fruit or vegetables to speak of, according to Heffer, *and* precious little meat . . .

Luce told himself for the second time that he had made a bad mistake: he should have stayed in London. No glory was coming his way out here, even if he made a good job of being Governor; and there would certainly be no money, apart from his salary, because it was already quite obvious that these Puritan peasants were too mean and too righteous to offer a bribe and possibly too poor anyway: they wallowed in their poverty as though it brought them closer to Heaven.

The next item on Luce's list was establishing an island currency.

"Money," he said to Heffer. "Currency." And noting the blank look on the man's face, said impatiently: "Without a legal currency and a credible rate of exchange we can't have trade! We have to establish trade, so we need currency. You can't go on exchanging things. Using sugar as money is absurd. 'A pound of sugar is worth a penny' –" he laughed cynically and then smiled understandingly at Heffer: these sort of things were beyond the understanding or competence of soldiers.

"But we *have* a currency, sir," said a startled Heffer. "We use it all the time now."

"Ah yes, some metal coins your fellows have stamped out with a hammer and die, no doubt. No, I mean a proper and acceptable currency which has its own intrinsic value, based on silver or gold."

"Around here we deal only in gold: *reals*, pieces of eight and dollars," Heffer said, still puzzled by Luce.

"But they are *Spanish*!" Luce protested.

"They're solid gold," Heffer said stubbornly, and remembering a phrase of Mr Yorke's, added: "Gold takes on the nationality of its owner!"

"Yes, yes, my dear fellow," Luce said soothingly. "I quite understand, but I'm talking about a great deal of money: enough to finance the working of this island."

"Well, we seem to have had enough so far, and if we run short we can probably get more."

"Yes, yes, quite," Luce said, his patience getting strained, "but a country's money is simply tokens unless there's gold or silver to back it. That is what a treasury and mint are for!"

"Well, I don't know how much you had in mind, sir, but Mr Yorke seemed to think it would last us."

Luce was now getting angry with this sheep of a general. "Yorke, Yorke, Yorke . . . that's all I hear from you," he said crossly. "Mr Yorke says this . . . Mr Yorke says that . . . Mr Yorke thinks this . . . And pray tell me just how much money does Mr Yorke think is needed?"

Heffer glanced through the pile of papers in front of him and found a particular sheet, which he put on top.

"I don't know that Mr Yorke ever said how much he thought would be *necessary*," Heffer said, "but –"

"Ah, now you see!" Luce exclaimed, "you can't administer an island this size on the casual opinions of clodhoppers, you know."

"No, sir," Heffer agreed. "What sort of figure had you in mind?"

"Well, I brought £48,000 with me in the *Convertine* and have the authority of the Committee for Trade and Foreign Plantations to start a mint here."

"What metal would you use for the coinage, sir?"

"Well, to start with it will have to be copper, and the coins would be tokens."

"We can let you have gold, sir, if that would be better," Heffer said slyly, pleased with himself that the bait had so easily lured this pompous ferret of a man into the trap set in front of him.

"Oh yes," Luce said patronizingly, "how much had you in mind?"

Heffer looked down at his list again. "Well, we have about half a million pieces of eight. Most of those are in the Treasury, with just enough in circulation to let us trade. A piece of eight is worth about five shillings, so that'd be about £125,000 you could re-mint. But maybe you don't like the idea of gold?"

Heffer deliberately misinterpreted Luce's stunned look. "You'd prefer silver, Your Excellency? Now, let's see," he pretended to consult his list. "Yes, we've got more than two hundred pounds of silver in the Treasury, still in the original loaves, wedges and cakes that the Spanish cast 'em in. That could be melted down for silver coins, though I must admit, sir, the folk round here are not partial to silver coins on account of silver tarnishing and there being so much gold."

"But . . . but . . ." Luce stammered, and Heffer again deliberately misunderstood him.

"There are several sacks of cobs, too, sir. Fact of the matter is that once those cobs were counted out to give the buccaneers their share, no one thought to make a note of the total."

"*Give the buccaneers their share?*"

Luce screamed the sentence at Heffer, who grinned happily. At last he could see how much fun Mr Yorke and Sir Thomas must have got out of playing with him in the past, but now he, Major-General Heffer, had his own mouse to tease – for a brief while, anyway.

"Yes, sacks of cobs, chests of emeralds – I see there were two hundredweight of them, and they're still in the Treasury. Pearls – yes, one hundred and fifty pounds of them – from the island of Margarita, on the Main coast. Then there are the chests with seven hundredweight of gold and silver ornaments – plate, candlesticks, jewellery and that sort of thing; I suppose you could melt that down for coins, too: all bulky sort of things and hard to value except by weight. You can't put a price on workmanship."

Luce, speaking almost incoherently like a man in a dream, stammered: "But where did all this – this treasure – come from?"

"Oh, Mr Yorke brought it in to start us off," Heffer said nonchalantly, knowing this was the chance to get his own back after a lifetime of slights, sneers, snubs and humbling jokes from his superiors.

"But – I mean, where did Mr Yorke get all this wealth?"

"He's a wealthy man," Heffer said. "He'll be here soon, if he received your message, so you can ask him yourself."

And that, Heffer told himself, means I've avoided the responsibility of revealing any more of Mr Yorke's business.

"This man Yorke," Luce persisted, "isn't he just a pirate?"

Heffer shrugged his narrow shoulders and licked his large and protruding teeth, which had a distressing tendency to dry so that the inside of his mouth stuck on them, giving him the appearance of a grinning ewe. "He's saved the island from starving – that was at the beginning. Then he captured Santiago and took what we needed of the Spaniards' great guns – they're the ones we have out there in our batteries. Then he brought in all the gold and silver and suchlike. Some people might call him a pirate: others might regard him as lord of the manor. Frankly, sir, I don't know what you'd call such a benefactor . . ." He had put just enough emphasis on the "you'd" that Luce glanced up and, to distract attention from the deep flush spreading over his face, said abruptly: "You'd better give me that list."

But Heffer was fast learning of the perquisites of power and he politely shook his head. "This is my own copy, sir; I'll have another one drawn up for you."

As Ned and Thomas walked the few yards from the jetty to what was always referred to as "Heffer's place" but which looked as if it was to become (temporarily at least) Government House, Thomas said: "Y'know, Ned, it seems only yesterday that we were rescuing old Heffer from his mutinous colonels."

"It wasn't so long ago, either – I noticed their bodies are still hanging in chains from the gibbets at the end of the Palisades."

"No, I suppose it wasn't. My ears still ring from the pistol shots in that damned little office of his."

"'His office', my dear bishop, is likely to be the island's new council chamber."

"Who *is* this fellow Luce?" Thomas asked. "I've never heard of him."

"Aurelia heard somewhere that he was knighted for this job."

"Where's he been for the last few years?" Thomas asked shrewdly.

Ned shrugged his shoulders. "With the King in exile? Compounding with the Roundheads? Pouring the Protector's ale? Hiding in the woodshed? Who knows – twelve years is a long time. Presumably he wasn't a very naughty boy because he's been given this job."

"That doesn't follow," Thomas was doubtful. "General Monck – sorry, the new Duke of Albemarle – persuaded the

King to grant a general amnesty for all but the very worst scoundrels . . . This fellow might be a splendid Royalist who fought bravely for the King, but he might equally well be a thoroughly wretched scoundrel who compounded his way out of trouble."

"We'll soon see," Ned said cheerfully. "One look at Heffer's face will tell all: he's already spent hours with the man, handing over the reins."

"On the other hand, remember this fellow Luce has also spent hours listening to Heffer," Thomas said with a chuckle. "They're probably both very confused! By the way, who else is summoned to the presence?"

"Damned if I know. I suspect we're the first two lambs; the tradesmen will follow later."

By now the two men had reached the house, acknowledged the salute of the sentry (whose uniform had been hurriedly modified to disguise its Roundhead origins), and been handed over to an elegantly dressed man of about thirty, bewigged and twirling a gold-topped cane like a bandmaster, and who had introduced himself as "William Hamilton, the Governor's private secretary, you know; his major-domo."

"I don't like the major-domo," Thomas growled as they followed him. "One more flounce and he'll turn into a yard o' lace . . ."

The secretary led the way to Heffer's office, knocked and, at an answer from a voice Ned did not recognize, flung open the door and walked in, standing to one side and announcing: "Visitors for His Excellency the Governor!"

Oh dear, Ned thought to himself; the Governor has not yet trained this tame spaniel to distinguish between tradesmen and scoundrels like buccaneers.

Ned looked at the man seated at the head of the small table and saw a ferret complete in almost every detail, right down to the urine-coloured hair peeping out from the edges of the wig and which matched a ferret's fur. Pointed face, sharp little hungry eyes, small and yellowed teeth and the skin freckled like pepper on cold pork. So this was Sir Harold Luce. Well, Ned would bet His Excellency had never fought in the King's cause; he did not have the appearance of a man who had ever smelled powder or considered fighting for anything but his breath.

The ferret face turned to Heffer and said casually: "You had better introduce these men."

Heffer, already standing, turned to Ned. "Sir Harold Luce, may I present Mr Edward Yorke, and Sir Thomas Whetstone. Gentlemen, your new Governor, His Excellency Sir Harold Luce."

Luce nodded but made no attempt to shake hands. "Please be seated."

Ned looked at Heffer, and guessed that Thomas was doing the same.

"Whetstone? Whetstone? Aren't you Cromwell's nephew?" Luce asked querulously.

Thomas shook his head. "No. Oliver Cromwell, to whom I presume you are referring, is dead. I *was* the Lord Protector's nephew until a merciful but tardy God gathered him to His bosom."

For a full minute Luce worked out the sentence. Was it a declaration by Whetstone that he was a Roundhead? Was it a sarcastic reference by a Royalist to Cromwell's death?

Thomas tugged his well combed, square black beard, and inquired politely: "Is Your Excellency one of the Northumberland Looselies or are you of the Denbighshire branch?"

The Governor's face had first gone pale, but now it was becoming purple. "*Luce*, Whetstone, not Loosely."

Thomas looked down at his clothes. "What's loose, Your Excellency? I'm afraid I don't understand."

"My name, Whetstone. It is Luce." He spelled it out, enunciating each letter.

"Oh, I beg your pardon. I must admit that I didn't *think* you could be one of the Northumberland Looselies. Have it your own way, then; Loose it is."

Thomas managed to convey enough relief in his voice that Luce was left appearing as though he had been masquerading and, Ned realized, knew too little of the knightage to challenge Thomas about two families Ned knew had just been invented on the spur of the moment.

"Yorke," the governor snapped, but before he could continue Ned held up his hand.

"Your Excellency, no doubt you have brought a copy of the table of precedence with you?"

"Of course."

"Well, out here among the Caribbee Islands, quite apart from what they might be doing in Europe, we use the conventional method of address."

"Well?"

"Can't think how I mistook his name," Thomas mumbled, as though chiding himself for mistaking a gamekeeper for the owner. Then he said, loudly and clearly: "What Mr Yorke means is that in England you'd be seated at the table well to leeward of both of us and out here we peasants still hold on to the social graces. Thus if we address *you* as 'Your Excellency', you address *us* by our titles and observe precedent. I am a baronet and Mr Yorke is an earl's son, but prefers just the plain 'mister'. You, I imagine, are a knight by a very recent creation."

"And supposing I refer to you as 'Whetstone' and 'Yorke'?" Luce said sarcastically.

Ned stood up quietly, followed by Thomas. "We bid Your Excellency goodbye. If you'll permit me to misquote from the *Faerie Queene* – 'So with courteous *congé* both did give and take'. Not quite the 'both' that Spenser intended, but it must serve."

As Luce's face twisted into the hurt look of the man who could not see what he had done to offend anyone, Heffer leapt up in a sudden spasm, sending his chair flying. "You're not sailing, gentlemen?"

"Yes, I have a feeling we shall be happier in Tortuga."

"You mean you are taking all your ships? All thirty-three?"

"Yes, but you'll have the *Convertine* to guard you for another week or so."

By now Heffer's alarm warned Luce that something he did not yet understand had gone badly wrong; that adopting the high hand (but, damnation, he *was* Governor) with these two fellows had perhaps been a mistake.

"Gentlemen, gentlemen, you must excuse me: this is the first full day of my governorship, so forgive me for not appreciating all the social niceties. Please resume your seats, Sir Thomas and Mr Yorke; we have much to discuss."

Thirty-three ships? Luce realized that must mean just about every ship in the anchorage, apart from the *Convertine*. Did they all belong to this fellow Yorke? That would mean they were all pirates! Jamaica threatened by thirty-three pirate ships, and he had not yet slept two nights here . . .

As soon as both men were seated and Heffer had picked up his chair, resuming his place white-faced and flustered, Luce said as amiably as he knew how: "All those ships out in the anchorage, Mr Yorke: they belong to you?"

"No, Your Excellency. Only two."

"Who owns the others, pray?"

Ned shrugged his shoulders. "Blessed if I can remember. Let me see . . . Five are Dutch, one is a Spaniard, there are a couple of Portuguese . . ."

"Nine are French," Thomas said.

"Ah yes. One is Sir Thomas's, of course."

"Diana's," Thomas corrected.

"I beg your pardon, Your Excellency. That one belongs to Lady Diana Gilbert-Manners. Sir Thomas is – er, the master."

"That makes a total of twenty," Luce said.

"Does it, by Jove!" Ned said. "You've a sharp mind with figures. Whom have we forgotten, bishop?"

Thomas scratched his head and then slapped the table. "Damme, we forgot the English! Eight English. So with His Excellency's twenty, that makes twenty-eight. Then there are the five prizes from Portobelo."

"But . . . but . . ." An appalled Luce was stammering now, "most of those ships belong to foreign countries; ones which don't have Jamaica's welfare at heart . . ."

"Oh, don't worry about that Spaniard, Your Excellency," Thomas said reassuringly, "he's a splendid fellow; one of our best captains."

"I don't know what you mean by 'our' but Spain is no longer our enemy; a peace has been signed. *Obviously* the news hasn't reached you yet."

"It hasn't and won't make a scrap of difference when it does, Your Excellency," Ned said quietly. "Not a scrap."

Again the ferrety face began to turn purple and Heffer wriggled uncomfortably: this meeting was not proving the success he had hoped.

Ned turned to Luce, twisting his chair slightly. "Your Excellency – we'd be grateful if you'd bring us up to date with the happenings in England since the Restoration; then perhaps you might confide in us, ah, some indication of your instructions?" And, Ned thought to himself, if you expect more tact than that, you are nearly eighty degrees of longitude too far west.

Luce nodded judiciously, as though considering what State secrets he could reveal. "Well, you know the most important facts: our gracious King is back on the throne and is relying on the Duke of Albemarle (who was of course General Monck before his ennoblement) to run the country's affairs. You mentioned Spain – well, I can reassure you on that point: the King has just signed a peace treaty with Spain."

"Most encouraging," Ned said, and reflected on the letter from his elder brother George which the *Convertine* had brought out. George, who had inherited the title and the estates on their father's death and had been with the King during the royal exile in France and Spain, warned that the King had signed a secret treaty while in exile in Spain.

"Oh yes, it is," Luce said. "Indeed, the King of Spain has already sent an ambassador to the Court of St James, the Prince de Ligne, a most charming gentleman."

"And what did the ambassador demand, as a reward for Spain's hospitality during the King's exile there?"

Luce looked puzzled, and Ned asked innocently: "Was not a secret treaty signed with Spain which would come into effect on the King's Restoration?"

Luce stared down at the papers in front of him. "If it was secret, Mr Yorke, then I don't think it's any concern of ours."

"Oh, it's our concern all right: I just wondered if you had later news about it, or if the Duke had confided his views?"

"My lips are sealed," Luce said primly, squeezing them together until they vanished, leaving the tiny eyes and nostrils as the only marks on his face.

Thomas, who had read the letter from Ned's brother, roared with laughter and slapped the table again. "Well, your lips might be sealed, Your Excellency, but if you are going to survive out here in Jamaica, within musket shot of the Spanish Main, you'd better keep your ear to the grindstone and your nose to the keyhole!"

"Grindstone . . . keyhole? I don't –"

"I think Sir Thomas is hinting that although we are but

yokels, we do have friends in England watching our interests," Ned said mildly.

Luce eyed both men with wary suspicion. "What have you heard, then?"

Ned looked at Thomas doubtfully then shook his head. "No, Your Excellency, it wouldn't be fair to burden you; you'd only worry. Later we'll pass it on to General Heffer – I suppose you still command the island garrison, General?"

Heffer nodded cautiously, wondering what Ned had heard.

"If your information concerns the interests of this island, I demand that you tell me!" Luce said angrily.

Ned looked at him contemptuously. In appointing Luce, the Duke of Albemarle was either paying off an old debt or getting rid of a nuisance, but either way Jamaica was the loser. A Governor who did not want to understand the actual position out here (compared with what he had been told in London) was an even bigger liability than Heffer.

"Very well, I'll tell you, Your Excellency," Ned said patiently, "not because you 'demand' it but because your ignorance is a liability to us –"

"Damme sir, I'll not stand for your confounded insolence!"

Ned stood, followed a moment later by Thomas. "My apologies, Your Excellency, we embarrass you, but since your lips are sealed so that we cannot hear any more news of the danger in which the island stands, we'd better sail back to Tortuga."

Even without Heffer's appealing look, Luce realized that his "I am the Governor" bluster was simply antagonizing these two men. He also realized that they owed him nothing and all too clearly did not give a damn for his authority. And, he noted, Heffer seemed very anxious to placate them.

"Oh, do sit down again; you're a sight too touchy to deal with governors," Luce said, trying to sound jocular but, like all weak men, determined not to apologize again. "We are all concerned with the wellbeing of Jamaica, so we have the same interests."

"I doubt that," Thomas said sourly, "not judging by the pathetic little bag of money the Duke gave you to run this place. Each one of those ships out there uses more than that to buy the week's rum."

"Yes, well," Luce said lamely, not realizing that Thomas

was only guessing, "do please tell me what you've heard."

"Surely you must know," Ned said brusquely, "the King signed a secret treaty with Spain promising to return Jamaica and Dunkirk, and now the Prince de Ligne is in London demanding them both."

"Oh, *that*," Luce said offhandedly. "Yes, I heard about that," adding pompously, "these are matters of State."

"So you don't mention them to yokels, eh?" Thomas exclaimed angrily. "'Matters of State' like this are our daily bread. Our lives in fact. 'Matters of State' are stupid decisions wrapped up in flowery language!"

"Well, I have to be discreet."

"Your Excellency," Ned said crisply, having decided that it was time to put his cards face-up on the table, "Europe is one world and the Caribbee another. Treaties signed in London, Madrid, Paris, Lisbon or wherever you care to name, do not have the slightest effect on us out here.

"I told you the nationalities of the owners of our ships. The Frenchmen and Portuguese don't give a damn with whom France and Portugal are at war; they fled their countries years ago because of persecution. The Dutch are refugees from Spanish persecution in the Netherlands –"

"And the English?" Luce interrupted shrewdly.

"Originally we were Royalists escaping from Cromwell's régime, or men and women he had transported, prisoners of war or those sick of Puritanism. Now we have settled down here, trying to remake our lives again."

"A pretty speech," Luce said sarcastically, "but how does it concern me?"

"Because," Ned said slowly, now enunciating each word very clearly and carefully, "whatever the Spanish say in London and Madrid, whatever treaties they might sign, whatever agreements they might make with England, out here in the Caribbee *there is No Peace Beyond the Line*. No peace, no trade."

"You're exaggerating," Luce said contemptuously.

Heffer suddenly looked up. "He's not, Your Excellency. No Peace Beyond the Line – that is the prayer every Don says before he sleeps o' night."

"The Line, the Line – what the Devil has it to do with us?"

"Dear me," Ned said wearily, "I never expected to hear a

Governor of Jamaica speak those words. Briefly, Spain forbids any country to trade with her possessions out here. Not just trade, but forbids them to sail in the waters or enter her ports. The actual Line is a particular degree of longitude a few hundred miles west of the Azores. Anything west of that – the Americas, the Caribbee islands – all is 'Beyond the Line'."

"But that's nonsense – you *do* trade with the Main," Luce said.

Ned shook his head. "No, we don't 'trade', we *smuggle*. And if anyone is caught by the Spanish authorities he is handed over to the Inquisition, or sent to the salt mines, or put to work in the quarries, cutting out stone to build more fortresses."

"But that's absurd! I'll send a despatch to London!"

"Don't waste your time," Ned advised. "London knows all about it and, in answer to your next question, does nothing. Any moment the Spanish may attack and try to recapture Jamaica. What will the King do to defend it? After all, he's already signed a treaty giving it back to Spain."

"But I was told nothing of this in London," Luce wailed.

Thomas gave a throaty chuckle. "Nor were you given any ships to protect your new kingdom – even the *Convertine* is spared only long enough to bring you out, and she has orders to return home as soon as she's provisioned and watered."

Luce looked wildly from Ned to Thomas and then to Heffer.

"What can we do if the Spanish attack us?"

Heffer, in what Ned saw was probably the most daring act in his whole life, said in a lugubrious voice: "Pray, Your Excellency, and put your trust in the buccaneers . . ."

"Buccaneers? But they are simply pirates! The King didn't give me a commission to come out and entrust this island to a gang of pirates!"

"Then, he should have done," Heffer said unexpectedly. "They've saved it for him up to now and filled the Treasury with gold *and* kept the Spanish sufficiently frightened that so far they haven't dared make a regular attack."

"But they're just pirates!" Luce repeated helplessly, almost whimpering as he slowly realized the position he was in. Should he pretend illness and return to England in the *Convertine*? What illness, though? The Duke would see through that. Obviously, the Duke had known the situation out here when he gave him the job. Luce saw with a clarity which chilled the room that he was trapped between the deceit of an almost bankrupt Court in London and the murderous Spaniards out here. He tried to grab the conflicting ideas racing through his mind. Admittedly, these fellows in Jamaica have survived so far; there are plenty of prosperous plantations in the other islands, which are even more vulnerable than Jamaica. But remember, none of the other islands is such a threat to the Spaniards as Jamaica, which sits astride the route of the plate fleets to and from Cartagena. The other islands are small and Spain does not need land. Jamaica, though, is a dagger at its throat because of the plate fleet.

Heffer said quietly: "Yes, 'just pirates', Your Excellency, but Mr Yorke is their leader and Sir Thomas is his second-in-command." He took a deep breath. "In view of your attitude, I reserve the right to resign my commission and return to England in the *Convertine*: you shall have that in writing just as soon as this meeting is over."

"Oh come, now," Luce said hastily, "let's discuss this like reasonable men. After all, I –"

"We are not reasonable men," Thomas growled. "We are drunken pirates, the outcasts of nearly every country in Europe. We've not abandoned God; He's abandoned us. Drunkards and lechers we are – we whore all day and carouse all night and on Sundays sleep off a week of sin, and we are not the sort of people to whom a Governor holding the King's commission should introduce his wife or mistress. Is that not right, my worthy General? Was it wise of you to introduce the Governor to such scoundrels, rapscallions and heretics as us? Does he *know* how much I owe in gaming debts in London? Does he *know* I live in vigorous sin on board my pirate vessel with a most beautiful member of the aristocracy? Are you wise to keep such things secret from the Governor?"

Heffer began laughing and both Thomas and Ned stared at him. They had always assumed that when Heffer's unfortunate sheeplike face and head had been constructed, a malignant Nature had also omitted a sense of humour and the muscles necessary to pull his features into a smile.

However, having plucked up enough courage to threaten to resign, Heffer decided that, after all these years, he liked this new feeling of freedom. "My loyalty," he told Luce and was pleasantly surprised to hear himself saying it, "is to Jamaica and the King, not to any other individual."

"Well spoken," bellowed Thomas, again thumping the table. "There you are, Your Excellency, you'd never believe that a few months ago old Heffer here regarded my rascally Uncle Oliver as second-in-command to the Lord himself, would you? But Heffer has at last learned the one and only lesson that concerns the safety of Jamaica, and which I pass on to you. *If the Spanish come, they've got to come by sea.* Have a sampler made up with those words embroidered on it and hang it on the wall where you see it the moment you wake up in the morning."

While Thomas was making his little speech, using both arms as though beating time, Luce had been thinking quickly. Obviously, he needed these two men, both to help him govern Jamaica and – he shuddered – prevent him from ending up on a Spanish rack. He had been a fool not to have realized it sooner: these men were right: no one in London gave a damn about the safety, future or welfare of an island acquired almost as a whim and which the King intended giving away.

Even if the King changed his mind (because of the protests of the London merchants who now had interests in the West Indies), no one was going to push Jamaica's case at Court because that would only emphasize the King's error in the first place . . . But, Luce realized, he personally was stuck with it. There would be neither honour nor advancement if he managed to secure the island and get it properly governed; on the other hand, if he failed no one in London would grieve overmuch, so he would probably end his days in a dank Spanish dungeon.

"Very well, gentlemen, in confidence, I'll reveal my instructions –"

"No thank you!" Ned's interruption was quick and firm. "Tell us officially or not at all. This 'in confidence' is simply blackmail: it ties our hands so we can't do or say anything without you declaring: 'But I told you that in confidence.'"

"Your Excellency," Heffer added, "you should realize that even with our garrison disbanded (no, I'm not giving away secrets: everyone will know about that in a day or two) the Spaniards will still be out there. They'll discover within a few weeks that we no longer have a garrison – and their King already knows the value *our* King privately places on Jamaica."

"Well? What's all that got to do with it?"

Heffer stared squarely at Luce. "You don't seem to understand, Your Excellency, that you have few friends out here. In fact, none except the buccaneers."

Ned also turned and looked Luce straight in the eye. "And don't count on the buccaneers unless you make an agreement with them so that they can trust you. Remember, when the King promised Jamaica to Spain, he wasn't even on the throne – he had no right to do it."

Luce gestured to both Ned and Thomas. "Very well, you are the leaders of the buccaneers. As General Heffer has more than hinted, my first task is to pay off and disband the Army."

He thought a few moments. "No, I'll start earlier so that you can understand the sequence of events. As you know, both France and England have signed treaties with Spain. I know nothing of the secret treaty concerning Jamaica and Dunkirk apart from the London merchants protesting to the Duke about their trade interests out here. However, the Privy Council has set up a permanent committee to deal with the West Indies – with 'Trade and Foreign Plantations'. I report to this committee."

Ned asked: "So the Committee for Trade and Foreign Plantations drew up your instructions?"

"Well, I think they had received instructions from the Duke, but they actually drew up the new constitution for us. And a very fair one it is, too," Luce said defensively.

"Constitutions are luxuries that can wait," Ned said warily. "Tell us about the orders you have to carry out immediately."

"Well," Luce said apprehensively, "I have to withdraw all commissions granted to privateers and order the captains to return to port."

"Oh, so at least the Privy Council did not regard us as pirates, because it knew we all have commissions signed by the then acting Governor. It was just you who regarded us as pirates. Anyway, what ports do these privateers return to? Lisbon, Brest, Cadiz, Bristol . . . ?"

"All that was just a misunderstanding," Luce said hastily. "But you appreciate that now with the peace signed, your position has changed. Without commissions you are no longer privateers – or buccaneers, if you prefer the word."

"No," Ned said sourly, "without commissions we are simply pirates, if you prefer the word."

"But it's not what I prefer; that's the legal position," Luce said with a return to his old primness. "We are now at peace with Spain. Remember that."

"I hope I never have to remind you of your words," Ned said bitterly, "but do remember Sir Thomas's injunction about the Spaniards, and my reference to 'the Line'."

"Oh, I will, I will," Luce said eagerly, anxious to change the subject. "Now let me tell you the rest. It has been decided that everyone granted land in Jamaica shall pay no rent for seven years. Of course, new settlers must be Protestants and obey the laws of England."

Thomas started laughing, a laugh which began deep down and shook the table on which his elbows rested. "The laws of England . . . isn't that splendid, Ned? Most of the Army he's about to disband are the sweepings of Roundhead jails; most of the present settlers were transported by Cromwell because they were prisoners of war, or had been naughty boys, stealing sheep and laughing on Sundays, fornicating and even blaspheming, too. Who are the 'new' settlers going to be?"

Luce flushed. "Well, you hardly expect prosperous folk to leave their homes in England and come out here, do you?"

"Of course not; that's why I'm asking."

Luce sorted through several sheets of paper. "Well, yes, the Privy Council is agreed that convicts will be transported here as settlers – but no murderers, burglars or 'incorrigible rogues'."

"Ah, that rules out defaulting politicians," Thomas commented, "so perhaps we're luckier than we deserve. What now happens to poor old Heffer's Army?"

"Ah, yes. He tells me he had 1,523 men (plus 550 I'll refer to in a moment) and I have £12,247 to share out among them, their pay up to date plus a gratuity."

"So, clutching their pay and their gratuity to their

bosoms," Thomas said sourly, "what do they do then? Swim back to England?"

"Of course not," Luce said, having appeared to take the question seriously. "They will settle here."

"Despite the ban on 'incorrigible rogues'?"

"They're already here," Luce said, nimbly avoiding Thomas's trap. "But General Heffer will not be left entirely defenceless; I have instructions to keep a force of 400 infantry and 150 cavalry for the defence of the island –" He glanced down another page of written instructions and ran his fingers along a line. "Yes, to be kept 'as long as is thought fit for the preservation of the island'."

"Very wise," Thomas said judiciously, his tone making both Ned and Heffer look up. "Five hundred and fifty men . . . fewer than one man at every mile if they're placed carefully round the island. They'll hardly be able to see each other, let alone roister and gamble. Very shrewd men, the Privy Councillors."

"I'm sure General Heffer will make the best possible use of his force," Luce said hurriedly. "Now, the fort which you have built here on Cagway is to be called 'Fort Charles' –"

"It already is," Ned said, "in honour of the King."

"– and the whole spit, or peninsula, on which it and this building and the market stand, is to be called Port Royal."

"What excellent taste the Privy Council has," Thomas said.

"Now for the important part, which will affect those soldiers who are disbanded, along with everyone else. Every male and female over the age of twelve now living in Jamaica or arriving within two years is to be granted thirty acres of 'improvable land'."

"Hard luck on bachelors and spinsters," Ned commented. "A married man with a large family will receive a large estate – and no rent to pay for seven years."

"Do you want to hear about the new constitution?"

Ned shrugged his shoulders. "Well, since we're just sitting here, I suppose . . ."

"Well, the Governor will rule with a council of twelve locally elected men. The Governor and council –" he began reading again, "– 'will obtain and preserve a good correspondence and commerce with the plantations and territories of the King of Spain,' but if the Spanish governors refuse," Luce explained, "then all this will be done by force."

"By what force?" Ned asked innocently. "You will have 400 infantry and 150 cavalry, but how do they get across to the Main – to Cartagena, say, or Santiago, or Ríohacha, or Vera Cruz, or Havana in Cuba, to wield 'force'?"

It was Luce's turn to shrug his shoulders. "I assure you, gentlemen, that I understand my problems better now than I did when I first read these instructions.

"But let me finish. The Assembly (the Governor acting with the council) will make laws to remain in force two years, and no longer, unless approved by the Privy Council in London."

Thomas sniffed, doubtful and wary. "That means we're ruled entirely from London," he grumbled. "If they don't like a law, they don't approve it and it lapses after two years. But how will they know what's needed out here? They've shown no signs of doing so up to now. Stupidity reinforcing ignorance . . ."

"We'll have had a couple of years' benefit from it," Ned said, "and after two years we can pass other laws almost identical and that'll give us another two years . . ."

"Now, here's the final thing and I should have mentioned it earlier," Luce said hurriedly, not liking the loopholes being revealed. "I am to form a militia of five regiments, and each regiment is to be named after the particular area where the volunteers were recruited."

Ned sighed. "So we'll have the Port Royal Volunteers, commanded by the butcher with the candlemaker as second in command, and with three sawyers, two coopers, one potman and a rheumatic pickpocket as the fighting force. Five regiments, Thomas: I haven't seen five horses in the last five days!"

"I take it that you two gentlemen have no objection to me putting your names forward for election to the council?" Luce asked.

Thomas laughed and again the table trembled. "By all means do. I want particularly to be on the committee responsible for 'preserving a good correspondence and free commerce' with the Dons. And you, Heffer, you'd better start pacing out the positions for the sentry boxes for those 550 soldiers of yours. In the meantime, Your Excellency, Mr Yorke and I will open a few taverns and bordellos and we'll see if we can't get our hands on some of that £12,274 you will soon be giving to those dry-throated and womenless soldiers . . ."

Chapter Three

"Well, there they are," Ned said tapping the parchment of twenty-eight creased and stained commissions which he and Thomas had collected from the buccaneers, using their visits to explain the situation now that the Governor had arrived with a new constitution.

"None of the captains liked the news," Thomas said, more to tell Diana and Aurelia than comment on it.

"I should think not," Diana said. "If this shows what the Privy Council know about the Spanish, the Caribbee Islands and how to choose men to be governors, I hate to think what's happening in Barbados and Antigua, or even the Isle of Wight and the Isle of Dogs."

Thomas gave a bitter laugh. "Lopez made the most interesting comments, and don't forget he's Spanish. He said two things. First, that obviously our King has secretly converted to Catholicism and knows he has to curry favour with the Pope by returning Jamaica to His Most Catholic Majesty, and second, among our King's advisers is someone in the pay of Spain – probably a Catholic who was in exile with him and who drafted that secret treaty handing over Jamaica and Dunkirk."

Aurelia asked: "Do you think Lopez's right?"

Thomas glanced up at Ned, who nodded. "It sounds possible. I don't think the Duke of Albemarle is involved in the religious aspect, but obviously someone in the pay of Spain (or a Catholic fanatic) has the King's ear. It's the only way to account for Jamaica and Dunkirk – the Duke knows the bitter fighting for Dunkirk, and as for the place's importance to England, it doesn't matter whether it was Roündhead or Cavalier keeping out the Dons."

"Is Lopez likely to tell other captains what he thinks has happened in London?" Aurelia asked.

"Yes, he has to, out of loyalty to them."

"He wouldn't take your assurance that he was wrong?" Diana asked.

"Would *you* give anyone such an assurance?"

"No, I suppose not. What happens now, Ned? Do we all depart for Tortuga and forget we are just starting to build ourselves houses and clear land for planting after finding guns and gold for this island?"

Thomas sat down with a thump, his fingers beginning to curl the ends of his beard. "Thanks to the Portobelo purchase, none of us has to worry about money, and this fellow Loosely or whatever his name is can't avoid confirming Heffer's land grants to us, so we can go ahead and build the houses and clear the land, but . . ."

"Exactly," Aurelia said. "That 'but' . . . the island will have no Army, except for 550 pathetic buffoons spaced round the beaches, and no ships to protect it because the buccaneers will get bored and go after purchase: the Restoration of Charles II doesn't make the Dutch, French and Portuguese buccaneers suddenly love Spain. But you two men are going to enjoy clearing land and building houses and dressing up to attend council meetings whenever this buffoon Luce decides to call them. *Quelle blague*," she said disgustedly. "Do any of the buccaneer captains want a cook?"

"There's no holding a French lady once she gets going," Diana said laughingly. "Can I say my Catechism now?"

"Go ahead," Ned said ruefully. "You'll have to say '*quelle blague*' in English, and anyway, the Spaniards won't be here before Michaelmas!"

"Thank you, kind sir, for that reassurance. First, if you two leave the island now for Tortuga, it means that Luce blunders along with the help of a few misguided tradesmen as councillors. Poor old Heffer – who at last has learned a few lessons from you – will be left with no allies."

"Good point," Thomas grunted, "but do we really *care*

what happens to the island now? Hasn't London cast us off by giving us back to Spain?"

"*Going* to give," Aurelia said. "They haven't done it yet."

"It's the anchorage, not the island," Diana said. "But anyway, I'm not going to waste all that work we've done pegging out the foundations for our house. We have at least six months before we need worry about the Spanish. Five months, perhaps four – how many? Anything can happen by then."

Ned shrugged his shoulders. "The Dons haven't the ships over here to do us much harm – yet. But what's going on in Madrid? If they feel strongly about Jamaica, then they've got to dig the money out of their treasury and fit out enough ships to send a fleet to deal with us here. And collect the silver and gold and gems that have been piling up in Cartagena and Vera Cruz for shipment to pay Spain's debts. The Spanish King will soon be defaulting on his loans from the Fuggers and the other bankers in Europe. So sending out a fleet (if he can afford it) would serve two purposes."

"I doubt he can borrow the money to fit out a fleet," Thomas said.

Ned disagreed. "He might be able to borrow more because the bankers know they won't get a dollar more of interest or principal for years unless the Dons get at least one plate fleet from the Main. The last was years ago, from Vera Cruz. The Spaniards' treasury is really in the silver mines out here, which means the King can't spend a dollar of it until he ships it home."

"What you mean," Thomas said, "is that the bankers will have to risk more money to get their original loans back."

"Yes. Risk throwing good money after bad. Bankers hate that."

Diana smiled and held her hands palm uppermost. "Then we need to be more frightened of the bankers than the Spaniards!"

Ned nodded. "For many years Spain has been using her money to try to force converts to her religion, but I begin to think that bankers must be shaking their heads now over a new loan which might end up bringing Spain to its knees faster than an invading army!"

"None of which," Diana reminded them, "helps us decide what we do. If our new King gives us away to Spain, it doesn't matter about bankers. What about us? What do you think, Aurelia?"

"I agree with you about the house. I've ridden over those mountains so often and been bitten by so many mosquitoes, that I'd like to see it finished. Clearing the land for planting – when we know if we keep the land or give it to a *hidalgo* – can wait until later. We have time, haven't we Ned?"

"I think so, but whether we have time or not really depends on what the buccaneers decide. They long ago elected me their Admiral, and Governor Luce's arrival doesn't change that. But now he's cancelled their commissions will they go on using Port Royal as a base? That's what matters. If they don't, many merchants and chandlers will be ruined."

"They'll still attack the Spanish or smuggle?" Diana asked.

"Of course they will. It's the only life they know!"

"How does that affect you?" Aurelia asked quietly.

"If I remain their leader, I'll be a pirate as far as the English are concerned, because now we're at peace with Spain."

Thomas interrupted by holding up his hand. "But what about that 'forcing a trade' clause in the Governor's orders?"

"That is to follow attempts at doing it peacefully!"

"Well, you don't think the Spanish will agree to a peaceful trade, do you? It's a contradiction. People either trade or they don't trade – you can't force 'em. The third method is the one we've always done – smuggle. Anyway, that sort of decision about trade would have to be made in Spain, and it'd take months to get an answer back from Madrid. Six months at least."

"And the buccaneers are not going to stay here idle and drinking rum and chasing the women in the bordellos, for as long as that."

"No," Ned said firmly and, winking at Aurelia, added: "There's such a poor choice of women for them, too."

Luce wasted no time in appointing his legislative council and both Ned and Thomas were notified that they had been chosen to serve. The following day they received a notice in the morning that they were required to attend a meeting that evening at "the Governor's residence" in Port Royal. This, a postscript added, was the house previously occupied by the acting Governor.

"He's got to be trained," Ned grumbled. "Evening meetings mean we have to fight our way through swarms of mosquitoes. Why not morning meetings? Or even afternoons?"

When they arrived for the meeting, Ned and Thomas found five large candles burning on what had been Heffer's desk, which was surrounded by chairs on three sides, the fourth side having only one chair on which the new Governor was to sit. Heffer emerged from the small crowd when Ned and Thomas came into the room and, keeping them to one side, said quietly: "The Governor has asked me to introduce you to any councillor you might not know . . ."

"Don't know any of 'em," Thomas said bluntly. He looked at the men, still standing round talking. "That doesn't surprise me. Sorry-looking lot, aren't they?"

"Er . . . well, they're tradesmen, of course, and not used to this sort of thing. You gentlemen are going to have to be patient and teach them."

"Teach them!" Thomas exclaimed. "What do *we* know about councils? Ned gives the orders to the Brethren and they obey; on board my ship I give the orders and the men obey. No discussing and debating!"

He was thankful Diana could not hear him and as he caught Ned's eye he saw the same thoughts were crossing his mind about Aurelia. The sisterhood of the Coast, the identities known only to the two men, had more influence than all the Brethren!

"No, quite," Heffer agreed. "But now we have a Governor and a legislative council, so you gentlemen must keep to the agenda! Your turn will come last."

Ned stared at Heffer: it was the first time he had heard the man say anything which sounded even whimsical, let alone amusing. "If the agenda is your responsibility, write down just one item: 'Any other business'."

"I've already done that," Heffer said. "The final item. That's *your* turn!"

Heffer found he did not have to lead Mr Yorke and Sir Thomas to the other councillors: as soon as they realized who the two men were, they hurried across the room and formed a line. Ned was amused to notice that already they had decided their own order of precedence, probably based on each man's prosperity.

The first introduced by Heffer was a squat and fat-faced man with a jolly manner who was obviously quite in awe of Ned. "I'm O'Leary, the ship chandler – I'm glad to meet you, sir. I hope I can look forward to having you for a customer."

Ned grinned and shook his head. "Not unless the Dons stop supplying us for nothing!"

O'Leary laughed cheerfully. "Don't let the Governor hear you say that – I hear we're supposed to be at peace with Spain now."

"Has anyone told the Dons?" Thomas made no attempt to keep his voice low as he introduced himself.

After O'Leary came Kinnock, the island's pawnbroker, whose narrow and mean-looking face had already marked him down in Ned's mind as a moneylender, pawnbroker or apothecary. His skin was white and he was one of those unlucky men who perspired heavily, both naturally and because he drank heavily.

His pallid complexion was emphasized by a sharp red nose so heavily veined that it appeared to be covered with crude purple lace. A pair of long moustaches once blond were now stained by the smoke from pipe tobacco and sagging because they formed a natural catchment of the perspiration streaming down his forehead and missing his eyebrows. His tapered beard was so thin that it reminded Ned of a discarded paint brush.

Kinnock obviously realized that Nature had treated him unfairly and equally obviously was under no illusion that most men disliked him. However, he made the mistake of assuming his unpopularity was due to his trade, whereas it was caused entirely by his ungracious manner, obvious meanness and obsession with the value and price of everything.

He had no sooner been introduced to Ned than he was fingering Ned's sword. "That's from Toledo, Mr Yorke, I'll stake my reputation on it. Where else can you find gold wire inlaid like that? Any time you want to sell it, Mr Yorke, you call on me!"

"I'm sure Mr Yorke will," Heffer said hastily, and turned Ned so that he met the next person. "You don't know Mr Fraser, who imports most of our cloth and thread," he said, and before he could complete the introduction Fraser was shaking Ned's hand with a firm grasp, and turning to do the same with Thomas.

"I've been wanting to meet you two gentlemen for a long time," he said eagerly. He was a burly man, round-faced and cheerful – every child's idea, Ned thought, of a kindly uncle who brought a present when he visited.

"Yes, I've wanted to thank you. Without you and your men, we tradesmen here would long ago been killed by the Dons – or be trying to scratch a living in somewhere like Barbados!"

Ned smiled and then said: "General Heffer and his men played a part, too, don't forget."

"Best we *do* forget it," Fraser said amiably, eyeing Heffer. "The only thing his men could do against the Spanish is let their trollops give them the pox!"

Heffer flushed but did not argue – an indication of Fraser's wealth, Ned thought – or the accuracy of his comment.

"Tell me, Mr Yorke," Fraser asked quietly, "what have you heard about giving the island back to Spain? Giving us all to Spain, rather."

Ned thought of the fate of the bearer of bad tidings. "I'm sure our new Governor will soon have something to say about it – after all, this is the first meeting of his new legislative council."

"We'll send him packing if he tries to humbug us," Fraser growled. "The *Convertine* frigate hasn't sailed yet!"

Heffer coughed and took Ned's arm. "There are several more people you should meet before the council starts its meeting," he said hurriedly. "Please excuse us, Mr Fraser."

With two exceptions, the rest of the members echoed Fraser's question about the Spaniards. The two exceptions were men who Ned remembered were planning to set up a business importing slaves. From the Main, he assumed: the Spanish *asiento* claimed the monopoly of slave trading from the Gulf of Guinea to the Main and the Indies. To bring in slaves, this pair would first have to buy them from Spanish traders. Then Ned remembered how he knew of the pair: for a long time they had been protesting to Heffer about the Brethren's activities against Spain, complaining that the buccaneers were wrecking any chance of trade with the Main. At the time their protests had seemed ludicrous, but now, in the light of the news from England, they seemed sinister.

Parry, he was one of the men, a Welshman. Who was his partner? Shaw, that was his name. Parry had wanted to arrange for Spaniards to make an official visit to Jamaica – even suggested, so Heffer said, that their leader should be given some sort of present, a piece of silver plate or something.

Even the humourless Heffer had seen the irony of that, because any piece of silver plate given to the Dons must certainly have been captured from them in the first place. Although Port Royal boasted a silversmith (a very good one, as it happened) he was a wild man with a great hatred for the Spanish. Even now he was working on pieces of silver which were to designs that Aurelia and Diana had drawn for him, but anyone suggesting he did anything for a Spaniard (unless a buccaneer) was likely to get his throat cut, albeit with a silver knife.

Heffer pulled an enormous watch from his fob pocket and clucked like a scrawny hen recalling strayed chicks.

"Gentlemen, please be seated: the Governor will be here any moment." He looked at Ned and Thomas, and pointed to the two chairs on the right side of the desk. "If you two gentlemen will sit there . . ."

"Why?" Thomas demanded. "I like to face people."

"A matter of precedence," Heffer said mischievously.

Preceded by his secretary, William Hamilton, who marched with all the self-important strutting of an auctioneer and tapped the floor three times with his gold-topped cane, demanding silence, Sir Harold Luce walked into the room, bowing slightly as he held the scabbard of his ceremonial sword with all the wariness of a passing adult eyeing a playful child's broomstick.

"Forgot to put his face on," Thomas muttered. The Governor's expression fluttered between embarrassment, welcome and stern resolve.

"Good evening, gentlemen, pray be seated."

Obviously he had carefully rehearsed the phrase because in fact no one had risen: only Heffer was standing, having turned as if to greet the Governor.

"Ah, yes, well," Sir Harold said, manoeuvring his sword scabbard so that he could sit down safely, "welcome, gentlemen. I am sorry I have not yet met each of you personally – with a few exceptions, of course – but I wish to send the minutes of our first executive council meeting to London in the *Convertine*, which is due to sail tomorrow. Now," he said, his voice becoming brisker, "my secretary, Mr Hamilton, will give each of you a copy of the agenda for this first meeting of the council –"

"I hope this isn't a precedent," Fraser said.

"What isn't a precedent, pray?" a puzzled Luce asked.

"Giving us the agenda at the meeting. Doesn't give us time to consider any of the items."

"No, quite," Luce agreed warily, "but the *Convertine* . . ."

Fraser looked at the sheet of paper which the secretary had just given him. "Aye, well, I should send down word to the captain of the *Convertine* that he won't be sailing for a day or two – not judging from items three and four – aye, and seven, too. And we'd better start looking for a bigger council chamber, too. I've got barns better than this hutch."

Luce look startled. "Well, Mr – ah . . ."

"Fraser," the man said uncompromisingly, and spelled it out for good measure.

"Well, Mr Fraser, it all seems straightforward to me, I can't see any reason to delay the *Convertine*."

"There's no reason to delay the *Convertine*," Fraser agreed. "You'll need something bigger than a frigate to carry the minutes of this meeting to London after we've talked about the items on the agenda."

"To what items are you referring?" Sir Harold asked, not bothering to keep the chill out of his voice.

"Three, four and seven, of course!"

"Ah yes," Luce said, as though talking to a child. "But of course item number ten is the important one."

Fraser's finger ran down the list. "What, the one that says 'To hear the new constitution'?"

"Yes. I intend reading it to you."

"Why is that so important?" Thomas asked suspiciously, his eyes narrowing as he realized that Fraser had not caught the significance of the triumphant tone in Luce's voice.

"Ah yes," Luce said, and Thomas noted that he would hate that phrase before many more hours had passed, "the constitution gives the Governor power to dissolve the legislative council."

For a few moments the rest of the members did not grasp the meaning, but Ned asked at once: "What happens then?"

"Ah yes," Luce said innocently, "then the Governor rules the island by decree."

"You just give orders without being accountable to anyone, that's what you mean?" Fraser demanded.

"That's a crude way of describing governing by decree, but certainly –" Luce hesitated a moment and then decided to try to placate the men staring at him, "– certainly it means governing without the help and advice of you gentlemen."

"Well, let's get on with it," Fraser growled.

Luce nodded, and began reading from a paper in front of him: it was the King's commission establishing him as Governor of Jamaica, and conveying the King's greeting to the island's people. As soon as he had finished, Luce rolled up the scroll with a flourish and gave it to his secretary, who handled it as though any sudden movement might change the wording.

"Now," Luce told the seated men, "your names have been suggested to me as suitable members of the legislative council. You will appreciate," he said casually, "that few of you are known to me personally at this stage, so I might later suggest that certain of you resign to make way for – er, replacements."

"The naughty boys will be sent out of the room," Thomas commented to no one in particular. "Quite right too: can't have teacher upset, can we."

Luce tried to squeeze a smile to show that he could appreciate a joke, but obviously he suspected that Sir Thomas Whetstone was not joking. "Well, now you all have the agenda for this first meeting. As you see, I have already dealt with the first item, reading my commission. The second item simply says, as you can see, 'Agreement to serve'. As I have not yet received written acceptances from all of you of my invitation to serve on the council, I will assume that anyone not now withdrawing from the room is in fact accepting. Yes? Good, I am sure we shall work well together.

"Now we come to the third item, 'Paying off and disbanding the Army'. Yes, Mr Fraser," he said holding up a hand, "I know you want to speak on the subject, but first please allow me to describe my instructions from the King –"

"From the Secretary for Trade and Foreign Plantations, more likely," Thomas growled.

"Ah yes," Luce said. "The Secretary was speaking in the King's name, of course."

"Of course," Thomas agreed. "Please go on . . ."

Hurriedly, fearing more interruptions, Luce repeated what he had already told Ned and Thomas: he had brought out £12,247 to share among the 2,073 soldiers, representing their overdue pay and a gratuity.

"A total of less than six pounds a man," Fraser commented.

"That's the pay due to them, *and* a gratuity – what more can they expect?"

"Mr Fraser wasn't thinking of that," Thomas said, "he was thinking that £12,000 is a small price to pay for the defence of the island."

"Ah yes," Luce exclaimed brightly, "but four hundred infantry and one hundred and fifty cavalry will be kept as long as I think necessary."

"Five hundred and fifty men and a few score spavined nags?" Ned asked. "That works out at one man for every three miles of coast – providing that none is sick, and no horse has gone lame."

Luce shrugged his shoulders elaborately and held up his hands. "Gentlemen, gentlemen, I'm afraid all this is out of my hands. This was decided in London and these are my instructions."

Fraser sniffed contemptuously. "Just means that we still have to rely on the buccaneers to protect us."

"Oh no, it doesn't," Ned said quietly. "Read the next item on the agenda."

Fraser read aloud: "Item four 'Commissions and letters of marque'." He stared at the Governor. "What *exactly* does that mean?"

"Wait until we come to it, Mr Fraser," Luce said impatiently. "We must approach these matters in the correct order."

Thomas began laughing, a deep laugh which started in his belly and erupted like spasmodic explosions. "The correct order! Your Excellency has a splendid sense of humour."

"I fail to see any joke," Luce said stiffly.

"No, I suppose not," Thomas said sadly. "But these gentlemen will think you are teasing them. First you tell them they no longer have an Army – which, with respect to General Heffer, was a polite name for a rabble. Then, in the next item on the agenda, you are going to tell them you're sending away the very men who in the past have brought them guns, food, gold and silver. I can't speak for the rest of the council, but as far as I can see you'll have ruined the island long before you hand it over to Spain!"

At once several of the men jumped up, yelling at Luce, asking if Jamaica really had been promised to Spain.

White-faced, Luce stood up, forgetting the gavel lying on the table, and started to shout back, more from fright than because he had any answers. Thomas glanced at Ned and winked, and then saw Heffer watching and obviously struggling hard to keep the satisfaction showing in his face.

Finally the shouting men sat down, out of breath, but Luce remained standing, apparently dazed by his councillors' violent reaction and uncertain what to do. The skin covering his narrow face was even more shrunken and his yellowed teeth were bared, as though he knew he was cornered. His eyes flickered from left to right, as if he was looking for a bolt hole.

Finally Heffer came to his rescue, picking up the gavel and tapping the table. "Gentlemen, we are still discussing item number three, the disbanding of the Army and the formation of a militia . . ."

Luce, like a man suddenly coming from darkness into a well-lit room, sat down and numbly took the gavel proffered by Heffer. "Ah yes, number three. That does not call for any decision by the council, since I have my instructions: I was merely reporting to the council. The same goes for number four, so we move on to –"

"Surely Your Excellency is going to report to the council your instructions concerning item number four?" Ned asked quietly.

"You'd better," Fraser told the Governor harshly. "If the damned Dons had captured this island, I reckon they'd be singing the same song as you!"

"There's nothing to get excited about," Luce muttered, obviously fighting hard to keep the despair from his voice.

"You gentlemen *must* understand that we are no longer at war with Spain. The two nations *must* live together peacefully –"

"Aye, try telling that to the Dons," growled a man sitting next to Fraser. "'No peace beyond the Line' they say. They drew the damn' Line and we're the wrong side of it. Tell the Pope to scribble it out. Until he does, we need an Army and we need a Navy – or the buccaneers."

"Tell them," Thomas prompted Luce. "Tell 'em what the Committee for Trade and Foreign Plantations have decided about the buccaneers. The fourth item on your agenda."

"Sir Thomas," Luce said severely, "unless you stop addressing your Governor in that insulting tone of voice, I shall adjourn this council meeting."

"Have you ever seen a flustered cook throwing water over a pan of blazing fat?" Thomas asked conversationally. "In a few seconds she has the whole kitchen blazing. You've taken away their Army and now you're taking away what passes for their Navy. And," he added heavily, "those gentlemen in London are taking away their island. No –" he shook his head sadly, "– no one is going to invite *you* in for a rum punch."

As Luce sat open-mouthed, Ned stood up and slapped Thomas on the back. "Well, m'lord bishop, we can't waste the evening gossiping, so let's not take up any more of His Excellency's time."

With that he led the way to the door, hearing several voices agreeing with him and chairs scraping as they were pushed back.

"Yes," Diana said, "you were both very witty at poor Sir Harold Loosely's expense, but he won the battle."

"What do you mean?" Thomas said irritably, reaching across the table for the onion-shaped bottle of rum. "We told him exactly what we thought of him!"

"But the Army is still going to be disbanded and paid off, and all your commissions are cancelled," Aurelia pointed out. "You didn't make him change his mind."

"We couldn't," Ned said, "because it's not up to him. He'd been ordered to pay off the Army and cancel our commissions before leaving London. He can't change anything."

"Do you think he would – or at least try to persuade the ministers in London?"

"Sir Harold wears a wig," Ned said unexpectedly. "He's not used to wearing a wig. And his head itches. What does that tell us? Why, that his hair is still growing out. *He was a Roundhead!* Until the Restoration, he had his hair cropped in the fashionable Cromwell style. As soon as Albemarle put the King on the throne, Loosely (and many like him) put wigs on their heads to hide their revealing and now unfashionable 'Roundhead' hairstyle. Hair takes a long time to grow and itches in the process. Wigs are particularly uncomfortable in the Tropics. Now, what was I saying? Ah yes, Sir Harold is concerned only with the survival and glorification – and enrichment – of Sir Harold Luce. Like all governors sent out to the Plantations, he sees the job as an opportunity to fill his purse and start an apprenticeship which will eventually let him get his foot on the lowest rung of the peerage with a barony . . . it's the only way such people can make 'ladies' of their wives, you know."

"All of which," Diana said, "means he's no help to the people of Jamaica or the buccaneers."

"Bravo," Thomas said, "you've arrived at last. Old Loosely has probably taken off his wig and is dictating a despatch this very moment to tell his Council in London that he's had to dissolve the executive council after a few hours because everyone was nasty to him and that in future he will govern the island by decree."

"Until the Spanish arrive to take possession," Ned added.

"Exactly. 'Ah yes' Loosely realizes now that he's just the caretaker before the handing over."

"Caretaker in a haunted house," Aurelia said unexpectedly.

"Indeed, but the people haunting him at today's meeting were real enough."

Thomas refilled his glass, setting down the bottle with a bang. "Still, apart from those two would-be slave traders, most of the merchants were on our side."

"That hardly surprises me," Ned said. "The buccaneers are their best customers, whether simply at anchor here or buying supplies to smuggle to the Main. That chap Fraser, for example: he knows that thanks to the buccaneers half the cloth he sells here is eventually resold by Spaniards on the Main."

"Well then," Aurelia said, looking across at Diana for support, "leave the merchants to fight the Governor. They have a lot more to lose than we have. After all, the buccaneers only have to sail to another island. Once away from Jamaica they don't *need* commissions or letters of marque to smuggle to the Main or capture Spanish ships and towns . . ."

Diana nodded agreement but said: "For all that, in spite of any secret treaty the King might have been advised to sign or any idiocy the government might perpetrate in London, the fact is we all feel a loyalty to Jamaica."

"Yes, that's the damnable thing," Ned admitted. "We know England should keep Jamaica and we know any peace treaty with Spain will be brief and torn up the moment Spain thinks it to her advantage but . . . well, I suppose we're not the first Englishmen to realize that our country is our own worst enemy."

"That's pitching it a bit strong, Ned," Thomas protested.

"Is it?" Ned asked quietly. "Could Spain have made Jamaica's Army disappear by throwing £12,000 at the soldiers? Could Spain have driven more than a score of buccaneer ships away from Jamaica using a few written words? Could Spain without doing anything have ruined all Jamaica's merchants – because that is inevitable – as a free bonus?"

"He's right, Thomas," Diana said, cupping her generous breasts as though weighing them. "God knows, Thomas, you of all people should beware of trusting kings and courtiers and politicians. You're reasonably safe with pimps, prostitutes and panders, but guard yourself against the rest."

"What have we decided about us, then?" Aurelia was puzzled.

"I'm anxious to see our houses completed," Diana said firmly.

"You just want to sleep in a big bed again," Thomas growled. "As soon as you set foot on land you start eyeing me with a speculative look."

"There's no harm in that," Ned said. "I'm all for completing the houses – it'll give us something to do. We can always burn 'em down if the Dons come, and anyway we have our ships at anchor waiting for us. The buccaneers will go off to Tortuga, and they'll be quite happy without their Admiral for a few weeks."

He looked across at Aurelia, who was clearly picturing the completed house in her imagination. Or was she thinking of her last home, a lifetime ago in Barbados? She could only remember that place with a shudder, and the husband (since dead, admittedly) who had made her life a hell.

Looking back on it, Ned realized just how much he (and Aurelia) had matured since then. When he ran the family's Kingsnorth estate, and his neighbour had been the drunken sot Wilson, who bullied his French wife and treated her with contempt, Ned had fallen in love with her, but she had insisted on keeping her wedding vows.

Until . . . yes, Ned admitted that in a curious way Cromwell had done him a good turn because the Roundheads' planned seizure had stirred Wilson into such a frenzy that Aurelia had come with Ned when he fled in the *Griffin* with most of his staff. Since then . . . well, first Wilson had managed to get hold of Kingsnorth, and later Aurelia heard that he had died, so she inherited both the original estate and also Kingsnorth.

And now – for months, in fact since Wilson's death – they had been free to marry, but the only Protestant church in Port Royal was little more than a shack, and both of them wanted to pay for the construction of a new stone church. So Aurelia, for the time being, continued as Mr Yorke's mistress, not his wife; but no one paid any attention – they accepted the situation, in the same way they accepted that Thomas's hateful wife in England prevented him marrying Diana.

Would the Dons come before the church was built?

Chapter Four

While Ned rode off on his horse to talk to the carpenters, masons and labourers (now starting to dig trenches for the foundations), and inspect the temporary kitchen (with its oven made out of rocks and which provided daily meals for everyone on the site), Aurelia sat alone in the shade at the edge of the cliff.

The tamarind tree, shaped like a giant mushroom and with foliage so thick the shimmering noon sun could not penetrate, survived the perpetual buffeting of the Trade wind because it grew on the lee side of a range of hills running northwards to the sea. The hills ended abruptly at the coast in steep cliffs forming the western end of a bay and against which the northerly swells thundered even on almost windless days, sending fine spray drifting upwards in a salty mist.

Aurelia's tamarind – Ned and Thomas had been quick to name it as hers – was halfway along the western slope of the hills which would protect the house when completed. To windward, another range of similar hills ran parallel, plunging down to the sea to form the eastern end of the bay.

Ned had already brought the *Griffin* round to the north coast and sent in a boat to survey the bay. It was deep enough for both the *Griffin* and Thomas's ship; the holding ground was good and, Ned had told her, would be an excellent anchorage except during the northers of the winter, which brought rollers crashing against the cliffs with a ferocity that had frightened Aurelia the first time she saw them and helped Ned persuade her not to insist on building their house on the edge of the cliff. A constant view of the sea was splendid, Ned had agreed, but had Aurelia thought of the fine spray in the sea air? Polished silver tarnishing within hours; mildew as much of an enemy of cloth and leather as it was on board a ship. Paint would peel off window frames and shutters . . . the way Ned described it all, Aurelia began to think of sea air as a corrosive acid . . .

She settled herself on the stool after looking carefully on the ground in case it had stirred up a nest of ants which would crawl up her own legs, seeking bare skin to bite with vicious hot-needle nips. Then she unrolled the parchment plan of the house and looked at it for the thousandth time.

The architect must have spent as much time drawing the title of the house as the plan itself! *Yorke Hall, with Plantations and Lands* it said on a shield surrounded by elaborate cross-hatching indicating the nearby hills and valleys. Aurelia knew there was a second parchment indicating all land, rivers and streams, the big stands of trees and where various crops would best grow. The site of a proposed sugar mill was shown beside the largest river, along with the little houses, hospital, kitchens and the water cistern for the slaves who would eventually work the plantation.

The house seemed enormous. She looked at the plan and then the front elevation; then she shut her eyes, trying to picture the completed building. Yes, rectangular and on two floors, its roof giving it a Norman look. The front entrance – that was impressive: high double doors opened out on to a stone balcony the width of the house and wide stone staircases curved round like horns at each end.

When she protested that visitors climbing the steps still had a long walk to the front door even when they reached the balcony, Ned's explanation had been chillingly simple: whether they approached from left or right, they would have to pass the windows of three rooms before reaching the door. In times of danger those windows would be shuttered, and each double shutter (made of bullet wood) would have two keyhole-shaped gunloops carved in it, so twelve muskets – two for each window – could drive off any unwelcome visitors, from whichever direction they approached.

For several days Aurelia had teased Ned over the gunloops, saying that the Spanish would never come. "Spaniards!" he exclaimed finally. "I'm not worried about Spaniards; I'm concerned about the Maroons!"

The Maroons (originally called *Cimarróns* by the Spanish – the word meant "wild man", she remembered) still lived scattered among the mountainous ridges that were almost the backbone of the island. They came down in bands to loot and steal: they would set fire to plantation houses, burn crops, shoot settlers if they had the chance – Ned said they were fantastic marksmen – and drive off their cattle and donkeys, taking them back whence they came, into the thick forests of the Grand Ridge of the Blue Mountains or, if they came from the western end of the island, into the remote area known simply as "the Cockpit country".

Looking across the rolling hills and up into the mountains it was hard to think of roving bands of hostile Maroons. She could understand the Spanish freeing their slaves after the British attacked the island and gradually captured the important places. These Indian slaves were the native men who had looked after the great herds of cattle, wonderful horsemen and fine shots, who could lasso or shoot the cattle as required.

If one came from the eastern islands, negroes from Africa working in the sugar and tobacco plantations came to mind when one thought of slaves; but as one moved westward, to the big islands of the Greater Antilles, Cuba, Hispaniola and Porto Rico, the word slaves usually meant herdsmen, native Indians captured three or four generations ago by the Spanish settlers.

And of course, as Ned never tired of telling her, it was to the herds of cattle and the *Cimarróns* that the buccaneers traced their origins . . . As the Spanish fled from the big islands or moved on to the Main in their search for gold, they left behind herds of cattle and thousands of hogs, all of which bred happily because they had no natural enemies: only the *Cimarróns* (released by the Spanish, or escaped from captivity) hunted them.

Then when the small islands to the east, the ones standing like sentry boxes to stop the Atlantic invading the Caribbee, were later captured by French, British and Dutch who started plantations, it was only a matter of time before the white rebels and refugees from those islands also moved westwards, into the big islands which, except for the bigger cities like San

Juan, Havana and Santo Domingo, had been abandoned by the Spanish, with the *Cimarróns* running wild in the forests and mountains.

"Rebels and refugees" – well, they were: Protestant Frenchmen, Royalist English, Irish and Scots oppressed by Cromwell, Dutchmen escaping from a Netherlands where the Spanish were determined to turn everyone into Catholics . . .

These men were indeed rebels, she realized, but the majority of them were not rebels in the sense that they actually rebelled against a particular king or a government or a religious system, but rather it was a case that they did not conform to the pattern of life laid down in their own country. They did not necessarily agree with the Pope, or Cromwell, or Colbert, or whichever Spanish duke was ruling the Netherlands, and the price of disagreement (assuming the man escaped with his life) was getting out of the country – and being labelled a rebel.

These "rebel" French, British and Dutch from the islands to windward had moved westward in small groups, three men here, a dozen there. They made canoes from hollowed-out tree trunks and once they reached the shores of the Spanish islands they poached cattle and hogs, selling hides and lard to passing ships, or exchanging them for powder and shot. And these men, not surprisingly, were called the "Cow Killers" – not to be confused with the native *Cimarróns*. Their only enemies were rum, disease – and the Spanish, who hunted them down when possible, although whether because they objected to the men living among the bays and lagoons of their islands or because they could not bear having heretics round their shores, Aurelia did not know.

At first, the "Cow Killers" could not preserve the meat they killed – presumably they were often too far from the natural salt ponds that lined many coasts – and they saw the meat go rotten within twelve hours in the tropical heat. Yet the *Cimarróns* had a simple solution, which the "Cow Killers" adopted – they cut the meat into narrow strips and dried it in smoke over a slow fire. They dug a shallow pit for the fire and then built over it a grating of green wood, the whole thing being called a *barbecu* by the Indians, although the French called it a *grille de bois*.

A slow fire cured the meat by heat and smoke and the meat would then last a good six months, providing it was first dusted with salt. Beef, as she knew only too well, had little taste left by then, but hog's flesh was better. Anyway, the Indians called such meat *boucan*, and the "Cow Killers" soon found that by packing *boucanned* meat into their satchels and canoes they had food for long expeditions. Then because they adopted the custom of Caribbee Indians, the "Cow Killers" gradually became known as *boucaniers*, a word the English soon rendered as buccaneers.

"Boucan" – Aurelia laughed to herself over the word. Curing meat over a *barbecu* was, as she knew from long experience, a hot and smoky business, and people living along the Norman coast of France soon referred to a house with a smoky chimney as "*un vrai boucan*". Aurelia remembered she had first heard the phrase as a child, and now as an adult she was (at first she hesitated over the word, then found she was in fact proud of it) the mistress of the leader of the buccaneers, and her closest friend was the mistress of his second-in-command.

Diana – yes, a *ripe* woman, in the most glorious sense of the word. And Thomas was a lusty man, a man with a roaring laugh and an unquenchable thirst – yet sensitive and gentle. No, Ned became angry when she began to speculate over the love life of people she knew . . .

Eventually, some of the *boucaniers* built larger canoes and captured small coasting vessels from the Spanish, and from then on she supposed they were pirates, attacking Spanish villages, towns and ships whenever they had the chance.

But by the time the British had captured Jamaica and driven out the Spanish, the island was only too glad of the *boucaniers* to keep the Spanish away, and gave the owners of the ships commissions or "letters of marque" so that they could sail as privateers. A privateer, she learned soon after leaving Barbados, was a privately owned ship with a licence, or letter of marque, allowing it to act as a warship on behalf of the country issuing the licence. She did not think it a very fair system because the owner lost everything if his ship was lost (in battle or by shipwreck) and of course he had to pay for all damage. In return he could keep a certain percentage of what he captured from the enemy but, in the case of commissions issued in Jamaica, the King and his brother now took their share, a quarter, and there were plenty of hangers-on round the prize court who needed bribes . . .

No, as far as she was concerned, issuing commissions was just a cheap way of having a Navy, even if Ned had been elected the leader of the buccaneers, hence his title of Admiral of the Brethren of the Coast.

Now, apparently, all that was over – the new Governor of Jamaica (and apparently the King of England, too) had decided Jamaica did not need the buccaneers (or an Army, be it ever so small) to protect it: instead Spain was now a friend – she shivered at the thought – and all the commissions previously issued to the buccaneers were cancelled. So be it. At last she and Diana could have the houses built that they dreamed about. Yet if they were honest, she admitted that as soon as each was finished and furnished and they had lived in them for a few months, they would tire of them and wish themselves back at sea . . .

She opened her eyes again and found the sun's glare, shining under the tree, almost painful. From up here on the cliff, the sea, scattered with white horses, seemed strewn with winking diamonds reflecting the sun.

The house, she told herself, think about it! Two floors – not counting the ground floor which would be in effect the cellar, a series of arches allowing a cooling breeze to blow under the house and providing plenty of storage space for butts of wine and the like. Twelve bedrooms on the upper floor – that was probably more than they would need, but Ned insisted on building for a large family and with plenty of room for guests. Aurelia thought for a moment – say six children, that would be seven bedrooms including their own. Thomas would often be too drunk to go back to his own home, so an eighth for him and Diana. Four other guests. No, perhaps twelve was not being too generous. The first floor would of course be the main one. A small entrance hall, leading into a vast room as long as the house was broad: a room spacious enough to entertain a hundred people, Ned wanted, with room for those who might wish to dance. She admitted that the secret of a cool house (apart from having it built facing the right way, with sufficient windows for the breeze) was space. Crowd people together and they felt hot.

Take two people and put them in the same room at the same temperature, one at each end, and each would probably complain of feeling chilly.

Most of the servants would live in the three small houses built behind the main building. And there, beside the house, was the cistern – collecting all the rain from the roof. The men were already beginning to dig out the huge hole, but Ned had decided that Saxby must oversee the masons when they started. He had seen too many cisterns that leaked so badly that people were out of water by May . . .

She was glad that Ned agreed – indeed, insisted – that the trees should be left standing. In fact they had had to cut down and rout out the root of only one small tamarind tree, which had been growing exactly where the house had to be.

She heard Ned's horse neighing and, in the distance over the hills behind her, she heard another answering. And was that the thud of galloping hooves? Who on earth could be riding up to see them? The port was many miles away, and anyway Thomas and Diana, who had only left for their building site an hour ago, would not gallop in the heat of the day . . .

Ned left the sawyers, where he had been inspecting the trunk of a mahogany tree straddling the pit where they were just about to saw it into long planks, and walked along the track to meet the horsemen – the hoofbeats revealed there were at least two. He saw that they were Secco, the Spanish owner and captain of one of the buccaneer ships, and Gustav, a Dutchman who owned another.

Secco reined up his horse and swept off his hat, decorated with a green plume. "Admiral," he said breathlessly, "we're sorry to interrupt the building, but . . ."

"But what?" Ned said amiably. "You haven't ridden up from the port to show us how to cut planks!"

"The Spaniards are preparing a landing!"

"Is that all? You should have waited until we came down for more supplies."

Secco pretended to strike his brow and swore in Spanish. "And that's all the thanks we get! I am returning from Sinamaica in the Golfo de Venezuela when I meet Gustav who has been doing business –" Secco rubbed an index finger against his thumb, "– at Tucacas and we both heave-to for a drink of rum and a gossip.

"What do Secco and Gustav find to gossip about a couple of hundred miles north-west of Aruba? Ah, Mr Yorke, you might well ask!"

The sun was hot; the horses had swirled up dust which dried Ned's throat (but not, he noted, Secco's). Behind him the saw grunted its way along the mahogany trunk while to the right the masons' chisels and mallets in the little quarry alternated in a monotonous series of clinks and thuds.

Ned realized that Secco's report would take all afternoon unless he made the right responses. "I've no idea. But what *did* Secco and Gustav find to talk about when they met a couple of hundred miles north-west of Aruba?"

"The Viceroy's latest orders, that's what!"

The sun beat through Ned's coat and the heat shimmered up from the rock of the track. Who sent a loquacious Spaniard and a monosyllabic Dutchman with important news?

"And what *are* the Viceroy's latest orders?" Ned asked, hoping that the extra saw would soon be brought up from the port.

"To invade Jamaica, that's what they are!" Secco announced triumphantly.

Ned gave a loud mock groan. "The Viceroy gives that order on Mondays, Wednesdays and Fridays, and twice on Sundays."

"Is different," Gustav grunted, dismounting and nodding towards a nearby tamarind. "Is shade there, no?"

The three men gathered under the tree, hunching their shoulders because the lower boughs grew out horizontally like a ceiling.

"Why is it different this time?" Ned demanded.

"He calls ships to Cartagena," Gustav said, seeming to begrudge each word.

"And that's what I hear all round the *Golfo*," Secco said. "All ships to finish discharging their cargo and sail for Cartagena."

"*All* ships? Fishermen, fly boats, sloops?"

"No, no, no! That's what makes it serious," Secco said. "Only the big ships. The Viceroy's order gives the minimum size. Each must be able to carry so many quintals of corn.

Not" he added hurriedly, "that they are wanted to carry grain. There isn't that much grain in Cartagena. No, but it's significant that the ships are ordered to take on as much water as they have barrels *before* they go to Cartagena. We hear there is a great water shortage in Cartagena."

"Hmmm," Ned said, to give himself time to think and let Secco get his breath back.

"Water," Gustav growled. "For the troops they carry to attack Jamaica."

That makes sense, Ned thought to himself. All we need now is proof that troops are being marched to Cartagena: that battalions from Panama are being brought across the isthmus to join more from the Caribbee side. And that sort of proof will be hard to get. Troops cannot march on this side because there are no roads: they would have to be carried in by sea. In the ships the Viceroy has requested? Perhaps. And their horses, and the carts to carry their tents, and their field kitchens, and artillery and powder and shot?

But why? Trying to see into the mind of a Spanish Viceroy while standing in the shade of a tamarind tree with two buccaneers and two sweating and farting horses smelling ripe after their long gallop was – no, not a waste of time. Facts were facts, however hot the weather; it was easier to consider them in the cool, though.

If these two men now rode back to Port Royal they would gossip, and that would raise the alarm as effectively as half a dozen hoarse criers with handbells swinging. Gossip would reach the Governor and Heffer and the soldiers (who by now were anxiously waiting to get their back pay, which many of them probably saw as the key to Port Royal's rum shops and brothels, both long denied them since neither gave credit). Gossip would soon be regarded as fact, embroidered until a Spanish fleet had been seen on the horizon and priests in long black robes had been sighted striding down from the mountains, followed by mules dragging carts loaded with the racks of the Inquisition. Crowds, Ned thought soberly, were only slightly less gullible and easily panicked than vote-hunting members of Parliament in session.

Ned gestured along the track. "Come along, we'd better water your horses and give you something to eat. I want to ride over and have a chat with Sir Thomas. You'd better stay here until I get back. I don't suppose either of you wants to ride back to Port Royal tonight? No? Very well, we'll find beds for you in one of the tents."

Ned found Thomas down in the small quarry from which half a dozen men were cutting out rock in giant wafers, using pick-axes and thick chisels they drove between the strata with heavy mauls.

"Did you see Diana?" Thomas demanded nervously.

"No – not a sign of her: I rode along the coast. Why, do you want to talk to her?"

"God forbid!" Thomas exclaimed. "I'm hiding from her until she's cooled off a bit."

Ned deliberately asked no more: the couple quarrelled with (he suspected) the same ardour with which they made love and Diana's temper could be aroused as quickly as the ardour of any stranger seeing her for the first time.

"What brings you over?" Thomas asked. "Tiff with Aurelia?" he suggested almost hopefully, anxious for a companion to share his grouse against bullying women.

"No. Secco and Firman have ridden up from Port Royal. They've just arrived from the Main."

"Has old Loosely been upsetting them?"

"No, they've picked up some news from the Spaniards."

"Oh damn, have the Dons heard already that Charles is going to pay the rent owing on his exile by giving 'em Jamaica?"

Ned laughed drily. "No, it's a better yarn than that."

"What, has their wretched king, Philip the Fourth, suddenly become a sane Habsburg?"

"You ask for miracles! No, apparently the Viceroy in Panama has decreed that all merchant ships over a certain size take on all the water they can and sail for Cartagena."

"Why, does he plan to take the Vicereine and his large family and entourage on a cruise?"

"Not his family, his Army. To pay us a visit."

"Tell him he'll have to use some of the Governor's beds: we can't be expected to have guests until we get the roofs on our houses." Thomas held up a hand for Ned to help him scramble out of the pit. He brushed the dust from his breeches and then nodded to Ned. "Bit like the bridegroom wanting to start the honeymoon a week before the church service, eh?"

"Exactly. Why? Secco and Firman are certain: they heard the same story in several ports in two different provinces and both swear they saw ships taking on water as ordered. They're both sound men. I believe 'em."

"So do I, so do I," Thomas repeated. "Of course, the Viceroy might have just received orders to send some jolly soldiers over here to take possession of the island in the name of the worthy Philip the Fourth by courtesy –" he looked round to make sure none of the labourers were within earshot, "– of our own crazy Charles the Second. Stranger, isn't it, that Philip will be succeeded by another Charles II . . ."

"Do you think it's likely the Viceroy has received such orders?"

Thomas thought for a few moments. "I'm inclined to doubt it – but only because even the Committee for Trade and Foreign Plantations in London couldn't be stupid enough to forget to tell us we've been given away, kicking and screaming like an unwanted bastard."

"Old Loosely admits he heard the rumour in London but was not told anything by Albemarle: I'm prepared to believe him over that."

Thomas nodded agreement. "And although I've never met the Duke of Albemarle, I'm sure he wouldn't send an odd fellow like Loosely as Governor without warning him that his days in the job were numbered."

Ned said: "Why would the Spanish want to attack something that's going to be given them anyway? That's what puzzles me. Either they're preparing to accept Jamaica as a gift and the troops are simply taking possession, or they're preparing to attack it – it's as simple as that. Accept the gift idea and you accept that our new King has given us away; accepting the attack idea means old Philip is making a dastardly attack on a pearl in our great and good new King's crown."

"I can't see old Loosely rising to an occasion like this. He'll be petulant and stamping his foot or he'll have the vapours. What do you reckon we should do, Ned?"

"Most of our ships are still in Port Royal. If it's an attack, we'll have to put it to a vote. As you know, they're all very angry because Loosely took away their commissions.

Coming back a week later and saying 'Sorry, it was all a mistake: please chase those nasty Dons away' won't have them cheering and firing off salutes."

"I'll go and find Diana. Do you want to tell Aurelia you're going down to Port Royal? Diana can go across and stay with her: no point in taking both women with us."

"I'm taking Saxby," Ned said, "just in case we have to get ready to sail, and Aurelia won't stay here if she sees Saxby coming. And anyway, I have to collect Secco and Firman."

"All right, I'll bring Diana. Might get her into a cheerful mood. She's making a fuss about where we put the kitchen. Most unreasonable, she is."

His last words were lost to Ned, who was spurring his horse into a gallop.

Chapter Five

General Heffer came into the new council chamber, formerly his office, greeted the four men and said apologetically that the Governor was busy: could he make an appointment for them to see him tomorrow?

"You told him it was very important and urgent?" Ned asked.

"Yes: I said you had ridden over the mountains especially."

Thomas said sourly: "All this reminds me of some of the nonsense we had with you, Teffler, until you learned your lesson."

Heffer gave a wintry grin. "Yes, indeed; that's why I tried to impress on the Governor that there was some urgency . . ."

"Very well," Ned said, "then tell him this: first, he would be very unwise to disband his Army now; second, the Spanish are probably coming; and third, the buccaneers are certainly going. In fact they'll have sailed by noon tomorrow."

Although Heffer had by now learned never to doubt such remarks, he knew the new Governor's limited horizons. "Sir Harold would need a great deal of proof . . ."

Ned sighed and shook his head. "Heffer, you duffer, you'll never learn. We are refugees from England: even now my brother is trying to retrieve our estates which were confiscated by that thief Cromwell. In fact it now looks as if the King might give them to one of *his* favourites. So for the time being my own allegiance to the new King is qualified. But the majority of the *buccaneers* are foreigners: as long as they can use Port Royal as a base, they don't give a damn who sits on the throne in London. If the Spanish retake Jamaica – well, so be it: the buccaneers can use Tortuga as a base, or move down to the Dutch islands. So you'd better rouse out old Loosely so we can sing him our song or, from noon tomorrow, you are on your own and His Excellency can bombard the Dons with the coin he brought out to pay off the Army."

"Will you wait ten minutes?" Heffer asked.

When Ned nodded, he hurried from the room.

"I hate this place," Thomas announced. "It seems we've encountered more unpleasantness in this room than we've ever met in battle with the Dons!"

Secco took off his hat and scratched his head. "I'm not understanding the problem," he said. "Where is this new Governor? Is he ill? Why tomorrow?"

"You have this sort in Spain as well," Thomas said. "Give a man a bit o' authority and while his head swells like a bladder of lard his brain shrinks."

"We sail tomorrow?" Firman asked. "I need water, provisions; we were out a long time, this last voyage."

"Me too," said Secco. "Very little food and only a few gallons of water left on board. I must go out to the ship!"

"Wait, wait," Ned said. "We're only bluffing for the moment about sailing tomorrow: we're just getting the Governor into the right frame of mind!"

"He sounds a fool, like this man Heffer. A heifer, isn't that a young cow?"

"Yes, a virgin one," said Thomas. "That's why we feed him fresh grass. We'll be milking him by Christmas."

"Milking him? I do not understand," Secco grumbled, putting on his hat again after running the plume through his fingers.

The door flung open and the Governor came in, followed by a red-faced Heffer.

"Well, what's all this about?" he demanded.

"Good morning, Your Excellency. These two gentlemen bring –"

"Who the Devil are they, eh?"

"I was about to introduce them," Ned said, a warning note in his voice. "They're in a hurry, so we must be grateful for them sparing us their time."

Sir Harold looked them over. "Well, who are they?"

"Captain Secco and Captain Firman. Gentlemen, the Governor, Sir Harold Loosely."

"Luce, Luce!" Sir Harold said crossly. "What do they want?" he asked, deliberately avoiding talking directly to them.

"They want nothing, Your Excellency. They've brought something for you."

Luce looked at their hands and noted they were carrying nothing. "Well, what have they brought?"

"Information, intelligence, news: call it what you will."

"If it's anything to do with the nonsense Heffer has just been talking, I don't want to hear it," Luce said crossly.

Ned bowed and said quietly: "In that case we won't take up your time, Your Excellency." He held out his hand. "We had better take this opportunity to say goodbye."

"Ah, yes!" Thomas bellowed. "Goodbye and good luck, Your Excellency. By the way –" he lowered his voice, "– are you a Catholic by any chance?"

"Indeed not!" exclaimed a startled Luce. "Why?"

"Pity, pity. It often helps," Thomas murmured sympathetically. "The Dons are very excitable when they get their hands on a heretic – especially an important one. Great people for giving precedence at the rack, the Spaniards. Though to be fair, after racking you they only do you in to save your soul. Nod your head to show you repent as they give the garotte the last turn of the screw (you can't speak, of course, with the thing throttling you and breaking your neck) and they more or less guarantee you'll go to Heaven."

By now Luce had collapsed into a chair, his skin clammy, his forehead beginning to glisten with perspiration. He looked appealingly at Heffer. "What *is* all this nonsense about the Spanish?"

"I've no idea, Your Excellency," he said in the cheerful voice he had now adopted when dealing with the Governor. "I thought Mr Yorke and Sir Thomas had come to tell you about it."

"Well?" Sir Harold glowered at both men.

Ned shrugged his shoulders. "I'm sorry, Your Excellency, we'd all like to stay and gossip with you – even accept your kind offer of refreshments after our long gallop over the mountains – but we must hurry off: I have orders to give and all the captains have much to do, provisioning and watering."

"No you don't," Sir Harold yelped, like a dog protesting at his tail being trodden on. "No one sails from this port without my permission!"

"You had better send written orders to all the captains, then," Ned said quietly. "French, Spanish, Dutch . . . they won't take kindly to it; in fact they'll probably give your messenger a ducking! You ought to send your secretary with such important orders," he added. "That shifty fellow William Hamilton."

The Governor, by now white-faced, his eyes once again flickering from side to side as though looking for a way to escape, waved his hand. "All right, Yorke, I withdraw that. Now, what have you all come to see me about?"

"Warn you. We came to warn you. The Spanish Viceroy in Panama has sent orders to all ports on the Main that ships over a certain size are to water and sail at once for Cartagena."

Luce looked puzzled. "Is that all?"

"*All*," growled Thomas. "If you're the Governor of Jamaica, it's more than enough!"

"But I don't understand. What's the significance of that? It's not as if they're ships of war."

"What exactly *is* a ship of war?" Ned inquired sarcastically. "Surely a merchant ship carrying five hundred soldiers, field artillery, horses, powder and shot is a ship of *war*, especially if it belongs to your enemy and he intends to land those troops on your shores to cause you mischief?"

"But who says these ships *are* assembling in Cartagena, and *why* should the Spanish land troops on our shores?"

Firman grunted, as though unable to believe his ears. Secco took off his hat and inspected the inside of the brim. Ned stared at Luce while Thomas groaned as though wracked by twinges of rheumatism. Only Heffer remained silent and motionless, and Ned had the impression that the General was enjoying the baiting of the Governor.

"Where else would Spaniards be sending troops?" Thomas inquired innocently. "Are they still seeking the land of El Dorado?"

"Well, they're certainly no threat to us, even allowing that the Viceroy has called in the ships and proposes putting troops on board them. We now have a treaty of peace with Spain, which rules out any hostile act by the Viceroy such as you suggest."

Secco laughed and Firman gave another grunt.

Luce raised his eyebrows. "Why do you laugh, my man?"

Secco waved his hat, using it as a fan. "Señor, I am just a simple Spaniard, but I know how my own people think and act. I know about these ships because Spanish people in Spanish ports on the Spanish Main have just told me about them. In other ports they told the same thing to my Dutch friend here. A treaty of peace with England?" Secco laughed again. "I'll believe that matters when the Pope removes the Line. 'No Peace Beyond the Line', señor: no peace beyond the Line. You know where the Line is? Not many miles from the Azores. We are beyond the Line, Mister Governor; for us there's no peace with the Spanish. Not for planters, for their wives and children; not for governors and their wives and mistresses; not for buccaneers, whores, pimps, tavernkeepers . . . no peace for no one, mister. For you, maybe a golden garotte; but believe me, mister, it strangles you and – if you're lucky – breaks your neck just the same as an iron one."

With that, Secco jammed his hat on his head, took Firman by the arm and, with a nod to Ned and Thomas, marched out of the room. Ned and Thomas were just going to follow when the Governor waved at them to stay.

"What's all this nonsense about your people sailing?"

"You've taken away my captains' commissions, so they're not going to defend your damned island at their own expense," Ned said bitterly. "You don't believe the Spanish could possibly attack. We don't say they will but – an opinion based on considerable experience – we say they could."

"In that case you should stay," Luce said lamely. "You owe it to the island. You have a loyalty to the King, too!"

"Do I?" Ned asked, his voice weary. "Cromwell confiscated my family's estates claiming they were Royalist – which they were, of course. Now Cromwell's long dead and the King is back on the throne, and what's happening? I'll tell you, in case you didn't notice. The King has now taken over many of those confiscated estates and he's giving them away to his favourites. Although my father and brother went into exile with the King, this may be the reward for their loyalty –

the same treatment from the King as they received from Cromwell. As for us out here (and we are the people that did our best to protect Jamaica), our reward –" Ned looked Luce up and down contemptuously, "– our reward, Your Excellency, is to get a jobbernowl like you sent out to govern us. Well, we're still free men so we can refuse the reward."

"You insult me! You insult the office the King granted me! Why, I'd run you through!"

Thomas burst out laughing but managed to blurt out: "Even in your prime you'd have been hard put to run through a boiled potato!"

"Gentlemen, gentlemen," Heffer said, "all this won't solve our problems!"

"Aaaah," Luce cried as though in pain, "our problem is these damned buccaneers. Just because they buy a few provisions, all the tradesmen support them."

"They put gold in the treasury, Your Excellency," Heffer said quietly, "and guns in our batteries."

"Everything was stolen from the Spanish," Luce sneered.

Ned, who was walking towards the door, swung round. "Stolen goods, eh? Well, be careful we don't repent and take the gold back," he said coldly. "You told us you've brought out money from England to start a Treasury. My captains may decide that the Spanish gold and silver was just a loan . . ."

All the buccaneer captains, gathered on the *Griffin's* deck, listened to their Admiral's brief speech. Ned told them that the new Governor so far was simply carrying out instructions he had received before leaving London. "Not surprisingly, the people in London have little idea what is happening out here. They firmly believe that the new treaty with Spain means that the Spanish out here are our friends.

"The new Governor was even told to start a trade with the Main, and he is puzzled why he was laughed at in the first meeting of the executive council. I want you all to understand that the Governor means well; he just has to get a great deal more experience to help him decide what to do when things not covered in his orders from London start happening. So now listen to what Secco has to say, and after him Firman."

After both men had reported on what they had learned

about the Spanish ships, Ned asked the captains: "Any questions?"

There were several. Was the Governor now going to give back the commissions, so that the buccaneers could attack the Spanish – try to sink or capture those ships before they even reached Cartagena? Well, no, Ned said. Did the Governor really believe the reports of Secco and Firman? Ned had to shake his head. Was the Governor still going to pay off the Army and disband it, even though he had now heard the reports about the Spaniards? Again Ned had to report that the Governor was. When one of the captains asked if the Governor still expected the buccaneers to defend Jamaica and Ned reluctantly shook his head, there were shouts of "Tortuga! Tortue!"

The shouts increased until it seemed to Ned that all the captains were calling the island's name in English, French or Spanish. He looked round at Thomas, who muttered the single word: "Vote!"

Ned held up his hand for silence, and the shouting stopped. "Very well, some of you want to change our base. Remember, on the one hand we have here provisions and we can buy chandlery for our ships, but we have an English Governor. At Tortuga we are free of any interference, but we can't get provisions or chandlery. So we will vote. All in favour of moving to Tortuga?"

Many hands shot into the air, and Ned said: "Now, those in favour of staying here?"

Only three captains indicated they wanted to remain in Jamaica, one of them shouting angrily at the others: "You fools! There are no women in Tortuga! You'll just get drunk and because you can't have a woman, you'll start quarrelling."

Secco stepped forward, removed his hat with a flourish and turned to face his fellow captains. "Women? Where is the difficulty? Many of us carry half a dozen women on board. That way the food gets cooked, the clothes mended, and . . ."

"And . . . ?" echoed several captains amid laughter.

"Very well, that's decided," Ned said. "You'd all better get back to your ships and attend to provisioning and watering, and whatever else you need."

Slapping each other on the back like a group of boisterous

schoolboys let out of class, they made their way over the *Griffin's* bulwarks and down into their boats. Ned turned to Thomas.

"Well, my lord bishop, are we doing the right thing?"

Thomas shrugged his massive shoulders. "Depends whether or not we decide the safety of Jamaica is our problem or Loosely's."

"With old Heffer blundering around in the past it's become a habit, I suppose," Ned said, "even though Heffer now admits that but for us he'd have had nothing to hand over to Loosely."

"Diana's not going to like it," Thomas commented gloomily, "nor is Aurelia. They both want to finish the houses. Yesterday they were having long conferences about the sort of furniture they are going to have made. They've already decided both houses have the same, so the carpenters make duplicates."

"I'm staying here for a while," Ned said. "I'd like to get the house finished, too. And Tortuga is such a depressing place."

"Good," said Thomas. "That means I can stay with a clear conscience, and that means Diana will be in a good mood. But let's agree to keep away from the Governor: he's more stupid than I believed possible. He's bound to get a barony – unless the Dons get him first with a garotte."

Two hours later while the four of them were sitting in the *Griffin's* hot saloon talking of the problems of building houses, Saxby knocked at the door and looked in to report. "Secco's coming over in a boat with that Dutchman, Firman. From the number of boats visiting Secco's ship, the captains have been having a meeting. I wasn't invited."

Saxby had been foreman of Ned's plantation in Barbados, and commanded the *Griffin* when she was needed to carry cargoes for the plantation. When the Roundheads were about to seize the plantation and Ned decided to flee with Aurelia and those of the plantation staff who wanted to come, Saxby had sailed the *Griffin* with the Roundheads shooting at them. Now he commanded the *Phoenix*, which had been the *Griffin's* first prize. Saxby was a quiet, competent man who kept to himself – not, Ned knew, because he scorned the friendship of others but because he was a private man. Private except for his mistress, Martha Judd.

A Lincolnshire man, stockily built with a stentorian voice, Saxby had a curious past. Both he and his father had been farm labourers and were pressed into the Navy at the same time. Saxby had a great appetite for women and a dislike of hot liquors, so service at sea deprived him of his one pleasure and tried to pour down his throat the spirits he hated. After several years at sea (during which time he lost sight of his father) Saxby finally deserted, returned to his Lincolnshire village, and was still working there when the Civil War began. He was taken prisoner by the Roundheads and transported to Barbados.

Ned, recalling the story of the couple, remembered that Mrs Judd, wide-hipped, big-breasted, a woman with an enormous zest for life and for finding a man who could satisfy her and keep her respect, had been working as a housekeeper for a landowner at Banbury, in Oxfordshire, when the Civil War started. What, Ned had always wondered, had happened to Mr Judd? He never appeared in any of the stories (usually slightly bawdy) that Mrs Judd delighted in telling.

Anyway, as the Royalists were finally defeated the Banbury landowner had to flee, leaving his wife and children in Mrs Judd's care. Within days the house was attacked by Roundhead looters, who were also busy breaking the stained-glass windows in the local churches, whereupon an enraged Mrs Judd had set about them with two kitchen knives, changing them for a billhook as soon as she could get to the potting shed. Fortunately for Mrs Judd (and eventually Saxby) she failed to decapitate any of the Roundheads, who took her prisoner and ordered her to be transported to Barbados. On board the ship taking her to what she had anticipated would be a harsh, hot and loveless exile, she met Saxby, and both of them had ended up working on Ned's plantation. As Mrs Judd had once confided to Aurelia, instead of starting what she had expected to be the life of an overworked nun, she had become an overworked mistress, the wink at the end of the story indicating to Aurelia that it was not only in the kitchen that Mrs Judd worked hard.

Bawdy, lively, only too ready and certainly quite capable of taking charge in any situation, Mrs Judd had taken charge of Saxby, whose red complexion glistened, even if his blue eyes were often red-rimmed when he started work of a morning on the plantation.

If anyone was responsible for the transformation of Saxby from a seaman who had deserted and become a plantation foreman into the captain of a buccaneer ship and the equal of any of the other captains, it was Mrs Judd. Ned was not sure if the man's new confidence had come from his Lincolnshire forebears or from being clasped to Mrs Judd's ample bosom and eager thighs, but what mattered was that it had come at the right time.

Saxby returned to the saloon to report. "Secco and the Dutchman are coming alongside now. D'you want to see 'em on deck or down 'ere, sir?" he asked Ned.

"We'll come on deck," Ned said.

"You can't expect them to accept old Loosely's decisions," Thomas said as he stood up. "We don't even agree with them ourselves!"

"I don't, and I don't forget that most of the buccaneers are French, or Dutch, or even Spanish. But when we're here in Jamaica we have to accept whatever the Governor says – providing," Ned added, "we know that he's acting on government instructions. We might find ourselves defying him if he gets hysterical and starts issuing his own orders . . ."

Diana said: "Ned's right. Anyway, he'll soon run through his list of orders from London. Then the executive council can make sure he doesn't do anything too silly."

"He's got to *call* a council meeting first," Thomas pointed out, "and there's nothing to stop him leaving the executive council supping rum punch while that fancy private secretary, Hamilton, nails up decrees on the front door."

"You don't have to go up to the door and read them," Aurelia said.

"A town crier, that'll be the next appointment he makes," Thomas grumbled. "'Oyez, oyez, now hear ye, the Governor has decreed . . .' I can just hear it."

"I can hear the town crier's yells as the shopkeepers pitch him in the lobster crawl," Ned said, "and I can see the Governor's decree floating away as the town crier splashes his way back to the shore."

He led the way to the door.

Since both Secco and Firman seemed embarrassed, each waiting for the other to start, Ned asked amiably: "So what have you all decided to do?"

Secco looked relieved. The buccaneers were simply a group of privateersmen (former privateersmen, now that Luce had withdrawn their commissions) who had elected a leader whom they respected enough to follow and called him their Admiral. Nothing was written down: no orders were ever written. The only agreement – and that only an understanding between them all – was that when the Admiral led them, they obeyed him. There was nothing to stop any one – or indeed all – of the Brethren of the Coast, as they called themselves, refusing to follow.

"We . . . er, we did not like the Governor's decision . . ."

"Nor did we," Ned said, to help the man.

"And like you we do not like Tortuga. And we know what the Spaniards are doing . . ."

Thomas clapped his hands and laughed. "And the idea of all those ships sailing round to Cartagena was irresistible!"

Secco grinned and nodded. "Yes, Sir Thomas. Many of us think we can capture some, exchanging our small ships for bigger ones. I have fifty men crowded into my ship, for instance. I would like a bigger one, and then I can carry more men –"

"And your share of the purchase will then be bigger," Thomas said teasingly.

"My share as a captain stays the same," Secco said stiffly. "If I have more men, there are more men to share the crew's portion."

"Don't be so damned touchy," Thomas said. "I was only teasing you. Bigger ships and more men mean more purchase, so we all get richer."

"You don't want me to come with you?" Ned asked.

"No, sir," Secco said, and then corrected himself as Firman made a sudden gesture. "Forgive me, I didn't mean we don't want you to come. The message I bring is that the captains want to go after these ships, and if you and Sir Thomas want to stay behind to complete your houses, we shall understand. It is a raid of no importance, except in improving our fleet."

Ned nodded. "Good. I agree to that, and neither Sir Thomas nor I expect to share in the purchase. Just one thing, though. In time I may be able to persuade the Governor to be more – er, practical. For the moment, therefore, I don't want to quarrel with him."

"You want to leave the door open," Secco said, pleased with his knowledge of English idiom.

"Exactly. A door the Governor can come through to ask us for a favour, and a door we can go through, for whatever reason."

"I'll explain that to the Brethren," Secco said.

"And explain that the open door is the reason why neither I nor Sir Thomas want to know where you are all going. As far as we know you are all going to Tortuga because the Governor has taken away your commissions. If you all change your minds after you've sailed from Port Royal – well," Ned shrugged his shoulders, "that's your affair. Sir Thomas and I will be busy over on the north coast working as masons and sawyers – and perhaps tilers – before we see you again. Anyway, good luck to you all."

After the two captains had left, Thomas said: "They found the right answer without any nudges or winks from us."

"Yes, though I suppose it could be argued they're doing the right thing for the wrong reason."

"Wrong reason?" Thomas raised his eyebrows, but Diana said at once: "Don't be so dense. Ned means that the right reason – for the future of Jamaica – is that they're going to capture ships which might land a Spanish army on our beaches; but, in fact, they're off in search of the ships simply to capture larger ones for themselves."

"Let's not be too fussy," Thomas rumbled. "Otherwise we'll get as muddled as a convocation of bishops and start jabbering the sort of nonsense one expects from the Archbishop of Canterbury."

"A Canterbury gallop," Diana said unexpectedly. "When I was young and had my first horse, my father said I could ride only at a Canterbury gallop."

"What's that, riding facing the horse's tail?" Thomas asked facetiously.

"Riding at a canter, of course," Diana said.

"Slower than what we'd call a canter," Ned said. "Comes from the monks riding to Canterbury – their horses would amble, not *canter*. Irony, my lord bishop."

"I keep forgetting you come from Kent," Thomas said. "So you'd know all the scurrilous stories from Canterbury . . ."

Chapter Six

For the next week the work on the houses went sufficiently fast to complete the foundations, and both Diana and Aurelia walked round, jumping the trenches, and delighted to have at long last a real idea of the size of each room.

Thomas, who had been teasing Diana because she had not been able to visualize the sizes from the scale on the plans, admitted to Ned that his house was proving larger than he had expected.

"At least it'll be cool," he said.

"Like a barn," Ned said. "You'll be able to have the hens and the horses eating with you in the dining room."

"You wait," Thomas said gloomily, "as soon as it's finished, we're going to get dozens of visitors. They'll all be 'just calling in' as it gets dark, so we'll have to offer a night's lodging, and each of 'em will find an excuse to stay sennight."

"I thought you liked people: always surrounded by a merry throng of topers and gamblers – I thought that was when my lord bishop was in his element. A belly full of wine and slapping your last hundred pounds on the roll of a dice."

"Ah, that was before I met Diana," Thomas said reminiscently. "The sound of wine tumbling into a goblet was a musical waterfall and the clinking of dice a welcome descant – music to m' ears. Now – well, I hate the sound of dice more than a fusillade of musketry, and the music has gone out of wine and hot liquors."

"Ah, Thomas, now even your late and unlamented Uncle Oliver would be proud of you."

"Yes, and if only Diana was Lady Whetstone so that she was my lawful wife and not my mistress, he'd have made me one of his admirals. But no! I think he may have forgiven the gambling and the drinking and the wenching, but he knew I was a Royalist at heart and that he couldn't –"

He stopped for a moment, listening above the buffeting wind. "A horse. Don't say it's Secco back already! Two horses, in fact!"

"More likely a messenger from old Loosely bidding us to a council meeting to consider raising taxes to build him a residence more in keeping with his sense of his own importance."

"My word, we need some rain: just look at the dust those horses are raising. Recognize the men?"

Ned shook his head. "Strangers to me. I'm sure they're messengers from Loosely."

"He wouldn't spare a *couple* of men."

Aurelia had joined them and said: "Why try to guess? Just be patient!"

"Patience has never been a friend of mine," Ned said. "Ah, they've seen us. No, I don't recognize them."

"Sailors," Aurelia commented. "From their clothes and the way they sit a horse, they're more used to holding a tiller than reins."

The two men reined in and while raising their hats to Aurelia confirmed her identification if only by the lack of flourish and the cautious way they dismounted.

"Mr Yorke?" one inquired. "Mr Edward Yorke?"

When introductions had been made, it transpired that the men were the captain and the mate of a trading sloop. The captain, George Hoskins, a chubby and jovial man from the Isle of Wight, who, despite his obvious lack of experience with horses, was very bow-legged, explained that they traded between Jamaica and the eastern islands, starting at Barbados and taking on their final cargo at St Kitts and Nevis, and then bearing away for the long run to leeward which brought them to Jamaica while staying far enough south to avoid the Spaniards in Porto Rico and Hispaniola.

"Going back," he explained, "it's such a long beat to windward to lay up for Barbados that if it gets too brisk we ease sheets a little to go down south to Curaçao and see what the

Hollanders are offering. Drive a very hard bargain, does *mynheer*, an' o' course enough of their own ships trade northwards that they don't leave much pickings for us."

Ned realized that Hoskins was not to be rushed and in his own good time would explain why he had ridden over the mountains on what he obviously regarded as a dangerous and uncomfortable beast.

Finally Hoskins glanced at Ned and then Thomas. "St Martin and Anguilla. You know them?"

Both men shook their heads. "I know where they are," Ned said, "but I've never been farther north than Antigua. Don't the French and Dutch share St Martin? Anguilla – who claims that?"

"Whoever happens to be anchored in the bay on the north side," Hoskins said. "The island's almost deserted; it's just a good anchorage, 'cept in a west or north wind."

Ned saw that there was a reason for Hoskins asking if they knew two of the most insignificant of the dozen or so islands forming the chain known as the Windward and Leeward Islands. "What are they like, these two?"

"Well, on the chart St Martin and Anguilla look like a cooking pot with the lid held up across the top. The lid's Anguilla, which is separated from St Martin by a channel about seven miles wide."

As the man did not go on, Ned asked: "How do the French and the Dutch get on, sharing an island?"

Hoskins grinned. "About as well as you could expect: until any trouble comes over the horizon, they cooperate as little as possible. The Dutch own the southern half, the French the northern. A ridge of mountains cuts the island in half the other way, so it's really a bun divided into quarters.

"Anguilla is as flat as St Martin is mountainous. Flat as the pot lid I was talking about. Still, St Martin has some decent anchorages – off the village of Marigot on the north side; then on the south side there's Simson Bay (got its name from an Englishman who owned a plantation there, I shouldn't wonder) and a larger anchorage on the south-east corner with a reef protecting it. Very dangerous, both of 'em, when the wind goes south or west. Get embayed in a blow and you drag up on to the beach."

"All this is very interesting," Ned said, "but I'm baking

standing here in this sun, and you two must be thirsty."

"Aye, we are that," said Hoskins, who seemed to accept that his mate did not speak.

Ned led the way to the tent where Mrs Judd presided over what was somewhat grandiosely called the kitchen.

"'Ello," she said to Ned, eyeing the two strangers suspiciously, "what have you brought in? Not two rough sailors, I 'ope. I've got my reputation to think of."

"If we'd thought of that we'd have brought two dozen," Thomas said. "Ask our worthy friends what they want to drink, and offer them something to eat. Larks' tongue, nightingales' liver, unicorns' kidneys – whatever you happen to have at hand: they're not fussy."

"Boucanned beef or salt snapper, that's all we've got. Hot waters, o' course. Bread won't be ready for half an hour; that's a right fussy oven Saxby's built me – won't draw in this wind. Must 'ave found a load of special cold bricks. *And*," she added crossly. "the dogs piddled on the charcoal, so it's 'ard to get it started. What I'd give for an 'undredweight of proper sea coal."

Hoskins looked nervously at Ned. "I'm sure we don't want to be any trouble to the lady," he said.

"Oh, don't worry, Mrs Judd's just serving you the first course. Once she's had her grumble, you'll get a good meal."

"Dunno why I let Saxby talk me into coming up 'ere," Mrs Judd growled. "Reckon it's because 'e 'ates sleepin' alone."

Hoskins eyed her more carefully as she turned away to the table which half filled the tent. "Who is Saxby?" he asked Ned.

"A jealous man. Handy with a knife, though . . . Now," Ned said firmly, leading the men to the second tent which served as a canteen, "what have you been kind enough to ride all the way from Port Royal to tell us?"

"Oh, yes, well, this channel 'twixt Anguilla and St Martin, it's only seven miles wide, you understand?"

"Yes, so you told us. Coast flat on the Anguilla side to the north, mountainous on the French side to the south."

"S'right," Hoskins said. "Shallow, too. Four an' five fathoms in the middle, but a lot less at the sides."

"Indeed?" Ned said, wondering how long his patience would last. "Shallow, eh? Ships could accidentally run aground." He thought of the low ground on Anguilla, and the fact that it was the last of the chain, except for Sombrero, which was a barren rock. "Sandy bottom, I suppose. Once you're aground, you're stuck, if you happen to be running before a brisk Trade wind."

"Ah, you've guessed!" Hoskins exclaimed happily and, turning to his mate, said: "See, Mr Yorke's guessed! You don't get made the Admiral of the Brethren for nothing, just like I told you." He turned to Ned, grinning broadly. "Well, then, that's worth something, isn't it?"

Ned frowned, puzzled by the man's eagerness. "So far, you've described two islands and the channel between, and I've guessed that the channel is shallow. But neither I nor the Brethren give a damn; as far as we're concerned –"

"But the treasure!" the mate said suddenly.

Hoskins looked crestfallen. "Sorry, Mr Yorke, I've forgotten the important part. One of they Spanish plate galleons is stuck hard aground just off Marigot. They – that's the French – think she's laden, but she's got more than enough guns to drive off anything the French can bring up – trading sloops, fishing boats, canoes they use for conch diving . . . I don't reckon the French have a dozen muskets, let alone cannon. But that Don's there until his mates find him – or he breaks up in a gale o' wind. He's beginning to pound already. Leastways, he was when we left."

"When was that?"

"Just eight days ago. As soon as we heard what had happened we sailed for here."

"Hmm, you were sailing for Jamaica anyway," Thomas said. "Did you hear about it at St Martin?"

"Well, no," Hoskins admitted. "We were at St Kitts. That was our last place: we weren't carrying nothing to St Martin this time."

"Oh, so you haven't actually seen this galleon?" Ned asked.

"Not actually *seen* her, Mr Yorke, but we know the channel well enough. Look, I can draw you a chart, with soundings."

"Very well, I'll get you some writing materials. But eat first – sit down in here and Mrs Judd will feed you. I want to talk with Sir Thomas, then we'll come back for the chart."

As soon as they left the tent and walked over to shelter from the sun under the shade of a tamarind tree, Ned said: "A *plate* ship? What on earth would she be doing in *that* channel? If she's laden for Spain, she's hundreds of miles too far south . . ."

"And if she isn't laden with plate she's bound *from* Spain to the Main laden with needles and cotton, pots and pans for the worthy Spanish citizens waiting along the Main," Thomas said. "In which case she was probably chancing her arm, and taking a short cut to Cartagena through the Anegada Passage. She'd only have to be twenty miles too far south – likely enough after three and a half thousand miles across the Atlantic – and she'd land up just where she is."

"The Spanish pilot could hardly make a mistake like that," Ned pointed out. "That's the only place with such a narrow channel with high land to larboard and low to starboard. The Anegada's further north and seventy miles wide!"

"Think of that dam' haze," Thomas reminded him. "Sometimes you can see only a couple of miles. Or at night. They don't realize how far ahead of their reckoning they are. Scared maybe of getting too far north because of the Horseshoe Reef at the end of Anegada. Then – no breakers, no warning: the ship just slows up and stops. The leadline tells you you're hard aground on sand – and a brisk following wind telling you there isn't much chance of getting off."

"Very well, if she's come from Spain laden with 'needles and cotton, pots and pans', as you suggested and she's nine hundred miles to windward of us, then I for one am not interested!"

"Ah yes, Ned, but supposing she was making a bolt for it *the other way*, from Cartagena to Spain; just think, instead of risking the weather by rounding Cuba and calling at Havana before beating out through the Bahamas, and then up past Somers Island and over to the Azores . . ."

"You mean she'd break out into the Atlantic at Anguilla to face a couple of thousand of miles of brisk head winds! No fear, they're not that mad!"

"I didn't mean that. Just that she'd risk getting out into the Atlantic through the Anegada and then turn north until she's level with Somers Island. Then she'd be on the normal track of the homeward-bound galleons but she'd have avoided all the risks sailing past here and then round Cuba and the Bahamas."

Ned turned and faced Thomas, nodding his head slowly. "My lord bishop, imagine yourself the captain of this wretched galleon laden with silver ingots, gold cobs and gems by the sackful. Are you dodging the enemy or the difficult navigation?"

"Well, mainly the enemy, of course, but –"

"But *there's no enemy now*! Remember Spain has just signed a treaty of peace with our newly restored King, so the Dons have ensured the English heretics won't attack their plate fleets any more."

"But the heretics don't have ships of war out here anyway!"

"Indeed they don't, so the Dons are probably sure they have nothing to fear. Their ambassador to the Court of St James will have reported to Madrid already that the new Governor of Jamaica was sent out with orders to cancel all the privateers' commissions and start a trade with the Main –"

"Which the Dons know they won't allow!"

"Which the Dons won't allow, yes, but they haven't yet told the English King they won't allow it! So, my lord bishop, from the Spanish point of view now is a very good time to send off a galleon laden with plate! And to send it by the shortest route because the English Court has already agreed to stop privateering. If you were the King of Spain – or, since he is a busy fellow, his Minister of Finance, desperate to pay off those importunate Italian and Austrian bankers – wouldn't you send out a frigate or something to Cartagena, telling them to hurry over a galleon with as much plate as she can carry?"

"Why only one, Ned? The Dons aren't short of silver on the Main!"

"No, but they're short of ships. Supposing this was the only galleon in Cartagena that was seaworthy?" A sudden thought struck him. "Supposing, my lord bishop, that's why the Viceroy has called in all the large trading vessels around his coast? Supposing he is going to use them to carry more plate to Spain because the Dons in Spain can't afford to fit out the galleons and the *flota* because the money to repair ships and buy sails and cordage is still on the Main, still in ingots of gold and silver, useless until it arrives in Spain?"

Thomas suddenly grabbed Ned by his coat. "And think, Ned, these are the very ships the Brethren have gone off to capture – before they get to Cartagena!"

"Yes," Ned said calmly, "it's called 'Cutting your nose off to spite your face'."

"It's too late to stop them, I suppose, but they'll go mad when they realize the ships would have been loaded with plate if only they'd waited . . ."

"Well, we can't do anything about it, so let's find out whether we're talking sense or just daydreaming."

Thomas looked puzzled. "How do we do that?"

"By asking a question we should have asked at the beginning."

Thomas took off his hat and scratched his head. "What's the question and who should we ask?"

"We ask Hoskins which way the galleon was going when she ran aground. Was she coming westward into the Caribbean from Spain – or was she beating her way out eastwards into the Atlantic heading for Spain?"

The galleon had been going eastward, towards Spain. She had gone aground in Potence Bay, just east of the village of Marigot, because she stood on too far (Hoskins had heard that just a ship's length would have made all the difference) before tacking towards Anguilla. Seamen watching from the village reckoned she was making all of eight knots at the time, running up on hard sand and then slewing round to head west as they tried to tack, so that her stern dragged over a small shoal of rocks, damaging the rudder.

"You didn't mention the rudder before," Ned commented crossly.

"What difference does it make?" Hoskins asked, aggrieved. "I told you she was hard aground and there was no chance of getting her off. I can't tell you all the damage. There may not be any more; still, having a broken rudder – and probably unable to rig a jury one – is bad enough. But did those rocks stove in some planks as well? For all I know she might be resting on the bottom, her holds full of water. Usually hard to tell from a distance whether a ship aground will float off or she's holed. Only a few inches rise of tide, you realize."

"We know all that," Thomas growled, "but be sure there's

nothing else of importance you've forgotten. Is she in range of French batteries?"

"There's only a small fort on the top of a hill at the seaward side of the village of Marigot. Not even a fort, really; just a built-up battery. Perhaps a couple of guns. Never heard tell of them being fired, and I first saw the battery at least twenty-five years ago, when I were a boy, so I reckon the termites have weakened the platform so much by now no one'd dare walk on it, let alone put match to a gun."

Ned nodded, and waved a piece of paper. "You're sure of the soundings you've put on this chart?"

"Yes – that's the channel I always follow when I anchor off Marigot. We come in from the west and go out by the west, that's why there aren't soundings beyond into Potence Bay, where the galleon's stranded."

"I noticed that," Ned said. "By the way, you know what Potence Bay means in English?"

Hoskins shook his head. "Haven't concerned myself with it."

"Don't," Ned said drily, "it means 'Gallows Bay'."

"Well, sir, you going after him?"

It's curious, Ned noted, how the English always referred to their own ships as "her", while enemy vessels became "him". Certainly Latins usually referred to their own ships as male, so was there any significance in the fact that the English considered their own female? Did Englishmen not wage war on females, even in the guise of ships of war?

"Most of the Brethren have sailed," Ned said.

"I saw three at anchor off Port Royal," Hoskins said.

"My *Griffin*, Sir Thomas's *Peleus* and Saxby's *Phoenix*. Hardly a match for a galleon, even if it is aground. And the French in Marigot might feel they have a claim on her."

"They can claim all they like," Hoskins said contemptuously, "but the only way they'd ever capture her is to starve out the Dons, and that'd take months because she's provisioned for Spain."

"You think we should anchor round her, just out of gunshot, and start a siege?" Thomas asked sarcastically.

Hoskins flushed and said: "There must be a way, Sir Thomas. I have only thirty men, otherwise I'd try myself."

"Look," Ned said, "you'd better start off back to Port Royal, otherwise you'll get benighted. Thank you for the information. If we go after her and get her treasure, I promise you'll get a look in."

"How much?"

Thomas growled: "How do we know, until we capture her? Anyway, it'll be more than you deserve! Mr Yorke is very generous. If we take our three ships, that's three captains. You won't even smell powder or take any risks!"

"Supposing the rest of the buccaneers come back in time to go with you, what then?"

"Then you still get a reward. You'd still be a rich man, judging from our last purchases, but don't worry," Thomas said, "they won't be back in time."

Sitting at the table in the tent which served as a canteen, listening to the saw (which sounded like a bull spasmodically gasping for breath) and the chinking of maul and chisel against stone as the masons faced up the rock, Ned smoothed out the chart drawn by Hoskins.

With a finger Thomas traced round the edge of a soup stain on the bare wood of the table. "It's a temptation, Ned."

"We need a pair of scales. Put the chances of treasure in one pan, and the consequences on the other."

"Never been much of a person for worrying about consequences, Ned; nor have you."

"Not until now. This time the consequences could be much more serious. Officially we're at peace with Spain, so if you and I and Saxby go off and deliberately attack a Spanish plate ship, we're probably guilty of treason because we're waging war on a friendly nation. Certainly we'd never be able to return to Jamaica."

"I see what you mean," Thomas said. "The women would lose their houses."

"That, and the fact we've a monarchy again. I always thought of Cromwell and his Roundheads as a passing phase: the English would eventually get over him, like recovering from a nasty disease you caught from a passing beggar. It all took a dozen years, but now the King is back; England's a monarchy once again. But if we're forbidden to enter every acre the King rules because we're accused of treason, it won't change in our lifetime. Exiles for the rest of our lives. Where shall we spend our old age, Thomas?"

Thomas grimaced but said: "You're quite right, Ned, but don't forget what's in the other pan of the scales. How much plate do we need for a lifetime? How much plate does a galleon carry?"

"A lot more than we can stow in our three ships, but where could we sell it? We'd end up like the Dons, tons of silver but we can't use a penny of it."

"Well, Ned, although I can't speak for Aurelia I'm damned sure Diana will agree with me: let's first try to get our hands on the plate. We can start worrying about the consequences if we have some silver and gold stowed in the holds! After all, here we're only leaving –" he gestured towards the site of Ned's house, "– the trenches we've dug for the foundations and a few sawn planks and faced stones. If I can exchange them for my share of a Spanish galleon, old Loosely's welcome to mine. Don't forget Loosely's only the first of a string of fools to be Governor here – even if the King isn't giving the island back to Spain."

"I've just realized that your share might be the whole lot," Ned said ruefully. "The *Griffin* can't sail at the moment: you remember there was that soft patch in the mast? Just before we left Port Royal I told Lobb to make a new mast and step it . . ."

"So first he's got to find the tree, fell it, lop it, get it carried down to Port Royal for the men to shape it up with adzes, fit the ironwork for the topmast . . . Three weeks?"

"At least," Ned said lamely. "I'm sorry, Thomas, but with all the rest of the ships sailing for Tortuga, I thought we'd have at least a couple of months to get the houses built, and it seemed a good time for Lobb to do the mast work. He's a good man," Ned added, "he won't waste time once he's started."

"You weren't to know about this galleon," Thomas said. He reached across and took the chart, and then he looked squarely at Ned. "Supposing I go up there with the *Peleus*? I can have a good look round and rattle the bars loud enough to keep everyone quiet until you arrive. After all, by now the Dons might already have patched themselves up enough to escape. We'll find out how Lobb's getting on before I sail;

then we can arrange a rendezvous so that if I find the Dons *have* gone, I can meet you and save you going all the way."

Ned nodded. "Very well, then. Take Saxby and the *Phoenix*, and I'll follow as soon as I can."

Thomas held up his hand. "No, let Saxby stay with you. The *Phoenix* will only slow me down, and you can use every one of her men (and Mrs Judd) to help Lobb's crowd. There won't be any action until the *Griffin* and the *Phoenix* arrive, I promise you that."

"Let's go and tell Saxby and the women," Ned said. "Diana is the only one who'll be smiling . . ." He looked round the site. "So now all the sawyers and masons and carpenters are going back to being sailors. I don't think many will mind much."

He saw Aurelia walking towards them. She had seen Hoskins and his silent mate ride off and now, knowing she would not be interrupting any conference, she was coming to find out the reason for the strangers' visit.

Thomas listened while Ned explained because he wanted to describe to Diana all the details of Aurelia's reaction. Aurelia's final comment left Ned dumbfounded and Thomas laughing.

"Thank goodness: I'm sick of being eaten by mosquitoes and stabbed by sandflies, and I'm tired of the grating and grunting of that saw and the way the masons have to peck, peck at the stone, like a *pic*. How do you say – like a woodpecker!"

Chapter Seven

In the shimmering heat the four of them rode the length of the Palisades, the long spit of sand and scrub on which Port Royal was built and which formed the south side of the great anchorage. They led such a motley crowd of tanned and bearded men, dressed in little more than rags (none was going to wear decent clothes while working as a labourer on shore), that Ned turned to Thomas.

"There's a man called Falstaff in one of Shakespeare's plays that I saw at a playhouse near the White Hart, in Southwark, when I was a boy. Falstaff is pressing men to be soldiers but careful to take a good percentage of men who'll bribe him well to let them go free. He says: 'I have misus'd the King's press damnably', and grumbles because the quality of the men is so poor, blaming 'the cankers of a calm world and a long peace'. Looking back at my rogues," Ned commented, "I can see that the cankers of building a house and a long time away from the ship have made them soft!"

"Stepping a new mast and sending up the topmast, and then swaying up the yard, followed by a few hundred miles slogging to windward – that'll soon remind them of the happy life of a sailor!" Thomas growled.

"How awful the *Griffin* looks without the mast," Aurelia said. "Just an old box sitting in the water . . ."

Ned pointed ahead to where a group of men standing in a line seemed to be performing some complicated dance. "There's our new mast, lying on the ground with the men shaping it up with their adzes."

Diana, riding astride and dressed in a long skirt which had been joined and seamed down the middle so that she wore what were in effect voluminous breeches, said: "Don't let's stop to watch them. I feel faint even watching a man pick up an adze. It always seems he's bound to chop off his foot."

"They don't, though."

"They do, though, Thomas. Remember when we went down to that shipyard in Bursledon – one of the two brothers who owned it walked with a crutch."

"Perhaps his wife had stamped on his bunion."

"An adze, while he was shaping up a keelson. And don't argue, Thomas, because I asked him while you were flirting with the wife."

"Lobb has only just started on the mast," Ned said.

"How can you tell from this distance?" Aurelia wanted to know.

"That two-wheeled thing with an arch-shaped axle that they use to move tree trunks – you can still see the track of the horses' hooves and the wheels in the dust. It rained a couple of days ago – we passed through the muddy patches – but those marks in the dust –"

"Yes, my dear," Aurelia said amiably, "but how long before we can sail?"

"Lobb will tell us, but from here it looks as if there's at least another week's work with the adze. Lobb's chosen a thick tree so that he'll be left with the heartwood, but there's a lot to be trimmed off."

Lobb, waiting for them, looked anxious: the first he knew that Ned was returning to the ship was when he saw the approaching column of men. The former second mate of the *Peleus* and the mate of the *Griffin*, and acting as master while Ned was away, was a Man of Kent, coming from Little Chart, near Ashford. He had a particular loyalty to the Yorke family, Ned had once explained to Aurelia with a straight face, because as a young man before being transported he had regularly poached over the Yorke estate at Godmersham, a few miles away.

Ned slowed down to tell Saxby to take the men straight out to the *Griffin* – Lobb was bound to have a couple of boats at the little jetty – and warn every man that could handle an adze that he would be needed tomorrow. In the meantime, half a dozen men could return the horses and mules to the livery stable and bring the account back with them.

"Now," he said to Thomas, "let's see what Lobb has to tell us about his problems."

Lobb had plenty to say. After raising his hat to Aurelia and Diana, and helping them down from their horses while, much to the two women's amusement, Ned and Thomas dismounted painfully, swearing that every muscle in their thighs had been torn adrift, he came up to Ned and shook his head. "T'ain't the mast, sir. There's so many shakes in the yard we need a new one. It's this heat driving down on the wood all and every day: just dries out the natural oils and the wood cracks like thrice-baked biscuit."

Ned looked over to where the men balancing on the top of the tree trunk were chopping with their adzes as though hoeing a trench.

"You haven't found anything suitable to shape up?"

Lobb waved at the forests covering the hills across from the anchorage. "Trouble is, most of this timber is foreign to me. I'm all right shaping up a piece of fir for the mast and spruce for a yard, but damn me if I know out here what's springy enough for a yard."

"Aye," said Saxby, "might be springy enough when you cut it, but will it stiffen up in three months' time, when the wood starts drying? A stiff yard will go bang on us in the middle of a gale o' wind."

Thomas said: "If I can be of help: I know just the tree for yards. Stays springy in all seasons, doesn't get shakes as long as you keep it well oiled, and we'll be able to find one of a decent diameter, so you don't wear out the adzes trimming it to size."

"Thanks," said Ned. "Why don't you call the men, and keep back a couple of horses so that –"

Thomas looked at Lobb. "Shall we go now? We'll find a tree and you can mark it. I want to sail tonight."

Lobb looked startled but hailed the men collecting the horses and mules into a string. "Wait a moment, Sir Thomas, I'll find myself an axe."

The deck of the *Griffin* looked like an abandoned ship's chandler: coils of thick tarred rope represented the shrouds;

heavy wooden discs each with three holes drilled in them, forming the corners of a triangle, were newly tarred and piled up in a pyramid. They were the deadeyes fitted to the lower end of the shrouds so that laniards could be reeved through the holes and those in the chainplates in the hull and hauled tight so that each shroud was taut as it did its job of supporting the mast.

The yard condemned by Lobb was lying along the deck, almost obscenely naked to a seaman's eye now it was stripped of sail, halyard and braces, as well as the rope suspended under the boom, the stirrups, on which men stood hunched over the yard as they reefed or furled the sail.

Ned walked over and inspected the spar. Lobb had not been exaggerating, and the answer to the question "Why did no one spot it earlier?" was that at sea the wood was protected from the sun much of the time by the sail, but it was routine in harbour to send down the sail so that chafed areas, rips and worn reef points could be repaired.

A month or more at anchor here, with the sun scorching down on the unprotected wood, produced those shakes, or splits. Any mast or spar was bound to get shakes – that was natural, and the reason why spars were oiled, so that water running down into the cracks would not set up rot, but this yard had seen too many scorching hurricane seasons; for too many days the sun had beaten down on it at noon, when a standing man cast a shadow no wider than the brim of his hat. Yes, some of the shakes were wide enough for a man to slip in a hand edgeways.

Ned thought of beating nearly a thousand miles to windward to reach St Martin and Anguilla. Many times these Trade winds blew as strong as a gale but out of a clear sky and kicked up a big head sea. That was when every mast and spar and inch of rigging and yard of canvas was tested. Too many captains trying to make do had to limp back into port under jury rig, often with hatches stove in and cargo damaged, or else nothing more was heard of them or their ships . . .

There was the sail spread out over the poop, with half a dozen men working on it, each with a rawhide leather palm looped over his right hand to give a solid backing to the needle, like a monstrous thimble, as he stitched.

Ned realized that the sail was draped over skylights and the companionway, acting like an enormous blanket. The saloon and their cabins would be scorching hot, starved of any cooling breeze. Saxby, who was standing with him, grunted and said: "Think you'd better come and have supper with us in the *Phoenix*, sir. I'm sure Mrs Judd would be honoured. We'll all be able to watch the *Peleus* sail. Might even give her a gun or two in salute – just enough to scare the Governor!"

Ned had just noticed that Aurelia was hurrying up the companionway, obviously hot and flustered. "Oh Ned, it's an oven down there!" she said. "It'll take hours to cool down."

Ned glanced at Saxby: "We accept your invitation," he said, and explained to Aurelia, who looked relieved. "Tell the men to move the sail when they've finished for the day," she told Ned. "We must get some air down to our cabin, or we'll never sleep tonight."

Saxby and Mrs Judd proved to be excellent hosts for what was the first social visit that Ned and Aurelia had ever made to the *Phoenix*. Because Saxby had been the foreman on the estate in Barbados and Mrs Judd had ruled in the kitchen, there was at first a shyness. Ned was hard put to keep a straight face: the sight of Mrs Judd acting shyly had something of the shire horse pulling a light gig. She wore a very low-cut silk dress of a dark green: the very full sleeves were open down the front and held together by clasps of what looked to Ned to be gold and rubies. The skirt was wide and the whole dress seemed cunningly designed to disguise her hips, which were rather too wide, while emphasizing her breasts, which were full and seemingly anxious to leap out over the top of the dress, which was edged in a darker green lace.

The four of them watched the *Peleus* sail and Saxby let his men fire each of the guns on the larboard side as the ship passed, Thomas and Diana waving from the poop. The smoke of the guns set Mrs Judd coughing and she was soon cursing Saxby. "You're like a small boy. Any excuse to make a noise – look how you've startled all the birds. Who'd have guessed there were so many pelicans. Now all the terns are squawking. Really, Saxby!"

"Got to give Sir Thomas a good sendoff," Saxby said complacently. "After all, he's going to be the gamekeeper until we get up there."

"If he finds as much silver as you say there is, he'd better start polishing it. As sure as my name's Martha Judd, I still think we was wrong to give all that gold to the government here. That General Heffer looks like a sheep and he has the brains of a sheep –"

"You ought to meet the new Governor," Saxby interrupted.

"Well, anything'd be an improvement on a sheep."

Ned said: "Not always, I'm afraid. Sir Harold Luce looks like a ferret."

"As long as he doesn't stink like one," commented Mrs Judd sourly. "Well, there's the *Peleus* going out of sight. Let's go below and sample some of that wine you've been boasting about, Saxby."

The *Phoenix's* saloon was large, airy and comfortable: panelled in mahogany, it had settees built in on both sides and across the after end of the cabin, with a table set in the middle and the steward (or Mrs Judd) able to serve from the forward side. A large open skylight over the table allowed a comfortable and cooling draught.

Noticing the silver goblets, cruets and silver cutlery already set out on the table, Ned realized that Saxby had after one of the raids taken part of his share of the purchase in silverware, instead of money. What more natural and sensible? Saxby came from a humble family but was now (thanks to buccaneering) a wealthy man, and he liked to have around him, where he could touch it, some symbols of his wealth. Perhaps Mrs Judd was content to polish it, for the same reason. The goblets were very good examples of the silversmith's art. Italian? Spanish? Obviously the couple enjoyed them.

"Lobb tells me he's been hearing about some of the Governor's new ideas," Saxby commented.

"Surely Sir Harold hasn't had another meeting of the executive council?"

"No, he has a crier now parading round Port Royal, ringing a bell and telling all who care to listen (not many, Lobb says!) about his latest decrees."

"Gunpowder!" Mrs Judd said as she walked into the cabin and put down a carafe of wine with a thud.

Ned looked startled and Saxby explained. "All foreign

ships visiting Port Royal – no matter whether or not they're carrying cargo – will have to pay a tax of so many bushels of powder."

"Hmm, he's starting to build up an arsenal, eh?" Ned said.

Saxby shook his head. "No, that's not the way people see it. Only two foreign ships have been in so far and had to pay it, and Lobb says the powder was afterwards taken on shore and then, at night, tipped into the sea. He reckons – and so do I – that Luce wants to make sure the buccaneers don't use the port. If the foreigners among them keep losing powder in taxes, Luce reckons they'll stay out."

"Call it a hint," Mrs Judd said as she poured the wine. "But when the Spanish come he's going to have to do more than drop hints to get anyone to come and rescue him."

"The fact is Port Royal is the best base for us. We'd just trained Heffer when they sent out this man Luce," Ned said glumly.

"You must train Sir Harold now," Aurelia said. "In the long run it will be worth the trouble."

"You can never train a ferret enough to trust it," Ned said. "Just when you think you've succeeded, it nips you the next time you pick it up."

Saxby chuckled, obviously recalling some episode from his life in Lincolnshire. "Or else the damned animal stays down the burrow eating the rabbit it's just killed and won't come out."

"That's Luce," Aurelia said, "crouched in the burrow sulking and eating."

"And stinking," Mrs Judd said. "Nasty things, ferrets. My first husband kept them. Grew like them, he did."

"*First* husband?" Saxby said. "Wasn't that Judd?"

"Judd was my last one. I'm talking of the first," Mrs Judd said, and Ned wondered if Saxby realized that although the late Mr Judd was the last husband, he probably was not even the second. Did she wear them out and toss them aside? Well, Saxby obviously was not a jealous man, and he looked strong enough. If Martha Judd has any sense, Ned thought, she'll realize there are not many Saxbys in the Caribbee. At that moment he saw her watching one of the silver goblets as she poured the wine and realized that Martha Judd was quite happy with her lot, thank you: Saxby, silver to polish and a life of freedom was all she sought. She was wise enough to know what she was looking for and recognize it all when she found it.

By the time they had dined and gossiped and one of the *Phoenix's* boats had taken Ned and Aurelia back to the *Griffin*, their cabin had cooled down. After Aurelia undressed and was sitting at the foot of her bunk combing her long blonde hair, she asked: "If the galleon is carrying plate, and if we capture it, Ned, what then? Where do we go? We won't be able to come back here."

"Jamaica isn't the centre of the world, darling."

"No, but the world gets small if the King decides that by attacking a Spanish ship we have committed treason."

"Small!" Ned exclaimed. "You forget Europe!"

"I don't want to go back to Europe," Aurelia said flatly. "Nor do Diana and Thomas. You know that Thomas can't go back to England – he has too many debtors, and anyway, he'd never be able to stay away from the gambling tables. Especially now he's rich."

"England isn't the only place in Europe, dearest."

"Where do you suggest, Spain? They'd welcome us there – but I don't want to be greeted with a rack and a garotte!"

"What about France – or even Italy?"

"Ned, we'd be as welcome in a Catholic country as the plague!"

"Perhaps the King won't have us charged with treason," Ned said. "Anyway, it'd take months for Madrid to hear about it and instruct their ambassador in London to protest . . ."

"You forget the Governor here: he will hear about it within days. He might charge you himself: after all, I'm sure he received instructions covering this sort of thing before he left London."

Ned sat up in the bunk. "It's been a tiring day, darling. Put down that comb and come to bed."

"I'm not tired," Aurelia said, "that's why I'm giving my hair a good combing."

Ned looked at the breasts with their pink nipples dividing the long hair as it fell in cascades. "I'm not tired either, but come to bed."

The sun was already bright one morning a week later, but had not begun to scorch, when Ned inspected the new mast. A dozen men were still balancing themselves along the top of the tree trunk, tapping away like patient labourers hoeing sun-baked soil and shaping it into a long tapered cylinder. The adzes, looking like short-handled hoes, were sharp and enough chips of wood were scattered over the white sand to stop the glare.

Ned walked to one end and sighted along the great log. The men were shaping it skilfully and one of them, holding up his hand, called: "Right, all off! We've got to turn 'er."

All the men jumped off, put down their adzes and picked up short lengths of wood. Standing evenly spaced along its length, they pushed the levers under the tree and heaved down so that it turned a few inches.

Then, adze in hand, each scrambled back on top and began cutting once again, the chips of wood flying. "Another six inches all round," Lobb commented. "Then we can start shaping up for the ironwork."

"Pity we couldn't make new ironwork to fit this mast," Ned said. "It'd save us time, too."

"The only man with the right thickness of ironwork is the blacksmith here," Lobb growled, pointing to a small building half a mile away, "and he must have started cutting firewood and weaving baskets. He tells a fine tale and his boy works hard with the bellows, but I wouldn't trust him to shoe a dead horse, let alone go to sea with any mastwork *he* made."

"Pity our best blacksmiths have gone off to Cartagena," Ned said.

"I was going to talk to you about that one day, sir," Lobb said. "With not a blacksmith among the three ships, *Griffin*, *Peleus* or *Phoenix*, we ought to start looking for one."

"Or train one of our own. We had a couple of men making ironwork for the house."

Exactly a week later, as Ned and Saxby stood with Lobb watching men with tongs heating up a mast band in a rudimentary furnace before slipping it into place over the completed new mast, and while carpenters nearby shaped up the new yard, an excited seaman ran up from the jetty.

"The lady sent me over," he gasped to Ned. It was curious

how the men never called her "Mrs Wilson", and Ned knew it was less a question of not referring to her dead husband, whose vile reputation the seamen knew about, than a wish to refer to her instead as his wife. "The lady says a boat's coming round Gallows Point with three men in it, and they're sailin' it, but through the glass they look too weak to row up to the *Griffin.*"

"Well, for God's sake –"

"The lady's already sent a boat to take 'em in tow, sir, an' my boat's ready to take you out to the *Griffin.*"

Ned stared at the man, puzzled. Why on earth was Aurelia getting so excited over a boat being sailed in by three tired men?

"What the Devil's wrong with the boat?" he demanded.

"Nothin' *wrong* with the boat, sir; s'just we recognize it as being one belonging to the *Peleus* . . ."

Chapter Eight

Ned looked at the three men lying on the deck on tarpaulins. The sun had scorched and blackened their skin; starvation stripping away every ounce of spare flesh had left the bones in their bodies protruding – yes, Ned realized with horror, like those of a body left to hang on a gibbet. Worse, their flesh had that aged, dried and shrunken look of meat that had been boucanned.

Their eyes were shut; the sockets seemed enormous, emphasizing cheekbones and giving them an oddly Indian appearance. Ned remembered seeing them on board the *Peleus*.

"Stand back, sir," Mrs Judd said as she moved in to crouch beside the men, a leather bucket full of water beside her. She began dipping a cloth in the water and rubbing down the man nearest her.

Ned suddenly realized that Aurelia was standing beside him. "What happened?" he asked.

"They can't talk yet. They've come in one of the *Peleus's* boats, though: you know Thomas had all his boats painted in what he calls his livery, red and yellow."

"And Mrs Judd?"

"She and Saxby saw the boat and came over immediately. Mrs Judd learned this –" she gestured at the water, "– from an Indian. A man left for days in the sun like these poor fellows has all the water dried out of him, so you keep his mouth moist while you bathe his body to restore the water to the flesh."

"Why not give them a good drink of water?"
"We tried that, but they can't drink properly – I think their throats are too swollen. So we're just wetting their mouths as well."
Were they mutineers that Thomas had cast adrift? Had the *Peleus* sunk and these were the only survivors? What about Thomas and Diana, two people so full of life and love and zest it seemed a blasphemy even to think of them as drowned? Thomas with a mug or a sword in his hand always looked happy; a soldier or sailor of fortune who appeared the most independent of men – until you realized that he was incomplete unless Diana was with him (which she usually was). And Diana, dark-haired, always heavily tanned, proud of her body in a way few other women were – or dared to be. Diana talking to Thomas, and standing so close a breast brushed his chest, yet there was no coquettishness, just that they needed to touch each other, as though touch gave a deeper meaning to mere words. To see them standing together talking was to think of them making love – not because of a lewd curiosity but because their happiness together was so open and obvious – so natural, in other words.
He felt Aurelia's touch on his arm and looked down at her, guessing that the same thoughts were going through her mind. "Ned, I'm frightened for them."
There was no mistaking who "them" meant. The three men Mrs Judd was nursing, shouting at seamen to bring more buckets of fresh water, would be able to talk soon – but how long was "soon"? An hour, five hours, a day? Whether or not the King gave Jamaica back to Spain, whether or not the Ferret ever understood that Spain would always be the enemy of all foreigners who dared sail into the Caribbee – none of it mattered now. What mattered was what those men had to say.
"Supposing they're mutineers?"
He felt Aurelia shudder as he realized he had spoken his thoughts aloud. "I thought of that and then when I looked at them lying there like boucan, I was ashamed," Aurelia admitted. "But I suppose it's possible."
"What doesn't seem likely is Thomas casting such men adrift in a boat. He might hang mutineers from the yardarm: but a boat? It doesn't seem like him."
Aurelia nodded. "Diana wouldn't let him. Landing them to

take their chance with the *Cimarróns*, yes; marooning is common enough."

"And Thomas had only four boats. He wouldn't want to lose one for the sake of getting rid of three mutineers," Ned added.

"There may have been more men," Aurelia said. "These three might be the only survivors. But Thomas didn't cast them adrift," she said firmly. "That's not his way. Something awful has happened, Ned. I can feel it. Will those men live?"

Martha Judd heard the last few words, which were almost a cry of distress from the Frenchwoman, and she looked up from her sponging. "They'll live," she said crisply. "The sun's burnt 'em so badly they'll be in agony for a few days, but they'll live. Send for Saxby – he's down in their boat seeing if he can find out anything – and tell him to bring me some rum and I'll try rinsing their mouths out with a more familiar taste than water: it might bring 'em round quicker. Come *on*," she snapped, squeezing one of the men's scrotum and watching his face for any reaction to the pain. "Ah, this one's coming back to us." She walked round and crouched beside the second man, repeating the test. "This one, too," she said. "He's even groaning. Probably thinks he's arrived in Paradise. Just think," she said, winking at Aurelia, "a man arrives in Paradise – and there's Martha Judd to greet him with a clutching hand . . ."

Saxby soon arrived with an earthenware jug of rum. "Who's it for, you or them?" he asked Martha.

She ignored Saxby's teasing. "Well, what have you found out from the boat?"

"Precious little," he admitted. "All the oars are on board, and so are three pistols and three cutlasses. There's just one small water *bareca* and that's empty and the bung is missing. Seven notches cut into the aftermost thwart – probably chopped with a cutlass to mark each passing day. No compass, no signs of food, not even a shred of boucan."

Knowing Ned could hear his report, Saxby said: "There you are sir. They wasn't sent off on some expedition and got lost, else there'd be a compass. Three pistols and three cutlasses makes me think there was just the three of 'em. Yet three's an odd number of men to be doing anything with a boat: two oars one side and one the other. Don't make sense, but I don't reckon four started off, otherwise there'd be a fourth pistol – or at least a cutlass."

Saxby saw Martha Judd reaching over to the third man's scrotum and watched incredulously as she squeezed hard. "Here, Martha, what the Devil d'you think you're doing?"

"Quickest way to a man's heart," she said, picking up a fresh cloth and dipping the end into the rum. She knelt down at the first man's head and rinsed the inside of his mouth, squeezing the last few drops carefully so they did not fall directly into the throat.

The man stirred and then coughed. He then gave a loud groan. Martha Judd looked up at Saxby. "You see, it works."

Because the *Griffin* was without mast or rigging there was nowhere to sling hammocks on deck, so once Martha pronounced that her water, squeezing and rum treatment had worked, the three men were carefully carried below and put into hammocks.

Mrs Judd was forward in the galley preparing some thin gruel when the first of the men recovered consciousness. He did it so suddenly that he took Ned, Aurelia and Saxby by surprise. Muttering "Wemmeye," he clutched the sides of the hammock and tried to sit up.

Aurelia was beside him in a moment, making noises like a mother comforting a child as the man repeated, his voice rising in panic: "Wemmeye, wemmeye?"

Ned was the first to realize that the man was asking "Where am I?" and said, slowly and clearly: "You're on board the *Griffin* in Port Royal."

"Oh Gawd," the man muttered, "'spected Dons!"

Ned looked at Saxby, who shook his head. "Why should he expect Spaniards?"

Did he expect Jamaica to have been taken by the Spanish? Unlikely, Ned thought. Did he realize he was in Jamaica or had he expected the boat to arrive in Hispaniola?

Ned asked Aurelia: "When you sighted their boat, it was sailing, but did you see any of the men moving?"

"Not actually moving, no. With the glass I could see men and they were obviously exhausted. From their positions," she explained, "we could see that. We did not think they could row."

"When our boat towed theirs up alongside, did the men move then?"

Puzzled at the questions, Aurelia shook her head. "No, they were already unconscious, and our men had to lift them on board. Why do you ask?"

"I think these men have been unconscious for hours, if not days. This fellow didn't know he's in Port Royal. He was expecting to find himself in Hispaniola, a prisoner of the Dons. The western end of Hispaniola is a hundred and fifty miles to windward of here. I think that boat has been sailing itself for two or three days, and just a chance of the wind and current brought it into Port Royal."

Aurelia shuddered at the thought. "Supposing the boat had drifted up on a beach out of sight of us," she murmured. "Another mile or two to the eastward . . ."

"Think of what'd happen if they'd landed in Hispaniola, in sight of the Dons ma'am," Saxby said. "But best of all, don't think about it: they landed among friends, and they're three lucky fellows."

Ned looked down at the man again, and saw his eyelids flickering. He bent over and spoke clearly to the man. "Can you hear me?"

"S'right, can 'ear yer," the man muttered, and added: "Sir."

"Do you know who I am?"

"S'Mister Yorke, innit?"

"Yes. What's happened to the *Peleus*?"

"Dons got her. All of 'em. We was goin' woodin' an' waterin'. Dons agreed to give us water an' let us collect wood. All lies, tho'."

The effort of talking exhausted him and he seemed to doze. Ned left him a few minutes and, despite Aurelia's protests, shook him awake again.

"What happened to Sir Thomas and Lady Diana?"

"Orl gawn, sir; Dons got 'em. Only us escaped 'cos we was acrorst the bay, fishin' . . ."

"Where? Where did all this happen?"

"Wessen end P' Rico," the man mumbled, and Ned was not sure whether he was going to sleep or lapsing into unconsciousness.

"What's the name of the port? What bay?" When the man

did not reply he tried Martha Judd's trick, and said loudly: "Where were you watering?"

"Bokker somewhere," the man mumbled.

"Boquerón?"

"S'right, sir." Then he murmured, "Sorry . . . gotta . . . sleep . . ."

"Oh, you're a cruel man!" Aurelia accused Ned. "This poor *matelot* – you bully him with questions even though he's probably dying!"

The skin of Ned's face tightened. "If necessary, I'd have killed all three of them for the information I've just got," he said harshly. "Their lives against eighty or more in the *Peleus*? But it wasn't necessary, anyway."

"But the Spanish must have killed Thomas and Diana and all the rest of the *Peleus*'s crew," Aurelia said, beginning to weep as the full significance of what she had just said sank in. "Oh Ned, no plate galleon, *nothing*, was worth that."

"The Spanish won't have killed them yet. A cat likes to play with a mouse. Saxby, go across to Lobb and the rest of our men. Gather them round and tell 'em what we've just heard. Then ask them to work night and day until we get the mast stepped and can sway up the yard and bend on the sails."

"Aye, that's the way to do it," Saxby said. "What was that place in Puerto Rico?"

"Boquerón. It's the long bay on the western coast at the southern entrance of the Mona Passage."

"Reckon there's much we can do, sir?"

Ned shrugged his shoulders, avoiding looking at Aurelia. "I hope so. You know what a garotte looks like."

Next day, as the men of the *Griffin* and *Phoenix* hurried to get the mast ready to be towed out and stepped in place using sheer legs rigged on the ship, a canoe brought Sir Harold Luce's secretary Hamilton with a message for Ned.

Hot and tired from helping to rig the sheer legs – two roughly trimmed tree trunks lashed together at the top so that when raised they would form a large upside-down letter V – Ned did not know the young man had arrived on board until Aurelia came up to tell him: "There's a message from the Governor."

"Take it – I'll read it later."

Aurelia, dressed in seamen's clothes because she too was helping, said: "No, it's a young man with a message."

"If the Governor has any message for me, let him put it in writing," Ned said crossly, shouting an order to seamen standing ready aft to haul on a rope.

"Oh Ned, this poor young man has come all the way out in a fisherman's canoe with the message," Aurelia said. "Give him a minute!"

"Pretty young fellow with a silly blond beard, dressed like a haberdasher?"

"Well, he's –"

"That's 'Shifty Hamilton'! Send him off in his canoe!"

"Ah, Mr Yorke," the young man said, having followed Aurelia across the deck, "this sailor told me you were busy, but . . ."

Ned stared at Aurelia. Yes, she wore seamen's clothes; yes, her ash-blonde hair was piled on her head and covered with a scarf. But the face, even though sun-tanned . . .

"Don't listen to these rough sailors," Ned said, "they'll tell you anything. I've been waiting here for days for you to bring me a message from the Governor. What does Sir Harold say – that couldn't have been written in a letter and delivered next week?"

Hamilton, oblivious to Aurelia (whose face was flushed with embarrassment and anger as she realized that the young man was either unaware or uninterested in the fact she was a woman), said: "Sir Harold asked me to find out about the boat that came into the harbour yesterday."

"Did he?" Ned said politely.

"Er, yes, he did. There were men in it."

"Is that so?"

"Yes, three men."

"Well, now you can go back and tell Sir Harold all about it."

"But . . . well, that's *all* I know."

"What else do you want? The names of all their wives? How many children they have?"

"I'm sure Sir Harold will want to know where they came from, and why they came here, and what they want."

"I'm sure he will," Ned said, signalling to the seamen at the rope to start heaving. "Excuse me, I've work to do," he told Hamilton.

"But Mr Yorke, what shall I tell Sir Harold?" Hamilton asked plaintively.

"Tell him what you've just told me."

"But he'll want to know more. They tell me at the jetty you are hurrying to get that mast on board so you can sail. Is that because of the men?"

"How many men are rowing the canoe that brought you out?"

"Two. I was –"

"Tell them to row you back, now."

"But I must –"

"Unless you want to swim. Can you swim?"

"But Sir Harold will –"

"Good day," Ned said, turning his back on Hamilton and watching as the inverted V of the sheer legs rose up in the air, forming an arch which could be used to raise the mast.

Hamilton turned to Aurelia, hands held out pleading.

"I should go," Aurelia said crossly, "or he'll order *me* to throw you over the side."

The next caller was Saxby, who had just come over from the *Phoenix*.

"Had a bit o' luck sir. Both those Spanish seamen I signed on when we took the *Phoenix* as a prize know Boquerón, and guess what? The *Phoenix*, when she was Spanish before we captured her, was anchored in Boquerón for eight weeks while they used their boats to load sugar and cotton and hides from the shore. They both know it well – both the bay and the village, and even some of the towns and villages nearby. They used to go to Mass at various places because the priest of Boquerón was defrocked while they were there. Some trouble with his two servants. *Two*," Saxby said contemptuously, "and he got caught."

"One can't resist the hot-blooded *señoritas*, Saxby," Ned said.

"Indeed you can't," Saxby agreed, "but these were young men. Anyway," he produced a folded paper from his pocket, "my men have drawn a rough chart, complete with soundings. They're sure of the soundings and bearings because they used to put down fish traps every night and they didn't buoy them, else the local fishermen'd steal 'em, so they relied on bearings to find the traps again."

Ned unfolded the chart which Saxby had redrawn in ink and saw it had plenty of detail. "Hmm, a convenient little coral island with palms in the middle to mark that outer reef. And mangroves growing on coral to mark the entrance of the reef protecting the bay. A lake and marshes just inland near Boquerón. Ah, there's San Germán, about nine miles inland. Isn't that where the old church is? Mayagüez is further along the coast – probably the most important port around there. Look at that town called Cabo Rojo a good three miles inland. I thought '*Cabo*' meant 'cape'. Oh, that's the town up there: the cape itself is right down here, miles away to the south, ten miles at least, the real south-western tip of Porto Rico. Well done; tell the men I appreciate their care. I'll have a talk with them later – they've probably some ideas where we might find our friends."

Saxby shook his head, looking sombre. "Reckon all we'll find is graves, unless they throw the bodies on the town midden."

"We'll see," Ned said, "but in the meantime keep those sort of thoughts to yourself: the men must think we can rescue them. Men'll take chances when there's a hope."

"True, sir, I haven't mentioned my doubts to anyone else."

"Is this my copy of the chart?" Ned held up the paper, folding it and tucking it in his pocket when Saxby nodded. "By the way, we'll need a couple of your boats to help tow the mast out this evening, when the wind has dropped, and every man you can spare to help parbuckle it on board. And you, of course. Lobb took the mast out with the sheer legs, but he's never put one back. I think he'd like to have you standing beside him."

"He learns fast," Saxby commented. "If you ever find someone to replace him, I'd be glad to have him."

"I've no doubt you would," Ned said. "Let's get on shore and see how Lobb's getting on. I'd like to get that yard on board this evening, too. By the way, the Governor has been inquiring about the boat with the three men from the *Peleus*."

"I guessed as much: I saw a canoe bringing out that fop of a secretary. What did you tell him, sir?"

"Nothing. He'd heard from somewhere – the secretary, I

mean – that we were going to sail as soon as we get this damned mast stepped, but has no idea where – or why."

"That's right, let's keep Sir Harold guessing. Probably thinks we're going off to meet the rest of our ships and seize Cartagena!"

"If he's scared about what we might do, think of the Spanish Governor! In fact, when the Dons find out they're losing ships, they'll blame me. Still, if they complain to Madrid, giving dates, we can probably prove to Sir Harold that we were still in Jamaica sawing planks and digging trenches . . ."

"He'll probably confiscate your land," Saxby said, "just out of spite."

"I've thought of that, and Sir Thomas's too, especially if he's been killed by the Dons. Still, we can play the game of 'if' all night," Ned said, walking towards the entryport, where a boat waited.

At noon next day, with the mast stepped and men grunting with the effort of swaying up the yard and reeving the running rigging, Martha Judd reported to Ned: "Two of those men can answer questions now. The third's got a fever and is delirious. I've had his hammock slung up forward so he doesn't disturb the others."

Ned nodded and waved to Saxby, who followed him down the ladder. Going from the harsh brightness of the sun into the half darkness below, Ned paused for a minute to let his eyes make the change.

"Martha says one of them is delirious," he told Saxby.

"Not surprised. They looked like boucan when I first saw them. By rights they ought to be dead. Remember those notches? I wonder exactly how long they took to get here?"

"It's about six hundred miles from Boquerón, but I doubt they know the date they left. I still can't get over that boat sailing itself into here."

Saxby said: "It's not surprising really, if the boat sailed along the coast with a following wind. The wind then funnels in through the entrance, and the tide was making, so the current'd help carry them in. Might have been a different story with an ebb tide."

"That was one of the first lessons you ever taught me about

seamanship, Saxby: always make a landfall on a flood tide, so that if you accidentally go aground, the tide's still making and will probably float you off. Even if the rise and fall is a matter of inches!"

Saxby laughed cheerfully as he led the way to the two men in the hammocks. "I must admit you seem to have remembered everything, sir, but at the time I didn't think you were paying much attention."

"That was before I ever thought we might have to use the *Griffin* to escape from Barbados," Ned said. "It took Cromwell to show me my own neighbours could be my worst enemies."

He reached the first hammock. "How are you feeling?"

"Much better, thanks Mr Yorke," the man said. "Mighty sore from the sunburn but not so weak. That Mrs Judd is feeding us up as if she's going to cook us for Christmas."

"She may well be planning to do that. Now, tell me what happened – first, why did Sir Thomas go into a Spanish port?"

"Water," the man said simply. "Y'see sir, most of the casks had been left empty while Sir Thomas was up in the mountains starting to build his house. When he came back and said we was sailing, well, the mate sent the casks on shore to fill 'em, but Sir Thomas thought he was just having the water changed so we had it fresh: he didn't know most of 'em had been empty for weeks."

"What's that got to do with going into Boquerón?"

"Leaving the casks empty all that time, sir, the staves dried out. We didn't pay much attention when we filled 'em – just reckoned they was weeping a few drops of water and it'd stop once the wood took up, that's what we thought, and o' course we stowed 'em below out of sight and sailed that same evening, an' you watched us go from the *Phoenix*."

"And the casks were still weeping?"

"Yes, sir, though we didn't know. We were abeam of Cow Island, this end of Hispaniola, when the carpenter came up and reported a lot of water in the bilges, and when Sir Thomas went below to see what was happening he tasted it, and it was fresh, not salty.

"Well, we checked the casks – at least, we thought we did. We didn't move them all and reckoned about half had been weeping. We guessed the casks that weren't weeping weren't leaking, and that was our mistake."

"In what way?" Ned asked.

"Well, sir," the seaman said shamefacedly, "they weren't weeping because they were *already* empty: they'd lost all their water and the outsides had dried. We found that out much later when we was hoisting up a cask just as we got to the eastern end of Hispaniola, just starting to cross the Mona Passage. The cask came up light. We rigged up the tackle on the next one, and that came up empty too. Then we got down in the hold and started shifting the casks a bit sharpish. No water. Well, maybe we had fifty gallons all told."

"What did Sir Thomas decide to do then?"

"Well, sir, I only heard the gossip, but it all put him in a mortal rage because he was in such a hurry to get to St Martin, and after all the beating we'd done to get where we was, he weren't keen on running six hundred miles back here to get more water. He reckoned the casks were wet enough inside so the wood would be swelling gradually so they'd take up.

"Now this is just wot I 'eard, sir. Sir Thomas reckoned that because of the new peace treaty wot's been signed with Spain, that the governors – viceroys, that's what they're called, leastways I think so – would have had orders from Spain, or at least news of the treaty.

"So 'e reckoned 'e'd chance 'is arm and anchor off a Spanish port and send a boat in to ask for a safe conduct to send in the rest of the boats to fill the casks. Offered hostages, too, 'e did."

Ned saw the man was perspiring with the excitement of telling his story. "Did the Spanish take him up on the hostages?"

"No. I 'eard they pretended to be offended at the very idea. Come and take all the water you want, they said. Five or six wells right at the village of Boquerón, a few 'undred yards back o' the beach, with a track to roll the casks. It all looked so easy, an' the Dons so 'elpful. Fooled us all, they did. Our men start rolling the casks up the track – leastways, all they could get in the boats. The three of us was off the ship."

"How did the three of you escape?"

The seaman now looked embarrassed. "Well, to be honest sir, we all fancied a bit o' fresh fish, so as soon as – I shouldn't be admitting this – soon as Sir Thomas and the lady was out of sight below and the other three boats ran up on the beach and started rollin' the casks, we went off in the fourth boat with fishin' lines. Not far – not more'n a quarter o' a mile. We'd put the lines down and was rowin' slow when we heard shots an' the next minute saw a crowd of Spanish soldiers gallop along the track to the boats and some fishermen come out of the bushes behind the beach, and they drag the boats down to the water and start rowing towards the ship. We watched for a minute or two, then guessed what was going on. We moved so's the ship was between the Dons and us, so the soldiers couldn't see us, and rowed out of the bay, and the minute we got through the reef and clear the land so we 'ad a bit o' breeze, we hoisted the sail. The Dons must 'ave seen us then, but they didn't worry."

"Why couldn't you catch fish to eat?" Saxby asked.

The seaman shook his head angrily. "We did, big ones, an' every time they broke the line and we lost the 'ooks."

"The pistols and cutlasses?"

"Well, Mr Saxby, we was also guarding the ship, as you might say –"

"No, I wouldn't," Saxby interrupted coldly, "the Dons took the ship, didn't they?"

"– well, yes Mr Saxby, but we weren't daft enough to go off unarmed. We took a pistol each and a cutlass."

"Very useful, the cutlasses. You could cut a notch in the thwart each day and keep a reckoning."

"Mr Yorke," the man said, directing his appeal to Ned, "we admit we was wrong goin' off fishin', but three of us couldn't 'ave 'eld the ship against all them Dons – three boats full o' 'em – and if we 'adn't escaped, you wouldn't know nothing about wot 'appened."

Ned nodded. "That's the only thing in your favour. What's the last landmark you remember?"

"The other two was unconcherous, o' course, but I just saw the eastern end of Jamaica. I wasn't making much sense by then; just hollering for help although the land must have been ten miles away, p'raps more. A long 'ard sail it is, from Boquerón to Port Royal."

Ned looked at the man in the second hammock. "Did you hear all that this fellow said?"

"Yes, Mr Yorke, an' what you an' Mr Saxby said, too."

"Has he forgotten anything that we ought to know – about the *Peleus* and Sir Thomas, and the men?"

"Nothin', sir. To begin with the Dons was all nice an' friendly. Proper took Sir Thomas in, they did – I was with him when he went on shore the first time, with a flag of truce. Everyone was nice – not just the mayor but the fishermen: even the little kiddies came out an' smiled an' waved."

"Very well," Ned said, "we'll be sailing in a few hours. Mrs Judd will be going back to her own ship, but you'll be looked after. As soon as you're fit enough you'll have to help work the ship."

Chapter Nine

A brisk wind settled down from the east as soon as the *Griffin* cleared Port Royal. Ned commented sourly to Aurelia while they inspected the chart spread on the saloon table (the ship pitching into the head seas and rolling with a corkscrew effect was both tiring and irritating): "Draw a straight line directly into wind and sea, and that's our course for Boquerón, six hundred miles of this crashing about!"

A ruler with one end on Port Royal and the other on Cabo Rojo, at the south-western tip of Porto Rico, close to Boquerón, showed the course as a straight line if the *Griffin* could sail directly into the wind, but she had to keep tacking, the wind first on one side and then on the other, the ship progressing like a crab scrabbling along a narrow gully.

For four hundred miles the mountains and forests of Hispaniola would lie to the north of them, a land barrier preventing the *Griffin* taking long tacks to the north, so that the crab might well have been lamed, able to take long strides to the southwards but only short ones to the north.

Once out of Port Royal there had been the familiar beat to windward as far as Morant Point, the eastern end of Jamaica; then the seas had become wilder and – although it might have been their imagination – the wind freshened as they crossed the 120-mile gap to the western end of Hispaniola which further north became the Windward Passage between Cuba and Hispaniola.

Tack, tack, tack, with the *Phoenix* following astern at the *Griffin*'s heels like a well trained dog. By now spray and the occasional sea sweeping the *Griffin*'s decks had washed away the evidence of more then a month in port. The whiskery tails of frayed ropes had been cut off before serving or resplicing, wood shavings from the final tapering of the yard to take the end fittings for the braces, pieces of old canvas cut from the sails when they were being patched . . . all the scraps that the wind blew to hiding places behind coamings, gun carriages, the tails of ropes made up on kevils – all were sluiced over the side. But if the constant spray and the occasional sea washed the decks clean, some of the water found its way down through the deck seams, working its way past the pitch and the caulking beneath it to drip usually on to a sailor's last dry blouse or the cook's bag of rice or flour.

Water, Ned had noticed years ago, never dripped directly into the bilge, where it would do no harm and the pump would later clear it; no, as if directed by a wilful spirit, it fell on any dry object that would be damaged by salt water. A keg of gunpowder, a wooden box (assumed to be waterproof) of wheel-lock pistols which were not inspected until too late to stop the pistols rusting despite the grease smeared on them, sacks of freshly boucanned beef, a bag of clothes . . . all were sodden by the time the *Griffin* had thrashed her way up to Cape Gravois, at the Jamaica end of Hispaniola, and once again tacked south-eastwards. The men at the helm kept steering as close to the wind as possible, without slowing down the ship, but as soon as Hispaniola's mountains were low on the northern horizon, almost a grey smear like a distant cloud, and the *Griffin* was tacked north again, they found that because the ship's usual leeway had combined with a strong west-going current driven by the Trade winds, by the time they reached the coast of Hispaniola again they were depressingly close to Cow Island in the wide and shallow bay beyond Cape Gravois, having made little progress towards Boquerón.

As they tacked south-eastwards yet again, Ned inspected the rigging with Lobb. They found, as expected, that the ropes of the mainmast shrouds had stretched so that now the shrouds on the lee side were much too slack.

"Not dangerous," Ned said, shrugging his shoulders, "but if there's much more stretch we'll have to find a quiet bay on the lee side of one of these headlands and go in to anchor, so we can take up on these lanyards."

Lobb looked up the mast with a critical eye: the masthead was gyrating like a man waving his stick in the air and drawing imaginary circles on the blue sky; the sails were bulging with the weight of the wind, but there was no sign of chafe on the canvas nor the peephole of blue warning that the stitching of a seam was beginning to part.

"A new mast and green wood," Lobb commented, "so it's got plenty of spring in it. Enough to take care of those slack shrouds, I reckon."

With the sun dipping down towards the western horizon and darkness due in a couple of hours, Ned began timing the length of each tack. He had already noted that the *Griffin* had stayed on the last tack to the south for three hours. It was well over a hundred miles from Cow Island to the two islands off the end of the next bight – Alta Vela (which, as its name implied, looked from a distance like a high sail) and Beata Island, which was just lodged off Punta Beata, the southernmost tip of Hispaniola. With this damned current running so strongly to the west and heading them, they would be lucky to sight Alta Vela by nightfall tomorrow . . .

Aquin Bay, tack to the south-east . . . Tack to the north-east . . . Cape Raimond, tack to the south-east . . . So the *Griffin* and *Phoenix* worked their way eastward: Cap Jacmel, False Cape, Alta Vela, Punta Beata, Punta Avarena, Punta Salinas . . . Ned noted them down in his log and was thankful he had several Spanish charts, taken from captured prizes, which he could piece together to give a continuous picture on parchment of the coast. On the evening of the third day he called Aurelia on deck and pointed to the land lying on their larboard bow: flat, with mountains beyond and what seemed to be the mouth of a river well to the east.

"That's where Cromwell's plans for the Caribbee started to go wrong." When Aurelia looked puzzled, he explained: "Out of sight over there to windward is the city of Santo Domingo, where Admiral Penn was supposed to anchor his ships and land General Venables and his army to capture the whole of Hispaniola . . ."

"Don't laugh at them, Ned," Aurelia said. "If they hadn't failed here and then gone on to take Jamaica instead, we'd have had nowhere to go after escaping from Barbados!"

Out of curiosity Ned held on to within five miles of Santo Domingo before ordering the *Griffin* to tack yet again to the south-east. There were plenty of flat stretches of coast, and he could imagine the nervous Penn and the indecisive Venables slowly passing their objective as the following wind and the current carried them on westward . . . to a marshy stretch of coast where thousands of their men would perish from disease. Poor planning, poor leadership and poor troops had thwarted Cromwell's plans (grand enough, Ned admitted) and left the Spaniards still owning Hispaniola.

Finally, after tacks which took them into San Pedros de Macoris and La Romana (with Catalina Island lying just off it), they reached the south-eastern tip of Hispaniola, which looked on the chart like a rabbit's head nibbling a piece of lettuce which was Saona Island.

Once they tacked clear of Saona Island and could no longer see any more of Hispaniola to the north, Ned sighed with relief and showed Aurelia their position on the chart. They were now entering the Mona Passage, some sixty to seventy miles wide, separating Hispaniola from Porto Rico. It showed on the chart as a neat, parallel-sided channel between the two big islands, with the tiny deserted island of Mona almost exactly midway.

There was another small island, Desecheo, at the northern end of the Mona Passage, much closer to the end of Porto Rico. "Very convenient, that one," Ned said. "We can make long tacks north-east now, and as soon as we sight Desecheo it'll show us where we are, so we then tack to the south-east until Mona gives us our position on the other leg and we can tack again."

Aurelia ran her finger in a straight line from Saona Island, through Mona Island, and into the bay of Boquerón.

Ned nodded and said: "Yes, it's easy to see why Thomas chose Boquerón to look for water. It was the nearest place with a sheltered bay and took him only a few miles off his course to St Martin."

Aurelia then ran her finger eastwards from Cabo Rojo at the end of Porto Rico, passing the towns of Guánica, Ponce and Jobos to the headland at the far end of Porto Rico. She continued in a straight line, eventually reaching St Martin while leaving many smaller islands (the Virgin Islands, the chart said) to the north and one, Santa Cruz, to the south. Santa Cruz? That would be St Croix in French.

"We are getting so close now I am getting more frightened, Ned," she said, holding his arm.

"We faced bigger odds at Santiago and Portobelo than we'll ever find here," he said reassuringly.

She shook her head. "No, I didn't mean that. I mean, when we land at Boquerón, or wherever you decide, and find out."

Ned, for the moment engrossed in the chart, was not concentrating on what she was saying.

"Find out what? It's all here on the chart. It looks quite straightforward." A moment later he was trying to put his arm round her, bracing himself against the roll of the ship as she started sobbing. "Oh Ned, Ned . . . No, I mean when we find out about Diana and Thomas: if they are still alive . . ."

Alive, dead or just locked in a dungeon? Ned had asked himself those questions almost hourly, it seemed, since the three survivors had first landed in Port Royal. Alive – well, to be still alive meant that the Spanish authorities did not know or guess two things: Thomas's real identity and that he was second-in-command of the buccaneers, of the Brethren of the Coast. Diana's fate was wrapped up with Thomas's, of course. If the Spanish neither knew nor suspected, then there was a chance that both of them were being held under an easy form of arrest somewhere near Boquerón while the local mayor, or *alcalde*, sent a messenger to the island's capital of San Juan to know what the Governor wanted doing. And providing no one knew the identity of the prisoners, there was a chance (a slight chance? good chance?) that they would be freed, and the *alcalde* would be told that he could also release the ship. Thomas had broken no law – he had every right to call in for water and supplies, and he had been scrupulous, using a white flag. But . . .

Dead? In that case, the Spaniards knew (or had discovered) Thomas's identity, or guessed it from the name of the ship. They would probably have put him on the rack to try to discover what he was doing as far east as Porto Rico, but even if they knew one of their plate galleons was stranded off St Martin, they would never guess that Thomas was on his way to look at it: they knew the buccaneers had twenty or thirty ships, and the lure of such an enormous haul of gold and silver would bring them all out – there was no chance that the Governor of Porto Rico had yet heard of any raids on the ships called to Cartagena.

So Thomas would have been put on the rack, and perhaps even Diana (with Thomas being forced to watch). Thomas alone would reveal nothing, but Ned pictured himself being forced to watch Aurelia on the rack. Would he talk to save Aurelia from the agony? Yes, he would, most decidedly. And Thomas? It was hard to say, because if Diana could speak, she would tell Thomas to shut up . . .

If they discovered who Thomas was, then the Spanish would certainly kill him. But the peace treaty with England? Ned knew the answer to that almost before he asked himself the question: Spain would never consider the peace treaty applied "Beyond the Line", and all buccaneers caught "Beyond the Line" were executed.

Which left the third alternative: Thomas and Diana left to rot in a dungeon. Ned remembered the dungeons at Santiago and Portobelo. Prisoners were kept there with thick and rusty chains round legs and wrists, so that every movement caused chafe which developed into sores, sores which became gangrenous . . . Just rice and water to eat, and rats to share it . . . And likely enough the priests trying to get hold of them, two heretics whose souls should be saved by stretching them on the rack.

The garotte or the rack. Poor Thomas and Diana. Ned hoped that if it was death by the garotte they were executed separately: for either of them having to watch the other being garotted would be worse than death itself. The garotte was barbaric. Hanging was quick because, even if the hangman was a bungler, at worst the victim was suffocated by the noose, and became unconscious in three or four minutes, probably less. But the object of the garotte was that it could – according to orders previously given to the executioner – take hours to kill a man. He pictured the garotte itself, and shuddered.

The most refined one he had seen – they varied, of course – was simply a hinged metal collar fitting round the neck and which could be tightened by a threaded rod joining the two halves, slowly throttling the victim before (when the rod had been turned sufficiently and the collar had contracted enough) breaking his neck. The cruder and more usual garottes were simply hinged collars of a smaller diameter than a man's neck, the two ends being joined by a threaded rod which turned to bring the two ends together, usually strangling the victim long before it could break his neck. Or her neck: being a heretic was not a man's prerogative. And the earliest garottes were simply a rope noose round the neck, tightened by twisting a stick . . .

Alive or dead or in a dungeon: well, Ned was certain that the final decision would not rest with the local *alcalde*: the Spaniards were experts at passing on a decision to the next senior man, and so they should be: the whole system of government on the Main (in Spain, too, he assumed) inflicted harsh penalties on any of the King's servants who made mistakes.

So probably the decision about Thomas's fate had already passed through several hands. The *alcalde*, or perhaps even the garrison commander in Boquerón, if there was one, would certainly know exactly what to do when an English ship came in and anchored and sent a party on shore with a white flag, asking for a safe conduct to get water. They would know that with no English possession within three or four days' sailing, the ship's company must be desperate for water.

So they would grant the safe conduct and, as soon as they were on shore, seize the men and the ship. None of that needed any superior's permission; any child would know what to do, as would any shopkeeper, innkeeper or priest. Seizing heretics, buccaneers – indeed any foreigner (except a smuggler bringing in items they wanted) – was second nature.

The *alcalde* or garrison commander would then send a messenger to his next senior, and the decision what to do next would eventually reach the governor of the province. How many provinces in Porto Rico? A dozen or more, he guessed, and where was the capital of the one covering Boquerón? The charts did not help, but most likely it was San Germán (pronounced Her-mun), which had been important enough more than a century and a half ago to have the first church built in the New World.

Very well, but the provincial governor at San Germán would most certainly not decide for himself, even though the governor of the whole island was many miles away (at least a hundred, from the look of it, since most roads tended to go along the coast and, like Jamaica, Porto Rico had a spine of mountains that effectively cut it in two, into the northern and southern halves). Two days riding to San Juan, at least a day's wait for the governor's decision, and a couple of days' ride back to San Germán. Another day to pass the orders to Boquerón – that made six days.

All of which meant, Ned realized, that the decision could have reached Boquerón (or wherever Thomas and Diana were imprisoned) at least – well: it would take the *Peleus* a week to get to Boquerón. Say they were captured ten days after leaving Port Royal. For seven of those ten days Ned and the *Griffin* had been putting in the new mast, so they had three days in hand. More than a week for the *Griffin* to reach Boquerón – so they were four days behind so far, and by then they would have only reached Boquerón, not discovered anything.

Ned was thankful that Aurelia knew nothing of the way Spain administered its colonies in the Main. Every Spaniard had by law to live in a community, either a large village or a town: no one, or no family, could live in isolation. No Spanish possession on the Main could trade directly with another – everything had to go back across the Atlantic and through Spain, adding enormously to the costs, apart from making it subject to special taxes. The most powerful man was always the head of the Church, whether the priest of a village, the bishop of a diocese or the archbishop of a province. No mayor or governor, even if he was Guzman, the Viceroy of Panama, would dare argue with the Church. In Spain, Ned realized, the Cross was a great deal mightier than the Crown . . .

He rolled up the charts, made sure that Aurelia had recovered after her glimpse of the possible fate of Thomas and Diana, and went on deck. The sun sparkled from every hurrying wavetop as it raced on to the westward; every few moments silver darts rose up from the sea, skimming up the sides of crests and down troughs before landing again after a flight of anything from ten yards to a couple of hundred. *Poisson volant* was their French name; the Spanish knew them as *pescado volante*, the English as flying fish. It was impossible, in any language, to describe that bluish-green dart, the grace of its ridge-and-furrow flight over the wavetops. And what tiny wings. Often they flew on board, the light thuds bringing up the seamen with buckets to collect them for a meal. Ned had once inspected one closely. Although it was long and slim, the wings grew from a body which had become rectangular, and when he thought of the weight of the fish in relation to the area of its wings, and then compared it with a bird, which was so much lighter yet had bigger wings, he was puzzled how it could fly. Come to that, he was puzzled how anything could fly.

Ah, now they were tacking north-eastward and there was Desecheo, a speck almost dead ahead while Porto Rico was beginning to form a very low grey line on the horizon to starboard. They were still too far away for it to be a blur; it was no more than the line on a good piece of paper made by a newly sharpened pencil. And there on the starboard beam was Mona Island, sitting straight-sided like a cooking pot on a stove.

The *Griffin* butted her way to windward; spray like sudden tropical showers kept the foredeck running with water; the foot of the sails was dark where the spray reached up and soaked the flax. The whole ship groaned as she thumped down into a trough and then drove up the side of an approaching wave, seesawed over the crest and dipped once again to the trough.

Invigorating for fifteen minutes, Ned thought ruefully, but damnably monotonous for days on end. Nor was there the chance of breaking the monotony by having a race with the *Phoenix*: Saxby sailed his ship well, and Ned always knew when he had overstood the mark, because the *Phoenix* would tack first, and he or Lobb would grin ruefully and give the orders for the *Griffin* to tack. It had happened so often that they no longer bothered to joke about Saxby dropping a hint ... Ned had once broken the monotony by suggesting that Saxby was going about because Martha Judd was refusing to cook on that tack.

It was lucky (although not surprising) that the *Griffin* and the *Phoenix* each had a couple of Spaniards among the crew. In fact, the more Ned thought about it, the more surprising he found it that they did not have more. In both ships the English, Welsh, Irish and Scots were almost a minority:

Dutchmen rubbed shoulders with Frenchmen, and there was even a man from Poland, though Ned was hazy about exactly where Poland was. Between France and Russia, he knew.

The Pole spoke his own energetic brand of English and as they had sailed along the coast of Hispaniola the man had been disappointed that it was not necessary to set up the rigging because, as he carefully explained to Ned, sometimes when anchoring in a quiet bay to set up the rigging, along the beach you could find zeeyamber. The word had puzzled Ned until the Pole, Miroslav, had produced from his pocket a small griffin, beautifully carved in amber. "I keep as your wedding present," he explained to Ned. He had made it himself from one of several pieces of amber he had. Before leaving Poland, he told Ned, he had served an apprenticeship with one of the amber master craftsmen of Poland.

"Where did you find the amber you have?" Ned asked. "In Hispaniola?"

The man shook his head. Amber was washed up on the beaches of the Baltic coast of Poland, and men with nets fished for it as though they were catching shrimps. The amber, he explained, was sap from pine trees which many centuries ago had hardened into rough lumps, and somehow the pine trees and the amber, or both, had rolled into the Baltic, the lumps of amber eventually washing up on the beaches.

The Pole was a true artist delighted to find an interested audience, because Lobb had come across the deck to listen, and as the *Griffin* thrashed her way to windward he began to explain.

Amber was found as a roughly shaped piece only distinguishable from a small rock or pebble by its lighter weight. No, he said, it did not then have this deep tan colour. The colour varied, of course: amber found in Hispaniola, for instance, was lighter, more golden, but he preferred the darker colour from the Baltic: it had more depth, more substance.

The size of the chunks found by the men on the Baltic beaches varied from the size of a thumbnail to this (he held up three bunched fingers) and, if they were lucky, this (a clenched fist). Once the amber arrived at the *atelier*, it was put on a small raised table so that the craftsmen could walk round and inspect it, deciding what its natural shape suggested to them. Yes, it was going to be cut and filed and shaped and then polished, but no one wanted to waste any of it, and no true craftsman wanted to miss making the best use of the particular piece's natural shape, quite apart from the original folding of the resin sometimes causing holes or folds. Once the design had been decided, one of the craftsmen and his apprentice (the best had several, like a good artist had pupils) would start work.

How long did it take, and what tools? Miroslav shrugged his shoulders and grinned. He had started to work on this carving of a griffin soon after joining the ship, and fortunately among the pieces of amber he had one which was tall and narrow, just wide enough for him to get the wings right, though the raised leg nearly caused a problem because it stuck out so much farther than the head and beak. The only tool used up to now had been his knife, which also served as a chisel and a file.

"But you *could* have made a griffin *couchant* – which means it is sitting with wings folded," Ned said.

Almost shyly, Miroslav pointed to the heavy gold signet ring that Ned was wearing. "That one," he said.

Ned's family crest was a griffin and Miroslav had wanted to carve one like that. Ned felt both embarrassed and flattered: embarrassed that the man should use a piece from his valuable store of amber, yet flattered that Miroslav should want to carve not just a griffin, but a griffin with wings raised and standing on three feet with one forefoot lifted.

Ned asked to look at the carving again and, with the same shyness, Miroslav said: "Please do not tell the lady I make it. I want it to be a surprise present on her wedding day."

"Supposing we never get married?" Ned asked, intending to tease.

The Pole suddenly looked distressed and in his excitement held Ned's arm. "But you must, sir: she is a woman among women. Never again you meet one like her. This griffin –" he pointed to the amber carving which Ned was holding, "– will bring you much luck and many children! I know it: I bring people luck."

Ned gave him back the amber. "We shall marry, Miroslav," he assured the man, "but in the meantime you continue bringing all of us luck: we're going to need it for the next few days."

Miroslav agreed and then, understanding that both Ned and Lobb admired his workmanship, said: "I have a request to make, sir."

Ned nodded, wondering what was coming next.

"I need a piece of shagreen so that I can give the amber a final smoothing."

Ned looked questioningly at Lobb, who said: "We haven't got a piece left on board – the carpenter used the last to smooth the saloon table for you, sir. But it's not hard to catch another shark. Can I take a piece of boucan and bait the hook?"

"Are a shark's teeth sharp enough to bite it?" Ned asked sarcastically. "I think it's wearing out *my* teeth."

"Oh, it will, sir," Lobb said lightly, "but the shark doesn't have to eat it regularly like us! And by the way," he said to Miroslav, "it's up to you to flay the shark and nail out the skin to dry. You want the shagreen, and the only way to get it is to prepare it yourself. We have salt and alum on board."

"I shan't want the whole skin," Miroslav said. "What shall –"

"Sell it to the carpenter, or anyone else wanting to rub something smooth. We have enough sharks in these waters to set up a business selling shagreen."

Miroslav, a faraway look in his eye, said almost to himself: "If only I could get more amber from Hispaniola, I could set up an *atelier* in Port Royal. Would people in Jamaica buy my amber?" he asked Ned.

Ned thought of all the spare money in the island, where the tradesmen became rich in a year selling to buccaneers who spent their gold even faster than they acquired it. Wealthy tradesmen might not appreciate Miroslav's artistry, but their wives would.

"Yes. Carve the finest articles you can, trim them with gold, and charge high prices. If you never lower your standards, you'll never have to lower your prices."

"And I'll get rich selling you shagreen," Lobb said with a grin. "Anyway, Mr Yorke and Sir Thomas will always be good customers, buying amber for their ladies – wives *and* daughters."

At the mention of Thomas's name, all three men looked instinctively at the thin grey line on the horizon representing Porto Rico. "Yes," Miroslav said soberly, "I have to look after my customers as well."

Because the two Spaniards belonging to the *Phoenix* had been transferred to the *Griffin* before the ships left Port Royal, Ned was able to have the four of them sitting on the deck in front of him as he leaned against the breech of one of the *Griffin*'s aftermost guns.

First he confirmed that they knew the survivors' story (two of those men were now recovered enough to be out of their bunks and employed on light day work, though careful to keep their bodies out of the sun). Then Ned passed round the rough chart of Boquerón which they had drawn.

"You can see it's inside and on the edge of quite a deep bay which is almost closed by this reef across the entrance. There's just that gap in the middle of it, and the *Peleus* sailed through it, anchoring very close to Boquerón village. That heavy line is the way from the jetty to the wells where they were going to get fresh water.

"But first we have to avoid two other reefs – Bajo Corona Larga, about five miles out and stretching north-south for a couple of miles, and then Bajo Resuello, two miles out and also running north-south for a couple of miles.

"Once we've passed them and reach Bahia de Boquerón, we find the whole bay almost completely closed off by the Bajo Enmedio, which is like a gate. Luckily there is a gap in it, a channel about four hundred yards wide but with more than thirty feet of water.

"And, as you can see from the sketch, the channel is marked for us by those clumps of mangroves growing on the coral. The coral comes up sharply on both sides of the channel, so if the sun is up we'll be able to see the channel clearly. Sir Thomas beat through it, so . . .

"Once we're inside the bay we've plenty of room, with depths of twenty or thirty feet in most places, except right close in to the shore. So let's hope we get a good sun and not too much wind . . ."

The four men nodded. The water should be clear – because of the Trade winds the western side of a large island was almost always in a lee; an onshore wind kicking up a sea and stirring up enough sand to make the water murky was rare. The art of pilotage in these clear waters was knowing what the different colours of the sea meant when translated into depths of water. Well offshore, a rich dark bluish-purple meant almost infinite depth, and as you approached land the blue gradually became lighter, changing into green. Not the murky and depressing green of northern waters, but a lively pale green which, as the water shallowed, became like shot silk and warned a prudent pilot that (if he was not already doing so) the man with the lead line should be busy calling out depths.

Interpreting all the greens came only with experience, because they varied not only with the depths but the light. A pilot faced with finding his way through a difficult channel strewn with rocks and coral wanted the sun over his shoulder, going into the water. If it was ahead it reflected off the surface like a mirror so that one could not see anything below. Rocks and coral reefs (especially staghorn coral which, as its name implied, grew up with wide antlers), and shoals of sand with fields of turtle grass on them, showed up brown. There was, for brown, a simple rule: the darker, the shallower.

For all that, it was a bonus when clumps of mangrove sprouted up on a reef. Mangrove, Ned reflected, must be one of the strangest trees (or were they really bushes?) that grew in the Tropics. Instead of a mangrove having a main trunk with branches, it comprised dozens of springy stems, or branches, like very young ash saplings, which rooted in shallow water. Each grew up to a height of three or four feet and then curved down again into the water, sending out roots before pushing another branch upwards. This in turn curved down so that in time the mangroves formed a swamp which was almost impenetrable, with thousands of thin boughs climbing up or down or across, so springy it was almost impossible to cut a way through using a machete, and never more than about ten feet high, and with roots growing just below the surface, a tangled web ready to trip any man unwary enough to try to wade through the shallow water in which they grew. And on the roots grew tree oysters, sharp-edged discs which cut like knives . . .

It was curious that the mangrove (which seemed to be the

natural home of swarms of mosquitoes) should have one particular warlike use – supplying slowmatch. Strips of mangrove bark, dried in the sun (after being hammered flatter), made excellent slowmatch. Providing one was careful to watch its thickness, or plait it into a strip, it burned evenly, like a regular fuse. More important, while regular slowmatch made in England was hard to get, mangrove match only entailed a visit to a swamp. Ned recalled the enormous explosions when the buccaneers had blown up the fortress at Santiago in Cuba, and the fort at Portobelo: the humble mangrove bark, beaten and dried, had burned steadily down to the kegs of powder . . .

The four men were sitting patiently waiting for him to resume: they had seen that his thoughts had left them, and they were content to wait for them to come back from wherever they had been.

"Yes, well," Ned said, "my plan is this." Then he came to a stop. He had no real plan, he had to admit to himself; he was hoping that something would come to mind as he talked with these men; that they would say something which made obvious to him the way they could all set about rescuing Thomas and Diana and the rest of the men from the *Peleus*. "Yes," he said, starting to improvise, "well, do you think the four of you can row to the village and land, and make the local people believe this is a Spanish ship?"

The men looked questioningly at each other, and then one, who seemed to be emerging as their leader, nodded his head vigorously. "Yes, we can, *Capitán*, but first we must do some things."

"What sort of things?"

"Make a Spanish flag and hoist it. Paint out our name on the transom – it does not matter that we do not have a Spanish one there. Think of a Spanish name for the ship, though, so we can tell anyone who asks – the *alcalde* and the *aduana* will want to know."

"That's easy. You can choose a suitable saint's name."

"Yes," the seaman said, and Ned suddenly remembered he was called Julio, "all Spanish ships are called by saints' names. The flag, and the name," he said, counting them off on the fingers of his left hand with the index finger of his right. "If we are to pretend that we are the officers –" he raised a questioning eyebrow to Ned, who nodded, "– we shall need some smarter clothes." He touched the fourth finger. "We'll row ourselves, just in case – if we had men waiting in the boat who did not speak Spanish and children came down to the boat asking questions – as they'd be sure to do . . ."

"Armour," Ned said suddenly. "We still have some Spanish breastplates, backs and helmets stowed on board – yes, and some Spanish swords and pistols."

Julio, the seaman who was obviously going to be the leader, banged his brow. "I had forgotten them! Two of us can wear armour and carry swords: that would be in order. The '*Capitán*' and the mate need not wear armour, but swords, yes. They'd be useful to salute the *alcalde*."

"And you think you could find out what has happened to our people without raising suspicions?"

"Is easy," Julio said confidently. "I ask about the *Peleus* – after all I will have seen her at anchor – and as soon as they tell me that she is English and just captured, I offer to buy her."

"You'll look silly if they say yes!" Ned said.

"No sir: you give me enough Spanish money to pay a deposit. A bribe really. I tell them I have the rest of the money on board, and we must draw up a contract. That will give me an excuse for returning to the ship as soon as possible to tell you what we have discovered. I say I must inspect her, too – so later we have an excuse for boarding."

Yet the more Ned thought about it, the more impossible the whole expedition became. How were a few score buccaneers to rescue all the people from the *Peleus* if they were shut up in some dungeon ten or twenty miles inland?

"Very well, you'd better sort out the armour and the pistols and swords. Check the leather straps on the armour – you know how leather rots in this climate. And you'd better start going through my wardrobe and Mr Lobb's. We all seem to be about the same build."

He thought for a minute and then asked Julio: "The *Griffin* is English-built. Do you think she'll pass for Spanish?"

"No one in Boquerón would be able to tell," Julio said contemptuously. "Fishermen, a few soldiers, the mayor, a customs officer, the priest . . . Once they've made sure we're not another English ship come in for fresh water, they'll be occupied with thinking up ways of getting things from us free. And the *Phoenix* following us in – well, she's Spanish-built anyway."

"It's so peaceful here," Aurelia said quietly. "Listen, you can hear the land birds singing. There's a kingbird. And doves, listen to them talking to each other. And there's a donkey protesting about something. And we're not rolling!"

Ned understood her sense of wonder because he could hardly believe it himself. The bay was set well back into the land as though a giant had bitten a great mouthful: with the entrance facing west and the land encircling the ships on the other three sides, the *Griffin* was anchored five hundred yards south-west of the village of Boquerón, the anchor down in a sticky mixture of sand and mud. The afternoon sun mirroring off the sea gave the impression that Saxby's *Phoenix* was floating in the air. Beyond the *Phoenix* the *Peleus* swung at anchor, with only one man – probably a Spanish sentry – visible on deck.

The land round the bay was a dark-green collar of mangroves growing ten or a dozen feet high, except where they had been cut down for the village of Boquerón and its small jetty, a small beach nearby where the fishing boats were hauled up (and made a sudden splash of colour) and, south of them, a narrow gap in the mangroves, just wide enough for an open boat.

This was the entrance into a mile-long but narrow lagoon lying just behind the mangroves and parallel to the sea. Ned could see salt pans just where the mangroves ended in the south-west corner of the bay, squares divided up like fields and shaped into moulds by banking holding in the sea, so that the sun evaporated the water, leaving behind the precious salt.

With the glass he could distinguish small pyramids of salt, brownish white, glistening on the landward side of the pans, ready to be taken away on carts and sold to preserve meat or fish. Was salt Boquerón's main industry? Did they send it to Spain? The main source of salt was of course the province of Venezuela, but exporting it from the Main meant licences and taxes . . .

"To be anchored in Spanish waters and no forts shooting at us," Aurelia said suddenly, pointing at the peaks of three hills to the south of them. "Forts – or gun batteries, anyway – on top of them, with that reef across the entrance, would close the bay like a cork in a bottle! Just think of it, Ned, here we are anchored in the Bahia de Boquerón. Beyond the mangroves by the salt ponds is the Laguna Rincón." She turned to face westward. "There," she said, "that reef growing out from the shore – that's the Bajo Palo. Then the channel we sailed through, the Canal Sur. Then the main reef in the middle with those funny clumps of mangroves growing on them, looking as though they're growing on the sea – oh, I've forgotten: what's that one called?"

"Bajo Enmedio," Ned said. "You forgot that headland –" he pointed to the cliffs forming the southern side of the entrance, "– that's Punta Melones and the one opposite is Punta Guanaquilla. They're the only names I know. I doubt if there are any more because there's only the one village."

"Melones, Laguna Rincón, Bajo Enmedio . . . they sound so musical. That headland, for instance, 'Melons' it would be in English, but how much better it sounds in Spanish, 'mellow-nays'."

"What do the other names mean?" Ned asked.

"You're straining my Spanish! *Laguna* is obvious, and anyway it's a lagoon. 'Rincón' is a town not far away. Bajo Palo . . . well, *bajo* is a reef, and *palo* means a log, or a stick. A *palo mayor* is a mainmast, so I'm not very sure about the reef. *Enmedio* has me beaten. Guanaquillo is probably a place, no particular meaning. Bahia de Boquerón – well, *bahia* is bay and Boquerón is just a place name, though I remember the Spanish word *boquete* means a narrow entrance."

"Well," he said brightly, "let's make up some names."

"It's no good, darling," she said gently, "we just have to wait as patiently as we can for the boat to come back. Meanwhile, let's just enjoy the hills and the mangroves and the fish jumping out of the water . . . How green it all looks, the hills so fresh, and –" she broke off and began sobbing, and Ned took her in his arms.

"Steady," he murmured, "don't let the men think we've given up hope."

"I haven't given up hope of Julio; it's just that it seems impossible we'll ever be able to rescue Diana and Thomas, even if they're still alive."

"We mustn't get upset when the Spanish play tricks on us: we play tricks on them. Don't forget Portobelo."

She nodded, wiping her eyes. "Ned, I think I'm changing. Once I thought I'd always be content being at sea with you in the *Griffin*, but now we've started to build the house . . ."

"Now we've started to build the house," Ned echoed, "you've been thinking that it's time we settled down and . . ."

"Well, we've enough money to live comfortably," she said. "For you, buccaneering comes easily; you love leading these men, and you do it well. But for me – well, the worry sends me crazy: I have nightmares in which I see the Spanish garotting you, or a cannonball smashing you into a pulp, or –"

"But I always come back safely, and anyway usually you're with us."

"I know, I know," Aurelia wailed, "but Diana gets the same nightmares about Thomas . . ."

"So what am I to do, then?" Ned asked, half angry and half wishing to placate her. "Plant sugar-cane, tobacco, and buy ships to collect dyewoods from the Moskito Coast?"

"Ned," Aurelia said, holding his arm, "both you and Thomas are going to have to accept that Jamaica is secure now: you've beaten the Spanish, you've provided the big guns for Heffer to put in the batteries to defend Port Royal, you've provided enough gold from the Portobelo raid to establish the island's currency. Now both of you have one enemy left, and you've got to be in the island to fight them."

"Who on earth –?"

"The government in London! They have no idea of what it's like out here in the Caribbee islands, and for years to come they'll be sending out people as stupid as this man Luce and, *quelle blague*, these *bouffons* will destroy everything you've done unless you are there to argue or persuade them. This buffoon – it sounds stronger in English – Luce will never understand that Spain in Europe is one thing, but Spain out here is another. I think the French and the Dutch understand, but they don't own Jamaica, so –"

Ned pointed, interrupting her.

"Oh," Aurelia exclaimed, "here they come! Four of them, and the sun is shining on the armour of two of them. Oh, let us pray that he's managed to find out what's been happening. Just look at the *Peleus* – she looks so forlorn at anchor, with just that Spanish sentry . . ."

Chapter Ten

Ned did not think four men in a boat could take so long to get alongside the *Griffin* and board. Yes, Julio could not rush back because if any Spanish were watching from the shore they would be puzzled (or even suspicious) of such haste. Yes, the sun was scorching and the two men at the oars wearing breastplates and backplates must be as hot as steaming kettles – not that anyone in the Tropics ever saw a boiling kettle steam, unless it was a very cold morning in January . . . He was thankful that Aurelia was so patient: it was extraordinary how she understood him, a man born without patience.

Finally seamen were at the bulwarks taking the boat's painter and sternfast and Julio swung over the bulwark, landing on the deck with a thump. Grinning, he gave Ned a salute and then swept off his hat in a deep bow to Aurelia.

"From the silly grin on your face it seems the news is good," Ned growled, still irritated by the man's tardiness.

"What little we could find out was good," Julio said cautiously, obviously put out by Ned's manner and not understanding its cause.

Ned gestured to the square of canvas rigged up over the afterdeck to provide some shade. "Let's stand under the awning; it's so damned hot in this bay: the hills shut off all the breeze."

The other three Spaniards joined them, the two in armour thankfully undoing the straps and taking off their breast and backplates, revealing the shirts underneath sodden and dark with perspiration. Their hair was matted and flattened by the weight and heat of the helmets; where the edges of the helmets had rested, both had livid red weals across their brows below the hairline.

Julio, as if wanting his three countrymen to share in his report, waited patiently. A diving pelican hit the water with a splash a moment before one of the men dropped his helmet on deck with a clatter, and black-headed gulls circled uttering shrill cries, waiting for the pelican to sit squarely on the sea, water streaming from the bulbous pouch forming his lower beak and letting some small fish accidentally escape to provide a meal for the gulls.

"Well," said Julio, "we landed on the jetty and there to meet us was the *alcalde*, the *aduana*, the priest and the agent for the man who owns the salt pans behind the mangroves –"

"Come on!" Ned urged, but it was clear to Aurelia that Julio had reached his hour of importance, when he had the complete attention of the Admiral of the Brethren of the Coast, and he was not going to rush anything; a time of glory to be savoured, not gulped, but Ned would not understand that in a thousand years.

"– all very friendly and obviously wondering what they could get out of us. If you want to ship fifty tons of salt to Vieques – that's an island just off the eastern end of Porto Rico – the agent will pay well."

"No salt," Ned said, hoping to speed up Julio's report.

"Good," Julio said, "it's a truly vile cargo: the salt gets into every cut or graze when you're loading and it hurts, and if it gets wet and a few sacks burst, it makes a mess of the bilges."

"No salt," Ned repeated doggedly, fighting back an urge to scream at the man, "we are not salters."

"Well, I left these two in armour to guard the boat even though they complained of the heat," Julio said, nodding at the two men, "and Fernando and I went along to the mayor's house where we all had a mug of wine. Very bad it was," Julio said, shuddering and screwing up his face, as though expecting sympathy from Ned. "It was a wine that wouldn't travel ten miles in Spain before turning to vinegar, which is probably why it was shipped out here.

"So we drank and gossiped. I worked the conversation round to the *Peleus* – rather cleverly, I thought, eh Fernando?"

"Very cleverly."

"The *alcalde* said he thought she might be sold soon: he was waiting to hear from San Germán. I asked – very innocently, you understand – eh Fernando?"

"Very innocently."

"– if the owner lived in San Germán, because I might be interested in buying the ship. I thought that was a clever approach," he told Ned, who nodded.

"The *alcalde* laughed in a strange way. 'You could say so,' he said, 'but there's no need for you to go all the way there: I shall be hearing very soon.' I thought it best to let them drink more of that terrible wine, tho' I realized it might have killed them before it loosened their tongues!

"Eventually, the *alcalde* admitted that she was an English ship – it was very cunning, eh Fernando, how I said she seemed to be foreign-built?"

"Very cunning," Fernando repeated obediently.

"Then, confidentially, he told me that she was English, and how she had sailed in on the seventh of this month and sent a boat to the jetty with a white flag, asking for water. The *aduana* then described how he had galloped to San Germán for soldiers, who rode in just as the priest had roused out the fishermen to have their boats ready. The rest we know – the soldiers caught our seamen on shore with the water casks, and the fishermen then rowed the soldiers out to seize the *Peleus*. Three soldiers were killed."

"How did that happen?" Ned asked.

"Well, there was a fight on board: Sir Thomas ran one through with his sword: the lady shot one with a pistol and a third was drowned."

"Drowned?" Ned exclaimed.

"Yes, Sir Thomas threw him over the side and, because he was wearing armour, he sank at once."

That would be enough, Ned thought. In Spanish eyes, both Thomas and Diana were murderers. It was irrelevant that in English eyes the Spanish had broken their word and were behaving like pirates, and Thomas was quite rightly defending his property against attack. And as murderers they would be tried and sentenced to death. Had the sentence already been carried out? There was no point in hurrying Julio; like a flood or ebb tide, he moved ponderously at his own speed.

"I made it clear how shocked I was at this brutal behaviour by the English," Julio continued. "I said I hoped the rack and the garotte were doing their job."

Ned felt himself going cold at the matter-of-fact way that Julio phrased it; but the man was Spanish; to him the rack and the garotte were as familiar a part of life as a donkey and cart.

"The *alcalde* said the man when put on the rack a few days later claimed to have shot one soldier and killed the other with his sword, but other soldiers had seen the woman firing the pistol, so there was no argument."

"What happened then?" Aurelia asked, knowing she would burst into tears if Julio kept her waiting any longer.

"Death," said Julio.

Aurelia collapsed on the deck while Ned felt the ship and the bay swirling round him as he tried to go to her help.

Julio himself was almost in tears as, once Aurelia had recovered, he began to explain. He had crushed his hat – Ned's hat, in fact – and screwed the plume into a ball before he could get both Ned and Aurelia, still white-faced and trembling, to listen as he finished his report.

"The *alcalde* was quite definite – wasn't he Fernando?"

"Quite definite."

"So that was the sentence of the court after they had heard the evidence and after the torturing," Julio said.

"That's enough," Ned said abruptly, watching Aurelia. "I'll hear the rest some other time."

Both Julio and Fernando looked puzzled, and finally Fernando, with a nervous glance at Julio said: "Sir, there's more to hear."

"I realize that," Ned snapped, "but the lady has heard enough. Surely you realize that Sir Thomas and Lady Diana are our closest friends? Were our closest friends," he corrected himself, but neither Spaniard realized the significance of the change in tense.

"We know they're your friends, sir," Fernando persisted, "that's why you should hear the rest of the report."

Aurelia said: "Let them finish, Ned: I've got over the first shock."

As Ned nodded, Julio took a deep breath as if to ward off interruptions by sheer staying power. "Well, the court sentenced the two of them to death for murder, and the rest of the men of the *Peleus*, sixty-one of them, were sentenced to death for piracy –"

"Where was the trial held?" Ned interrupted.

"San Germán, on the fifteenth of the month. But the court has to get the approval of the Governor of Porto Rico (who is in San Juan) before carrying out a death sentence, and the Governor insists on having the full minutes – is that the word? A complete report of everything said at the trial? Ah, good, well, he has to have the minutes – in Spanish, of course.

"These are needed to send to Spain. But, of course, Sir Thomas, Lady Diana and the three or four men of the *Peleus* who were questioned gave their evidence in English. Apparently, all this had to be translated for the minutes and the translations – every page of them – marked with a notary's seal that they are correct.

"The only notary in San Germán died a week before the trial, and the translations took several days, so by the time another notary had been found who could read English – there was one in Mayagúez – many days had passed. So the minutes, properly notarized and also signed and sealed by the president of the court, were sent off to San Juan on the twentieth."

"So we are just too late," Aurelia said, numbed.

Julio glanced up suddenly and stared at her. "No, *señora*, I think we might be just in time. Today is the twenty-third."

"Just in time? But they're already dead!"

"The three soldiers who boarded the ship, yes," agreed Julio, "but who cares about them?"

"But you said 'Death'," Aurelia forced herself to say, although her voice was faltering, "when we asked what had happened to Sir Thomas and Lady Diana."

"Ah yes, I did say 'Death'," Julio said, and this time Ned caught Aurelia as she fell towards the deck.

"But they're not dead *yet*!" Julio suddenly screamed, frightened that for the second time he had caused the Admiral's lady to collapse. "'Death' that was the sentence of the court. But alive they still is," his grammar beginning to collapse under the strain. "Not dead yet, you understand! No one, except the two soldiers and the man in the armour. *Madre de Dios*," he exclaimed, hurling the remains of Ned's hat down on the deck, "a few miles from here are they, locked up in the town jail, all of them, and waiting for us to rescue them!"

After a near-sleepless night, when both he and Aurelia had tossed restlessly in their bunk and it was far too hot to hold each other, Ned had tried to work out several mathematical problems.

Somewhere locked up in San Germán were Thomas, Diana and sixty-one men: sixty-three people in all. Here on board the *Griffin* he had fifty-nine men and himself and Aurelia, sixty-one in all. And on board the *Phoenix* were forty-seven men, Saxby and Mrs Judd, forty-nine in all.

So, leaving aside men who would have to be left on board to guard the two ships, and including the two women, he had one hundred and ten people to attempt the rescue of sixty-three. Assuming it was successful, at some point he would be traipsing around the Spanish countryside with more than one hundred and seventy people, some sixty of whom would be unarmed. Twelve miles from Boquerón to San Germán . . . Spanish cavalry could spit them all without risk or much effort.

The beginning of the rescue depended on more than one hundred buccaneers (and two women) managing to get from Boquerón to San Germán without being spotted. That should not be too difficult – land at night, and keep off the road – track, rather, from what Julio said. The main thing would be to avoid houses, but it was hilly, almost mountainous country in places and in the darkness people could fall down crevasses, stumble into ditches dug out of rock, and break limbs. Goats suddenly starting up with their high-pitched cry would startle men trying to creep silently; the packs of dogs lurking round every village, scratching over the middens, would start up a chorus of barking. The only advantage that Ned could think of was that in two nights' time there would be a full moon. The light from the moon was even now streaming through the skylight and falling on Aurelia as she lay naked on her back, one arm thrown up above her head on to the pillow, her long hair framing her face, the twin peaks of her breasts crowned with the rose-pink summits of her nipples, the slight curve of her belly merging into the mount of Venus . . .

He thought of waking her and trying to lose his worries between her thighs, but he knew he would not lose them; they would be thrust away for an hour but they would return as surely as the tide turned or the sun rose.

One thing was certain: given the present odds, it would be madness to blunder off towards San Germán without having more details about the track they would follow and the position and type of building in which Thomas and his people were held.

So, at what would seem to the Spaniards a normal hour, Julio and Fernando could go on shore, have another chat with the *alcalde* and his cronies, and then hire a couple of horses and ride into San Germán: it would be a natural thing to do, and the two men rowing them on shore could return to the *Griffin* and, eight or nine hours later, keep a watch on the jetty ready to collect Julio and Fernando on their return and, Ned hoped, with all the information he needed.

After breakfast, as he stood on deck giving last-minute instructions to the Spaniards, Lobb hurried up. "Look at the jetty, sir; who are all those people?"

Ned reached for the perspective glass which was kept in the drawer of the binnacle box and pulled out the tube to focus it. Yes, there was the *alcalde*, recognizable because of his sagging belly, the *aduana* with his goatlike beard, the priest in black ... Why were all the fishing boats gathered at that side of the jetty, the men in them standing up? And the priest was talking to them. And who were those twenty or so men in long robes? Monks? Yes – but what were they doing here in Boquerón?

He handed the glass to Julio, who had been nodding knowingly. The Spaniard took one look and shut the glass before putting it back in the drawer.

"I forgot to tell you, today is a *fiesta*. The Blessing of the Boats – it ensures good fishing," he explained. "The monks – the men you can see in long robes – are on a pilgrimage round the whole island. They come from a monastery near San Juan, and other groups of them are visiting all the towns and villages. It's something they do every year around Easter. Don't forget it's Good Friday in three days' time ..."

"I hope all this doesn't mean you'll find it difficult to hire a couple of horses to take you to San Germán," Ned said.

"No," Julio assured him. "What's more, the *alcalde* will be more talkative. Everyone can drink as much as he likes at *fiesta*. I'll wait until the boats have been blessed before I go on shore, otherwise the priest, who is probably *borracho* by now because he drinks heavily, will want to bless our boat, too, and as it is a good Protestant boat it'd probably start leaking in protest."

"You have enough money to hire the horses?" Ned asked.

"Enough to buy a dozen!"

"And you remember all the questions I want answered?"

"Yes, sir, and Fernando has a good memory, too."

"And you –"

Ned stopped as Julio held up both hands. "Please, sir," he said, "Sir Thomas is also one of our leaders as well as your friend."

"I'm sorry," Ned said impulsively, shaking Julio's hand.

Bats were just beginning to jink round the ship as darkness fell and the damp hay smell of the shore drifted invisibly over the ship. The seamen always came up on deck now in an anchorage like this just to watch in near-disbelief as the bats weaved through the rigging and round the mast. They had long since given up betting each other that one of the creatures would hit something and fall to the deck stunned. Now every man in the ship was listening as well as watching the bats and sipping rum.

"Ah," one of them exclaimed, "here they come!"

In the silence that followed Ned listened and in the distance finally heard the creak of oars pressing against thole pins and then the faint splashes as oar blades dipped into the water and lifted again. The boat had gone in at twilight, even though Julio and Fernando had not appeared, with orders to wait for them amid the buzzing mosquitoes.

Suddenly they heard Julio shouting, announcing his arrival: doing just what any watcher on the shore would expect, Ned realized: the jovial master of the ship returning on board after a happy day spent on shore.

The night began to feel chilly and, as Ned shivered, Aurelia held his arm in the darkness. A lantern hanging in the shrouds threw darting shadows as the ship rolled slightly; Ned reckoned there must be at least thirty bats flying over the hip. Maybe even fifty, he thought to himself. Or sixty. Think of anything to avoid trying to guess what Julio is going to report.

Julio was not drunk but a pedant could argue that he was not sober, either. He was tired, and like Fernando his clothes were covered with a light dust thrown up by the horses. Constantly wiping perspiration from their faces with the back of their hands had smeared the dust, giving them a startled, almost dazed look.

The two men stood before Ned who, as if to postpone listening to their report in case it contained more bad news, said: "You are hungry? Do you want to eat first? A drink?"

Julio shook his head. "Thank you, but no sir: we have just had supper with the *alcalde*, the priest and the commander of the garrison at Cabo Rojo – the man whose soldiers captured the *Peleus*."

"Very well. How did your journey go?"

"We have the answers to all your questions, sir. The road to San Germán is bad. It passes through several villages, I've never seen so many packs of dogs, the hogs walk along the track as though it is all one big farmyard, every family (I swear this is true) comprises at least twenty nosy children: the men and women can never rest o' nights. I defy a barren donkey to roam the streets without becoming pregnant."

"Oh," said Ned, for the lack of any other comment. "You'd better come down to my cabin and tell me all about it."

The cabin was hot and the lantern smoky. Although Julio's report – with many appeals to Fernando for confirmation of various points – was long, the facts it contained were not very encouraging. Nevertheless, when Ned sorted them out in his mind after Julio and Fernando had left, he realized that although the idea which had come to him earlier in the day might not work, it offered the only chance of rescuing the people of the *Peleus*.

Julio's supper with the *alcalde* and the garrison commander yielded the fact that the Cabo Rojo garrison originally comprised – in addition to the commander – a lieutenant, one sergeant, two corporals, sixty men and a cook. The total had been lessened by one corporal, whose body, still in its armour, must rest on the sea bed close to the *Peleus*, and two private soldiers, one shot by Diana and the other spitted by Thomas. Julio noted that the garrison commander, a drunken sot clearly sent to Cabo Rojo as a form of exile, was vastly amused at the way the corporal met his death: the corporal came from Villalba, in the far north of Spain at the foothills of the mountains of Galicia, and his heavy accent and the independent spirit of mountain folk had upset the commander, who came from Jerez de la Frontera, down in the south, and considered himself, as an Andalusian, among the country's élite.

More important, though, was that only four of the original garrison (a sergeant, two men and a cook) remained in Cabo Rojo: the rest, who had captured the unarmed men of the *Peleus* as they filled their water casks on land and the few left on board, had to march them to San Germán, and the *alcalde* there had kept them to act as guards. Three other soldiers had been left on board the *Peleus* as guards.

So much for Cabo Rojo and its garrison of four (plus the commander). The route to San Germán was very twisty; there were plenty of rolling hills and steep-sided valleys. Apparently San Germán itself, Julio had discovered, had been rebuilt several times in different places after being founded. Originally it was built so close to the coast that it was always being raided from the sea. Now it stood astride several hilltops, bunched together with the church more or less in the middle.

By dawn Ned had made up his mind about the rescue attempt, and immediately after they had finished their breakfast the *Griffin's* crew were busy with sail needles. Fernando was sent back to the *Phoenix* with orders for Saxby which would also start his men measuring, cutting and stitching.

At ten o'clock, Julio and Fernando were sent on shore again to drink with the *alcalde*. This time, Julio was told, he should say he wanted to inspect the *Peleus*, implying that he was more than halfway towards deciding to buy her, once permission came through from San Germán and a reasonable price could be agreed.

The boat came back shortly after noon, the two oarsmen no longer wearing armour: as Julio had explained, the *Griffin* (under her assumed name of a Spanish saint) was now thoroughly accepted, and there was no need for formality –

having one's boat's crew wearing breastplates was just such a formality.

It was Maundy Thursday and, Ned noticed, none of the fishing boats had gone out – because or in spite of the previous day's blessing? Interesting that neither the *alcalde* nor the priest (according to Julio) paid much attention to Lent in the privacy of their own homes.

Finally the boat was back alongside and once again Julio scrambled over the bulwark. This time he was not smiling; in fact, Ned saw with something approaching horror, the Spaniard seemed to have aged five years: his face was white and drawn beneath the layer of heavy tan and there was none of the usual spring in his step when he approached Ned. "Could we talk down in your cabin, sir?"

Ned seated him at the table and waved Fernando to sit on the settee beside him. Then he slid over the two mugs that Aurelia, after one look at the men, had put on the table, along with an onion flask of rum.

Julio poured rum into both mugs and drank quickly. "It's bad, sir," he began without preamble. "The *alcalde* has just received the word from San Germán. All of them are to be executed the day after tomorrow, Saturday. They're slipping it in between Good Friday and Easter Sunday."

Ned felt the familiar cold perspiration soak his body, then suddenly remembered that Aurelia had been standing just behind him. He jumped up and turned to find that she was now sitting on the settee at the other side of the cabin, white-faced, but trying to muster a confident smile for Ned. "At least they're still alive," she said. "They could have been executed today. We still have time."

Ned sat down again, thankful that she was still calm and hopeful.

Julio, wary because his past tactlessness had caused Aurelia to faint on deck, said with forced heartiness: "I was just going to say to Mr Yorke that we have plenty of time to get there for the ceremony."

Ned jerked upright in his chair. "The *ceremony*?"

Julio looked significantly at Ned and then glanced at Aurelia, who said quietly: "Ignore me. I want to know everything."

"Well," the Spaniard said, "it is going to be a public execution. The Iglesia de Porta Coeli in San Germán is a church built on top of a large mound with a couple of dozen wide steps (thirty or forty feet wide) leading up to the west door. In front of the steps is a large *plaza* which can hold a crowd of – well, a thousand or more. The steps are like a section of a – in Spanish, an *anfiteatro* –"

"Almost the same in English," Ned said. "An amphitheatre, like the Romans used."

Julio nodded. "All the important people in San Germán will watch from those steps. Sir Thomas and Lady Diana and the mate of the *Peleus* will be garotted in the *plaza* in front of the steps; the seamen of the *Peleus* will all be shot, two at a time, against the wall on the north side. Everyone, *alcalde, aristocracia*, butcher and baker and salter – and their wives and children – will get a very good view of everything," he said bitterly.

"Will there be many priests there?" Ned asked casually.

"Every priest for miles around, I suppose," a startled Julio replied, "with those from the Porta Coeli in the front row. No doubt they'll offer everyone the Last Sacrament just before the final turn of the garotte or the musket shots. It is all intended as a spectacle to impress the people with how they are being protected from pirates and buccaneers."

"And the monks?"

"Well, yes, if there are any from that monastery still visiting nearby towns and villages they'll be there for certain. No one misses a good execution. I doubt if San Germán has ever before seen a *mass* execution."

"No, I suppose not. Now listen carefully, and put yourself in the place of people living in San Germán: soldiers, mayor, priests – anyone, even small boys begging, and see what faults you can find in this plan. What might give us away, in other words."

Next morning the hollow and monotonous tolling of the single church bell at Boquerón woke them and reminded them that it was Good Friday. Lobb listened for a minute or two and then shook his head. "That's an iron bell," he said. "Probably had their original bronze one stolen years ago, long before even the Cow Killers started making raids."

"How are the tailors getting on?" Ned asked.

"Julio and Fernando have inspected them all. Some of the fussier seamen are making last-minute alterations."

"And pistols and cutlasses?"

"One or other issued to every man and some have taken one of each. I've checked matches with each man. All of them have spare ones in their pockets."

"And the cutlasses?"

Lobb shrugged his shoulders. "No need to put a sharp on any of them – still larded from Port Royal and no sign of rust, and sharp. Just as well. I didn't want to get the grindstone up and have it screeching away – they'd hear it on shore and might get suspicious."

"Tell me when Julio gets back from visiting the *Peleus*."

"Ah," Lobb said, "I was going to mention it to you, sir. Those sentries don't patrol the deck any longer, and since Julio will be able to confirm that there are only three of them, I don't think we have to bother much. Two or three of our men – from those we're leaving behind to look after the *Griffin* – can go over there tonight and deal with them."

"Good, you seem to have everything ready. I want the men to get some sleep if they can. Twelve miles – say three hours' walking in the darkness, and dawn is about six o'clock. So we'll start from here at half past two in the morning. That gives us half an hour to put all our party on shore, and then three hours to get near San Germán. We have to hide until about ten o'clock tomorrow morning so that we then have an hour to make a dignified arrival. The execution is arranged for noon."

"I doubt if the Dons will be punctual!"

"No, probably not," Ned agreed. "But we can't afford to be late . . ."

Chapter Eleven

The church – a simple whitewashed building with a tiny open-sided belfry perched on top of the roof like an afterthought above the arched west door – seemed poised over the crowded *plaza*. The bell tolled slowly and because it was small and the noise was quickly dispersed by the wind, it sounded like the call of a muffin man, or some other tradesman, rather than a summons to watch the execution of sixty-three people.

As Julio had predicted, the wide steps leading up to the church were crowded with people, the bright colours of their clothes emphasized by the peeling white west wall of the church high above them. Priests in black robes, thirty or forty women whose silk shawls of gay colours shone in the sun and who wore mostly black mantillas, many men in elaborate hats with bright plumes – the leading citizens, obviously, all as excited as if they were about to watch a bullfight or a play.

At the foot of the steps, five yards away (just far enough from the bottom that the crowd of dignitaries could see them clearly), were three wooden chairs, and seated in them, ropes binding their arms and legs, were Thomas, Diana and the *Peleus's* mate, Mitchell, all three slumped, despite the ropes, as though exhausted. On the ground beside each chair was an iron hoop which, apart from a rod projecting outwards, looked as though it belonged to a small barrel.

A soldier holding a musket stood behind each chair, but a whole file of soldiers lined the north side of the *plaza*, muskets resting on wooden rests, and facing them were all the *Peleus's* seamen, legs tied at the ankles and wrists tied behind their backs. Men that Ned recognized as normally clean-shaven had a month's beard; all of them had the pallor which came only from being shut away in the darkness. Each had sunken cheeks.

Parallel with the wall was a row of young trees planted at four-yard intervals. A seaman was tied to each of the three trees in front of the soldiers, their arms held backwards round the trunks and tied by the wrists: obviously they were intended to be the firing squad's first target.

To one side of the file of soldiers facing the *Peleus* men was their officer, a corpulent man in a bright green doublet edged with gold and with white silk facings, the sleeves slashed to reveal more white silk. His breeches, cut very wide in a style which had gone out of fashion in England fifty years earlier, were in a very pale green, but his hose was the same darker green as his doublet. However, his hat was the crowning glory: a dark yellow bird's nest of a hat had been heavily trimmed with gold, and the single larger plume seemed gilded. How had he done it, Ned wondered: shaken gold dust over it?

His enormous sword, slung from an ornate leather strap that went over his right shoulder and ended in a scabbard on which gold wire was sewn into elaborate patterns, was the most magnificent Ned had ever seen. No doubt it was one of the finer swords wrought in Toledo, and Ned was sure the steel blade was also decorated with the inlaid gold wire work for which Toledo had long been famous.

Many monks in long robes were scattered among the crowd, their cowls thrown back because of the heat, their hands clasped in front of them, their eyes generally fixed on the ground in front of them, as became holy men who had devoted their lives to a particular religious order and whose vows of celibacy made them conscious of the number of plumply provocative women in the crowd.

Two things distinguished this crowd from any other. First, although the people were packed shoulder to shoulder (but kept back from the *Peleus* men by the line of soldiers) neither they nor the dignitaries on the church steps were chattering noisily: instead everyone seemed to be speaking in hushed voices, as though awaiting the arrival of a famous man rather than the execution of more than half a hundred scoundrels.

Second, there was tension. Ned felt it even though his Spanish was far from fluent. He had never seen a bullfight but he had often been told of the tension which gripped the crowd before the first bull was let into the ring: they seemed to be holding their breath and they all sighed when they first saw the bull charging through the open gates and heard its hooves thundering on the sun-baked earth.

Ned stood almost alone between the bottom of the steps and the edge of the crowd in the *plaza*. Had they raised their heads, Thomas and Diana could have seen but not recognized him. Julio stood beside him, occasionally muttering a comment; indeed, his task was to give Ned a commentary on what was happening, based on his own experience of Spanish life and what people in the crowd were saying.

The sun was scorching and almost directly overhead: Ned looked down and found the shadow he cast was little wider than the brim of a Roundhead's hat. Perspiration ran down his spine and he had to wipe his brow frequently as it trickled into his eyes.

Suddenly the bell stopped its tolling. The great west door of the church began creaking open and everyone on the steps turned to watch as though this was what they had been expecting all along.

The first man coming out was splendidly dressed; the cloth of his jerkin was a rich wine red and round his neck was what Ned guessed must be if not a king's at least an archbishop's ransom in gold chains.

"The *alcalde* of San Germán," Julio muttered. Following him, walking ponderously as though carrying a heavy but invisible load, was a corpulent man in cope and mitre, two young boys carrying the train of his long robes.

"A bishop – probably of the province," whispered Julio.

The next two men wore uniforms similar to the officer already standing in the *plaza* but even more ornate, and behind them were two younger officers, obviously aides.

"The military governor of the province and his deputy, I should think."

The people on the top few steps drew to each side, leaving an open space for the newcomers. The bishop stepped forward and everyone in the *plaza* and on the steps not only stopped whispering but seemed to freeze.

The bishop began talking in a deep, sonorous voice, sentences drawn out and each ending on a sorrowful note.

"He's talking about the wickedness of pirates, buccaneers, heretics, sinners – just about everyone," Julio muttered.

"Turning on his friends, eh?"

Julio nodded. "Now he's congratulating the military governor for capturing so many wicked English pirates, buccaneers, heretics and sinners . . ."

The bishop waved to the crowd, his arm swinging as though brushing aside a bough, then turned and made way for the military governor, who began speaking to the crowd in a sharp voice, as though giving them orders, but spoke in what Ned recognized as a clear Seville accent which he could understand.

"There," the commander cried, pointing at Thomas, "we have the leader of the buccaneers, the famous Sir Tomás Witstone, the nephew of the heretical Cromwell, and sitting next to him the infamous woman who has whored the length and breadth of these seas in his company. And over there –" he waved at the seamen standing by the north wall, "– are their minions. All have just been tried before the court, all have been found guilty. All –" he turned and bowed respectfully at the bishop, who bowed back, "– have been given the chance of confessing their sins and recanting their heretical beliefs, but they have turned their faces away."

He paused, seeming to swell like a bullfrog mating, and then bellowed: "All are now to suffer death!" He pointed down at the officer in the *plaza*, who had now drawn his sword and was holding it pointing horizontally in front of him. "Begin the executions!"

The officer barked out an order and the file of soldiers cocked the locks of their muskets and then bent their heads to sight along the barrels at the three men lashed to the trees. Ned already had counted the file of soldiers. Twenty-one muskets. Seven shots for each man. The officer had allowed for some poor shooting . . .

The officer, having satisfied himself apparently that all the musketeers were now ready, bowed to the bishop and raised his sword so that it pointed up vertically. In a few seconds it would flash down and the first three seamen would be shot dead.

Ned pulled aside his robe, raised his pistol, and fired. The officer seemed to shrink as his sword clattered to the stone paving, his plumed hat tilted and flew off like a wounded bird, and then the man's body slewed round and fell to the ground.

At the same moment all the monks in the *plaza* tore off their robes, producing pistols and cutlasses, and started shouting "Griff-in, Griff-in" at the top of their voices, pushing their way through the startled crowd to the wall to begin slashing the ropes holding the seamen.

Ned and Julio, sharp knives in their hands, ran the few yards to the chairs and cut Thomas, Diana and Mitchell free. Saxby, Lobb and Fernando appeared out of the now frightened crowd, and while Ned lifted up an almost helpless Diana and carried her in his arms into the anonymity of the crowd, the other men helped Thomas and Mitchell to stand. Both were so weak and cramped that they had difficulty in walking, and finally the two Spaniards lifted them over their shoulders and followed Ned.

While the crowd of men, women and children fell over themselves in panic as they made room to let Ned pass through, Aurelia and Mrs Judd, both still in monks' robes, faces darkened with dust to make them appear mannish and unshaven and their hair tied down, walked beside Ned, each waving a pistol and Mrs Judd shouting blood-curdling threats in English at the frightened Spaniards.

A young man in the crowd who suddenly ran towards Ned waving a sword paused for a moment as Mrs Judd bellowed at him but, recognizing a woman's voice, started running again.

Mrs Judd calmly aimed her pistol and shot him, his sword sliding along the ground in front of him as he lurched a pace and then collapsed, his legs folding under him.

An enormous tamarind tree, its dense branches spread out horizontally like a parasol only a few feet above the ground and shading the far end of the *plaza*, had been chosen as the rallying point for the buccaneers.

Ned, beginning to lurch as Diana started wriggling, was unable to hear what she was saying because of the screams of the crowd trying to push back to make room for what seemed to them to be the leader of a party of mad monks.

Finally he stopped, heard Diana shouting that she could walk now, and set her down. As she slid from his shoulder, one magnificent breast surging from a torn bodice, she gasped: "Where's Thomas?"

Ned looked behind and pointed to Thomas only a few yards away. His feet were hardly touching the ground and he had one arm draped round Saxby's neck, the other round Lobb's.

"They almost killed him on the rack," Diana said. "He can't stand."

"He doesn't need to!" Ned said impatiently. "Come on – we're making for that tree!"

Then the yells and screams of the crowd began to fade as Ned heard a chorus of shouts growing over his right shoulder: the seamen, shouting in a variety of accents "Griff-in, Griff-in . . ." as they were cut free, picked up the cry from their rescuers and began running towards the tamarind tree.

Ned heard shots from the same direction, followed by agonized screams of wounded men. As all three women hesitated Ned said savagely: "Get to the tree! There's nothing you can do!"

Diana, although able to hurry, was finding it difficult to walk in a straight line. Ned took her arm and found himself momentarily fascinated by the movement of the bared breast. At that moment Mrs Judd bellowed more threats to the crowd in front of her as the people fought each other to make way, and Ned was proud to see Aurelia waving a pistol and screaming equally terrible threats in Spanish. The sight of a clearly enraged but beautiful woman monk waving a pistol at them left no doubt what she meant.

At last the four of them reached the tree and Mrs Judd turned with her back to the trunk, empty pistol waving threateningly. "Come on dearie, stand by me and look fierce!" she told Aurelia. "All right now?" she asked Diana. "Nice breast, but you've never suckled brats, that's for sure. But tuck it away for now, dearie, in case it rouses lewd thoughts in the minds of these 'eathen Dons!"

Diana blushed, and Ned laughed at her embarrassment in such surroundings: pointing pistols, pointing nipples, pointing fingers: at the moment all seemed to be chaos as Diana struggled with her bodice.

Then between the other two men Thomas lurched up, followed by Mitchell. "Ned," Thomas gasped, "there I am sitting ready to meet my Maker but instead I meet you!"

"Sit down and rest," Ned said. "We've still a long way to walk."

By now the crowd in the *plaza* was thinning as scores of panic-stricken Spaniards escaped along the track running beside the church. As Ned watched them for a moment he was surprised to see bodies sprawled at the top of the steps. By now the first of the ragged seamen, still shouting "Griffin!", reached the shade of the tamarind and began whooping as they saw Thomas and Diana.

"Saxby – you and Lobb go over and see how they're getting on freeing those men," Ned snapped, "and make sure all the Spanish soldiers are accounted for. I counted twenty-one with muskets and there were eleven others."

"Their commanding officer is dead, no doubt about that. Fine shot o' yours," Saxby said as he hurried off across the *plaza*.

"I suppose I should address you as 'Abbot'," Thomas told Ned. "When do we set off for the monastery?"

"Just as soon as all our men are back here. I hope we have enough stretchers for the wounded – that shooting sounded bad."

"Stretchers? Do you mean to say you've brought stretchers?"

"We've brought poles and we've brought pieces of rolled up sail cloth into which we've sewn open-ended pockets on the long sides, so we just slide the poles in to make stretchers strong enough to carry portly folk like you, my lord bishop!"

"I'll walk!" Thomas protested.

"Oh no you won't. You, Diana and Mitchell and any wounded go on stretchers. We're in a hurry to get back to Boquerón. We don't have time for invalids like – hello, what's this?"

Four of the *Peleus*'s seamen had stopped in front of Ned, obviously waiting to talk to him.

"Excuse me, sir, but we . . . well, we want to present this 'ere to you, as a kind o' . . . well, a token," one of them said.

With that he brought a large and ornate sword in its scabbard from behind his back and presented it to Ned, who recognized it as the one which the commanding officer of the Spanish soldiers was going to use to signal the first of the executions.

Thomas saw Ned hesitating and growled: "Take it, Ned! That dam' sword was going to signal the end of each of us. You might as well have something to remember today by."

Ned took it, and Aurelia, tucking her pistol in her belt as though it was a comb, helped Ned put the leather strap over his head. "Say something!" she whispered.

"I – er, well, thank you." Then he remembered something. "Those bodies on the top of the steps?"

"Ah yes, sir. We caught the town governor and his deputy – the governor was the one that made the speech after the bishop – and a few others: the ones that watched the torturing of Sir Thomas and the lady, and were then the judges at the trial."

"What did you do with them?"

The man turned and waved towards the church. "You can just see 'em at the top of the steps."

Ned was puzzled. Why had the military governor and the bishop waited, instead of escaping when it was obvious the prisoners were being rescued? He asked the seaman, who gave a dry laugh. "We heard the speeches and one of the men understood enough Spanish to guess the rest. So as soon as you shot the captain, sir, and we were freed, we got cutlasses and ran up the steps and – well, we executed them what was going to be executioners."

"Quite right, too," Thomas growled. "I take against bishops and governors who put me on the rack for hours to make me change religions, and put Diana on as well and make me watch, and then sentence us to death at the end of it."

"Don't worry about him," Diana said, "he always gets these attacks after he's killed a few deserving Dons."

Ned waved to the groups of seamen hurrying across the square, all of them shouting "Griff-in" in chorus, so that the name must be echoing through the whole town. The men started running, forming up breathless round the tamarind.

Finally Ned saw Saxby with the last group. They were carrying three men. By this time some of the *Griffin*'s men who had earlier reached the tree were preparing the stretchers, and Ned called: "We'll need six."

Saxby strode up. "All here now, sir. Had to leave two men for dead, and we've three wounded."

"What happened?"

"The firing squad. Our fellows made them drop their muskets and a few watched over them while the rest cut the *Peleus* men free. They never reckoned on the Dons having pistols, but half a dozen o' 'em did . . ."

"What happened to the soldiers?"

Saxby shrugged his shoulders. "There's no chance of any of them following us, sir."

Seamen now had the stretchers ready and while the three wounded were put on them, a protesting Thomas again demanded that he be allowed to walk.

"My lord bishop," said an exasperated Ned, "we've given offence to just about everyone in this town – apart from anything else, they put on their Sunday clothes to see more than sixty of you executed and they were cheated. They may well saddle their horses and chase us with billhooks and scythes and swords and curses just to show their annoyance, so we need to hurry. Because of over-indulgence in the past you are in no condition to hurry. So – on the stretcher!"

Within five minutes the column of more than one hundred and seventy buccaneers was marching out of San Germán, led by Mrs Judd, still in her monk's robes and singing bawdy songs, beating time with her empty pistol.

As they approached each village, Mrs Judd waved her pistol in the air and, keeping time, led the seamen in the shout "Griff-in . . . Griff-in . . . !" As the roar swept over each street, doors slammed when the inhabitants ran for shelter and the usual packs of dogs started barking from the safety of clumps of trees.

Ned walked between the stretchers carrying Thomas and Diana side by side and was startled to find both of them feeling guilty about the whole episode.

"Just because of those damned water casks!" Thomas said crossly. "I should have known they'd dry out, left empty for weeks. I knew the wood wasn't seasoned."

"That fool of a carpenter didn't tell you of the seepage and the water he was finding in the bilge until it was too late,"

Diana said.

"I know that," Thomas growled, "but having lost the damned water I should have run back to Port Royal for more. Fact is, Ned, beating to windward day after day leaves your brain numbed. You're stunned. I must have been mad to send in that flag of truce at Boquerón. *Me*, trusting the Dons," he said disgustedly.

"I was as bad," Diana confessed. "What with the King signing the new peace treaty with Spain, and old Sir Harold Loosely being so huffy when you pointed out that what's decided in Europe doesn't affect us out here . . ."

"You were just getting thirsty," Ned said jokingly. "Anyway, we've got you out. One of our Spaniards – you remember Julio? – Well, he's been trotting back and forth, pretending he's the owner and master of the *Griffin*, and he's so well in with the mayor of Boquerón they've nearly agreed on a price for him to buy the *Peleus* prize!"

"Good for him. Right at the moment I'd sell her cheap!"

Three hours later, preceded by the roars of "Griff-in . . . Griff-in!" they all arrived in Boquerón to find the boats of the *Griffin* and the *Phoenix* pulled up on the beach waiting for them and not a Spaniard in sight.

"Oh yes," Ned told Thomas, "there were three Spanish soldiers left on board the *Peleus* as guards. They'll have been dealt with by now."

As seamen launched the boats and were about to carry the stretchers across the sand to them, Diana held out her hand to Ned. "We haven't yet said thank you. But I wish you hadn't let Aurelia take such a risk, even if a monk's robes become her . . ."

"I tried to make her and Mrs Judd stay here. Still, but for Mrs Judd shooting him dead, you and I would have been spitted by that madman who ran out of the crowd."

Thomas said: "When do you want to sail, Ned?"

"Your water casks are still up by the well empty. Let's get them filled and then leave for St Martin. I wonder if that galleon is still there?"

Chapter Twelve

Led by the *Griffin*, the three ships weighed anchor and, with the last of the day's offshore breeze, sailed out through the Canal Sur, the channel between the reefs which were marked on the starboard hand by the small clumps of mangroves sprouting from the end of the Bajo Enmedio.

Aurelia, standing beside Ned at the taffrail, looked back astern into the quiet bay, ringed by mangroves and palms (most of which, seeming to bow, leaned slightly to the west under the constant pressure of the Trade winds).

"Apart from the visit to San Germán, I've enjoyed every minute of our stay in Boquerón Bay," she said. "It's so peaceful. Palms rustling at night, the birds singing – land birds, Ned, singing for the joy of it, not your miserable sea birds that only squeal and squawk when they're fighting over bits of fish . . ."

"You appreciate it now we're leaving, but you weren't so happy before we rescued Diana and Thomas!"

"Of course not. Anyway enjoying things is the memory of them; they never seem so much fun at the time . . ."

"You seemed to be enjoying yourself running across the *plaza* with Martha Judd, waving a pistol and screaming French and Spanish words I've never even *heard* before!"

"Just as well you haven't," Aurelia said, blushing. "I didn't know I knew them. They just – well, they just came out in the excitement."

"Very effective they were too," Ned said drily, signalling to Lobb to give the order to harden in sheets and braces as the

Griffin finally passed through the channel. Ahead on the starboard bow, he could just see more clumps of mangrove, rows of small rocks and waves breaking lazily on the Bajos Resuello, reefs which protected the channel into Boquerón from the west but left a wide channel to the south. This went past three points, Melones, Moja Casabe and Aguila, before allowing ships bound to the east to cross the Bahia Salinas and then round the appropriately named Cabo Rojo, recognizable because of the red cliffs forming the south-western tip of Porto Rico.

An hour later the *Griffin* reached down to Cabo Rojo, followed by the *Phoenix* and then the *Peleus*. Off the cape the wind had been fluking – no doubt swirled round by Cerro Maraquita, a mountain about a thousand feet high at the end of a row of peaks which, standing back from the sea, ran parallel with the south coast of the island.

"Here we go," Aurelia said as the sea became choppy, "beat, beat, beat ... You know, Ned, once we're back in Port Royal I never want to beat to windward again."

"Ladies with floppy bosoms should never be made to beat to windward," Ned said, "and gentlemen only rarely. But we're only about two hundred and fifty miles from St Martin."

"Yes, two hundred and fifty in a straight line," Aurelia said crossly, having been caught before, "but how many miles do we have to *sail*, with this everlasting tacking?"

"This time we'll stretch down to Guadeloupe or Dominica – about three hundred miles – and we shouldn't be hard on the wind, unless it blows from the south-east."

"Why are we going so far south?" Aurelia asked suspiciously. "That'll put us a couple of hundred miles south of St Martin."

Ned gave an exaggerated sigh. "There I am, making it easier for us all, and you start looking suspicious. Once we've had a good sail to, say, Dominica, we ease sheets and reach up to St Martin with the Trade winds comfortably on our quarter."

"Except they'll blow hard from the south-east all the way from here to Dominica, and then back north-east as soon as we arrive, so we have to go on beating all the way to St Martin."

Ned laughed and held his hands out, palms uppermost. "Of course, my darling. Obviously you're a witch who can foretell the future. But if, instead of steering south-east for Dominica or Guadeloupe, I steer due east, direct for St Martin, do you know what the wind will do?"

"It'll back to the east and head us," Aurelia said promptly. "That's why I said I'm sick of beating to windward."

As the *Griffin* rounded Cabo Rojo, revealing a coastline stretching to the eastward lined with mangroves, with dozens of small cays scattered just offshore and many long dark patches in the water showing where coral reefs reached up within inches of the surface, Aurelia unexpectedly said: "That's where I'd like to live. No mountains – except those well inland – no cliffs, and with all those cays and reefs to protect it, no rough seas . . ."

Ned looked at the small chart he was holding. "The first village along there is called Parguera, and it's about three miles nearer to San Germán than Boquerón. Seems not to have any fort or gun battery, so there's probably no garrison."

"Just the place for us," Aurelia said. "Can't we call and see if anyone has a large house to sell?"

"Yes – if you fancy piloting us through reefs scattered up to three miles to seaward, most of them running east and west like gates in front of us and a foot of water over them!"

"We should have walked down from San Germán," said Aurelia. "We wouldn't have had the sun in our eyes, as we did going back to Boquerón."

"Well, the Spanish seem so unfriendly that perhaps we'd better finish building the house in Jamaica first. Let's see what mistakes we make with it."

"The first mistake," Aurelia said bitterly, "was to think of building a house on an island claimed by Spain when there's such a government in London."

"Such a King," Ned said.

"It's the same thing. Oh Ned, you're so wrapped up with loyalty to the King you don't realize that your feelings are like a great river: everything flows one way. You're loyal to the King, or government, but you can't see that to them you are – well, a scribble on a piece of paper, a number, as important as one of those waves approaching us."

"You don't understand loyalty to a cause or a country," Ned argued, hurt by her words. "I can't describe it; it's just inside me, like appreciating beauty, or being revolted by wanton killing."

Aurelia was suddenly angered: Ned's attitude was an outrage against her practical attitude towards life. "You and Thomas and the buccaneers have saved Jamaica several times. Without you, England would have lost it years ago.

"Now the new King is too mean to send out even one of his ships to help protect it. In fact the new King," she said contemptuously, "shows his gratitude by promising to return the island to Spain, and then sending out this *bouffon* Loosely as the island's Governor.

"And what orders does he give the wretched Loosely? – why, pay off the Army and get rid of the buccaneers.

"Ned, don't trust kings or governments, and this Loosely is just the first of dozens of *parvenus* – assuming England holds on to Jamaica – who will come out here (just as they will go out wherever England has colonies) and strut and puff for a few years and then go back to London to be given a title for all their puny efforts . . . England will ruin her colonies by burying them under a heap of knighthoods and baronies.

"I wonder, Ned, if she really deserves to *have* any colonies: it's people like you that win them for her, and it is people like you that get cheated by the men in London who are not even faces, let alone names."

"Oh, we have names," Ned said, watching the *Phoenix* and the *Peleus* luff until they were in the *Griffin*'s wake. "The Duke of Albemarle, for one, and despite what you say, I think that as soon as he finds out exactly what's happening out here, he'll prove a good friend."

"Mark my words," Aurelia said gloomily, "watch the men who came back from Spain with the King. Oh yes, I know they showed their loyalty by going into exile with him (and I know your father and brother were among them); but some were Catholics, and I think everyone knows that the new King is, to say the least of it, sympathetic to Catholics. Very well, Ned, watch out. The minute the, *comment dit-on?*, the Secretary for Trade and Foreign Plantations is a Catholic, Spain's interests will come first. What the Pope wants is what matters. The Pope wants Jamaica returned to Spain, and a

Pope drew the Line giving Spain most of the New World."

"If the Jesuits could hear you . . ." Ned said.

"If the Jesuits could hear me, they'd make sure I never spoke another word. And remember what I've said. This man Bennet, Sir Henry Bennet – watch him. He's a strong Catholic; he went into exile with the King and he has the King's ear. Watch him, Ned. If ever he becomes the Secretary of State then Jamaica is certainly lost and we must think of settling somewhere else. The Bay Islands? Perhaps we should sail up there and inspect them."

"Cheer up," Ned said, "let's get to St Martin and see if we can help the Spanish with this stranded galleon. If we lighten her of a few tons of gold perhaps she'll float off the sandbank . . ."

He pulled open the binnacle drawer and took out the perspective glass. He studied the coast carefully, commenting: "Low cays, reefs and mangroves. This is no coast on which to make a landfall at night . . ." He thought for a minute or two. "Perhaps we ought to short tack along here. None of us know this south coast of Porto Rico and having once had a sight of it the knowledge might come in useful."

"Just as long as the sea is no rougher," Aurelia murmured.

"No, and now the light is going the offshore breeze may set in for the night, so we can stretch along here comfortably without beating."

"You aren't going to see much of the coast once it's dark," Aurelia pointed out.

"There's a hundred miles of it, and the night breeze will be so weak I doubt if we'll make much progress over the current. The scene won't have changed much by the time dawn comes round."

In fact dawn next day found them approaching Guayanilla, the second port along the coast, and as they tacked again they could just see the port of Ponce, the island's second largest city. When Lobb commented that the name, which he pronounced in the English way, was a strange one, Ned explained it was named after Juan Ponce de León, who visited Porto Rico while still searching for the Fountain of Youth. Ponce, Ned added, was pronounced "Ponthay" in Spanish, and "Juan" was "Hwan".

Ned found himself explaining more Spanish a few hours

later as the three ships tacked seaward again after passing a small island some five miles offshore. Called Isla Muertos, it meant "Island of the Dead". Why? Lobb wanted to know. Ned shrugged his shoulders. "Your guess is as good as mine. Perhaps they hanged pirates on it – though why they'd row out this far I can't think. Maybe people living on it all died of the plague. Or ships run on it at night and the bodies are washed up on the shore."

Aurelia said: "Cities named after dead explorers – even if they were looking for the Fountain of Youth – and islands of the dead: don't let's become like the Spanish, obsessed with death."

Finally, as the *Griffin* tacked south-east again at the south-eastern tip of Porto Rico and was followed round by the *Phoenix* and the *Peleus*, the eastern end of the island began to fade to the northwards and they could see another island ten miles further eastwards.

"Crab Island," Ned explained. "The Spanish call it Vieques, and I've no idea what *that* means. Beyond Crab Island, much too far away for us to see now, are a line of low cays running eastwards from the end of Porto Rico to meet another island, which in English is called Snake Island and the Dons call it Culebra, which means the same thing, snake or serpent."

"Porto Rico means 'rich port' in Spanish," Aurelia said suddenly. "That's an odd name to give a whole island."

"Well, go on," Ned said encouragingly.

"Well, calling the capital San Juan, St John, seems strange too."

"I'll let you into a Spanish secret," Ned said. "When Columbus first sighted the island, he called it San Juan, after St John the Baptist, and when he discovered that fine port on the north side of the island, he called it Porto Rico because he was sure he would find plenty of gold to send to Spain. But somehow, when the news of his discoveries reached Spain, there was a muddle, so that the island was called Porto Rico and the port San Juan."

"Doesn't seem worth beating up to Vieques to look for crabs," Lobb said lugubriously. "They probably muddled that with the Island of the Dead . . ."

"Anyway," Aurelia said, "the next island we sight is Dominica or Guadeloupe – is that right, Ned?"

"We might sight Santa Cruz, which is about fifty miles away, but it'll be on the northern horizon."

"Santa Cruz? Another Spanish island?"

"Yes, but call it St Croix if it makes you feel more comfortable," Ned said, "even though it's not French."

"Why don't we capture it so you can rename it and give it to me as a present?"

"Of course, darling. It must be as big as St Martin and Anguilla put together, so we'll collect it on the way back – unless your arms are too full of bullion."

From the moment they tacked away from Porto Rico the wind backed to the north-east, giving the three ships an easy reach towards the chain of islands running almost north and south, like a row of sentry boxes separating the Caribbee from the Atlantic. A shifty-looking little Welshman named Williams was the first to sight land late one afternoon, and Lobb was the first on board the *Griffin* to identify it.

"South end of Guadeloupe," he said confidently. "I recognize those three peaks – that's the volcano, La Soufrière, but we are too far off to see if it's smoking." He looked at Ned. "That's just what you said, sir: just about midway between Dominica and Guadeloupe!"

Ned unrolled the chart he had just fetched from his cabin. "So St Martin lies up there, to the north of us, and the wind looks as if it's going to veer, which will be most obliging of it. Anyway, we don't want to get too near Guadeloupe – those mountains cut off the wind for miles to leeward."

He gave Lobb a new course, to the northwards. "It's like a road, this last stretch up to St Martin. We'll find Montserrat to larboard and Antigua to starboard. We gallop up the middle, leaving Barbuda and St Barthélemy on our right, and Nevis, St Christopher, St Eustatius (usually known as St Kitts and Statia) and Saba on our left."

"And then what?" Aurelia asked.

"And then we come to St Martin on our right, with Anguilla just beyond. Then we stop the carriages, water the horses, and pay a visit to the French on the north side of the island."

"Why not call on the Dutch on the south side?"

"The galleon is supposed to be aground on the north side,

so it's nothing to do with the Dutch. Anyway, I'm hoping that neither the French nor the Dutch have managed to do anything about her. Our arrival will certainly keep the French interested, but let's hope they don't have suitable ships in Marigot."

"Ned," Aurelia said, "I haven't said anything before because I was afraid you'd think it was because I'm French, but aren't we going to risk upsetting the French if we just arrive and attack the galleon, which is so near to the St Martin coast?"

Ned grinned ruefully. "If the French have captured the galleon already, we'll be too late; but if the galleon is still there aground, they'll be like a toothless fox starving outside a rabbit hole. If we come along with the right ships and a good plan, perhaps we can strike a bargain with the French: give them a share of the purchase and they'll look the other way."

"You haven't mentioned anything about a good plan before, Ned. What are you planning?"

"I wish I knew," he admitted. "Until we see if the galleon is still there, and how she is lying, it's useless even to think about it."

"I suppose you'll want me to act as the translator when we call on the mayor of Marigot," she said. She thought a moment and then added: "I haven't any suitable clothes, you realize that, don't you?"

The sail northwards between the islands was something that Diana would always remember even though, as she commented to Thomas, she had sailed thousands of miles through the Caribbean.

By now she and Thomas had recovered from the torturing although Thomas, looking at some of the black-painted metal bands round the oiled wood of the mast, had immediately protested that they reminded him of the garottes waiting on the ground beside their chairs in San Germán, and later that same day Mitchell had, without comment, sent a man aloft to paint them white.

Diana, inspecting her body in their cabin using the tiny mirror, said: "At last the bruises have almost faded. The advantage of being suntanned is that you don't notice so much the horrible stage when they turn yellow."

Thomas watched her as she turned slowly. "You don't look any taller, so the rack didn't stretch you permanently!"

Diana shuddered at the memory. "It surprises me that it didn't hurt so much when they were winding it up to stretch me, even though I thought my arms and legs would pull out of their sockets. What hurt was when they let go: that was when I fainted. It was like being kicked in the back by a mule."

"I was the same," Thomas said, reaching for his breeches. "I say, that's some bruise you have on your left breast."

"That's where they pinched me with those tongs. They are swines, you know, stripping off all my clothes like that."

Thomas grunted. "Well, I didn't mind that so much; I took against them when they started winding you up on that damned machine. I kept remembering all the stories I'd heard of men having their arms and legs torn out."

"Yes, but they weren't scourged at the same time. It's very painful having a wild-eyed priest whacking your belly and breasts with twigs. The look in his eyes!"

"What was he looking at?"

"Not my fair face, I assure you! I thought his eyes would pop out!"

"Can't fault his taste," Thomas commented. "I'll scourge you myself if you go on twisting and turning like that!"

"But not with twigs," Diana said, walking towards him.

Later, when they were both standing on the foredeck of the *Peleus* as she drove north before a brisk south-easterly wind, Diana said: "This is the kind of navigation I enjoy. One just has to count. We've passed one big island to starboard –"

"That was Antigua," Thomas said.

"– then a smaller one we could just see –"

"Barbuda."

"– and the mountainous one to larboard and the little one sticking up like a tooth . . ."

"Montserrat and Redonda."

"Now there's this big one to larboard. Just look how it starts low down, then rises to that peak, and then goes down again."

"Like a young woman's breast. Like your breast before you grew into a proper woman. Used to be a volcano."

"Did I?" Diana inquired innocently. "Don't you think hot fires still rage inside me?"

"Oh yes, they just need me to stoke them now and again," Thomas said, "but if you're keeping a count, that island's Nevis. The light must have been bad when he first saw it, because Columbus thought it had snow on it, hence the name."

"Just look how the cloud forms right up at the peak," Diana said. "As though an artist is painting it in."

"Both St Kitts and St Eustatius have peaks like that. In fact you can see cloud forming above St Kitts. There, just north of Nevis."

Diana looked with the perspective glass. "Not just cloud but a great black thunderstorm! It's just starting to bubble up now! Oh, it's rising so fast!"

"They'll be glad of the rain. Antigua and Montserrat looked parched and there's much more brown than green on the slopes of Nevis."

Diana suddenly pointed ahead and up in the air. "Look – a huge white swallow!"

"Ha! That's a tropic bird. Don't you recognize it? Look at its tail when it passes overhead."

Diana shaded her eyes and watched. The bird flew with strong but unhurried strokes of its wings, looking at first like a great tern, and in a direct line, as though having sighted the ship from a long way off it was investigating. "Oh! I see what you mean about the tail – it's so long – and why, it's only two feathers! As long as the bird itself – longer, in fact. But they do split just like a swallow's tail."

"You don't remember the first one you ever saw?"

Diana looked puzzled. "No. In a way they're just the opposite of frigate birds, white instead of black. I hate frigate birds – they seem evil, but the tropic bird – look, he seems so independent!"

"The first one you ever saw," Thomas reminded her, "was in the middle of the Atlantic. You were quite upset because you thought it was lost, with the nearest land fifteen hundred miles away!"

"Yes, I remember now. It was flying as though so determined; as though it knew where it wanted to go but had taken the wrong turning. And look, there's another!"

"They live in colonies near high cliffs, so there are probably a number round Nevis and St Kitts."

"This sea," Diana said, "what a wonderful deep purple. And with the glass I can see how it turns green, and then a very light green as it reaches Nevis. Outlying reefs, I suppose."

Thomas suddenly took the glass, searched a section of the horizon just south of Nevis, and said: "You're not much of a lookout!"

"What did I miss? Anyway, I was just looking at the island."

"There are a couple of sail over there."

"Spanish? Anything for us to worry about?"

Thomas grinned and shook his head. "Just two small local sloops, fishing from the look of it. They'll have a tale to tell when they get in, how they saw three enormous sail heading north . . ."

"But people will see us from the island, won't they?"

"Perhaps not. The capital is on the other side, and if it's like most of the other islands, the plantations will be that side too, where the rain falls."

Diana took the perspective glass back and examined the slopes of Nevis again. Much of it was covered with bushes, the occasional tamarind standing out, its dark-green mushroom shape growing from a circle of shadow. She felt the hot sun penetrating the cloth of her blouse, and the deck planking was scorching under her bare feet. She thought then of the flies and the mosquitoes and the sandflies, the thirst that seemed ever-present on a tropical island, and the narrow interests of planters who went for weeks without seeing a new face on their plantations. And the rumbullion and mobby . . . most men in the Tropics drank too much, to help pass away the time, as though the drinker was hurrying to reach the end of his life. And mobby, made from fermenting potatoes, had to be drunk the day it was made, an easy excuse for taking a few extra mugs.

"I'd hate to be a planter's wife," she said unexpectedly, startling Thomas.

"I'd hate to be a planter," Thomas said, "but what provoked that announcement? Not afraid I'm going to buy a plantation, are you?"

"There are a couple of plantations on this side of Nevis – I can just see the dark green of the sugar-cane with the glass. I was thinking of the life the planters must lead, and –"

"You are suddenly frightened that once we have the house built in Jamaica, I'll turn into a planter, eh?"

"Not so much that," Diana said frankly, "but that you'd take to hot waters, just to pass the time."

Thomas looked her up and down. "Men take to hot waters to pass the time when they haven't anything else to do. Not many wives come out here, you know. Most of the women have been transported – whores, beggars and those sort. None the worse for that," Thomas added, "and once here they often turn out to be real princesses, if they meet the right men."

Diana laughed and looked coquettish. "Oh lah, sir, coming out here was the making of me! Before that I was just Lily, the cheapest whore in Cheapside, but out here I met a real gentleman what set me up with rich clothes –" she tugged at her worn blouse, "– and real leather shoes –" she lifted a bare foot, "– and now I'm back to being a whore who gets taken advantage of but now never a guinea is put in her purse."

"True, Lily, true," Thomas said with mock sadness. "The dreadful story of how you became a poor sailor's doxy should be a lesson to all the legions of the fallen women that my uncle Cromwell transported to the Indies." He nodded his head. "Of course, my concern for these poor young women's welfare is well known; indeed that's why Ned always refers to me as 'my lord bishop'."

Diana looked directly at Thomas and smiled lewdly. "Indeed? Aurelia told me it was because you once confided to him, when you were more than usually drunk, that you dreamed of making love to me on a church altar."

Thomas flushed and coughed. "Well, that's Ned's story. I've never been inside a church with you."

"No," Diana said thoughtfully, "nor you have."

Later, on board the *Griffin*, Ned said: "That must be St Barthélemy almost dead ahead. We'll have it abeam by nightfall, and soon after dawn tomorrow you'll see the Dutch side of St Martin. I believe the Dutch spell it 'Maarten', but I prefer the French way."

"You're prejudiced, sir," Lobb said, grinning at Aurelia.

She clapped her hands. "Think, in a day or so I'll be hearing French spoken by Frenchmen – the first time for many months. Years, in fact, apart from the buccaneers."

"Well, you can't expect your luck to hold for ever," Ned growled, and then suddenly stiffened. "You're still a French subject!"

"No, I'm not," Aurelia said firmly. "I became English when I married Wilson. I don't lose that just because Wilson died!"

"Of course not," Ned corrected himself hurriedly. "Just for a moment – well, you were only saying a few days ago about trusting kings and governments . . ."

Lobb said: "Anyway, I think madame could give a very good account of herself as an Englishwoman who happens to speak good French."

"You should have heard her cursing those Spaniards in the *plaza* at San Germán," Ned said. "Sounded very Spanish and earthy to me!"

"What time does the moon rise?" Aurelia asked sweetly. "It should make those islands there, Nevis, St Kitts and St Eustatius too, look like fairy islands!"

Chapter Thirteen

As the *Griffin* ran northwards from St Barthélemy with the Dutch side of the island of St Martin sitting four-square on the horizon ahead, the sun rose on the starboard hand, tinting several small islets a rose colour that just managed to soften their harsh and jagged lines. A constant swell put ragged white collars of breaking water round every rock and it was still early enough for the sea itself to be a harsh grey, the rolling crests flecking with red.

"So that's the *mynheers*' half of the island," Aurelia commented to Ned, pointing ahead. "Well, they seem to have chosen all the mountains! That line of peaks running through the middle is a spine; it looks like a sleeping iguana."

"I wish I knew if this damned south-east wind was going to hold for the rest of the day," Ned said crossly.

"Why don't you like it now? It's brought us up from Guadeloupe at a spanking pace!"

Ned pointed over the starboard bow. "Just look at all those islets and isolated rocks lying between us and the eastern side of St Martin."

"Why should they put you in such a bad humour?"

"Marigot is on the opposite side of the island – on the far side from where we're heading. If we sail down the western side and the wind backs, we'll have to beat up to Marigot."

"Beating just a few miles? I don't mind that!" Aurelia said. "Why are you worrying? If you want to avoid the risk of having to beat up to Marigot, let's dodge about among those rocks and islets and sail round the east coast, so we'll be running free, whether the wind has backed or not!"

He continued staring at the island ahead, a blue-grey lump: too far away to distinguish the natural colours yet.

"Oh Ned," Aurelia said impatiently, "it doesn't matter! Go whichever way round you want."

Ned sighed theatrically. "I'm sure Thomas doesn't have to put up with this sort of bullying from Diana. She cossets him and is understanding when he has problems."

"I don't know what makes you think that! I've noticed Thomas does exactly what Diana says, although perhaps not at once, just to save his pride. At least *he* doesn't treat her like a mistress who comes running to bed as soon as he calls."

"What's wrong with that?" Ned asked innocently. "I always do what you say *and* I come to bed the minute you call. That's if I'm not already there, waiting for you."

Aurelia made a face. "If you're not careful I'll give in and marry you. Then I'll demand my rights as a wife."

Ned inspected a group of islets on the *Griffin*'s starboard bow and then tucked the glass under his arm. "I always had the impression that mistresses have more privileges than wives."

"Oh yes," Aurelia agreed sweetly, "when her lover dies she has no responsibilities whatsoever: no money, no home, no rights . . . The poor wife has all the worry of being left her husband's fortune, his house, his estate . . ."

"Unless there's a son, in which case she's moved out to the dower house and becomes a plump dowager and an indulgent grandmother living on the charity of her son."

"All right. I'm persuaded now," Aurelia declared, "I remain your mistress."

"It was the running to bed that decided you," Ned teased.

"No, I don't fancy the dower house. England is probably crowded with dower houses, all cold, damp and gloomy." She shivered.

Ned thought for a moment. "Well, you'd have a choice of three Yorke dower houses. The nicest is the one on the Godmersham estate. It's near Ashford in the lee of the Downs, and is far from gloomy. A stream runs through the garden, plenty of fruit trees . . . When I was last there, plenty of flowers too. The one on the Ilex estate – well, you'd probably find that too big; nine bedrooms, a kitchen with a spit large enough to roast an ox. And of course you'd be cheek by jowl with your nephew, who'd have inherited the title from brother George and be living at Ilex."

Aurelia pretended to be considering the alternatives. "Yes, the Godmersham house does sound possible, but still, England is so *cold* ... and the long, long winter, as bad as northern France. No, I shall stay in the Tropics to be warm, so I won't marry you. But I warn you, as your mistress I shall demand emeralds and rubies, and gold rings and chains and brooches..."

"None of which you have already?" Ned asked with raised eyebrows.

"Oh," she said airily, "I do have a few trinkets you've given me and which I can wear when I go back to live in Barbados, a cast-off mistress. Don't forget I still have the estate there that I inherited from my husband. Not that I shall ever set foot in it again because it would remind me of what a terrible man he was. But I could sell it and buy another. One large enough to attract another lover."

"Yes," Ned agreed with mock seriousness, "and then you'll realize what a wonderful lover you had before..."

"It's a risk I'll take," Aurelia said. "If he's after my money at least he'll be kind – until he gets it, anyway. So you're going round the west side of the island?"

"The chart I have doesn't show half these islets; just a few scribbles," Ned said. "But along the west coast there's nothing to worry about, nor round to Marigot."

Aurelia shivered, and Ned noticed. "What's the matter? Do you want your cloak?"

She shook her head. "No, I just wish I could see the other side of the island. I'm beginning to feel *timide*. How big is a galleon?"

"I've never seen one, but four or five times as big as this ship, I suppose. But it may not still be there. I've stopped thinking about how many weeks ago we first heard about the damned thing. If they've had any bad weather she could have broken up. A few weeks of northerly swells lifting her and bumping her down again could break her back or send the masts by the board ... Or the French might have brought in ships and captured her; all the gold and silver could be on its way to Paris by now..."

"Cheer up," Aurelia said, "but if you're going to satisfy your mistress's greed, you'll need better luck than that."

An hour later, when the sun had lifted high enough to raise the shadow from the western side of the mountains, the *Griffin*, followed by the *Phoenix* and the *Peleus*, reached the southern tip of the island, finding a deep half-circle of a bay almost entirely closed by a reef. Ned saw that the reef in fact made the bay into a natural port, and in addition to a ruined jetty there was a small fort on the western arm. More interesting was the fact that there were twenty or more sloops anchored close to the remains of the jetty, and on the beach beyond there were several pyramids of salt. A minute or two later, as the *Griffin* was lifted on a swell wave, Ned saw a big lagoon behind the beach – probably an enormous salt pond. It was surprising the whole place was not called Salt Island – most of the inhabitants must (judging from the mountainous land) be salters – or goats!

"That reef must give very little protection when the wind pipes up from the south or west," Ned commented to Lobb. "But while it stays in the east, these sloops can unload cargo into boats, or take off salt. Carry it down to Curaçao, I suppose. All that salt –" he gestured to the piles on the beach, "– with all those mountains means *mynheer* can't grow much. If the French have any flat land, they got the best bargain!"

"How did they decide who had which half?" Lobb asked.

Ned laughed drily. "I don't really know, but there's a story (no doubt told by the French) that it was agreed a Frenchman and a Hollander should stand back to back and, at a signal, start walking in opposite directions round the coast. That was to be one end of the frontier, and the other would be where they met. The Frenchman got farther round – giving the French the larger portion – because the Hollander was also a trencherman and stopped for a hearty lunch."

"To be fair to the Dutch, I can't see a Frenchman missing a good meal," Aurelia said doubtfully. "But if the French part is like this, all mountains and valleys and cliffs, I don't think either of them got a bargain (except in salt) if they wanted to plant sugar or tobacco, or even vegetables to eat themselves! The mountains look beautiful enough, but only goats can appreciate them. And water . . . both sugar and tobacco need plenty, but does it rain much?"

As the three ships sailed along the coast, they saw that the mountains with their rounded peaks soon curved inland, leaving a flat plain like a shelf to form the western corner of the island, with long sandy beaches.

"Low land, shallow water," Ned said to Aurelia, who looked puzzled.

He explained: "Where the land is low, as it's now becoming, usually the sea gets shallower. Where there are high mountains and cliffs, you'll find the sea is generally deep right up to the shore."

Aurelia, looking ahead over the *Griffin*'s bow, nodded. "I can see the water changing colour. It's becoming a lighter blue, and where that furthest bay curves inland, it's light green."

Ned searched the coast with his glass. These mountains were high but beautiful: in every case the slope up to the peak was smooth and gentle; each mountain had trees growing on the lower slopes and usually they thinned out to give way to smaller trees, little more than bushes, and finally shrubs which were so green that from a distance each mountain seemed covered in a green carpet. Only occasionally a sharp edge of rock showed where some fall had made a crevasse.

A slight movement on the lower slopes of one mountain showed a herd of cattle grazing and, a little higher, he could distinguish goats. Then he saw a village of half a dozen buildings tucked in the lee of a small hill, then another village at the end of a long beach had fishing boats pulled up to the mangroves. A few wisps of smoke, from cooking fires or *boucans*, were the only signs that people lived on the island.

The Dutch here must (apart from the salt) make their living by trading with the other islands: buying and selling goods that were brought out from the Netherlands. The Dutch, he admitted, were the best merchants in the Caribbee. They were also the most successful smugglers to the Spanish Main. Judging from their part of St Martin and from what he had heard about St Eustatius, just in sight as a grey lump on the southern horizon, the Dutch were more interested in trade than farming: on the British and French islands, from Grenada up to Guadeloupe, but especially Barbados and St Kitts and Nevis, sugar and tobacco ruled supreme. And cotton, of course. Three crops which together made men rich and then ruined all too many of them with the hot waters.

There was a dreadful irony, Ned mused, that a man devoted his whole life to his sugar plantation, getting from it wealth every time he sent a ship back to England laden with sugar and barrels of molasses. Nevertheless, that same sugar-cane produced rumbullion, with which that same man drank himself insensible every night after passing the day in a drunken haze.

Slowly the drink would make him careless: careless about how his plantation was run, careless of his dress, his manners, his accounts, his honour and his wife. Slowly but quite inexorably his own rumbullion would kill him, and in the process would ruin the estate. In a way it was what had happened to Aurelia's husband (although he was also a complete scoundrel). A man spent a brief lifetime digging his own grave after fashioning his own shovel.

Gradually Ned could distinguish the low tongue of sand marking the corner of the island and which stretched out to the west like a pointing finger. Somewhere back there they had passed an invisible line which divided the island, because this low area must be French. They had the best beaches and probably they were growing crops behind the mangrove forming a low barrier at the back of the sand.

As the *Griffin* came up to the sand spit Ned could just glimpse the western end of Anguilla seven or eight miles away on the far side of the channel between the islands. With the sheets hardened the *Griffin* came on the wind after rounding the spit and Ned saw Anguilla continuing to stretch away eastward into the Atlantic – and what a difference: that island was flat, reminding him of Romney Marsh and Dungeness.

As he looked at St Martin again he could see that the flat land was slowly beginning to rise again to the eastward, but there was no sign yet of the little town of Marigot – nor of the galleon.

Gradually, as the *Griffin* sailed hard on the wind towards the middle of the channel between the two islands, with the *Phoenix* and the *Peleus* following closely in her wake, Ned could see that the north-western coast of St Martin was scalloped by bays and short headlands, each a little shorter than its neighour beyond. Sailing eastward, Ned noted, was like peeling skin from an onion: passing one spur revealed yet another bay and yet another spur. Some bays had small sandy beaches with one or two fishing boats dragged up well clear of the water.

By now the *Griffin* was a third of the way across the channel towards Anguilla. Once again Ned looked back at St Martin and across the top of a low spur, where the land dipped, he saw in the distance the white speckles of a small town, obviously Marigot. The galleon was supposed to be aground beyond it. If he could see Marigot (or part of it, anyway) should he be able to see the galleon?

Aurelia asked the question a moment later and, answering instinctively to delay disappointment, Ned said: "Not necessarily – there's another much smaller bay just beyond the town. Remember, it is called Gallows Bay."

"Ah yes, the Baie de Potence. Perhaps the people of Marigot don't want to look out of their doors and see a row of gallows . . . *Quelle blague*, I can't make up my mind whether I want the galleon to be here or not! Half of me wants it to be gone so we can go back to Jamaica; the other half wants it here so we can capture it . . ."

Ned laughed softly and made sure no one else could overhear him. "To be honest, that's just how I feel. So I shan't be disappointed whatever we find. Certainly, we'd all be delighted with a good purchase, but in my imagination that damned galleon gets bigger every time I think about it. If it's as big as I think it is (assuming it's still there!) our three ships don't stand a chance, unless we can think of some trick to play on the Dons."

Ned and Aurelia stood together on the afterdeck looking over the *Griffin*'s starboard quarter while Marigot opened up. As he had guessed, it was in a wide moon-shaped bay. The western half comprised just a rocky headland; then it curved round to a flat beach backed by mangroves: with the glass, Ned could just distinguish small fishing boats hauled up in front of huts, and brown specks on the sea turned out to be small logs cut from palm trees, obviously markers for fish pots.

The bay's eastern curve ended at the town of Marigot, which was built at the point where the first of the mountain peaks (the north-western end of the ridge running across the island) sloped down to form the flat western corner. A rocky hill, like a redoubt, stuck out in front of the town and a much smaller bay, presumably Gallows, began. On top of the cliffs forming the side of the hill – Ned strained his eye, refocusing the glass – there was a flat platform, a ledge surrounded by a rough stone wall. A gun battery to defend Marigot and its anchorage? From there guns could fire along the low beach to the west, northwards over the shallow Marigot Bay, and also round to the north-east, into Gallows Bay itself.

All right, he told himself, now he had to take a careful look. He had quite deliberately started his inspection from the west, slowly creeping up, as it were, on Marigot. Now he had inspected the low coast and the ridge of peaks coming down in a series of valleys behind Marigot like waves breaking on a beach. He had looked at Marigot, the rocky bastion in front and its gun platform. Now for Gallows Bay itself.

The galleon, bow to the west, her stern to the Atlantic end of the channel, was aground and heeled towards them, to the north. Heeled slightly – just enough to notice, but so little that if she had been afloat the master could have corrected it by shifting some cargo to the other side.

He handed the glass to Aurelia and waved to Lobb, who was standing on the fo'c'sle, watching the colour of the sea ahead of the *Griffin* and making sure there was no reef in their path that the Spanish chartmaker had missed. Lobb was also inspecting the island of Anguilla, noting as best he could from this distance the positions of bays and their usefulness as anchorages. The chart showed the main port was on the north side of Anguilla, simply a village at the head of a deep bay.

When Lobb joined him, Ned pointed at Gallows Bay and Aurelia, having finished her inspection, gave Lobb the glass.

"So it's still there," she said to Ned. "And enormous. I've never seen such a big ship. But why are all the yards down on deck? The masts look so *bare*, like trees without boughs. And she's heeled towards us."

Ned gestured towards Lobb. "Let's wait and see what explanations John has to offer!"

Lobb finally shut the glass with a snap and turned to Ned, grinning cheerfully. "So she's still there. Bit o' luck that. I'll bet Sir Thomas and Saxby are rubbing their hands, too."

"What do you make of her?"

"Well, without having taken soundings all round her and judging from what we've seen of this channel so far, I reckon she's stuck there for good. Because she's heeled towards us we can't see just how much more water she needs to float – that'll be obvious once we get a look at her other side – but from the angle of heel I reckon she needs four feet. The rise of tide round here must at the most be a foot at Springs. She probably drove up a foot or more – perhaps at the top of the Springs – before they could furl the sails, and I reckon there's been some strong northerly winds and swells that have pushed her up another foot or so. I'm sure that's why all her yards have been sent down – to reduce windage and because the swells were making her roll badly. Rolling gets her further on to the sandbank – her keel acts as a lever, like someone rolling up a beach, using his elbows.

"I see four boats at her bow. She hasn't got a boat boom rigged, so that's probably been carried away. Anyway, with this easterly wind she's got to hang 'em off the bow, not the stern. All her boats – I reckon four are as many as she carries – are there, so presumably all her people are on board. And –" Lobb lifted the perspective glass again, adjusted the focus and had another look at the galleon, "– yes, it's even clearer as our bearing changes. All her gunports are open – on the upper-deck anyway – on the landward side, and I'm certain the guns are run out."

"That *could* be just to get weight as far outboard as possible because she's heeled the other way," Ned said, not because he thought that was the actual explanation but he was interested to hear Lobb's reply.

"Even if all those guns are run out it wouldn't be enough to correct that heel. The master will long ago have shifted over the cargo and ballast, and if that hasn't done the trick, then running out guns won't help."

"Why run them out, then?" Aurelia asked.

"To shoot at the French, I reckon. Or make the French think they will."

Ned nodded. "That's what I thought. They can probably train them round just enough to roll a few cannonballs through the streets of Marigot. The eastern side of it, anyway, because the hill with the gun platform on top protects the rest."

"What about the gun platform shooting at the Spaniards?" Aurelia asked. "Surely the galleon is within range?"

"Within range, yes," said Ned. "But do the French have any guns up there? When were they last attacked? Who do they have to fear? Even supposing they have two or three guns, when was that wooden platform built?"

Lobb said gloomily: "Or perhaps they've done some sums. They have at the most three guns but the Dons have at least a dozen on that side, probably more. The French can't sink the galleon because she's already sitting comfortably on the bottom. If she has two or three hundred men on board, all armed with swords, pistols and muskets, they're probably stronger and far better trained and armed than all the able-bodied Frenchmen in St Martin . . ."

"Once he knows who we are," Aurelia said, "the French mayor of Marigot should welcome us with open arms."

"The situation certainly isn't as I pictured it," Ned admitted. "I'd expected we'd end up quarrelling with the French about who was going to capture the galleon. Anyway, we'll soon see. You can tack in towards Marigot now," he told Lobb. "We should be able to lay it nicely. We'll anchor off the town, putting the hill with the battery between us and the galleon!"

By now all the *Griffin*'s seamen were on deck, lining the bulwark on the starboard side, and from the snatches of comment borne along in the wind the men were impressed by the sheer bulk of the galleon, though none seemed particularly overawed. For a moment Ned was irritated: like Lobb and Aurelia, they took the whole thing in their stride. *Mr Yorke will find a way.* That was the damned trouble; everyone expected Mr Yorke to perform miracles. Well, Santiago and Portobelo had been attacks on towns and forts. But what about that galleon? Did they expect him to cast a spell on her so that when they woke up tomorrow morning she would have shrunk to a quarter of her present size?

Chapter Fourteen

Ned watched the Governor General carefully. Charles Couperin was much younger than he had expected: perhaps a year or two past thirty, he was slim, with a face that verged on thin but was tanned, strong white teeth (a striking comparison with his deputy, who had a row of teeth protruding from a large mouth like a battered portcullis), a narrow hooked nose and ears which were pointed, adding the hint of foxiness.

Charles Couperin had started off being alarmed by their arrival: he had met them at the crude landing stage, politely wary as Ned introduced Thomas, Saxby and Aurelia. Obviously he had been watching Ned and Thomas more closely than the others. Aurelia in her split skirt and her hair crammed under a broad-brimmed hat which kept the glare of the sun out of her eyes had been taken for a man until Ned introduced her and Couperin, turning with a polite greeting, found himself staring at a beautiful woman who, smiling, answered in perfect French.

Couperin's residence was a couple of hundred yards back from the jetty, a large, wooden-framed house recently whitewashed. If any women lived there, they had been ordered to keep out of sight. A male black slave dressed in what was intended as a livery modified for the Tropics took their hats, and Couperin led them into a large room which obviously he used as a parlour.

Both he and Ned had surprised each other: Ned had not enunciated his own name very clearly, and it was not until he began to describe their voyage from Jamaica that Couperin suddenly exclaimed, in good English: "The Buccaneers! You are the Admiral of the Brethren of the Coast! And this gentleman – you, sir, must be the nephew of the late – *comment dit-on*?"

"Lord Protector," murmured Aurelia, "Oliver Cromwell."

"I am," Thomas admitted, "but that was a matter of chance. Had it been up to me, I'd never have employed him as an ostler, let alone chosen him for an uncle!"

Couperin nodded but was too polite to smile, obviously trying to recall what an "ostler" was.

Finally, when all the formalities were completed, Couperin raised his eyebrows and asked politely: "Do you intend to stay long in St Martin?"

Just as Couperin had been surprised to find that Ned was in fact the leader of the buccaneers, so Ned had been surprised to discover that Couperin, while the Governor of St Martin, was officially also the Governor General of the much more prosperous island of St Christophe, better known to the English as St Kitts. Apparently the French half of St Martin came under the rule of St Kitts.

Ned smiled, to take any sting out of his answer. "You will forgive me for asking how long *you* are going to stay here?"

Couperin shrugged his shoulders, thought for a few seconds, and considered the fact that the French and the English were friends, while out here, anyway, France and Spain were enemies.

"As you may have noticed, you are not the only visitors to Marigot . . . ?"

"Well, intentional visitors," Ned said. "We have sailed in, anchored, and come on shore to present our compliments."

"True, true," Couperin said cautiously. "But is it wisdom or accident that led you to drop your anchors so that the hill hides you from the ship in the other bay?"

Thomas laughed drily as Ned said: "Wisdom. That ship does not – at first glance, anyway – seem to be French-built. Nor does she seem to be properly anchored. The only cable we have been able to see leads out on her quarter. And, of course, she is heeled and her yards have all been sent down on deck. Is the captain a friend of yours?"

"*Touché*," Couperin said, adding: "She is the reason why I am here and not at my office in Saint Christophe."

And, Ned thought to himself, now is the time to stop this gentle jousting and start bargaining. "Your negotiations with the Spaniards have not been – well, they have not come to a satisfactory conclusion?"

"When a –" Couperin looked at Aurelia for help, "– a *voleur de grand chemin*?"

"A highwayman," she said.

"Ah yes. When a highwayman aims a pistol at an unarmed person, it is less a matter of negotiation than *force majeure*."

"Indeed it is," Ned agreed. "You have no ships, and no guns in your battery on the hill –"

"Oh yes," Couperin said, "we have some guns up there. Three. But the wood of the platform is rotten, and termites . . ."

"So you cannot fire them."

"No, but that is not a problem."

When Ned raised his eyebrows questioningly, Couperin said: "I mentioned *force majeure*. If we fired a gun – a single gun, even a pistol – at that Spanish ship, they would bombard the town of Marigot. Unfortunately the hill protects only a third of the town."

"Are you sure they will open fire?"

"I have the captain's promise," Couperin said drily. "In writing, in fact. Do you wish to see his letter?"

Ned shook his head. "What happens now? It could take a year to get that ship afloat – if a hurricane doesn't destroy her first."

"Ah, yes; we pray for a hurricane! But we have not enough French ships or troops to do anything about the Spaniards, and within a week or so help will be arriving for them. From Cartagena," he added.

"From Cartagena? Are you sure?"

"Oh yes, I am very sure," Couperin said bitterly. "My own ship is on her way to Cartagena – has probably arrived by now – to fetch help."

So this Frenchman was working with the Spaniards! Ned glanced at Thomas, who looked puzzled. Aurelia suddenly said something in French to Couperin, speaking so quickly and unexpectedly that Ned missed it.

When Couperin answered, using an expression Ned did

not understand, Aurelia explained: "The Spaniards took the ship in which the Governor General had come over here from Saint Christophe and sent it off to Cartagena. Monsieur Couperin is marooned here – at least, until another ship arrives from Saint Christophe."

"He wasn't thinking of going anywhere while the Dons are aground out there, was he?" Thomas asked her, as though Couperin was not in the room.

"No, I have no plans," Couperin said with an easy smile. "Apart from anything else, I'm hoping that when they return the Spaniards will give me my ship back."

Does he know? Ned was not absolutely sure. If the galleon had run aground in the darkness, then the French might think she had come in from the Atlantic, from Spain, and was loaded with only an ordinary cargo. Surely they must have found out she was in fact bound *for* Spain – the men who had brought the news to Jamaica had known. Was Couperin playing some deep game? Perhaps. Had he made some bargain with the Spanish, letting them use his ship to go for help in return for a substantial reward? If so, Couperin was foolish to think that the Dons would keep to the bargain.

So – did he know the ship was almost certainly laden with gold and silver and gems intended for the King of Spain's treasury? The more he thought about it, the more puzzled Ned became. Was Couperin a prisoner in his own island, threatened with death and destruction if he did not leave the Spanish alone so that they could send up ships to carry the bullion and gems back to Cartagena, leaving the ship herself to rot or fall to pieces on the sandbank which was clearly never going to yield her up?

Or was Couperin quietly dealing with the Dons on his own behalf, as Charles Couperin, shipowner, not Charles Couperin, His Excellency the Governor General? Had the Spanish stolen his ship – or had they chartered it? Had the Dons threatened to raze most of Marigot – or had they paid off Couperin so that the galleon was left in peace until help arrived from Cartagena?

Ned admitted to himself that he would probably have trusted Couperin but for the appearance of his deputy, who combined the shifty amiability of a dishonest horse coper with the bland deceit of a bishop. The man nodded after every statement by Couperin, as though approving it, yet Ned was far from sure the man spoke English.

So? Ned was wondering just how much to reveal to Couperin. He found he wanted to hear Aurelia's opinion: she had an instinctive feel for people. And Thomas – he was rarely wrong. Saxby, too, seemed to be able to judge people as well as he could ships and horses.

Ned turned to Couperin and said frankly: "I would like to talk with my friends. After that," he added by way of encouragement, "we may have a suggestion to make."

Couperin stood up at once. "There's no need to go out in the scorching sun," he said with a bow to Aurelia. "Please make yourselves comfortable here. Call the servant if you wish for something to quench a thirst – that is the English phrase, isn't it? – and I and my deputy will sit in the shade of the palm trees that you can hear rustling behind the house."

As soon as they were alone, Thomas growled: "Is he telling the truth about his ship or spinning us a yarn?"

Ned looked at Saxby. "I believe his story that the Dons have stolen his ship to fetch help."

He turned to Aurelia. "And what do you think?"

"I believe him, too. He's frightened for the town – village, rather – and I suspect that every penny he owns is in that ship, which is why he's worried that he won't get it back."

"And what do you think, apart from not being sure?" Ned asked Thomas.

"I trust Couperin: his deputy worries me, though: I'd be wary of telling him the time o' day in case he stole my watch!"

Saxby said quietly: "And what do *you* think, sir?"

At that moment Ned saw the galleon again in his imagination, and the fleeting picture made up his mind for him. "I believe him."

"You didn't a few minutes ago," Thomas said shrewdly.

"No, I didn't. I thought the Dons might have struck a bargain with him."

"What changed your mind?" Aurelia was curious.

"The galleon's guns. Those facing the town are still run out, and from what I could see with the glass, trained round forward ready to fire. They don't help right the ship. If Couperin had struck a bargain with the Dons, those guns would have been run in and the portlids closed – especially as these heavy tropical showers must drive in through the ports and soak everything."

Thomas nodded judicially. "You're right Ned – as usual. Obvious really when you think about the guns still run out, but the trouble is the rest of us can't seem ever to be able to spot the obvious. Shall I call Couperin back?"

Once the Governor General had returned, still upset that his guests would take no refreshment, Ned said: "I wanted to talk to my friends about the reason why we have come to Marigot, and your problems."

"Ah, my problems," Couperin glanced at his deputy and then said "You are a fortunate man, Mr Yorke: you have friends you can trust and with whom you can discuss your problems and your plans." He held out his hands, palms uppermost. "I am the Governor General. The people look to me. If I asked their opinions, they would think me indecisive. I would lose their trust."

Ned nodded sympathetically. "The buccaneers are called 'The Brethren of the Coast', and they elected me their leader. That's the important thing: I can lead, but I can't force them to follow. They follow only if they agree with my plans. If not – well, I suppose they go their own way, though it hasn't arisen, so far."

"But I thought there were many of you," Couperin said. "Twenty or thirty ships. I see you have only three."

Ned laughed and decided to tell Couperin the truth, or at least enough of it to explain why the whole buccaneer fleet was not anchored off Marigot. Couperin listened carefully and as soon as Ned finished, made a point Ned had not yet thought about.

"If your buccaneers are capturing the ships approaching Cartagena, they might catch mine. Which means – apart from anything else – that this Spaniard here gets no help . . ."

"Well, I promise you that you'll get your ship back!" Ned said. "But let's leave that aside for the moment and consider this galleon. Have you any idea what cargo she's carrying?"

"Gold, silver, gems, I suppose . . . perhaps a few tons of leather, coffee, herbs. But mainly bullion. But you know that!"

Ned nodded, and Couperin glanced at his second-in-command as though inviting comment. Ned realized that the man must after all speak English.

"Why you here?" the man asked abruptly.

Ned looked at Couperin as he answered. "We are interested in the bullion."

"But it is ours!" the man spluttered.

"At the moment it belongs to the Spaniards," Ned said mildly. "No doubt they want to keep it!"

"But this is our island – France's, I mean." Couperin said. "So now the gold and silver is ours."

Ned raised his eyebrows but said nothing.

"It stands to reason," Couperin said lamely, as if backing up his deputy. "The galleon goes aground a few yards from one of our forts and the Spanish can't refloat her. What are we supposed to do, eh? Leave the wreck to break up, so the gold and silver is left to the fishes?"

Thomas coughed apologetically, as though unwilling to make a point which could only cause embarrassment, like a parent trying to discipline a wayward child in front of visitors. "But the gold and silver won't be left, will it, because the moment the Dons get back from Cartagena with your ship and few of their own, they'll unload all the bullion and take it away."

Couperin nodded and grinned. "You're forgetting that, aren't you," he chided his second-in-command.

The man shrugged and Ned saw that he had forgotten but was in no mood to admit it: clearly he regarded the English as the same sort of people as the Spanish, greedy folk who were standing between him and many tons of bullion – so much gold, silver and gems that it made the phrase "a king's ransom" sound like the spare coins a royal treasurer kept slung over his shoulder in a leather purse to pay for any trifles that caught the royal eye.

And, Ned admitted to himself, the man was right about the plate: the galleon probably carried enough bullion to pay all of Spain's expenses for another year or two, paying for its Army and its Navy, as well as anything else the King wanted (like fitting out more galleons and a *flota* to collect his wealth from the Main) and, of course, the men o' war to protect them from the enemies waiting just over the horizon . . .

Couperin suddenly stood up and began pacing back and

forth across the floor, the inch-high heels of his boots thudding on the planks, punctuating a silence. The seat of his tan-coloured breeches was stained from the leather of a horse saddle; his stock needed washing; the lace of his collar curled over like a dying leaf. He looked tired: not the weariness of a bout of sudden exertion but the tiredness of constant worry lasting too long.

He stopped in front of Ned so that he was looking down at him. "We have the same interest in this galleon," he said. It was a comment and, Ned hoped, the preliminary to a proposal. "You want the bullion and so do we."

Ned shook his head. "By 'we', I presume you are referring to the English and French governments. But as far as I am concerned, the English 'we' refers only to the three ships you see anchored out there."

Couperin shrugged his shoulders and said ambiguously: "There's no need for us to be particular. Gold and silver have the same mysterious magnetism, whatever one's nationality!"

"Agreed," Ned said, and decided the time had come to talk of definite proposals. There was no point in leading with a low card, either. "Your problem as I see it – and please correct me if I'm wrong – is that you have a plate galleon aground close to your town. You do not have the ships to capture her, and at any moment she can bombard you – as her captain has already threatened. So here in Marigot you are powerless, with your tiny battery of three guns unable to fire even a salute for fear of the recoil driving the guns through the wooden flooring."

"That is putting it harshly," Couperin said soberly, and then added, "but accurately, too."

"Nor is that all," Ned said without changing the pitch of his voice. "Not only can you do nothing about the galleon or its cargo, but within a few days the Spanish will be back to unload the ship, leaving you with an empty wreck. The only thing of any value left to you will be firewood eventually drifting up on the beach in Gallows Bay."

"You speak frankly enough," Couperin admitted, "but you are right. But now answer me a question: what can *you* do to get your hands on the bullion? Don't forget the Spanish regard England and France as allies: whatever you do, they'll bombard Marigot, and it'll be no good me protesting that it's nothing to do with the French!"

Ned nodded sympathetically. "Yes, you are in a helpless position," he said, and left the sentence hanging.

Thomas grunted. "Yes, quite helpless. Hopeless, too. I'm glad I'm not you, my dear fellow," he said sympathetically. "You're in an impossible situation!"

Aurelia caught Ned's eye and said in French: "Your Excellency, you are like the grains of wheat caught between the grindstones. What do you propose?"

Couperin sighed and sat down heavily in a rattan chair. He took a square of lace from the capacious pocket in his sleeve and mopped his face. "Madame," he said fervently, "at the moment I wish I was back in France inspecting my vineyards. As it is, I find myself in St Martin facing two formidable enemies."

"*Two*, Your Excellency?" Aurelia repeated, as though incredulous. "Why *two*?"

"Well, I have the Spanish threatening on one side, and the Brethren on the other, and whatever I do Marigot will be destroyed."

Aurelia seemed charmingly puzzled and looked helplessly at Ned. "Surely that isn't how you see it, *chéri*, is it?"

"Well, I never thought His Excellency would even consider that he had to decide between the Spanish and us, I must admit." Ned was pleased with his "more in sorrow than anger" tone.

"But he wasn't actually saying that, *chéri*," Aurelia said. "I had the impression he was accidentally caught between the two of us, without having any choice about taking sides. Your Excellency," she said, turning to Couperin. "was that not what you meant?"

"Yes, madame, you are correct: I have no choice."

Well, Ned thought to himself (and guessing from the expression on Thomas's face that he too considered it was the right moment), now we throw you a rope. "Your Excellency, you probably don't know how the Brethren share their purchase. Indeed, I doubt if you know what 'purchase' means in the sense we use it."

"I don't," Couperin admitted, "though I have always been curious about the method."

"Well, each captain owns his own ship, and has to pay for the rigging, repairs, and so on. So the whole purchase is shared out among the Brethren according to an agreed scale. The captains get the largest shares; then come mates, carpenters, surgeons, gunners, right down to seamen. There is an agreed scale for wounds – a man losing say, an eye and a leg, gets so many extra shares, and fewer if only one leg. On this expedition we have three ships and thus three captains, so any purchase would be divided accordingly."

"Supposing you were joined by another captain," Couperin asked casually.

He's testing the bait, Ned thought, just swimming round and round and seeing how it tastes. Gold and silver are for strong stomachs.

"Had another ship of the Brethren come along," Ned said just as casually, "of course he would have shared equally. At the moment three ships have a third each: had there been a fourth, each would have had a quarter."

"Supposing it was a small ship?"

"Ah, I didn't make that clear. Our three ships do not share exactly so that each gets a precise third. No, it depends on the number of men in each ship. The actual size of the ship does not matter except that it usually governs the number of men she carries."

"Most interesting," Couperin said. "If I had a ship and enough men I'd ask if I could join you!"

He has nibbled and swallowed the bait, Ned thought to himself. He waited until the silence in the room had the emptiness of an echo.

Ned pretended to be puzzling over something and then finally said: "I'd have to discuss this with the other captains, of course; but if we regarded the French half of St Martin as a ship and you her captain, I can't see why you should not be entitled to a quarter share. We'd have to agree on how many men you supplied, of course . . ."

"What good would all that do?" demanded the deputy. "The galleon isn't captured!"

"Yes," Ned said as though making an obvious correction. "I was just making a suggestion: after all, His Excellency is worried about damage to Marigot if the Spanish bombard – and of course, his ship."

"It's all crazy," the man muttered to Couperin. "They've three little ships and perhaps a dozen guns between them. Any attack they make on the galleon will be like flies landing on a horse – except the Spanish will bombard us."

"He's quite right, of course," Ned told Couperin, "but what our friend obviously does not know is how a fly suddenly stinging a horse in the right place at the right time can cause a stampede. However, it needs more than half an ounce of courage to go after a ton or so of gold!"

"What is your plan, then?" Couperin asked.

Ned stared at him and then looked deliberately at his deputy. "That information is worth the galleon out there and all the bullion on board her," Ned said quietly. "Just remember, we sacked Portobelo – which the Dons thought was impregnable – and captured enough gold to make pieces of eight the currency in Jamaica. You may have heard of our raid on Santiago de Cuba, too?"

Couperin nodded soberly. "Yes, I've heard of them. Who hasn't! Who led those raids, you or your predecessor, that Dutchman who died?"

"Mr Yorke, did," Thomas said gruffly, "and to be quite honest, I'm damned if I can see what good you or St Martin can be to us. You can't capture that galleon even though it has been sitting in front of you for weeks like a broken-winded horse. We knew how we'd take her the moment we heard about her back in Jamaica."

And, Ned thought to himself, if you believe that you'll believe that highest peak over there, the Pic du Paradis, will suddenly turn upside-down. But Thomas looked so sure of himself that, Ned realized, both the Governor and his deputy believed him. So now was the time to go back out to the ships and let the two Frenchmen make up their minds. And the English, too.

Chapter Fifteen

"I almost believed myself," Thomas chuckled as he poured wine in the *Peleus*'s saloon. "D'you think that fellow Couperin believed me, too?"

"Of course." Ned kept a straight face. "I thought we'd all come on board to hear you explain how we are going to do it."

Thomas was crestfallen and glanced at Diana, who looked back at Thomas as though she would sooner make love at that moment than make plans. "Thomas's plan would consist of slapping the *Peleus* alongside the galleon with a crash and boarding in the smoke," Diana said affectionately. "Thomas is very good at *doing* if you point him in the right direction. As a *planner* he leaves much to be desired; in fact he usually leaves it to you, Ned. I thought you'd have noticed that by now!"

"I though it was the drink," Ned said. "That, or . . ."

"That as well," Thomas said contentedly. "More wine Saxby? Dear Mrs Judd, wine or rum? I hope you don't subscribe to these slanders being flung around by my common-law wife?"

"There are as many common-law wives in this cabin as common-law husbands," Martha said sternly. "If it was left to the wives, we'd soon have that galleon captured and the bullion transferred."

"Ah," Thomas winked lewdly, "common-law wives have weapons not available to any sort of husbands. But still, three against so many?"

Mrs Judd shrugged her shoulders and pushed her empty mug across the table. "We have our ways. If the three of us rowed slowly past that galleon, I can guarantee you could come along ten minutes later and find an empty ship."

"Not Sirens on the Rocks, but sirens in a boat, eh?" Thomas said. "What would you do when the Dons caught up with you?"

Mrs Judd managed to make the whole of her considerable bulk look coy. "Any sacrifice would be worthwhile if it let you get your hands on the bullion."

"I'm not sure it'd be such a sacrifice in your case," Saxby growled unexpectedly. "Any ideas, sir?" he asked Ned.

Ned sipped the wine, thinking of what Mrs Judd had just said. Guile, stealth, subterfuge, deception, surprise ... all would be needed if they were going to seize the galleon before her guns started bombarding Marigot. The guns were already laid and run out, and the ship was not rolling to affect the aim, so there was no advantage in attacking at night: the Dons would just have to touch their linstocks to guns already loaded and aimed.

Dress the buccaneers in the three ships as voluptuous *houris* and have them follow Mrs Judd, Diana and Aurelia in a parade of trollops through Gallows Bay. Borrow fishing boats from the French ... Wait, there is an idea floating about there, shapeless at the moment, but an idea nevertheless. Tell that fellow Couperin that since he has no ship to offer, we'll settle for a couple of dozen open fishing boats ...

He looked up to find Thomas and Saxby both watching him, expecting to receive their orders. "Guile and stealth," Ned said, adding as much weight to the words as a hanging judge delivering his sentence.

Thomas and Saxby both nodded, but Aurelia glanced at Diana as Ned went on. "We have to decide whether to leave the Dons there for a day or two, until they forget we're anchored the other side of the hill, or to start worrying them at once: make them nervous, so they don't guess where the attack will come from."

"Where *will* it come from, Ned?" Thomas asked enthusiastically.

When Ned said he would give them the details later, Mrs Judd sighed, "He's going to use my body, I know it!"

"You mean you hope," Saxby said unsympathetically.

"You don't understand that there is a lot of woman here to love," Martha Judd grumbled, cupping her large bosoms in her hands.

Both Diana and Aurelia smiled, knowing that Martha Judd's sexual appetites frequently left Saxby like a wrung-out mop. Both had seen her naked enough times to know that despite her size there was not an ounce of spare flesh on her body. However Martha took her exercise (both women suspected it was mostly in bed), her body was in good condition.

"For the time being," Ned said, "let's concentrate on making the Dons nervous."

"So you've decided to make them jumpy, eh Ned?"

"Nervous people are more likely to make mistakes," he said portentously and hoped no one would ask what Spanish mistakes would help the buccaneers.

"What had you in mind?"

Ned remembered Couperin and his deputy going out in the garden to sit in the shade of the palms while Ned talked with Thomas and Saxby, and he remembered the gentle thud and emphatic curse as a ripe coconut fell from a tree, apparently just missing His Excellency. Coconuts floated down with the current; even in bright sunshine they could be mistaken for men's heads in the water, while at night it was impossible to distinguish – as many a buccaneer sentry had found to his embarrassment.

Were there any palm trees on the eastern side of Gallows Bay? No, there were tamarinds on the ridge of hills along the eastern side of the bay, and thick mangroves lined the shore. So floating coconuts were not a regular sight. With a little luck the Spanish sentries might never yet have seen any: raw seamen might not recognize a coconut even if it dropped on their head.

Ned sat upright on the settee and said: "The first thing we must do this afternoon, after giving His Excellency time for his *siesta*, is to make sure he is joining us, and agreeing to our terms."

"What are they?" Diana asked.

"Two dozen fishing boats and a hundred men, that's the equivalent of a ship. And two hundred coconuts delivered at night to the eastern shore of Gallows Bay. To windward of the galleon, in other words."

"Are we going into the bumboat business?" Thomas asked with a grin, "with Martha selling coconuts to the Dons? 'Sucking the monkey' the Navy calls it," he explained. "Some Navy captains won't allow hot liquors on board their ships, but don't mind bumboats selling fruit and vegetables. What you do, Martha, is strip the husks off the coconuts, pierce them and drain off the milk, then pour in rum. The sailors pay a good price because their officers don't mind them drinking coconut milk."

"'Sucking the monkey' indeed," Martha said scornfully. "If I'm going into trade with the Dons I've got more profitable things to sell than coconuts filled with rumbullion!"

"Indeed you have," Ned said, "but for the moment let's write down the scale for Couperin. Treat him as the captain of a single ship with a hundred men. That gives him roughly a quarter share."

"But he's only got fishing boats!" Thomas protested.

"And if all of them are lost, Couperin has to compensate the fishermen," Ned pointed out. "I doubt if much suitable wood for boatbuilding grows on this island. Ah," he looked up as the steward knocked on the door and announced he was ready to serve the first course.

Mosquitoes whined so loudly that they seemed to be right inside each man's ears. They rose in noisy swarms the moment he touched a bush, and walking along the narrow strip of sand between the mangroves and the sea stirred up sandflies, the tiny insects nicknamed 'no-see-'ems', whose bite was like the jab of red hot needles. Among the bushes on the hills behind them, goats and their kids protested at being disturbed in high-pitched bleats that, Thomas swore, could be heard over Anguilla.

Charles Couperin muttered to Ned: "You think we have enough coconuts?"

"Yes, and send your men away with those donkeys. If one of them starts hee-hawing the rest will follow, and we don't want a 'Donkey's Chorus' just at the moment so the Dons know we're here."

The Governor General gave the order and then came back

to Ned. "You have a – how do you say, a whimsical attitude, *m'sieur.* And your friend, Sir Thomas."

Ned remembered Charles Couperin's sober approach when they proposed he joined the buccaneers on a shares-of-the-purchase basis. The Frenchman seemed to walk round the idea for an hour, inspecting it from every angle, while his deputy walked round the opposite way. As Thomas commented drily afterwards, they wasted sixty minutes making a one-minute decision. "On your deathbed you might have been glad of those fifty-nine minutes," he told Couperin, who did not laugh.

"Whimsical? Perhaps. I suppose we'd prefer to die laughing than weeping."

"I prefer to stay alive," Couperin said, obviously puzzled.

"Ah, who doesn't," Ned agreed, "but we live in a wicked world and often don't have the choice. And make no mistake," he said quietly, "although we may say something lightly, usually a good deal of thought has gone into the idea."

"We realize that," Couperin said. "In fact that's why we took so long to make up our minds," he admitted frankly.

Ned, suddenly irritated, said: "I make it a rule never to trust a man who doesn't trust me." He intended the remark to be a warning to Couperin and added: "There are more than thirty buccaneer captains. Any one of them could betray the others, but we don't fear betrayal because we know we all have the same object..."

"Yes, I understand that now," Couperin said soberly.

Thomas left a pile of coconuts on the sand and walked up to Ned. "The wind's damned light – we're right in the lee of the hill – it's making the wind go over our heads."

"I know, but it's the current that's going to do all the work. The current is quite strong off the end of the headland – and it curves into the bay, right on to the galleon."

"How the Devil d'you know that?"

"While you were unloading the coconuts from the donkeys' panniers, I walked to the end of the point, threw sticks into the water and watched them drift."

"Hmmm, so now we have to shift all those blasted coconuts out to the end of the headland?"

"Yes, you'd unloaded them before I found out. Anyway,

:'s take three or four each and try 'em. They might drift dif-
rently from sticks."

"I think not," the Frenchman offered.

"Neither do I," Ned said, "but it all helps keep Sir Thomas
a good humour."

There was a brief pause while Couperin digested Ned's
ords and realized there had been no protest from Sir
iomas. "Ah yes, that is most important."

He walked with the two men and picked up an armful
coconuts. Land crabs scurried out of the way, disappear-
g down their holes, for which the men kept a wary
e: although many were large enough for coneys,
e holes usually went down vertically so that instead of
pping a walking man they were more likely to break his
kle.

As they trudged towards the headland, Anguilla was sit-
ıg in the darkness out of sight ahead of them, Gallows Bay
ı their left with the galleon in the middle, and Marigot town
as beyond over their left shoulder.

"Coconuts," Thomas muttered to himself, "we bombard
m with coconuts. If the King of Spain ever hears about this,
'll surrender, or die laughing."

"If it works," Ned said softly, "a lot of the King's officials
ill be punished with a garotte round their neck. I'm sure the
ing gets very haughty when he hears that buccaneers are
ending his money!"

Couperin laughed. Yes, he was beginning to understand
ese Englishmen. Joking passed the time; they were nearly at
e end of the headland and, listening to them, he had not felt
rvous. He had not thought once about the prospect of
ing recalled to Paris. Not until this moment, anyway, and
seemed a good deal less likely. Perhaps there was something
this light-hearted approach after all. Certainly he felt all the
tter for having made his deputy stay behind in the town.
iat gloomy face always seemed full of reproach. Was he
Couperin was startled that he had never thought of it before)
informer? Did he report secretly to Paris on the Governor
eneral's activities? As he stumbled along in the darkness
ouperin remembered reproofs from Paris, and often he had
en puzzled how they could have known. Yes, it was that
mned deputy! He recalled half a dozen episodes where only

he and the deputy had known of them, yet the repriman
had arrived.

Now, *parbleu*, the damnable deputy knew all about the ga
leon, and although he didn't know about the buccaneers' pr
cise plans, he knew what it was intended to do with t
bullion if they succeeded in getting it. If Paris ever receive
even a hint . . . well, Charles Couperin would never see h
vineyards again. The deputy, Couperin thought (with
light-heartedness previously alien to his nature), will have
meet with an accident . . . A bar of gold might fall on h
head! Couperin giggled to himself. Killed by his own gree
What a good epitaph. It was surprising how quickly the cen
etery up the hill was filling. Fevers, too much drink, drunke
quarrels . . . it was extraordinary how everything was final
resolved in the churchyard up the hill, just below the battery

By now they had reached the headland and Ned led the wa
out to the furthest rock, first placing his coconuts on tc
before scrambling up.

He picked up a coconut, looked round carefully to see ho
much room he had, and hurled the nut seaward as far as
could. He stood still, watching it. Then he threw two more
quick succession, and Thomas said: "Quite amazing ho
they show up, Ned. From down here they look just like me
swimming. The waves are just high enough to give them t
right amount of movement. We should have painted faces c
them!"

"If the Spaniards suddenly spotted a dozen men swimmir
towards them facing the wrong way, they might be puzzled

"All right," Thomas said, "no faces. Here are some mo
nuts."

Ned threw them in and, a couple of minutes later, adde
Couperin's armful to the flotilla which current and wind ca
ried across the bay in a gentle curve towards the black hulk
the galleon.

"Have the men bring up the rest of those coconuts, ar
pick someone with a strong arm to take my place up here
Before jumping down on to the sand, Ned stared into t
darkness. Yes, it was easy enough to see the coconuts and ye
they did look like human heads. Would they fool a Spanis
sentry on board the galleon? Would the sentry be awak
Would there even *be* a sentry?

"If those sentries don't sight the coconuts," he commented to Couperin," then it'll be our enemy's incompetence that wrecks our plan . . . !"

"You are likely to be disappointed." Couperin said. "No respectable Latin would anticipate an attack at night. Only you English (and perhaps the Dutch) could be so –" he groped for the word, "– so ungentlemanly."

All the coconuts had been launched from the rock and the long curve of black balls stretched down towards the galleon, watched by Ned, Thomas and Couperin and the half dozen seamen from the *Griffin* who had volunteered to help handle the donkeys.

Couperin paused in his pacing up and down the beach and said, almost accusingly: "It didn't work. All that trouble finding donkeys and collecting coconuts, and losing a night's sleep –" he scratched himself vigorously, "– getting eaten by the mosquitoes – to what purpose, I ask you: what good has it done?"

"Well, I don't know," Thomas drawled. "Let's see. We now know the set of the current into Gallows Bay, which even the Governor General didn't know before. We have discovered that thousands of land crabs live along this beach. We –"

"What the devil does all this matter?" Couperin asked angrily.

"Did you know whether or not the Spaniards kept sentries on duty at night?" Ned asked mildly.

"Well, no, not for certain."

"Don't you regard that as useful and important information?"

"Well, only if you are making a night attack," Couperin said doubtfully.

"You'd attack in daylight?" Ned inquired innocently and incredulously.

"As I have neither ships nor trained men, I can't attack at all; you know that!"

Ned paused for a moment. "I was wrong: they do have sentries!"

Across the bay they could now just hear voices shouting and then, making them all jump because they had been talking with lowered voices, a single shot rang out, the noise echoing round the bay, followed by a dozen more. Tiny winking red eyes along the galleon's upperdeck showed more men firing with muskets and pistols.

"Sentries – and at least a couple of dozen men either on watch or sleeping near their guns."

"Well," Couperin asked, and Ned thought the man was chastened, "what have we achieved *now*?"

"That I forecast the result of the race too soon," Ned said cheerfully. "They do have sentries, and men are on duty near their muskets. That means that they fear some sort of attack – and thought a couple o' hundred swimmers were about to swarm on board . . . which in turn indicates they don't know what the Devil is going to happen."

"And what is going to happen?" Couperin asked.

"Nothing much, until you've got rid of your deputy," Ned said evenly. "None of us like him very much. Don't forget you are the extra captain we've accepted into the Brethren for this job, and you can guess what happens to anyone we trust who then betrays us . . ."

Chapter Sixteen

"What will you do if Couperin doesn't sack that fellow?" Thomas asked as he and Ned paced the *Griffin*'s quarterdeck. "After all, the man may have been appointed by the authorities in Paris. Perhaps Couperin can't sack him."

"Well, we'll keep an eye on him. If necessary, he'll meet with an accident. It needn't be fatal . . ."

Diana came up with Aurelia. Both the women had been delighted with the story of the Spaniards fighting off the coconut attack: both were enchanted with the anchorage in Marigot. St Martin was different from the other islands. Diana said, "because the hills are softer and warmer. More curved. You don't get the feeling of jagged rock lying just underneath everything."

Aurelia agreed. "Think of Antigua – there the hills are lower anyway, but they're nearly always parched brown. Somehow – well, Antigua always seems to be a cringing beggar with his hands outstretched. And so many mosquitoes and sandflies; more than anywhere else."

"Marigot," Diana said dreamily. "I'll always remember it along with a couple of bays in Grenada." She let her memories move northwards, up the island chain. "St Vincent – nowhere there; Cumberland Bay always frightens me; I imagine voodoo and disease and death. St Lucia – beauty and corruption, like a lovely whore with a vile disease. Martinique – yes, a few bays. Dominica – those glorious rain forests but all the *rain* – no wonder the Spanish plate fleet coming from Spain often used to water there. Guadeloupe – no, nor

Antigua. Montserrat – all rocks and cliffs, and always the shi rolls. Nevis – yes, *that's* a beautiful island – the slope up to th top of the old volcano. That glorious sweep down from th top and then northwards to the beaches, as though an artis did it with a brush. We once sailed right round the island an you could see all the plantations spread out on the slopes, lik patterns on a quilt."

Aurelia nodded in agreement. "We were sailing up the wes coast of St Christophe one morning just before dawn. Gradually the island took on a lovely pink glow as the sun came u behind the island. The pink glow gave way to all the green and browns but there were still shadows giving shape to th valleys. And the little wisps of smoke showing where the villages and plantation houses were just waking up to begin th day. So beautiful . . . it makes me want to cry just to think o it. Why does one want to cry when remembering happ days?"

"Afraid they won't ever come back, probably," Ned sai gruffly. "Now change the subject or you'll have *me* in tears: remember that morning. Not a breath of wind; just th north-going current carrying us along."

Thomas sighed and looked at Diana. "Remember thos mornings in Cuba? Among the cays in the Queen's Gardens?" He explained to Ned and Aurelia: "Not a breath o wind, the fish jumping, the pelicans flying past and divin and seeming to wink, as though we were all in a big conspiracy to steal fish from the Spanish. You could see the sand bottom clearly at fifty feet: conches crawling along dow there, leaving trails; barracudas keeping still in the water hovering until they saw a target – then they'd be off like silve arrows. And dozens of other fish, some only the size of piece of eight. And such colours you'd hardly believe. Ther was a little one of such a blue that if you gave a king a cloak o that colour he would make you a duke on the spot (and th queen would probably poison your wine out of jealousy) The coral – all shapes and sizes, and it grows like great hedge under the sea. Oh well," he said, embarrassed by his enthusiasm, "you two have seen it all as well."

"A sensitive little heart beats strongly under that tattere jerkin," Diana said wryly. "Thomas likes to beat his ches from time to time, but it's like a cockerel strutting."

"If you go on like that," Thomas warned, "I'll talk about an old hen losing her feathers!"

"The galleon," Aurelia said. "Now we've alarmed the Dons with coconuts have you decided what to do about transferring the bullion?"

"Well, I know you think the coconuts were a great joke, but you may find they were worth ten thousand times their weight in gold."

A startled Thomas turned and stared at Ned. "You mean you really *do* have a plan?"

"If we find it works, then we'll say I had a plan. If it doesn't work, it was only an idea."

"Ned, my dear," Diana said sternly, "we don't care whether it's a dream or a nightmare, just tell us about it. Aurelia and I can't wait to look at all those emeralds they'll have from the province of Columbia, and the pearls from the island of Margarita. 'Margarita' is Spanish for pearl, by the way. We don't really love you, you know; we just collect jewellery – and gold, of course. We are not very keen on silver – too much polishing. But gems, big and bright, and well mounted in gold. Yes, necklaces and bracelets and rings . . ."

"It seems that if we dig deep enough we'll find your hearts under a pile of bullion and emeralds," Thomas growled. "An upsetting thought for someone with as sensitive a little heart as me, throbbing away under this jerkin."

"That idea," Aurelia reminded Ned. "Let's sit down under the awning and hear about it. Is it funny like the coconuts or serious, like rescuing Diana and Thomas at San Germán?"

That afternoon, after picking up Saxby on the way, Ned and Thomas were rowed in to the small jetty at Marigot. The little town was hot: the few houses seemed to act as ovens, while the big hill with the gun battery perched on top cut off the easterly breeze which had cooled them on board the ships anchored further out.

There was just enough wind several feet above the ground to rustle the tops of the palms, but the dogs and the pigs dozed contentedly wherever they could find shade. A pile of empty conch shells, a dapple of vivid pinks and yellows edging into browns, was a buzzing mass of flies. The fisherman who

dived them up had not cut the muscle holding in the animal a
the right spot, so that as each conch was wrenched from it
shell a small amount of the meat stayed in the pointed spire o
the shell, where the sun's heat soon rotted it and the stench, a
Saxby commented sourly, brought over all the flies whic
had been on duty on the other side of the village.

They found Couperin at his house looking tired, unstead
on his feet and with an onion-shaped bottle and a glazed pot
tery mug on a small table beside his rattan chair.

Once the handshaking was completed, Couperin motione
them to sit down in the other chairs. When Ned commente
that he looked pale and hoped he had not picked up a fever
Couperin shook his head. "There's a lot of work for on
man," he said, and Ned thought there was a curious inflexio
in his voice.

"You must leave more of the routine to your deputy," h
said.

Couperin shook his head sadly. "Ah, there's the tragedy,"
he said. "I have no deputy until another is appointed by Paris
My original deputy, the one you met, had an accident thi
morning. A fatal accident."

"How distressing," Ned said. "What happened, pray?"

"Thrown by his horse, poor fellow. The groom brought i
round to his door, he stood on the mounting block, and a
soon as he was astride the horse, it threw him. Broke hi
neck."

"Probably a piece of cactus under the saddle cloth,"
Thomas said politely. "It happens, I know. The rider'
sudden weight makes it jab the horse."

"Yes," Couperin said, "I'm sure that's what happened. Th
funeral is tomorrow."

"He was Catholic?"

Couperin nodded, and Ned knew that the formalities wer
now over: the deputy was dead, the funeral was arranged sc
there was no suspicion of foul play, and it was acknowledgec
that the buccaneers, being Protestant, need not attend the service.

"The galleon," Couperin said, looking at Ned hazily anc
forgetting to offer them drinks. "How are we going to dea
with the Spaniards?"

"Ah, first of all I must thank you for the coconuts."

Couperin's jaw dropped. "Oh, of course, you are more than welcome. If you want more . . ."

"Thank you," Ned said politely, "I know I have only to ask."

Couperin nodded, took a sip from his mug, and looked up at Ned. "You were going to . . ." he prompted.

"Ah yes, the Spaniards. That's what reminded me of the coconuts." He settled comfortably in his chair, the rattan squeaking in protest, showing it was both old and rarely used. "Well, we've seen that the ship has a total of forty-four carriage guns. There'll be a couple of dozen smaller guns that they mount on the bulwarks. Two hundred men, would you not agree? Ah, yes. Each with a pistol or musket. Well, perhaps not all: say one hundred and fifty. And the same number of swords – daggers, too, I expect."

Couperin nodded. "Yes. My estimate was higher, for both men and guns, but I had forgotten the smaller guns."

"And how many men can you muster?"

Couperin shrugged his shoulders. "Given a few days – two or three, anyway – about forty. Thirty, anyway. That includes the fishermen."

"We can land about two hundred men. They rather outnumber your thirty," Ned said pointedly, and watched as Couperin divided thirty into two hundred.

The Frenchman realized that Yorke, Saxby and Whetstone were together providing two hundred men. Each captain, he thought, was like a Roman centurion: he had (almost) a century of men. Each captain, that was, except himself, the Governor.

Couperin, thinking of his thirty, was thankful that Yorke had not asked him (yet, anyway) if the men would be armed. There were perhaps twenty muskets and ten pistols in St Martin, and he dreaded to think of the condition of the powder: it would be damp and caking. The slowmatch for the locks . . . well, better not to think about it.

"And weapons?" Ned asked.

Couperin decided there was no point in prevaricating: Yorke had the kind of eyes that could see through a greenheart plank. "Twenty muskets, ten pistols, poor powder, doubtful slowmatch," he said. "Swords of course, and we have the three cannon up in the bastion."

"Three canons equal one bishop," Ned said and as Saxb and Thomas laughed, Ned explained to a puzzled Couperin "A complicated sort of joke, A cannon, spelled with tw 'n's', is of course a gun. With one 'n' it is a religious rank."

Couperin laughed heartily and then said: "We use only on 'n' in French: *droit canon* – that's what the ecclesiastics ca 'canon law'. Cannon law and canon law – ha, the Spanish wi notice the difference! You are a *drôle* fellow, *M'sieur* Yorke. use the word in the English sense."

He lifted his mug, still not realizing that the other men ha nothing to drink. "I give you a toast – to much *drôlerie*! May i make us rich!"

"Yes, indeed," Ned said. "Which reminds me. We agree earlier that if you joined us, you would have a quarter share."

"Yes, a quarter," Couperin said, clearly doing his sum again. Thirty men as a proportion of two hundred. Sadly h watched his quarter shrink to a sixth, thought again and the smiled. A sixth of all the treasure in that galleon would stil leave him a very rich man, and now there was no deputy t share in it. Just small rewards for the thirty or so men and th fishermen. A sixth of the sixth would keep them quiet.

Couperin felt faint when Ned nodded. "Very well, w agreed on a quarter, even though we expected you to provid more men. Still, it may not matter now. And what I an going to tell you is for your ears only. Do not repeat it t anyone."

Ned finally jumped down from the breech of the aftermos gun on the *Griffin*'s starboard side, his voice hoarse fron having explained for the third time (once to each ship) th plan of attack. Just as his feet hit the deck, Lobb called an pointed towards the western headland forming the bay. Further out to sea, obviously tacking towards Anguilla befor tacking in again for Marigot, was a ship.

Ned grabbed the perspective glass which Aurelia ha snatched from the binnacle box drawer, pulled out the tube t the ring marking the correct focus for his eyes and examine the vessel.

She was perhaps half the size of the *Phoenix*. Heavy laden – her hull so low in the water that the waves, not particularly high, were occasionally sweeping over her foredeck. Guns –

gun port aft, so perhaps two guns. Just a small trading sloop bound for Marigot with a mixed cargo from somewhere. Then as he was going to take the glass from his eye, he caught sight of a second sail, another vessel on the same course and perhaps half a mile behind the first.

Not so heavily laden, about the same size, and armed with four guns, and neither ship flying any flag. Sailing in company "for mutual protection" – that made sense in these waters where anyone with a ship who was short of money could indulge in piracy. And, the Devil take it, a third sail! Three sloops bound for Marigot. They were not intending to go to Road Harbour, on the north side of Anguillia, because hey were hard on the wind, whereas they would ease sheets if they wanted to round Anguilla, at the western end of the island.

He handed the glass to Lobb. "Tell the men to forget what I've just said. My throat's too sore to raise my voice again."

With that he went down to the cabin, followed by Aurelia. "What ships are they?"

He realized that apart from his instruction to Lobb, he had not spoken a word. "Nothing to worry about," he said reassuringly. "Three small trading vessels bringing cargo to Marigot. Half a dozen men in each of them and they're heavily laden."

"What cargoes? Not salt, because they have their own salt pans here."

Ned shrugged his shoulders. "Potatoes? I haven't seen any growing here. Cattle, horses, hogs – not much land here for farming."

"But you told Lobb to tell the men to forget what you've just said," Aurelia reminded him. "Why should the arrival of these three sloops affect your plan?"

"Damned if I know until they get here," Ned admitted, "but it might mean Couperin has a few more men. They won't be in for another two hours and by the time they've gone on shore and Couperin has enough details to tell us about them, it'll be much too late for us to do anything tonight. That reminds me, I must send over to Thomas and Saxby and tell them of the delay."

"Don't forget those Spaniards coming from Cartagena,

Ned," Aurelia said anxiously. "You've said you think they'll send several ships . . ."

Ned shook his head. "Those chaps aren't the Dons: we've at least three days more before we see them, even if they made a fast passage in Couperin's ship. The wind has been brisk every day but it falls flat every night. You know what a wretched passage we had from Porto Rico, so you can imagine what a miserable sail it'll be from Cartagena to here: foul wind, foul current . . . and no doubt the bottoms of the Spanish ships so foul with barnacles and grass their speed is halved. Three days? More likely another week!"

"Where are you going now?" she asked as Ned buckled on his sword. "If you are going on shore I'm coming too: I need some exercise. And we can collect Diana on the way."

"I was just going to call on Couperin."

"M. Couperin is lucky," she said. "The way he looks at Diana and me, I suspect there are few women on this island, or St Kitts."

Couperin looked startled when he saw Ned, Thomas and the two women approaching his house along the narrow, sandy track. He hurried forward to greet them, kissing the hands of Diana and Aurelia in a way which reminded Ned that Aurelia's suspicions were obviously correct.

He waited until they were all in the house before asking Ned nervously: "Is there a difficulty? Have you changed the plan?"

Ned gestured towards the harbour. "For tonight, yes. Those three ships coming in – what are they?"

"Oh, just three sloops from St Christophe. Mine would have been with them, if those damnable Spaniards had not stolen her."

"What are they carrying?"

Couperin shrugged his shoulders. "The usual mixed cargo. They bring items needed here, but their most important job is carrying cargo from here to St Christophe. Hides, salt, some fruit . . . to be transferred to the next ship going to France. We never know when one will arrive, but we have warehouses in St Christophe where we can store it all."

"Fruit, for *France*?" Thomas asked.

Couperin laughed. "I'm sorry, I must correct myself.

hese ships – he waved seaward, "– bring pitch and casks for e people here to preserve the fruit."

Aurelia made some comment in French which Ned did not uite understand, but Couperin looked towards Diana and 'homas. "Excuse me, I will explain. In France such fruits as uava, prickly pear and prickly apple are rare delicacies for hich some people will pay a very high price. The only way f keeping them on the voyage across the Atlantic is to pick em before they are fully ripe, and then store them in a barrel ith pitch. The pitch, it seems, has properties that prevent e fruit from rotting without affecting the taste. Rather like lt preserving meat. Whereas we have our own salt pans – ost islands have – we have to bring up the pitch from Trini-ad. There's plenty there but getting it away from the Spa-iards is a problem. All of it is smuggled: that's why pitch is expensive."

Aurelia nodded in agreement. "We used to send some fruits England from Barbados packed with pitch in barrels. lthough the pitch is soft out here in this heat, it is brittle by e time it arrives in England and it is easy to break it away ithout damaging the fruit. If the fruit still isn't quite ripe, anging it up in a dark corner is enough."

"How much pitch will these ships be bringing?" Ned sked.

Couperin shrugged his shoulders. "Twenty barrels each, erhaps. Preserved fruit is a profitable luxury. Here in St Aartin they can grow fruit, and they can breed cattle for their ides. And there's salt. Sugar and tobacco – well, they grow ome sugar, but the tobacco smokes with an earthy taste, and he Dutch – who buy all they can – give such a poor price for that planters here are giving up tobacco altogether, except or their own needs."

"Hot waters," Ned said. "Do they make their own rum-ullion here in St Martin?"

Couperin shook his head, almost apologetically. "No, they ring it over from St Christophe. The three sloops you saw vill be carrying some, I expect."

"You are sure they're from St Christophe?" Ned asked asually.

"Oh yes, absolutely certain. As I said, mine should have een among them. They are owned by my friends."

"And as Governor General, in an emergency you can con mandeer the ships?"

"Well, I have the power to," Couperin admitted reluctan ly, "but you understand, they belong to my friends."

Ned nodded. "Your friends, but not ours. What you don commandeer, we can always take. You can always explain away to your friends as submitting to *force majeure* . . ."

"Yes, indeed: it would be a more tactful way," Couperi agreed.

"Just one ship, and part of some of the cargoes," Ned sai "That would be enough."

"Ah yes, *force majeure*. I shall have to make a formal prote to you, of course."

"Of course," Ned agreed. "In writing. As soon as we kno the name of the ships and can read the cargo manifests, we' draw up the protest. I'm sure Madame Wilson will make yo a fair copy – I would not care to trust my French."

Chapter Seventeen

Ned broke the seal of the letter from Charles Couperin and began reading. Couperin began with the names of the three ships – *Les Deux Sœurs* of Nantes, the *Sans Peur* of Toulon and the *Didon* of Honfleur. They had a total of twenty men on board, and he then listed the main items of their cargo. The *Didon* carried fifty-five barrels of pitch and the *Sans Peur* another twenty. The *Deux Sœurs* had mostly clothing – bundles of jerkins, breeches, stockings, hats, feathers and shirts, along with boots, not all intended for Marigot.

All three had bundles of barrel staves and hoops to be assembled in the island and used for carrying salt. The ships carried casks of rumbullion and one had a quantity of gin (Dutch, Couperin noted – presumably in case any of the English felt nostalgic about what foreigners regarded as the country's national drink).

Ned folded the letter and put it down, watched by Aurelia from the other side of the table. She gave him the whimsical, questioning smile that regularly made him fall in love with her again. "Well," she said, examining her finger nails, "what brilliant ideas has the Governor's letter stirred up in my lord and master?"

"Do you know Honfleur?" Ned asked unexpectedly.

"I've been there as a child, but I can't remember much about it. Tarred rope, rotting fish, paint, linseed oil – I seem to remember only smells. The ship's chandlers' shops fascinated me. I can't recall what they *looked* like, but what mysterious *smells*! Why do you ask? Honfleur must be as far from Paris as we are from Porto Rico!"

Ned waved towards the anchored sloops. "The *Didon* of Honfleur is just the ship we need."

"Stop talking in riddles!"

"I haven't put all my ideas together yet, but we need Thomas and Saxby over here, and their mates." He looked at Aurelia and grinned. "And Diana and Martha Judd too, of course."

While a boat went off with the message, Ned took out the inkwell and uncorked it, found a new quill and searched for his pen knife to cut a point, and then took a sheet of paper. He sketched the bay with Marigot at its eastern end, marked in the hill with the battery on top, and then drew in Gallows Bay, carrying the sweep round to include the headland from which they had launched the coconuts, naming it 'Coconut Point'. Then he marked in the position of the galleon.

After carefully wiping the quill and putting the cork back in the inkwell (and, after looking at his sketch, cursing that he had not shaken the bottle first: the ink was very faint), he shut his eyes and in his imagination pictured the night attack on the galleon. He was not conscious of Aurelia coming back to the cabin after telling Lobb to fetch the others, and she sat quietly sewing after tiptoeing round the table to look at the chart he had drawn.

When he opened his eyes, as though wakening from a brief nap, she looked at him with a raised eyebrow, and he smiled and nodded. "A plan. I'm not sure if it's practical, but I can't think of a better way of tackling it."

"You're going to set Martha Judd on to them?"

He sighed. "I thought of that, but poor Saxby'd be heart-broken if she went off with a handsome *hidalgo*."

"I see no alternative to leaving it to Martha," Aurelia said teasingly, hoping Ned would describe his plan. "It has to be a night attack but there's no moon. We'd need scaling ladders if we go alongside and try to board. They're expecting an attack and your coconut trick showed us their sentries are wide awake. And Couperin is frightened to death that the Spanish will bombard the town . . ."

"All looks hopeless, doesn't it?" Ned said blithely. "Let's leave all the gold and silver plate to Couperin, sail home to Jamaica and finish building our house."

"Oh you beast! Give me some hint!"

Ned looked down at his rough chart. "You'll hear all about it when the others arrive, but there are three main points. We've got to be able to *see* the galleon in the dark: we've got to be able to attack her: and we've got to take the Spaniards by surprise."

"Martha Judd, swimming out holding a candle – there you have it all: seeing, attacking and surprising. Aren't I a wonderful help?"

He walked round the table and kissed her. "We'll use some of the gold and silver to build a big church in Port Royal so that we can be married properly. In stone, and pews to hold a hundred. A minstrel's gallery. A peal of bronze bells. Have I forgotten anything?"

"Yes. I haven't yet agreed to marry you."

"A mere trifle," Ned said, kissing her again. "Ah, here they come: I can hear Thomas booming and Martha chiming. Let's go on deck and meet them."

After welcoming them on board, Ned pointed out the *Didon*. "Take note of her," he said. "Do you agree she looks the most weatherly of the trio?"

"All three must be reasonably weatherly," Thomas said. "After all, they crossed the Atlantic to get here!"

"She's the one I'd pick," Saxby said. "Why do you ask, sir: are we taking her as a prize?"

Ned laughed. "No, not a prize. Come below and pick holes in an idea I have. Couperin has sent out the cargo manifests – or at least an indication of what the three ships are carrying, and this idea occurred to me."

"I know," Thomas said, "we're all going to make our fortune by preserving guavas and bananas in pitch and sending them to London in the *Didon*. We'll also send Martha to set up a business at the Sign of the Golden Guava, next to Mr Wickes who sells hot waters to the gentry from his establishment at Black Friars, just by the Playhouse."

"You're not getting me back to England," Martha said emphatically. "Cromwell had me transported and I've been grateful ever since. Your uncle was a rogue in every other respect," she told Thomas, "but he got me out of the drizzle and cold into sunshine and warmth, and no one – not even you," she told Saxby, "will ever make me return to that miserable weather!"

"Well spoken." Ned said, "so Thomas will have to leave the guavas to rot on the trees. Now come on, we haven't a lot of time."

He sat at the head of the table and explained his plan, surprised at the end of it that everyone congratulated him and agreed it was the only possible one.

"There are three aspects as I see it," Thomas said, holding up three fingers. "The first is that there must be plenty of illumination, so that whoever is sailing the *Didon* can see where to go. But we can't wait for the moon." He folded one finger. "That leaves us with 'surprise' and 'means'. Only you could think of a way of surprising the Dons while they're actually watching us," he told Ned. "But I'm sure it'll work." He folded down the second finger, leaving only the index finger sticking up. "The means – well, as long as we don't have any trouble with Couperin, it should work. But we must remember there are enough Dons on board that galleon to seize Marigot."

"That did occur to me too," Ned admitted, "but even if they did they wouldn't stay. The ships are due here soon from Cartagena, and they'd take them back. The island is big enough for the French to hide in the mountains for a few days."

"We could have some of our men with muskets along the beach, just to discourage them," Saxby said. "Just enough to make them think Marigot is strongly held, so they'd keep away from the town."

"Yes, there are other bays to the eastward where they can be taken off by their friends from Cartagena," Ned said, "but our interest is getting the plate! Thomas, you and I had better go over and tell Couperin the glad news. In the meantime the rest of you can be getting your men ready."

He looked down at a list he had written. "Very well. Lobb, you will be responsible for lighting up the merry scene, so you'd better come on shore with us, and have a good look round. Saxby, you should start filling kegs and collecting boats." He looked up impatiently, listened to Martha and then glanced at Saxby, who shook his head helplessly. "Very well, Martha, you can go along with him. You can make sure the slowmatch doesn't go out. Now, Thomas – Mitchell and fifteen men had better get over to the *Didon*. You've got your list of what they need? Good. The *Didon* should be ready to sail within a couple of hours. Now Lobb should take ten men from the *Griffin* and ten from the *Phoenix*, all with muskets, and decide where he's going to place them, after dark. And remember, everyone must make dam' sure the Dons can't see anything you do. The galleon is behind the great hill, which Nature put there as a convenient screen. They can't see our three ships, nor the three sloops. They'll have seen the sloops arrive – and think no more than that: three small sloops laden with the usual cargoes."

Couperin listened to Ned describing the plan with all the enthusiasm of a man accused of murder listening to a hanging judge sum up the overwhelming evidence against him. Finally he shook his head. "I can't allow the *Didon* to be used like that."

Ned watched him without comment.

"And all those Spaniards! Why, you agreed there must be at least two hundred of them. They could capture Marigot – I've barely fifty men I can rely on!"

"That's twenty more than you mentioned when we were last here," Thomas commented sourly.

"And who is going to pay for all that cargo?"

Ned leaned forward. "I agree, Your Excellency. It is unfair to burden you with all this responsibility. After all, you will have to account to Paris for everything – ship, cargoes, perhaps even the capture of Marigot by the Spaniards for a few days."

Couperin looked relieved. "I am glad you understand the position I am in. I am sympathetic towards the Brethren of the Coast, and I admit I agreed to your earlier offer, but I must look after the interests of France –"

"And your own," Ned said sympathetically.

"– and of course my own responsibilities as Governor General of St Christophe and St Martin. Already I have had my own ship stolen. Commandeered, anyway, and I doubt if the Spanish will keep their word to return her. And I bear all this responsibility alone: since the unfortunate death of my deputy yesterday, I have no one to advise me."

"It is insupportable," Ned said gently, "and it is unfair of us to make these demands on you. The answer is clear to me, and I am sure you will agree. We cancel the agreement making you temporarily a member of the Brethren which entitled you to a quarter share. Thus no blame can rest on your shoulders. True, you won't get any of the purchase, but of course 'Nothing venture . . .'

"Instead of you commandeering the *Didon* and confiscating the few tons of cargo we need from the other two ships, we shall take all three ships as prizes, so they will go into the general purchase account. I am sure your friends are well insured, and no blame attaches to you: the vessels were captured by the buccaneers, and that's that – there was nothing you could do to prevent it."

By now Couperin, face drained white and hands shaking, was like the accused man after the judge had pronounced sentence. His dreams of gold and silver ingots, leather pouches of gems, even a few ornaments being given to him as his share of the purchase, with no one else to split it with (the original partner's funeral was being held tomorrow), had vanished. He had just talked himself out of a possible fortune.

"But . . . but well, surely –"

Ned interrupted him. "It is simple enough, Your Excellency. If you commandeer a French ship and a few tons of cargo, you stand a good chance of getting a fortune. But your duty to France, your sense of honour, your responsibility to your friends who own the *Didon*, all these prevent you from taking that chance. And believe me, Your Excellency, we respect your sentiments. You are a man of honour; we are but thieves sailing in from beyond the horizon." He stood up and bowed. "The only request I have, Your Excellency, is that since we told you our plan in good faith, you will in equal good faith not repeat it to a living soul."

"I – of course, Mr Yorke. I –"

"Otherwise," Ned said grimly, "there'll be a double funeral tomorrow."

Couperin leapt to his feet, his face now changing: gone was the look of fear, of apprehension and doubt. Ned stared at the man, unable to believe the sudden transformation.

"Monsieur Yorke, please: the *Didon* is requisitioned, along with whatever cargo you need from the other two ships. I will give the orders at once. All my men – fifty-two – are at your disposal: give me their orders and they will be carried out to the letter. There are times, *m'sieur*," he explained, "when Paris seems very near. Equally, there are times when Paris must be forgotten; when the emergencies we governors face are immediate and would never be understood by the *bufones* in Paris. Someone who has never been to these islands, who has never seen Spain's grip, can never understand."

Ned smiled and shook Couperin's hand. "London gives us the same problems. London and Paris – they could be on the moon for all the relevance they have. We live out here, *M'sieur* Couperin, and one must remember that. The Spaniards kill and rob us, not the elegant gentlemen in London and Paris."

He thought a moment. Fifty Frenchmen on the beach. Yes, that would save using men from the *Griffin* and the *Peleus*. Which in turn . . .

"Yes," he said, "so we are agreed: you help the Brethren and have a quarter share. In return we have the *Didon* and the cargoes we need, and your fifty men – led by you, eh?" When Couperin agreed, Ned gave him their instructions and then said: "Two good horses: you must give two of my men sound horses with good saddles. Can you do that? Not mules, horses."

"From my own stable," Couperin said eagerly.

"Good – have them waiting here for the men to collect tonight – any time from eight o'clock onwards. Eight o'clock our time," he emphasized, "not French time. *Everything* – success or failure, a fortune or our destruction – depends on those two horses. They have to gallop a mile in the darkness – less, in fact. But *gallop* they must!"

"Twenty miles if necessary," Couperin said. "You can trust me," and his eyes twinkled as he added, "this time."

Chapter Eighteen

Thomas bent over the binnacle, trying to read the heading in the faint light of a rush candle. "Who'd believe these dam' fools would use rush candles for the compass," he growled.

"I certainly would," Ned said, amused by Thomas's wrath. "No trader sails at night among these islands! They have more sense, since they can make every passage in daylight. I'm surprised there was even a candle in the holder!"

"I'll be glad when we get to Marigot," Thomas admitted frankly. "We don't have a good enough chart to take us round St Martin safely at night. We might as well be riding round the coast on horseback: we're just navigating from village to village. Let's hope the village opposite this island of Tintamarre still has some people awake and with lanterns alight."

"The channel is wide enough," Ned said unsympathetically. "I admit it's a dark night but you can just distinguish the shore."

"Just," Thomas growled. "In fact I can just make out Tintamarre. Once it's on our starboard quarter, we turn to larboard and then it is a dead run to Marigot. When do you want the two lanterns lit?"

"We have to start counting headlands as soon as we turn. Light the lanterns as we pass the village of Grand Case. Then there'll be four small headlands before we pass Coconut Point, about two miles. But before that our two horsemen should be able to spot the lights and start their gallop."

"That fellow Parker sits a horse well," Thomas said. "I was quite surprised."

Ned gave a dry laugh. "You surprise me, Thomas. Can't you guess what he was?"

"Ah, I see what you mean. A groom, or an ostler."

"A knight of the road – or so he claims. I can believe it, the way he tucks a brace of pistols in his belt and rides hunched up. Obviously you've never met a highwayman – not on the road, anyway."

"I haven't, though before I met Diana I thought about becoming one," Thomas admitted. "But as I'd lost everything at the gaming tables I hadn't enough money to buy a decent horse."

He looked down at the compass again and then peered into the darkness ahead of the *Didon*. He turned aft to speak to the man at the heavy tiller. "Stand by, we'll be wearing round to larboard in a couple of minutes."

Mitchell, the mate of the *Peleus*, was standing just in front of Thomas and received orders to prepare to trim the sails. Ned stood to one side, glad that for once he had no responsibility for handling the ship – not until the last few minutes, anyway. Once again they were skirting the French part, and he was alone with his plan.

He was a fool to be on board the *Didon*: he should have stayed in Marigot: it was there that things could (and almost certainly would) go wrong. To start with, supposing those two seamen with the horses did not spot the two lanterns which would be hoisted up the *Didon's* mast – or did not spot them until too late? Or else, as they galloped their horses put their feet into crab holes and broke their legs. And then Lobb, he thought – supposing his slowmatch goes out and he spends twenty minutes with flint and steel trying to light more tinder. And Couperin – can he be trusted to get his men into position – with muskets (provided by the buccaneers)?

What about Saxby and Martha Judd – had they made all their preparations and were they ready in position? If the horsemen and Lobb were the most important part of the plan, then Saxby and his men came next. And after Saxby – well, after Saxby, it was up to Ned Yorke. It was Ned Yorke's plan and like the hero in the last scene of a play, the last move of all, the one which meant success or failure, was to be handled by Ned Yorke.

He began to feel sorry for himself just as the helmsman and his mate leaned on the tiller, the sails flapped wildly and then filled with a thud on the other tack, and Ned could just make out a darker line in the night which was the north-eastern corner of St Martin.

"Time for the axes," he reminded Thomas.

Thomas bellowed at the dozen men waiting abreast the mainmast, sleeping in the lee of the hatch coaming. They jumped up and quickly began knocking out the wedges jamming the long battens that held down the tarpaulin over the cargo hatch. The tarpaulin was hauled off and while one man began cutting it into strips, the others lifted off the planks of the hatch cover. Quickly they chopped and split the planks into three-foot lengths and dropped them down into the hold and then tossed in the strips of tarpaulin.

"Carry on!" Thomas shouted, and the men began hacking at the deck planking with their axes. In the darkness Ned could only hear and feel, through the thudding of the planks on which he stood, that the men were working quickly and, judging from the ribald remarks, confidently, cutting small holes every few feet.

The men with the axes had finished their work and Mitchell was standing by with two lanterns when Thomas announced: "That's Grand Case on our larboard beam. That nearer black shape is Crole Rock, which stands tall a few hundred yards off the shore. Grand Case is just to the west of it – there's quite a bay here, like the one at Marigot. But we're steering a steady course and we'll pick up the headland at the end of the bay. That's the headland where we hoist the lanterns."

"Let's get 'em lit, then," Ned said. "Is the halyard ready to hoist them?"

"I checked it an hour ago, sir," Mitchell reported.

Ned saw the man's face lit up by the first of the lanterns. Mitchell waited a few moments to make sure the wick was drawing well and not smoking, and then shut the door and, in the light from the window, lit the second lantern. He then picked them both up and, calling to two seamen, walked forward ready to hoist them.

"Hoist away!" Ned called.

"I don't know if the fellows at Coconut Point will see 'em,"

Thomas grumbled, "but they've damned well blinded me. Can't see a thing."

"Always keep one eye shut when there's a light around," Ned advised. "Then, when the light's gone, you can still see in the darkness when you open that eye."

Thomas sniffed. "You were a bit late with that advice. It's the sort of thing a highwayman would know."

"Just as well you couldn't afford to buy that horse," Ned said, and heard the squeak of rope rendering through a block as the lanterns were hoisted up.

"They'll see them on Coconut Point all right," Ned said. "Look, they're even lighting up the foredeck and reflecting on the bow wave."

"There's just enough phosphorescence along here to help too," Thomas commented. "We must be making five knots – there, see how that surge sent out the bow wave and the phosphorescence is as bright as a couple of coach lanterns! I hope those two men got out to Coconut Point all right. All those land crab holes. Worse than hunting across land riddled with coney warrens."

"The men are probably perfectly safe," Ned said reassuringly, although made nervous that Thomas's fears ran parallel with his own. "They're probably out on the point, asleep in the lee of a large rock. Or else keeping up their courage with rumbullion."

"Ned, don't joke about such things. They *could* be asleep or they *could* be sucking at a bottle of rumbullion like a lamb at its mother's teats."

"Well, there's nothing we can do about it now," Ned said, "so remember what we told Couperin. *Drôle*, Thomas, stay *drôle*: all else is madness – as you well know."

"That's the headland at the end of Grand Case bay," Thomas said. "So start counting – one, and three more to go to Coconut Point."

Although the wind was light and steady, low swell waves creeping up under the wind waves on the starboard quarter made the *Didon* pitch at times so that as her bow dipped, she slowed momentarily until the wind, bulging her sails, thrust her forward again so that the bow wave chuckled. Cloud hid most of the stars although Ned had an occasional fleeting look at Orion's Belt and, low down on the starboard hand, the

Pole Star. If only it had been a clear night there would have been enough light from the stars to show up the land clearly. If only, Ned thought grimly. *If only* was another road leading to madness. If only there had been a moon . . . If only the galleon was smaller so the three ships could board . . . If only the Governor of Jamaica was not such a fool . . .

That is the second headland and, damnation, he could see the third and . . . the fourth, Coconut Point . . . and the sky over on the larboard bow is turning a faint pink and now going black again, becoming pink and then fading, as though someone is using a bellows to revive a dying fire.

"They were neither asleep nor drunk," Thomas grunted happily. "That's the only advantage of a dark night – a lantern shows up better." He moved closer to Ned and whispered: "You know, I think I'm more nervous than I was sitting in that dam' chair at San Germán staring at the garotte!"

"I should think so, too," Ned said drily. "All you had to lose then was your life; now all our gold and silver is at risk!"

"Those two lads must have spotted the lanterns the moment we hoisted them and then galloped like the wind round to Lobb," Thomas commented. "Those land crab holes . . . there must be hundreds of them between the point and the track round to Marigot."

Ned watched the pink of the western sky gradually deepening into an angry red, pulsing like a severed vein. The glow was not only growing larger but beginning to burn steadily.

"Lobb has done a splendid job – lighting all the scrub on the hill couldn't have been easy. I wonder if they pulled those three cannon clear? The battery and carriages are just a pile of rotten wood, but the guns themselves can be remounted. It might be quite a blaze. I thought he was just boasting when he told me he was going to set everything alight from the beach right up to the top of the hill!"

"It's quite a blaze all right!" Thomas said. "I can distinguish your features, and we've still a headland before we reach Coconut Point. By Jove," he exclaimed, "Saxby can probably see us by now! Let's hope the Dons don't spot *him*!"

"They'll be too puzzled about what's going on at the hill – at least I hope so. Look, that's Coconut Point – three palm trees, then the two rocks. You'd better get the men below. Mitchell! Lower those lanterns!"

The halyard squealed in the block aloft as the lanterns swayed down to the deck, and Mitchell and another seaman hurriedly untied the knots.

"What about Saxby?" Thomas exclaimed.

"If he hasn't already seen us, he'll soon spot us in the light from Lobb's bonfire as we round the point. Don't forget, he only starts five minutes early. Sorry, three minutes – though how he'll be able to judge that accurately I don't know!"

"He can see the point, he'll see us, and he can see the galleon. He knows what we're trying to do and he knows what his job is. So don't worry – don't forget Martha's with him!"

"Ah," Ned said with a melodramatic sigh of relief, "I'd forgotten her."

"Not sure Diana'll ever forgive me," Thomas muttered. "When she heard that Martha was going with Saxby and I told her she couldn't come with us . . ."

"I had the same trouble with Aurelia," Ned admitted, "but I left her in command of the *Griffin*. Not that she was very impressed by that. Thomas! Just look at those flames – if we can see them they must have reached the top of the hill. I think you'd better go to the hold – I see Mitchell's already down there with the lanterns. Check the draught."

Thomas hurried forward and Ned saw him swing a leg over the coaming and then scramble down the ladder into the hold. Ned found himself alone on the *Didon's* deck, apart from the two men at the tiller behind him.

"Can you see Coconut Point?"

"Aye, sir, see it fine. Pass it fifty yards orf, y' said?"

"There's deep water up to the two rocks, so take it as close as you like."

Ned knew he was talking for the sake of it: the men at the tiller knew exactly what to do. And now the *Didon* was passing the last headland before Coconut Point: it would all be over, one way or the other, in the next ten minutes, and the breeze chilled the perspiration on his brow. At least, he blamed it on the breeze.

Very well, so far – *so far*, remember – the horsemen at Coconut Point had done their job, and so had Lobb: the whole hillside was ablaze and lighting up Gallows Bay and the galleon, just as he had planned. He should – should be damned, he certainly *would* – be able to see the galleon very clearly the moment he reached Coconut Point and began steering round into Gallows Bay. Saxby should see the *Didon* approaching and, as Thomas had forcibly reminded him, be able to judge distances without fiddling around with minutes. That left Charles Couperin – was he ready on the beach with his fifty-two men and muskets provided by the buccaneers, ready to defend their town – if town was not too grandiose a title for the village? Large village, anyway.

And on the other side of the blazing hill, unable to see what the Devil was going on and probably dying a thousand deaths from worry, Aurelia was in the *Griffin* without even Lobb to talk to, and Diana was on board the *Peleus*, without even Mitchell. Martha and Saxby were the lucky couple – if sitting amidst all that gunpowder, holding slowmatch, could be considered lucky.

A couple of hundred yards. He hurried forward and leaned over the edge of the hatch coaming. Down in the hold, looking like prancing devils in the flickering lanternlight, were a dozen seamen, Mitchell and Thomas. They were pulling at barrels, tugging strips of tarpaulin as though rearranging the bedclothes of a loved one (but for all that giving the impression of men who had done their job properly and were now just adding a little gilding to what they knew was a lily).

"All ready?" Ned asked.

"All ready!" Thomas called back, "and the draught's fine; just look at those lanterns flickering!"

"We're a hundred yards from Coconut Point . . ."

"Not so many mosquitoes as the last time we were here!" Thomas commented.

Ned moved to the bulwark on the larboard side. It seemed he could almost touch the low cliffs, but a glance forward showed that the *Didon* would pass well clear of the two rocks. Fifty yards to Coconut Point. He could make out the colours of the leaves – Lobb's blaze would be seen in Anguilla, he thought, though what they'd make of it over there . . .

Twenty-five yards – and then with startling suddenness the *Didon* had passed the point and the whole of Gallows Bay opened up: there was the blazing hillside, a livid and pulsating red and yellow inverted cone, and there, squatting in the centre of the bay like a small, steep-sided island, black and menacing with shadows flickering across it, was the galleon.

No one on board was firing a cannon or a musket: with luck, the Dons might still be thinking the hill was burning because of someone's carelessness. Yes, the galleon's people were not alarmed: her four boats still drifted on their painters at her bow; her stern still faced the east and all was well.

Suddenly a huge red eye, like the setting sun, winked a mile over on the *Didon*'s starboard bow and as far to seaward of the galleon. A few moments later the thunder of an enormous explosion bounded among the mountains and then echoed and re-echoed back again. The rumbling had hardly died away when a second red eye winked in almost the same position and the noise of the explosion boomed across the bay to lose itself among the mountain peaks, and it seemed to Ned that both the *Didon* and the galleon trembled.

"Come round two points to larboard!" he shouted at the men at the tiller and hurried to the coaming. "Right ho, Thomas, start it up!"

"Saxby seems to have timed that right!" Thomas shouted. "Sounded as though we'd get our sides stove in. Ah!" he bellowed as the third explosion echoed across the bay and Ned saw red pinpoints along the galleon's side: startled Spaniards were now firing muskets in the direction of the explosions as though expecting an attack from seaward.

Now the galleon was dead ahead. The *Didon* was slowing as the short peninsula ending in Coconut Point cut off some of the wind, but Ned was thankful: it gave him extra seconds to pull himself together and more time for Thomas to make sure everything was going well in the hold.

A sudden thought struck him and he hurried aft, past the startled helmsmen, and stared over the taffrail into the *Didon*'s wake. Yes, her boat was still towing there safely, like a puppy on a leash.

Suddenly Thomas was standing beside him and men were tumbling out of the cargo hatch. "A minute to go," Thomas gasped, looking over the bow, "and we've timed it beautifully, by God!"

A fourth explosion boomed to seaward and the rattle of the Spanish muskets, firing at they knew not what, now sounded so loud that Ned's ears rather than his eyes warned him. Then he realized that, able to see only her transom, he had misjudged the distance: the *Didon* was a great deal closer than he had estimated, and Thomas had just made the same mistake.

"Into the boat, all of you!" Ned shouted, and as arranged Thomas moved to the tiller. "Come on, lads, haul in the painter and down into the boat and don't forget to keep an eye open for us!"

Dragging off his boots in case he had to swim, he watched the galleon's great black shape, stark now against the glowing red of the hill. "Come round to starboard, Thomas . . . that's enough . . . hold her there . . . Hurry, you men – you too, Mitchell, there's nothing more for you to do . . . Fine, Thomas, now larboard a point . . ."

And now there was smoke and flame roaring up from the *Didon*'s tiny cargo hatch and Ned was puzzled for a moment by the small red squares glowing at various places along the deck: then he remembered the men chopping with axes and Thomas's assurance that there was enough draught . . .

"The pitch and those bits of tarpaulin have caught all right!" Thomas shouted. "If we take much longer – that's the first of it," he exclaimed as a sudden flash of blazing rumbullion lit the *Didon*, "– if we don't get there dam' quickly it'll reach the powder which'll hoist us both into those hills!"

The *Didon* was rapidly turning into a floating torch and Ned cursed monotonously as the flames leaping up from the hatch almost blinded him. But there she was! "Helm hard over!" he shouted at Thomas and ran to help him at the tiller to swing the ship to larboard. Slowly – agonizingly slowly it seemed – the bow began to turn, and Ned was relieved that bowsprit and jibboom just cleared the galleon's quarter galleries. Then slowly, but inexorably, the sloop seemed to slide sideways to crash into the galleon's transom and stop, held there by the wind pressing on her sails.

Ned paused for a moment to make sure the *Didon* was definitely pinned, held by wind and current under the immense outward curve of the galleon's transom, and then he felt someone tugging his arm violently. "Come *on*, Ned!" Thomas yelled. "All that powder'll go up any second. Quick, over the side and –" he paused as the crackle of pistol shots overhead warned that the Spanish were firing down at them, still not understanding what was happening, or forgetting what El Draco had done to them half a century earlier off Calais.

"– over the side and swim for your life!" Thomas shouted again and, glancing back to make sure Ned was following, leapt on to the bulwark and jumped feet first into the sea.

Ned followed him. The water was warm! It was only in the few moments it took to drop into the sea that he had switched his mind from handling a fireship into swimming, and as he surfaced he saw, only a few feet away, the enormous bulk of the galleon with the *Didon* jammed across the transom like the fiery tail of a rocket.

Men were shouting in English and splashing showed that Thomas was swimming towards the noise. The world looked huge but absurdly distorted from sea level: there was the burning hill – glowing now, rather than flaming – and there was the galleon. And there was the *Didon*. He swam a few strokes and then stopped to watch the burning sloop. Acrid smoke from the pitch seemed to scorch the back of his throat – salt water and burning pitch smoke, a harsh combination. And still those stupid Spaniards were lining the galleon's taffrail, firing muskets and pistols down into the *Didon* as if expecting to be boarded by a hundred howling and heavily armed men scrambling up out of the smoke and flames – Satan's cohorts.

Thomas must be in the boat now, and he could hear him and Mitchell shouting. They sounded alarmed, as though they feared something had happened to him. And now the creak of rowlocks: damnation, they would get dangerously near the *Didon*. Ned shouted several times, heard an answering hail, and then began swimming towards the boat. The flames were taking a long time to reach the kegs of powder, he thought. Then, only seconds later it seemed, he was being hoisted and then parbuckled into the boat, coughing up salt water.

"Take a look, Ned!" Thomas shouted in his ear, hauling him upright on a thwart.

It did not matter that the powder took a little longer: the *Didon*'s mast and blazing sails had just tumbled down on to the galleon, stoving in part of the taffrail and holding the sloop against the galleon like a foal nuzzling its mother. Flames spitting up blazing pitch from the *Didon*'s cargo hold had started a fire on board the galleon and, as they watched, the galleon's great curving transom began to burn, driving back the men with pistols and muskets. The flames lit up the gilding on the quarter galleries: in the excitement Ned had not noticed it before, but the galleon's transom was beautifully decorated, carved wood carefully painted in gay colours. And there was the name, carved and gilded, *La Nuestra Señora de la Piedad*.

"Come on, Ned, we'll have a better view from farther away!" Thomas urged. "Which way do you want to go?"

"Round the stern and out to where Saxby should be watching." The seamen started pulling enthusiastically at the oars without waiting for Mitchell's order: they had first lit canvas strips round the barrels of pitch and then the thin, cord-like trails of slowmatch which led into the kegs of gunpowder. They had placed the casks of rumbullion so that as the pitch heated up it would burst the casks, spraying the hold with the spirit – hot waters indeed, Ned thought inconsequentially. They had left the hold at the last moment, they had climbed into the boat at the last moment, they had seen their Admiral and his second-in-command jump over the side several seconds *after* the last moment, and now all they wanted to do was to get as far away as possible before the first slowmatch burned its way into the powder, like a tiny red caterpillar crawling along a string.

Mitchell steered the boat towards Coconut Point until they were three or four hundred yards from the two ships locked in a fiery and fatal embrace and then gradually turned seaward.

"What the Devil's happened to that powder?" Thomas suddenly exclaimed.

"Looks as though the slowmatches have gone out."

"Six of them? Don't forget there are six kegs."

"Don't worry," Ned said, "the flames will be almost through the staves of those kegs. But why the heat hasn't done the job already . . ."

"Wasn't French powder, was it? That'd be so damp you could wring water from it."

"No, it was ours. Stop rowing for a minute or so," Ned told Mitchell, "we're far enough away now and it isn't often we can see such a sight."

The wind was driving the flames upwards at the galleon's ansom so that sails and rigging were starting to blaze, and so forward to piles of rope, the rigging on the yards which ad been lowered to the bulwarks, and the rolls of sails piled gainst the bulwarks.

"Look, sir!" Mitchell exclaimed, pointing towards the galon's bow, and Ned saw what seemed like dozens of ants warming out along the galleon's bowsprit and then scramling down rope ladders into the boats which had been left iere, wind-rode and clear of the hull.

"Ho, ho, ho!" Thomas said, giving an appropriately lood-chilling laugh. "A couple of hundred men in four oats? Half of them are going to have to swim for it when iey capsize . . . Ho, ho, ho – I doubt if a quarter of 'em can wim."

At that instant the *Didon* exploded: in the blinding flash led thought for a moment he saw the trees of the Pic du aradis green among the clouds – and then, as the sloop anished, so the galleon began blazing more fiercely but now louds of steam swirled up to mix in the coils of smoke, and hunks of blazing pitch scattered across her decks were inned by the wind into bonfires as though a bivouacked rmy was cooking meals. Ned watched speechless as thin nes of fire raced up diagonally from the deck towards the iasts and a moment later he realized that the tarred rope of ie galleon's rigging, dried by days of scorching sun, was atching fire.

A sudden puff of flame which burgeoned out into a small xplosion showed that gunpowder left on the galleon's deck or the guns threatening Marigot was now exploding. And ie flames, like a dreadful cancer, must be creeping below ecks towards the galleon's magazine . . .

"Very well, Mitchell," Ned said, "let's go off and find axby."

His calm voice fooled no one. "When her magazine goes p," Thomas said, "our ears will ring for a week."

"Just so long as the gold and silver sinks right there in shalow water," Ned said, "with all the emeralds and pearls eside them. Just a big enough bang to get the Dons off the hip, but not enough to split open those wooden crates and rack the royal seals on them."

As the men rowed, the oars creaking against the thole pins each man fell silent with his thoughts, and for the first tim each heard clearly the noise accompanying the destruction h had wrought. The flames attacking the wood of the galleon' timbers were crackling as though a giant was snapping tre trunks like twigs. A distant hissing puzzled Ned for moment until he realized it must be the hot hull of the *Dido* still being quenched by the sea. And the birds and dogs every laughing gull, tern, heron, king bird and pelican ha been roused out and was flying in circles or fleeing ami squawks of alarm; every dog in Marigot – and Ned had see large packs of them – was yapping, yelping or barking according to its size, and working itself into a frenzy. And like a querulous bishop trying to make himself heard in crowded brothel, at least one donkey was braying frantically its hee-haws like a saw blade binding in green wood.

The shouting from ahead proved to be Saxby challengin and Thomas bellowed the reply. Two minutes later bot boats were being held alongside each other and as Ned lear over the bulwark to talk to Saxby he felt himself being seize in the darkness.

A moment later, after a smacking kiss, he heard Marth Judd telling him: "That's to be going on with, until you g back to Mrs Wilson! Those bangs! What a blaze! What a nigh – better than my first honeymoon!"

"You must tell us about the second," Ned said, provokin chuckles, and then asked Saxby: "Did everything go a right?"

"Perfect here, sir. Just like you told us, we uncovered th kegs in the first fishing boat, laid the slowmatch, lit it an pushed it off to leeward. Then we rowed to windward lik madmen, towing the other three boats, and then we were jus preparing the second when the first went of! What a bang Oh," he exclaimed anxiously, "I hope you saw the flash an heard the bang, sir."

"Must have been heard over the whole island and i Anguilla, too," Ned assured him. "All four of them were per fectly timed."

"Yes, well, first we saw your two lanterns. Then we sav you lower them. Then Lobb started setting fire to the hill Made a proper job o' that, didn't he!" Saxby said, admirin he other man's work. Martha said: "And then we saw the *Didon* round Coconut Point and start her fireworks. I wish Mrs Wilson could have seen you tuck her under that Spa-iard's tail! But the Dons never did seem to realize what was appening to them!"

"No, that's right," Saxby exclaimed. "Why, they started hooting in our direction with muskets!"

"That's nothing!" Thomas growled. "They shot down at s with pistols – just as we were jumping over the side!"

"Sir," said Mitchell, "there's something going on over here, along the beach."

They all turned to see the flickering red spots of musketry ire.

"Couperin," Ned said. "He and his men are driving off the Spaniards as they try to land from the boats on to his beach."

"What a choice," Thomas said. "Those that couldn't swim ad to roast or drown. Those in the boats have the choice of eing shot or skewered by Couperin's men. Well, any escap-ng to hide in the hills will have a tale to tell their grand-hildren."

"Time we went home," Martha said. "Poor Mrs Wilson nd Lady Diana, their hair must be turning grey with vorry."

Mitchell waited until Ned said: "Does anyone want to wait or the galleon to blow up? No? Well, let's get back to our hips."

Chapter Nineteen

The galleon did not blow up. Ned, Aurelia, Thomas a
Diana were rowed round to Gallows Bay to wait for fi
light and see what had happened, and Thomas was the first
guess why they had neither heard the rumble of the galleo
magazine exploding nor found the bay littered with pieces
floating wreckage.

"Her magazine must have been flooded when she first we
aground weeks ago. What'll you bet me, Ned, that we fi
she was holed by rocks and when she heeled a bit the mag
zine flooded?"

"What about her captain's threat to bombard Marigot?"

"Just bluff. Run out a few guns and threaten the French
Couperin isn't fool enough to defy those muzzles and call h
bluff. He never for a moment suspected the Dons *were* bl
fing."

"But we saw powder exploding on deck," Ned said.

"Not much – probably a couple of kegs they managed
get out while the magazine was flooding, or which happen
to be there for use in the muskets."

"Dearest," Aurelia said softly, "does this mean you do
have to dive to get the gold and silver and emeralds a
pearls?"

"Marry her," Thomas said. "Don't let her escape, Ne
she's the only one with any brains round here. Not like th
feather-brained trollop that sticks to me like a limpet."

"I have infinite faith in Ned," Diana said sweetl
"Whether his men dive to enormous depths for months

ıd, or whether they just climb on board and hoist out the
ates, I know he will make us all very rich at the King
: Spain's expense. He'll find the loveliest emeralds and
ve them to Aurelia and me. Pearls, too. He'll be kind and
ving, as usual. Oh Thomas, if Aurelia had not found him
:st!"

"The two of you could share me," Ned suggested. "We'll
nd Thomas away on a voyage round the world."

Diana shook her head sadly. "A noble thought, Ned, and I
ank you. A noble sentiment I know Aurelia shares. But the
ct is that Whetstone owes me too much money to let him
ıt of my sight for more than a couple of hours."

Thomas coughed politely. "When you carrion crows have
ıished pecking over my impoverished bones, may I point
ıt it is now light enough to board the galleon? Shall I signal
our boarding parties? There's no sign of life in the galleon
ıt to be on the safe side we'd better let our men make a
orough search. There might be an inflamed prelate down
:low somewhere, waiting to ambush us with a red-hot
communication."

They waited while three boatloads of buccaneers swarmed
ı board, led by Saxby, who eventually came back on deck
.d waved them to the gangway. As soon as they were along-
le he shouted down: "Not a soul on board. We've found the
ıllion. I have a dozen men guarding it."

He led the way below where excited buccaneers holding
stols and lanterns were grouped round the door to the ship's
:ongroom, which they had broken open.

On one side of the cavernous cabin were more than a
ındred wooden crates made of thick boards and carefully
ped, each knot almost hidden in a big blob of red wax. It
ıs too dark to read from the doorway the words painted on
e side of the crates but Ned recognized them: they were full
silver, mined at Potosí, cast in various sized ingots,
ıipped up the South Sea coast to Panama, then carried in
.nniers on the backs of horses and mules across the peninsula
Portobelo, where royal assayers once again checked the
eights and the individual numbers stamped on the ingots
·fore packing it all up, roping and sealing each crate, and
atching it being loaded on to ships for the brief voyage from
e shallow-water Portobelo to the deep-water Cartagena,

where the galleons could get in without risking going aground.

There were the crates of silver; on the other side of the strongroom, equally neatly stacked, were fifty or more crates containing gold. And in between, nestling like small lambs on beds of thick straw, were leather bags, the cord round the neck of each also sealed with blobs of red wax. These held the gems and each bag weighed – well, Ned guessed about twenty-four pounds each. Emeralds by the handful from Columbia, pearls by the bucketful from the island of Margarita.

Thomas gave Diana's bottom a playful slap. "A quarter of all that belongs to the *Peleus*. I'll be able to pay off my debts and then maroon you on Anguilla."

"You forget I share in the purchase with the rest of the Peleuses. By the time I've compounded the interest, you'll still be in my debt. Mistresses like me, my dear Thomas, are very, very expensive!"

"Well," Ned said briskly, "it's time we fetched the ships round from Marigot: I'll feel much happier when I know all this plate is closely guarded by the *Peleus*, *Phoenix* and *Griffin*. Looking at all those red seals reminds me that Spanish ships are due here soon to take everything back to the royal treasure house in Cartagena . . ."

Aurelia said: "Wouldn't it be a good idea to fetch out the Governor so that he can see all the crates and leather pouches?"

"He can wait for his share, like everyone else," Thomas said offhandedly, but Ned realized that a Frenchwoman understood only too well the thoughts which would be running through the mind of a Frenchman. Was he being cheated? Were these Englishmen secretly carrying away some of the crates? Were they going through the purses of gems and removing the best?

"We'll go over and see Couperin now, Thomas. Saxby, please put the ladies on board their ships on your way back to the *Phoenix* – and will the ladies pass the word that we'll be getting under way in an hour to shift our berths round to here?"

Couperin was in his house, holding out his hat while a servant tied a wide strip of black cloth round the brim. "For the funeral," he explained. "The service starts in an hour. Well, *mes braves*, what a night, eh! I guarantee there is not a living Spaniard within ten miles of Marigot. Those we did not shoot down as they jumped out of their boats ran inland and by now are hiding themselves up in the mountains by the Pic du Paradis. One of the prisoners – we took a few so that they could answer some questions – said the captain was killed when he fell from the bowsprit (is that what you call it, that thick pole at the bow?) into one of the boats. Broke his neck. And can you guess what I discovered about the guns that he threatened he'd use to bombard Marigot?"

"Yes," Ned said. "They had no powder to fire the shot."

Couperin's face fell. "When did you discover that?"

"We suspected it last night when the ship didn't blow up, but we weren't sure until half an hour ago, when we found her magazine flooded."

"Why would they flood it?"

"When she ran aground she hit some rocks which stove in a couple of planks, so that although she was aground she was also sunk. That's why you didn't see any attempts to refloat her."

"I should have guessed," Couperin said. "I did wonder why they never used the boats to take out anchors to pull themselves into deeper water." He banged his brow melodramatically. "I am a fool. I wonder, but I do not realize I am asking myself a question that I should be able to answer. Not," he added, shrugging his shoulders, "that it would have made any difference because we could not do anything against them until you gentlemen arrived. Er, have you been out to inspect the ship this morning?"

"Yes, that's how we found out that she was sitting on the bottom."

The servant, finally tying the black cloth with a neat knot, left the room. Ned was amused to see the conflict showing in Couperin's face: manners prevented him from asking at once the one question that interested him, but avarice was trying to nudge its way to the front.

"The Spaniards you killed on the beach," Ned said conversationally, "when is their funeral?"

"Funeral? Funeral?" Couperin repeated, as though he had never heard the word before. "The dead we threw back into

the sea; the five prisoners are under guard in the hut at the en
of the jetty."

"What will you do with them when you've asked all th
questions?"

Couperin shrugged his shoulders. "Tell me, was the gal
leon much damaged by your ship of fire? Did you copy you
Francis Drake when he sent fireships into the Spanish armad
at anchor off Calais?"

"No, I didn't copy Drake," Ned said, "because the circum
stances were different. The ship is badly damaged: her tran
som is almost entirely destroyed, thanks to the *Didon*. Th
mizenmast burned through and went over the side. The top
gallant masts on the fore and main will come down in the nex
strong wind – most of the shrouds are burned through. Th
yards which had been sent down on deck (and the sails fron
them) are all burned."

"Our prisoners were very frightened," Couperin said. "I
is strange, but they were gabbling about the ship blowing up
Yet if the magazine was flooded . . ."

"The ship they were frightened of was the *Didon*," Ne
said. "She did explode and blew off the galleon's stern as yo
saw. The Spaniards probably expected more explosions
Don't forget, we've been planning all this for days so none o
it was a surprise, but it all happened to the Spaniards in te
minutes or so. They've been sitting here for weeks withou
anything happening – and then within ten minutes their shi
is blazing and they are jumping on shore from their boats – t
be shot down by your Frenchmen. It must be disturbing."

"Disturbing," Couperin repeated. "Yes, disturbing
M'sieur Yorke, you are *drôle*!"

"Yes, well, would you like to come out and look at th
ship? We have opened up the strongroom and we want t
begin making an inventory of all the bullion and gems befor
dividing it."

"Ah, yes, indeed. How much do you think there is?"

"I've no idea at the moment. Have you ever seen bullion?"

Couperin shook his head. "No, only dreamed about it."

"It doesn't look very exciting," Ned warned. "Most of it i
silver and cast in three different forms. There'll be loaves
each weighing about seventy English pounds; wedges, o
about ten pounds; and cakes, weighing only a pound or two

There'll be plenty of coins, minted in silver at Potosí and Lima. Gold doubloons, too, each worth a French pistole or an English pound. And pieces of eight (also called a dollar), each worth a quarter of a pistole or five English shillings. It can be cut into eight parts (hence its name) or 'bits', also known as reals, and worth an eighth of a dollar.

"What we call 'cobs' are known by the Spaniards as *cabo de barra*, or 'cut from the bar'. However, although a piece of eight is worth five shillings and silver and gold have definite prices, emeralds and pearls, and other gems – well, they're worth whatever people will pay. This galleon isn't carrying many gems –"

"What do you mean by 'many'?" Couperin asked.

"Well, we know about fifty years ago one ship alone carried two chests of rough (uncut) emeralds, and each chest weighed a hundred pounds. The difficulty out here in the West Indies, of course, is that there's no proper market for gems.

"Just remember a doubloon equals a French pistole or an English pound; a dollar or piece of eight is five English shillings or a quarter of a pistole; and a piece of eight, which can be cut into eight reals is also equal to a peso. A peso equals a dollar equals a piece of eight!

"Then of course you have maravedi. About fifty-nine of them equal an English pound, and 375 of them are worth a ducat. Does that help?"

"So how many pesos' worth of gold and silver would you expect this galleon to be carrying?"

"I don't like guessing when we are just about to count it all, but she may be the only plate ship to get away for Spain this year. So – an English frigate captured a galleon in 1655 with two million pesos of plate and gems. The Spanish King's royalty is a *quinto*, so a fifth of that is 400,000 pesos. Quite a loss! Four hundred thousand pesos is one hundred thousand pounds or pistoles . . . Let's hope this galleon is the same: we'd share four hundred thousand pounds or pistoles."

"Quite a loss for the King of Spain, but quite a gain for us," Couperin pointed out with a grin. "We shall not starve, then!"

"No, indeed. By the way, how do we pay your share? Bring it to your house? You should have guards. And the gems – shall we agree on a value for your share and give it to you in gold and silver, or would you prefer the actual gems?"

By now the figures which Ned had mentioned were being absorbed by Couperin, and he was dazed. Whether considered in pounds of weight or the actual value in doubloons or pistoles, Couperin's quarter share was enormous. And Ned realized there was an interesting legal question hanging over Couperin's head. Ned was thankful the decision did not rest with him. The facts were simple enough: a Spanish galleon laden with bullion had run aground on a French island. The two countries were not at war, but Spain maintained that no foreigners had rights "Beyond the Line", so Spain would argue that legally the French were not in St Martin and therefore had no rights. So there could be no question about the present ownership of the bullion: it belonged to Spain whether the galleon was sailing past or hard aground in Gallows Bay.

But France, England and the Netherlands did claim, administer, farm and trade from islands "Beyond the Line". Gallows Bay as far as the King of France was concerned was as much French as Calais Roads. Any wrecks in French waters belonged to France. To the King, Ned corrected himself.

Hmmm. The buccaneers had given the Governor General of St Christophe and St Martin a quarter share, but as far as the King of France was concerned the buccaneers had no right to the galleon. Still, he could not stop them making free with it. It followed that as far as the King was concerned, his Governor General had no right to make any arrangement with the buccaneers – yet the King's advisers might decide that a bird in the hand . . .

It might look very different from Couperin's point of view. If he accepted the quarter share on behalf of his King he might get into trouble from Paris for accepting a single piece of eight, or he might be in for worse trouble for not demanding all of it.

But Ned had more than a suspicion that Couperin was going to take his share and run. Put the Governor-Generalship of two tiny West Indian islands on one side of the scales and a quarter share in the galleon's bullion in the other and there was no doubt on which side the pan would crash own. What Couperin did might well depend on whether he ould get his ship back from the Spaniards. Well, there were ill the two sloops that came in with the *Didon*.

So where could Couperin go with a fortune? Ned was urious only because he found himself liking the man, who learly did not belong among the rumbullion-swilling plantation owners.

"Your wife might like some gems," Ned said.

"My wife?" Couperin gave a laugh which combined cyniism with sorrow. "My wife threw a glass of wine in my face nd returned to France three years ago."

"I regret my clumsy question," Ned said, unsure whether Couperin needed sympathy or congratulation.

Couperin waved his hand dismissively. "Thanks to you nd Sir Thomas, I am now a rich man. A free one, too. But a ealous one."

"Jealous?" Ned exclaimed. "Of whom? Of what?"

Couperin smiled. "Don't sound so alarmed. I am jealous of ou and Sir Thomas. Unfairly so, of course, because you deserve to have such wonderful –" he paused, to choose the preise English word, "– such wonderful companions."

Ned nodded. "We were lucky, and I hope we bring you uck, too. Now, let's go over and look at the bullion."

Couperin held up his hand, motioning him and Thomas to emain seated. "You are reasonably certain that my quarter hare will make me a rich man?"

Ned smiled and said: "It depends what you mean by a 'rich nan', but you'll be able to change the bullion into enough istoles to buy any plantation that takes your fancy, as many laves as you wish, live a life of luxury – and have as many companions' as you might reasonably need. That is, of ourse, unless you hand over your share to the King of rance."

"Yes, indeed," Couperin agreed, "the choice will have to e made, and that is why I ask you to remain a few more minites. What I am going to say – what I am going to ask you – nust remain confidential: otherwise my life might be foreit."

"You have our word," Ned said.

"Very well. In truth, I must tell you that being Governor General of these two islands is a task boring beyond belief.

The people I rule are drunken fools: they have larg
plantations and enormous thirsts. Why do I stay here? Because
do not wish to return to France. The cold winters, the rain
the constant need to be at Court to stay in the King's favou
and the plotting and scheming that goes on there – I am tire
of it. I like this climate, but it is dull. I have a great *ennui*.
have reached the stage where a routine visit to St Martin from
St Christophe becomes an exciting expedition allowing me to
get away from all the drunken planters in St Christophe. Bu
within hours I find myself among the drunken planters of S
Martin, listening to the same complaints and the same quar
rels: only the place names differ."

"Ah, sugar-cane, the evil mother of rumbullion, has much
to answer for!" Ned said lightly.

"Yes, I am tired of it. Which brings me to my question
gentlemen. If I presented myself with a ship and a crew, could
I join the Brethren of the Coast? What do I have to do to
apply? Do I pay to become a member? Do I deposit a bond
Who decides – you, Mr Yorke?"

Ned, dumbfounded, looked helplessly at Thomas, who
slapped his knee and gave a mirthless laugh.

"Let me explain who the Brethren are," Thomas said. "M
Yorke has been so responsible for their success that he is too
shy to talk much about them. First, they can be any national
ity. The captains own ships, but each differs from the othe
Brethren only because owning a ship means a larger share o
the purchase: that is only fair, naturally.

"Each member of the Brethren, whether a cabin boy or a
captain, is a volunteer. He follows the Admiral's orders
because he wants to, with this provision: he doesn't *have* to
join an expedition, but if he does, he then obeys the Admiral's
orders. Take the attack on Portobelo, about which you've obviously heard. That was Mr Yorke's plan. All the Brethren
followed him. But if before we'd started one of the captains
hadn't liked the plan he could have stayed in port.

"Everyone who comes gets a share of the purchase – so
much for the captain, for the ship, for the mate, the carpenter
sailmaker and so on down to the cook and cabin boy. If any o
them are wounded they get extra shares, depending on the
wound – there is an agreed scale. If any are killed, well, that
means more to share among the others.

"Every captain is responsible for the discipline of his own ship and once he agrees to join an expedition, then he also agrees to follow Mr Yorke. So far everyone has wanted to, anyway."

"I understand, and I accept the terms, but do you accept me?"

"If you have a ship, yes," Ned said, "and Sir Thomas didn't make it clear that a buccaneer captain abandons his normal allegiances. Your allegiance would then be to the Brethren, and until recently the buccaneers in turn had been giving their allegiance to Jamaica because they use Port Royal as a base. Until recently they have been defending Jamaica, but now they are moving to Tortuga."

"Which is French," Couperin said.

"France claims it," Ned said, "but can't hold it."

"True," Couperin acknowledged, "and that of course is the basis of everyone's quarrel with Spain: she claims all these islands but cannot control or use them."

"Well, if you have a ship, understand the conditions, and still want to join the Brethren, then welcome!"

"Thank you," Couperin said simply but sincerely. "Let's go and inspect the 'purchase' then," savouring the word as though it was a fine wine. "So now I am a buccaneer!"

"One thing occurs to me," Ned said. "You are getting a quarter share, and we offered that to save us from any interference by the French authorities. *After* we had agreed, we discovered that the French authorities – you, in other words – were in no position to interfere anyway. However, we had made a bargain, and that's that. But I want you to be clear at what point you become a buccaneer, and at what point you recruit your men, because they too are going to join the Brethren and will be entitled to a share in future purchases, and I don't want them coming to me in the future and claiming a share in this one."

"You are shrewd as well as *drôle*," Couperin said, "but rest assured that the men who helped me drive the Spaniards into the hills are going to be rewarded separately – we all agreed on a price, which comes out of my own pocket. Don't forget, at the time I hired them we did not know whether or not the galleon carried plate.

"They are also the men I shall bring with me when I get my

ship back. It was only after finding I could lead them and they would follow that I considered seriously asking to join the Brethren."

"Good, it's always worth having men around you that have smelled powder," Ned said, "and those muskets we lent you – keep them as a present. If you don't get your ship back from the Spaniards when they return from Cartagena . . ."

Couperin shrugged his shoulders. "I have two others to choose from. Neither is very big, but will do until we capture something larger."

Again Thomas slapped his knee and bellowed with laughter. "Spoken like a true buccaneer," he exclaimed. "The Dons build fine ships. The Hollanders are not so good because they have so little wood in the Netherlands and build for shallow waters. The French – yes, they're all right, as long as they don't build with that damned larch or Spanish oak. An English ship of English oak – that's the best of course."

"Of course," Couperin said politely, picking up his hat as he stood up and ripping off the black mourning band.

Lobb had found a small table and chair somewhere and set them up just inside the strongroom door, ready with paper, quill and ink. Saxby had already sailed the *Griffin* and *Phoenix* round to Gallows Bay and was anchored a hundred yards to windward of the galleon. Now he waited with Lobb to begin the inventory.

Couperin walked from one pile of crates and chests to the other, reading the words painted on the sides. Occasionally he slapped the flat of his hand against a crate, as if still not believing what he saw.

He turned to Ned. "This was all here, and I sat in my house afraid that the Spanish captain would start bombarding Marigot . . . and while I waited you were coming from Jamaica . . . And because of you . . ." He slapped another crate. "And those chests; gold and silver, it says so on the sides. There must be an emerald for every mistress in the world in those pouches."

"That's the way," Thomas said encouragingly, "always take the grand view! The buccaneer's secret (thanks to Ned) is to think on the grand scale. The Spanish shipment of silver and gems for the whole year is waiting at Portobelo? Right, let's go and capture it! All the guns defending Jamaica come from Santiago de Cuba which was regarded as impregnable by the Dons until Ned here decided we needed those guns."

"The grand view – yes. It reminds me of distant horizons. I have sat in my house in St Christophe for too long and seen only Nevis to the south and St Eustatius and Saba to the north; and when I'm here in Marigot I stare at the sea, but Anguilla is the only horizon," Couperin exclaimed enthusiastically.

"Be careful," Thomas warned, "sudden freedom can affect you like a very good but very strong wine..."

"Let's get the *Peleus* round here," Ned said, "then Mitchell can help Saxby, Lobb and Simpson with this inventory. By the way," he explained to Couperin, "usually each ship sends her mate along to watch an inventory being taken: that prevents any misunderstandings. Do you want to stay and watch – or send someone on your behalf?"

"What do the mates usually do?" Couperin asked.

Saxby laughed and answered for Ned. "They usually find the ship's spirit room and stay there getting happily drunk, leaving Lobb and me to count while a couple of men open the crates and chests for us and another couple seal 'em again."

"I won't bother," Couperin said. "I want to have a talk with my men and explain what you've been telling me. And I must get my ship ready. My ship, that is, if the Spaniards don't bring my original one back from Cartagena in time."

"Which will you choose?" Ned asked.

"The *Sans Peur*. You took the best one, the *Didon*," he added dolefully, "so I'll have to make do with what's left..."

"I thought all three ships belonged to friends of yours," Ned said, remembering a remark Couperin had made several days earlier.

"Ah yes, they belonged to friends of the Governor General. But he's become a buccaneer now, and buccaneers have no friends!" He thought for a moment. "The two sloops are your prizes – I forgot. Can I buy one?"

When Ned and Thomas went back on board the smoke-blackened galleon after anchoring the *Peleus* close to the *Grif-*

fin and *Phoenix*, they found the strongroom sounding like a busy carpenter's shop.

All the men were stripped to the waist, working in breeches and hose by the light of lanterns whose guttering wicks added to the heat. While two seamen levered open one crate, two others were busy hammering in nails to seal another.

"How is it going?" Ned asked Saxby, who gestured at the pile of papers on Lobb's table which were held down by a cake of silver, weighing about a pound and almost covered in assay marks and the Spanish royal stamp.

Lobb grinned and turned the sheet he was writing on so that Ned could read it. It was in fact the running total of gold, silver, emeralds and pearls.

"We're a third of the way through counting the silver, sir, and we've finished the gold." He gestured to the pair of small scales beside the pile of paper. "We've checked one chest of emeralds and one of pearls. Even allowing that the emeralds are rough and a lot will be lost in cutting, I've never seen such fine gems."

Ned had been reading the totals as Lobb talked. "Not as big as Portobelo, but it'll do – unless you find the remaining crates are filled with rocks."

Lobb grinned as he began writing down the number of sugar loaves, wedges and cakes of silver that the two men were taking out of the crate they had just opened. It needed both of them to reach down to lift out the sugar loaves, which weighed seventy pounds each, while the wedges turned the scales at about ten pounds. "How much longer will you need?" Ned asked Saxby, who looked at the rest of the crates and chests.

"About four hours, I reckon."

"Then we can share out?"

Saxby looked at Ned and then at Thomas. "Am I right in thinking you're in a hurry to get out of here, sir?"

Ned nodded. "We've no idea what ships the Dons will bring from Cartagena to collect their bullion. If there happens to be a galleon available, they might come in that. Perhaps a frigate or two; maybe three or four *petachas* and a frigate. But they're liable to cause us trouble."

"So if we could get clear of Marigot by nightfall . . . ?"

"That would be fine, because I don't think the Dons can get here from Cartagena before tomorrow at the earliest."

"Dividing all this plate and the gems among the three ships – four if you include that Frenchman – will take time. Supposing we brought the *Griffin* alongside – I went round taking the depths with the leadline as soon as I came on board: these galleons draw three times as much as the *Griffin*. And with all her yards burned there's no chance of them catching in yours, sir."

All the plate and gems would be on board the *Griffin*. It was the custom to share out the purchase before returning to port, but Saxby seemed quite content with what was his own idea. Ned looked at Thomas. "What about you and your people?"

Thomas gave a lopsided grin. "I think I can speak for them and assure you they'll trust you. We'll all meet in Port Royal and make the division there."

Chapter Twenty

As the four ships ran down the outside of the giant cocked thumb forming the flat and sandy peninsula of the Palisades, the long spit protecting the wide and sheltered Port Royal anchorage on the inshore side of it, Ned was thankful that the batteries which he had forced General Heffer to build (supplying him with the cannons for them after raiding Santiago) were still intact.

They were sailing close enough inshore to see that, except for a few small trading sloops, the anchorage was empty, so the rest of the buccaneers were either still attacking the Main or had moved to Tortuga. And there was no sign of damage to batteries or buildings, so there had not been any attack by the Spanish.

This was confirmed a couple of minutes later when Lobb, who had been standing on the foredeck with the perspective glass, called aft that he could see the flag flying from the flagpole in front of the Governor's residence.

"That won't please Thomas," Ned commented to Aurelia. "He'd sooner see it at half-mast and go on shore to find out he'd just missed old Loosely's funeral by a couple of days . . ."

"*Chéri*, promise me you'll try to be civil to Sir Harold from now on. He has a very difficult task," Aurelia said, "and for the first week or two – when you and Thomas took against him – he still thought he was in London."

"You're fair to him but hardly fair to Thomas and me," Ned grumbled. "We've defended this damned island for the

King, and even given it a currency – don't forget that but for us the piece of eight would not be the official currency of Jamaica, and without it what would we buccaneers and the tradesmen – and old Loosely – do for money? Why, he withdraws the commissions of the buccaneers and drives them away. The man is a fool, even by Court standards. Idiots like him belong in the Church or Parliament."

"In Parliament with your brother?" Aurelia asked innocently.

"Just because George is a peer it doesn't mean he is stupid – he never attends Parliament."

"He hasn't had much chance because he was with the King in France until the Restoration, and since then he's been busy trying to get the family estates back. So not *everyone* in Parliament is stupid."

"Enough to make George an exception," Ned said sourly and turned to look astern. Following closely in the *Griffin*'s wake (too closely for comfort, as far as Ned was concerned) was the *Sans Peur*. Couperin, making his first visit to Port Royal, was certainly following Ned's instructions that he was to follow in the *Griffin*'s wake.

The *Peleus* and the *Phoenix* were following on each quarter of the French ship. For the hundreds of miles run from St Martin, past St Eustatius, Saba, Santa Cruz, Porto Rico (like Hispaniola seen only as a thin grey line on the northern horizon) and now the south coast of Jamaica, they had maintained perfect formation, keeping each other in sight at night with lanterns but in daylight taking it in turns to investigate any strange sail seen in the distance. Seldom, Ned thought to himself, had any golden goose had such an attentive flock.

For that matter, the goose (with a galleon's cargo of bullion and gems stowed below) was lucky that no ship or fleet hove in sight to say "boo". There were always enough rumours – even definite reports – that the Spanish on the Main were expecting a fleet from Spain or had a squadron at sea, to make a voyage from somewhere like St Martin to Jamaica with such a cargo in such a small vessel a desperate venture. Santa Cruz, Vieques, Porto Rico, Hispaniola – all were Spanish islands, and although they were all to the north, the Main itself was to the south.

Lobb was giving orders to the men and the *Griffin* turned a point to starboard to avoid Gun Cay, and then a point to larboard to dodge a reef. Ned watched the *Sans Peur* as Lobb then ordered a large alteration as they turned northwards to thread their way among some more reefs.

Finally, the *Griffin* led the ships round the headland and into the anchorage, and started the long beat to windward, intending to anchor close to the jetty jutting out from the north side of Port Royal, opposite the Governor's residence and close to the lobster crawl.

Fresh meat, Ned thought, his mouth watering. With the meat market only a few yards from the end of the jetty, Ned knew one of Lobb's first tasks after anchoring the ship would be to send men to buy beeves and make arrangements to roast them. Everyone on board the *Griffin* was tired of boucanned or salt meat.

Aurelia smiled and patted his stomach. "It's not hard to guess what you are thinking about. Thomas and Saxby, too!"

"You and Diana will continue eating boucan, of course?" Ned inquired innocently. "By the way, is there any woman on the island who might suit Couperin? I think he's rather lonely."

"I *know* he's rather 'lonely', poor man," Aurelia said, "but at the moment I can't think of anyone who might interest him in a regular sense."

Ned shrugged his shoulders. "Well, those sort of introductions never work. Anyway, I don't know what kind of woman he likes."

"From the way he looks at Diana and me, I don't think he'll be too fussy. Anyway, I wonder how General Heffer has been getting on while we've been away."

"Either he's taken to locking himself in his office, or he's a trembling wreck, leaping into the air every time old Loosely calls him."

"Yes, I'm afraid it'll be one or the other." She paused, staring at the James bastion, which they were passing close on the starboard bow as Lobb tacked the ship. "Look, old Heffer has his men exercising at the guns!"

Ned thought for a moment. Exercising? But Sir Harold Luce had declared that he was paying off most of the soldiers. "Quick Lobb, you've got the glass – what are those men doing at the James bastion?"

Before Lobb had time to put the glass to his eye they all saw smoke spurting from the muzzles of the guns, smoke which began streaming off to leeward and was followed by distant thuds.

Without realizing he was doing it, Ned looked for the fall of shot, but there were no spurts of water between the *Griffin* and the bastion, and certainly no cloth-ripping sound of passing ball. He glanced astern just in time to see small fountains of water collapsing midway between the *Griffin* and the *Sans Peur*.

Lobb held out his arms palms upwards, in a gesture of despair. "They don't get any better, sir," he called. "Perhaps we should all wear round and pass closer!"

"Who do they think we are, Spaniards?" Aurelia asked.

"Heffer must have recognized the three of us when we passed the other side of the sandspit," Ned said. "I'm sure he didn't order these men to open fire."

"Then who did? Oh *no*!" Aurelia exclaimed. "Oh well, if you're right I'll take back all I said about him!"

The bastion also fired at the *Peleus* and the *Phoenix* as they passed but, as Lobb commented, their aim was so bad that the officer in charge of the bastion ought to have his hand slapped.

Ned noted thankfully that the *Sans Peur* had stayed close in the *Griffin*'s wake, even though Couperin must have been startled at being fired on when entering what he had been told was the buccaneers' home port. There had been no time before leaving Marigot (nor had it seemed the appropriate place) to give a detailed explanation of the English government's curious attitude towards Jamaica. Until he was absolutely sure that Couperin was going to prove an enthusiastic buccaneer, Ned was reluctant to reveal that there was a very good chance the English King intended to give Jamaica back to Spain (much as one might shut the front door and say thank you after having the use of a house for a week).

Poor old Charles: barely back on the throne of England before being blamed for everything that went wrong. To be fair, no king could be wiser than his advisers when deciding what to do in lands he did not know. As far as Ned could see, the men giving advice (whether to Cromwell or to the King) about the West Indies had always been ignorant fools. His own experience admittedly only went back to Cromwell, but there was no reason to think the present advisers were any better; in fact, the way things were going now it seemed that those round the King might be worse. Every fool whose horizon was limited to St James's was probably an expert (at Court) on West Indian affairs.

And now the *Griffin* was furling sails as Lobb brought her round to anchor. Ned smiled at Aurelia. Despite all the irritations there had been when they left to catch up with Thomas and the *Peleus*, it was good to be back. It was very easy to get angry with Jamaica when you were really angry with someone like old Loosely. You needed patience because the Looselys of this world, as soon as they realized that Jamaica could not provide them with either fame or fortune, had themselves recalled to England. Governors of colonies were ambitious men: each posting was a step up (they hoped!) the ladder whose lower rungs were made of money, nepotism and opportunism and whose upper ones were held in place with various orders of knighthood.

As the *Sans Peur* anchored to leeward and the *Phoenix* and the *Peleus* took up their usual positions on each quarter, Lobb came up to report, almost apologetically: "There's a fishing boat coming out to us from the jetty, sir, and I'm afraid it's bringing that mincing secretary to the Governor . . ."

"Make him brush off the fish scales before you allow him on board," Ned said, and Lobb grinned. Suddenly Ned felt too tired to put up with Sir Harold: not physically tired, but unwilling to truckle with a man who could never have made a spontaneous remark in his life; whose every sentence had to be examined because it had two meanings, if not more. Luce, he thought bitterly, was such a perfect trimmer it was impossible to understand why honest men had anything to do with him. He had survived and flourished under Cromwell; at the Restoration he had trimmed his sails and was now under way again, only this time in the King's service . . .

"And Lobb – if he's carrying a letter from the Governor, bring it down to me: I don't want to see the young man. Tell him I'm too busy."

Young man . . . the phrase came easily enough but Hamilton was about his own age and Luce was probably paying off his tailor by taking the man's son as his aide: that was how most of these youngsters started off. Well, it was possible for a tailor's son to get a dukedom by trimming, as the Duke of Albemarle had just shown . . .

Ned went down to the cabin with Aurelia and suddenly kissed her affectionately. She responded with equal warmth, and then held him at arm's length. "What are you up to now?"

"Nothing," he said innocently. "Why can't I just want to kiss you?"

"You can, and I hope you always do, but at this moment you have a look in your eye – a *cunning* look. What trick are you going to play on that poor man Hamilton?"

"Trick? What trick *can* I play on him? Damnation, we've just sailed into Port Royal, been fired at from the bastion by guns *we* provided and using powder *we* supplied, and you ask me what trick *I* am going to play? Better ask old Loosely what trick he's *already* played."

"All right, then, tell me why Sir Harold Luce had his guns fire on us?"

"That's easy. He's jealous of me because I have such a lovely Frenchwoman as a mistress."

Aurelia smiled but persisted. "Come on, be serious."

"All right. It's actually Thomas's fault. Sir Harold lusts after Diana. He's been reading the Song of Solomon again and Diana's breasts are driving him mad. Or the thought of them, anyway."

There was a knock on the cabin door and Lobb came in. "This fellow, sir: he hasn't got a letter. Says he must see you because he's got an urgent message from the Governor."

"Ned," Aurelia said quietly, "you promised . . ."

Ned made a face. "All right, bring him down, but stay and listen to what he says: one can't have enough witnesses when dealing with these people."

Sir Harold's secretary arrived with a thump, missing the last two steps of the companionway and falling in a heap at the doorway. Lobb stood behind him, unsmiling, as he stood up and straightened his jerkin, tugged at his lace collar and tried to wriggle his breeches lower: the fall had obviously pulled them tight under the crotch, and with Aurelia present he could do nothing more.

Ned glared at him as he stepped into the cabin, and before

he could say anything demanded: "Well, where is the written apology?"

"Apology? Sir, I bring a message from the Governor and –"

"Listen carefully. Sir Harold Luce's guns fired on my ships as we passed the James bastion. I want to know why, and I want a written apology."

"Very well, sir, I'll tell him that. But –"

"Delivered before I listen to anything he has to say," Ned growled. "Good morning to you."

"But sir, I have an urgent –"

"Trying to knock my head off with roundshot fired from guns I captured from the Spanish and gave to Jamaica is urgent," Ned said angrily. "You don't know just how urgent a roundshot sounds when it whistles past your ear but, if you'll excuse me, I am busy: we have to make a careful inspection of this ship to see what damage we received."

"Oh sir," the wretched Hamilton wailed, "I'm sure none of the shot hit your ship!"

"None hit my ship?" Ned suddenly roared at him. "Why not? Do you mean to say we captured those guns at Santiago, brought them back here, made Heffer build bastions, provided powder and shot, and after all that the damned gunners can't hit an innocent ship passing a hundred yards away? Not one ship but *four*! Blasting away into the middle of the covey, they were – and now you say they didn't hit anything!"

"No, sir," stammered Hamilton. "I didn't say they didn't hit anything –"

"Oh, now you admit your damned guns did hit my ships! Well, I want to know why they opened fire."

"Sir, I didn't mean that they actually hit your ships –"

"Ah, now you say they are such a crowd of dunderheads that they can't hit such close targets. That's what I was saying: the guns, powder and shot are just a waste."

"Sir, they thought you were Spanish!"

Ned appeared to freeze. "Oh, so I am Spanish now, eh? An enemy of Jamaica, of Sir Harold Luce and his blessed majesty the King. Not a traitor, just an enemy. Well, you –"

Ned knew that Aurelia's pinch would soon draw blood from his arm unless he looked at her. He knew her well enough to recognize that she was fighting hard to avoid laughing, and he had noticed Lobb duck out of the cabin a couple of minutes ago after seeing Hamilton tripping over himself.

"Ned," she said in a neutral voice, "I think this gentleman has a message for you from the Governor."

"I know that: he said so at the beginning. And I've told him that before I have any other communication from the Governor, I want his written apology for opening fire on us. Lobb!" he called. "Ah, there you are. Send on shore for those beeves. It'll take hours to get them slaughtered and roasted. And take this fellow away with you and send him home. Shoot at him if he tries to come on board again without that written apology."

Ned realized that Aurelia had moved close to him again and any moment there would be another pinch. He promptly sat down at the table and glared at the polished surface.

"But sir –" Hamilton cried, scuttling out of the cabin when Ned bellowed: "What, are you still there? Where are my pistols, woman?"

As soon as she could no longer hear Hamilton's boots clattering up the ladder, Aurelia said: "Ned, that wasn't funny: it was cruel. You are a bully."

"Why are you laughing, then?"

"I'm not laughing. I'm ashamed of you."

Ned stood up and kissed her again. He started to unlace the soft leather jerkin she was wearing but she pushed him away. "Not now! The Governor wants to see you!"

"Darling, if I have to choose between you and the Governor, you will always win."

At that moment they both heard Thomas's deep voice calling from the top of the companionway, followed by Diana who, Ned noted, always sounded as though she was inviting you to her bed, no matter what she was saying.

"What did that fancy boy want?" Thomas asked. "He was as white as a sheet! Lobb fairly threw him into that fishing boat!"

Aurelia jabbed Ned with her finger and turned to Thomas. "Ned was absolutely hateful to him. He came with a message from the Governor and we still don't know what it is – even though it's urgent."

Thomas raised his eyebrows, startled by Aurelia's sharp

tone of voice. “Why don’t we know? Was he struck dumb?”

“No, Ned completely confused the poor man with demands for an apology because the bastion opened fire on us.”

“I should think so too,” Thomas rumbled. “Fired on by our own guns!”

“But we weren’t hit!” Aurelia said, almost wailing with exasperation.

“Even worse! At that range they should have riddled us. That damned Heffer – he hasn’t the faintest idea of how to train his men, although we’ve told him enough times!”

“But the Governor – it’s urgent!”

Diana tugged Thomas’s arm. “Listen to Aurelia,” she said firmly, “because Ned is having one of his attacks. Just look at him: he’s just sitting there giggling like a young girl.”

“Very sensible of him,” growled Thomas, subsiding on the settee facing Ned. “What’s all this about, Ned? Aurelia looks as though she’s going to lay a clutch of hard-boiled eggs.”

Ned shrugged his shoulders. “I don’t know, to tell the truth. Our friend was mincing down the companionway when he missed his footing and arrived with a crash. After that everything went to pieces.”

“Yes,” Aurelia said crossly, “it did because Ned got the Devil in him. The poor man was trying to say the Governor wanted to see Ned urgently, but Ned was shouting – oh yes you *were* shouting – that he wouldn’t have anything to do with anyone on shore until he had a written apology from the Governor over that shooting business.”

“Steady on,” Thomas said. “Someone could have been killed by ‘that shooting business’. Never underrate a round-shot, I say.”

Aurelia looked despairingly at Diana, who took her arm and led her out of the cabin.

Ned looked up at Thomas. “I was a naughty boy, but I couldn’t resist it!”

“When shall we go over and see him – tomorrow morning?”

Ned nodded. “Quite soon enough.”

Chapter Twenty-One

General Heffer was, as Ned had suspected, sitting in his office with the door shut, even though it was a humid day with only a slight breeze to ruffle the jalousies and stir up tiny whirlwinds of dust. There was no sentry on the door. Had Luce already paid off the Army, keeping only the four hundred militia?

Ned banged on the door and walked into the room. Heffer might well have been dozing: he leapt from his chair, his startled eyes blinking in the familiar mournful sheep's face.

"Ah, Mr Yorke and Sir Thomas! Welcome back. I heard you had returned."

"You didn't see us passing yesterday?"

"Er, well, yes. With an extra ship."

"Did you order the James bastion to fire on us as we came in?"

"Indeed I did not! I heard the guns firing."

"Why?" Ned demanded. "Why at us?"

Heffer sat down after closing the door firmly and gestured to Ned and Thomas to be seated. "There have been changes here since you left. My role is – well, my title is now Quartermaster General. I am (I think) supposed to make sure the island doesn't starve and we don't run out of powder and shot for the militia. I also have to make sure the Governor is well supplied with lobster, and with turtles from the Caymans (he's very partial to turtle cutlets). Oh yes, I have to collect all the uniforms and arms from the soldiers now they're paid off.

As they have nothing else to wear and they haven't the mone to buy clothes (there isn't enough cloth in the island anyway let alone boots or shoes), the Governor has a crisis on hi hands."

"So that's why the bastion fired at us, eh?" Ned asked "We're not welcome, I suppose, after Loosely cancelled all th commissions and the Brethren left."

Heffer gave an unexpected gulping laugh, like a shee sneezing. "Ah, yes, as I just told you, things have changed But I'm only the quartermaster. I hear the Governor tried t send you an urgent message yesterday, but you gave hi messenger a dusty answer!"

"Yes, that's about it. What was the message?"

"Mr Yorke," Heffer said ironically, "I'm now only th quartermaster – the island's housekeeper. The Governo doesn't confide in me nor does he ask my advice. He asks n one's advice. If he wants to see you urgently, I'm sure it' over an urgent matter. I've just told you we have a clothin crisis. Or perhaps it's a turtle cutlets crisis – the sloop from the Caymans is two days overdue . . ."

"Nothing changes much," Ned said with a grin. "Quit like old times."

"Except that you're not humbugging me any more!" Heffer said thankfully. "I remember when I first met the pai of you. Buying grain you had stolen from the Spanish!"

"Captured, not stolen," Thomas corrected. "You talk a though my sainted Uncle Oliver was still alive. The King i back, Heffer!"

Heffer glanced at the door, as if making sure it was stil shut. "Yes, I know. He sent us the Governor!"

"Heffer," Ned said suddenly, "that's the third time you'v smiled, and you just laughed. What's the matter? Whenc came this ribald Heffer? Why are you so cheerful? I've neve seen you smile before, and as for laughing . . ."

Heffer smiled yet again, self-consciously. "Well, Si Harold is not an easy man to work for but he has all the responsibility now. I can assure you that I'd sooner be responsible for turtle cutlets than the safety of the whole island. An –" he took a large watch from his fob and flipped open th front, "– perhaps you gentlemen had better go and pay him your respects: someone will have seen your boat arriving a ie jetty, and he'll probably think I'm deliberately keeping ou."

Ned stood up. "Well, we'll call in after we've seen him. Jot to tell you about the urgent matter, but to see if you can nd some turtle cutlets for us. And who knows, we might ien sail over to the Main and get some cloth so that your ormer soldiers can hide their nakedness."

Hamilton was standing at the front door of the Governor's esidence, hands trembling, his forehead beaded with perspiration that owed more to nervousness than humidity.

"Ah, Mr Yorke! We saw you coming on shore – but then ou and Sir Thomas vanished!"

"We often do," Ned said. "It's a trick Sir Thomas learned n one of the Crusades. The Third, wasn't it, Thomas?"

"The Fourth," Thomas said.

"Ah yes. The Third was when you rescued Lady Diana rom the Sultan."

"No, no, no, my dear fellow: I rescued the Sultan from ady Diana," Thomas said, straight-faced. "The poor man vas in mortal danger of being transmuted into a eunuch."

William Hamilton's eyes had long since become glazed. Sir Harold . . ." he said weakly, "Sir Harold has –"

"The written apology waiting for us," Ned said.

"Er, well, I'm not sure –"

"Good day," Ned said crisply, "we have plenty of work to upervise on board our ships." As he turned, Hamilton said urriedly: "I'm sure Sir Harold is only waiting to –"

Ned knew that Hamilton was lying to save his master's ace, but now, having spoken to Heffer, he was curious to now what it was that Loosely regarded as urgent.

"Very well, tell Sir Harold we'll give him ten minutes."

As Hamilton turned to hurry into the house, Thomas growled: "At the most, and that includes time for the apology."

And there Sir Harold Luce was, sitting at an enormous lesk: the ferret face, wisps of urine-coloured hair poking out rom under his wig, sharp little hungry eyes, the face like reckled cold pork on the turn, the mouth open enough to eveal yellowed teeth.

Hamilton announced their names and Luce stared at them vithout speaking. Both Ned and Thomas stopped walking into the room, waited a full minute and then turned to go out again.

"Gentlemen," Luce said hurriedly, "welcome back to Port Royal. I was getting anxious about you!"

"So I noticed," Ned said, taking out his watch and looking at it carefully. "Welcoming us with the guns of the James bastion."

"Oh, *that*," Luce said, waving his hand as though to dismiss it. "Just a mistake; some fool misunderstood an order."

"Indeed?" Ned's eyebrows were raised. "Well, we haven't much time and no doubt the explanation is given fully in your written apology."

Luce's eyes flickered from one side of the room to the other, reminding Ned of a trapped animal. "Well, no, I'm explaining now."

"No you're not," Ned said quietly. "We haven't time to listen. You received my message that I have nothing to discuss with you until I receive your written apology?"

"Damnation, boy," Luce shouted, thumping his desk, "you don't send messages like that to the Governor, laying down conditions!"

"Oh, but I do," Ned said. "Why, we could tar and feather you and send you back to England in a turtle shell, and everyone in the island would cheer us. You've no Army, you've no idea what is needed here in Jamaica, and you gave the order to fire on my ships. You are the Governor, yes; your commission is no doubt securely locked away somewhere. But don't forget – if we are exchanging compliments – that I am the Admiral of the Brethren of the Coast, and if the rest of my men hear that you opened fire on me, they'll come back here and capture the island. You'll be marched along to Gallows Point and instead of sitting at a desk, you'll be hanging from a gibbet, the *late* Governor."

Luce realized that he had gone too far: in a very few seconds he weighed his own ideas of the respect due to his position and its powers against the buccaneers' ships – more than thirty, he recalled – that this wretched fellow Yorke led.

"Very well, I apologize, and if you'll sit down I'll draft the apology now. William! Ink, paper and quill. Hurry!"

Five minutes later, having read it carefully, Ned folded the ology, tucked it into the capacious pocket in the sleeve of s jerkin, and then consulted his watch. "Three minutes, Sir arold."

The Governor looked puzzled. "Three minutes? What out them?"

"You have three minutes left of the ten," Ned explained tiently. "You wanted to see me, urgently."

"My dear fellow, I can't tell you all about it in *three min-es*!"

"A pity," Ned said, and stood up, followed an instant later y Thomas, "You see, we don't set traps and fire on people at trust us: we say exactly what we can do or can't do, and at's it. We said ten minutes, and they have almost passed."

His face now red with indignation, his wig beginning to ip and revealing what Ned had expected, that the man's hair ill had not grown out after having been cut back to the shionable "Roundhead" style under the Commonwealth nd which was the main reason for the wig's popularity at e Restoration), Sir Harold whined: "You have the imper-nence to give me *three minutes*! Damnation, I am the Gover-or of Jamaica: don't you understand? The *Governor*!"

Ned turned to Thomas and nodded towards the door. Good day, Your Excellency," he said ironically, "I'm afraid e have urgent business on board our ships." He thought a oment and then added, much as a fisherman threw out bait fore casting his line: "We have to provision and water efore sailing again tomorrow afternoon."

"Sailing? So soon?"

Far from looking like a trapped ferret, Sir Harold, wig vry, eyes flickering like guttering candle flame, looked ore like a ferret dying painfully after being bitten by a viper. Oh please, Mr Yorke, and Sir Thomas, hear what I have to y. It is urgent! It concerns the very safety of Jamaica! The land has never faced such a crisis! We've no Army, no efences except a few bastions – you are my last hope, Mr orke!"

"Poor you," Ned said unsympathetically. "If things are as ad as that there's nothing we can do to help. Just four ships nd perhaps two hundred and fifty men – the rest are at Tor-ga or along the Main. Why, if you cleared the bars and rothels of Port Royal you'd find more men – most of your disbanded Army, probably. Fill 'em up with rumbullion and point them in the right direction and shout 'Charge!' – that's only a suggestion, but the best I can do at the moment."

"Please . . ." Luce pleaded, and Ned suddenly realized that the man was almost in tears. Yet Ned was sure that Luce was not to be trusted: he was the kind of man who interpreted someone's kindly act as a sign of weakness. Luce and his type had moral standards somewhere between those of a cutpurse and a highwayman stranded with a lame horse and a pregnant and shrill doxy.

Ned sat down again. "Very well, but please hurry, Sir Harold. You must realize we do not like leaving our ships in an anchorage where batteries open fire on us without warning . . ."

"Yes, well, it's the Spaniards, you see!"

"The *Spaniards*?" Ned exclaimed incredulously. "What about them?"

"They're preparing to attack the island – and (as instructed by the Privy Council in London, I assure you) I have just paid off the Army who are, as you commented, dispersed like chaff on the wind. With all their back pay in their pockets there isn't a hope of re-forming them."

"They're still wearing their uniforms," Thomas said. "Those in the bars, anyway. Might be a different story in the brothels."

"So what am I going to do?" Sir Harold asked desperately.

"These Spaniards," Ned said. "Who are they? What ships are they coming in? Who sighted them and reported to you? When did you hear about it?"

By now Sir Harold was so distraught that he answered Ned's last question, that being the only one he could remember. "The day before yesterday – the day before you came back. I've tried to keep it secret for the moment, to stop any panic. Just the bastions were warned to fire on ships."

"Panic," Ned said musingly. "With all the bars and bordellos full of your former Army, you couldn't start a panic on the island even if you set fire to all the savanna and arranged a week of earthquakes. But who told you?"

"Oh, the master of a trading sloop from Santo Domingo. A smuggler, but well educated and well informed. I questioned him myself."

"And what urgent information did he give you?"
"That the Spaniards have a powerful squadron at sea." He
used a moment, like a small boy savouring the spasm of
ar he had just experienced when picturing the ghost his im-
ination had summoned up. "Yes, a powerful squadron at
a. They have already captured one island and set fire to all
e ships. It looks as though they are capturing the Windward
ands one by one and then the islands to leeward: they've
ways forbidden other countries to be here in the Caribbee.
o Peace Beyond the Line', you know."
"Yes," Ned said. "I've heard the expression somewhere –
Portobelo, I seem to recall."
"But Portobelo is Spanish?"
"Yes," Ned said dreamily. "Full of mosquitoes, too. Never
en so many as there."
Thomas coughed and said, as though apologetically:
lease excuse my friend's nostalgia. The currency of Jamaica
the piece of eight – as a result of his raid on Portobelo . . ."
"Indeed," Luce said absent-mindedly. "Well, I am sure
e're all grateful."
"That 'powerful squadron'," Ned asked. "How many
ips and how many troops?"
"Eight ships, my informant said, which I estimate would
rry two thousand men – at least two thousand, probably
ore."
Ned nodded in agreement. "Yes, if they started at the
uthern end and worked their way north, that could be the
d of the English, French and Dutch in the Caribbee. Cura-
o, Bonaire and Aruba – probably started there (all the
utch trade is based on Curaçao). Then Barbados, La Gren-
le (if the French own it, but I think it's usually called Gre-
da), then St Vincent, St Lucia, Martinique, Dominica
. dear me, I needn't recite all the names because you must
now them all. Bit of luck," he commented, "that Jamaica's
e last in the line."
"But that's the point!" Sir Harold said excitedly. "They've
ken the islands up to Porto Rico. Now there are just Spanish
lands – Porto Rico, Hispaniola and Cuba! Surrounding us,
ey are, and the Spanish squadron bearing down on us.
hy, didn't you see any sign of it while you were at sea?"
Ned shook his head and turned to Thomas. "Did you see

any sign of the Dons? Ships, smoking islands, boats full •
refugees making for safety?"

'Not a thing," Thomas said innocently. "Mind you, w
weren't looking for anything like that. After all, we're on
buccaneers and my men were just drinking and wenchin
That reminds me, Ned, what shall we do with all tho
wenches? Can't get any work out of my men while tho
wenches are on board."

"I'd put 'em on shore," Ned said judiciously. "This islar
is very short of wenches and –"

"Gentlemen, gentlemen," Sir Harold pleaded, "only th
island stands against Spanish domination of the Ne
World."

"Probably not even this island by now," Ned said sadl
"After all, the last we heard from England was that the Kir
had agreed to give it back to the Spaniards as a sort of 'than
you' present for looking after him during part of his exile.'

"Yes, I'd forgotten that," Thomas said, turning to Luc
"Looks as though you've lost your job and will soon lo
your home. Still, I'm sure that as soon as you tell the Priv
Council what's happened they'll find you somewhere else t
stay. Unless you like England, of course. I find it rather col
myself, but perhaps you wrap up and don't mind it."

Ned saw that Luce was about to burst into tears, fear figh
ing frustration for possession of his face. Was now the time

"Your informant – did he mention any actual plac
attacked or taken by the Spanish?"

"Oh yes, he had all the details of one island and the ship.
The Spanish put everything to the torch: the man said it wi
be years before the town can be rebuilt."

"Where was it?"

"One of the northern islands. St Martin. Do you know it?

"Yes," Ned said gently. "Let me tell you about St Martin.

estselling Fiction